With You

JESSICA MARLOWE

lyric
PRESS

with YOU

JESSICA MARLOWE

First Edition

ISBN 978-1-949262-01-8 (paperback)

Editing by Kelly Hartigan (XterraWeb)

editing.xterraweb.com

Cover Design by Eight Little Pages

Interior Design by Lyric Press

Published by Lyric Press. For questions or comments, please contact info.lyricpress@gmail.com.

Visit Jessica at jessicamarloweauthor.com

❀ Created with Vellum

To my family and friends. Without their unending support and feedback, this book wouldn't have been possible.

To all the musicians and bands who have inspired and helped me through the long hours of writing and the even longer hours of figuring out self-publishing. The latter resulting in many a day where I thought my head would explode.

Thank you.

Dear Reader,

Thank you from the bottom of my heart for giving my novel a chance to entertain you. Your time is valuable, and I cannot express how much it means to me that you're using some of it reading Jack and Emily's story. I hope you enjoy reading it as much as I did writing it.

If you find any errors, I would be very grateful if you could contact me. Not only have I read my novel a bazillion times during drafting and editing, but it was also professionally edited and proofread. However, errors are inevitable, and I would like to make any necessary corrections. Please email me at jessica@jessicamarloweauthor.com with "Corrections" in the subject line.

Thank you.

Jessica

Attention: Exlcusive Offer

Want more? Sign up to my VIP reader group to get access to prologues, epilogues, cut or extended scenes, cover reveals, and insider updates exclusively for my subscribers.

Chapter One

APRIL 1ST, OAKDALE, NEW JERSEY

Emily's car came to a screeching halt. There was a crap ton of traffic for two p.m. on a Friday. Her bosses had closed the office early after a celebratory lunch because Bradford and Ross Marketing had just landed the Franny's Gluten Free Goods account.

It was a bright sunny afternoon, but a cold wind whipped around her car, reminding her that spring hadn't yet sprung. The diamond in her engagement ring sparkled in the sunlight, casting a prism of colors on the interior of her car. Three more weeks until she and Sully would be married, and she couldn't wait. She'd made the final payment to the vendors last week, and today she'd given the head count to the wedding coordinator at the Park Manor. Next week she'd have her final fitting.

Since her wedding to-do list was in order, Emily turned her focus on the changes she needed to make for her latest book. She had two weeks left before it was due to her editor, and she was behind. She'd thought writing a story where the two main characters were planning their wedding was a great idea, since she'd have lots of material to work with. Luckily for her, her wedding plans had gone smoother than her characters Elle and Stephen's had. They couldn't catch a break. Emily laughed to herself. Until now. Emily turned on her mini recorder and placed it on the seat next to her.

"Change Steven's dad's occupation to some job working at The Wellesley Hotel in NYC, where there will be a sudden cancellation for the date of their wedding. Her dress may suddenly be found at the shipper's facility, or better yet, a dress shop in town offered to replace her dress with one of their off-the-rack dresses, since she doesn't have time to order another one.

"Okay, next chapter will be the wedding rehearsal. Have Nicki, oops, sorry, Natasha, sneak off with Stephen's brother, maybe call him Tyler or King. Somewhere have Elle say *'She couldn't wait for their happily ever after to begin.'* Final chapter. The wedding. Start from groom's point of view. And maybe do an epilogue after a few months to check in."

Emily clicked the recorder off. The rest would come when she sat down to write. She'd written herself into a corner, and now she had the perfect way out. She'd have to make several adjustments to the manuscript in order for the ending to work properly, but two weeks should be plenty of time. Emily hadn't been able to write the final chapters where the wedding occurred and their happily ever after began, so getting the afternoon off was fortuitous. The blaring of a car horn pulled her out of her thoughts. She waved in apology and pulled forward. As was the way with traffic, it suddenly opened up as if there hadn't been any in the first place.

Emily pulled into the parking lot of her apartment

complex and parked. She snagged her pants on the corner of the door getting out of the car, but luckily the fabric didn't rip. April Fools' be damned. She was having a great day. She unlocked the door and hurried up the stairs inside her apartment.

Sully wouldn't be home until after seven, so she had at least four hours to work. She hung her purse from the railing and walked down the hallway. She was about to go into her office when a noise registered. It sounded like people having sex. Mrs. Locke, her downstairs neighbor, was a widow in her eighties, so Emily doubted it was her. Most of the other apartments in her section were empty during the day.

She caught a faint whiff of perfume. Heat flooded Emily's body, and her scalp began to tingle. She never wore perfume and didn't own any.

"Oh yeah, baby, like that."

Emily swallowed the panic that rose in her throat making it hard to breathe. *It couldn't be. It must be the television.* Except they didn't have a TV in their bedroom. She hadn't noticed his car in the parking lot, but then she'd been preoccupied with her story. She forced herself to continue down the hallway. Emily felt like she was floating as all the nerve endings in her body fired. She scrunched her eyes closed and took the final step into the doorway. She opened her eyes and wished she hadn't.

"Oh, Sully, yes!" the woman riding Emily's fiancé screamed.

Emily opened her mouth but nothing came out. She felt paralyzed, unable to scream, move, or breathe. She knew the exact second the little bitch riding Sully realized that Emily stood there because she turned her head as a slow grin broke across her face. *Tiffany.* One of the many girls from Sully's office who was infatuated with him.

Emily wanted to throw up, but there'd be time for that later. "Get out!" she screamed. Her voice was shrill.

The unrelenting squeak of the mattress finally stopped. Sully sat up; he was still inside that bitch. Emily couldn't read his expression, except it wasn't the least bit guilty. Seconds ticked by as the two of them just sat there staring at her.

Shock gave way to anger, and Emily said through tight lips, "Get the fuck out of my apartment. Now!" Emily spotted their pile of clothing on the floor. She lunged forward, scooped up their clothes, and went to the window. "Let me help you." She flung the entire pile out. The smell of his cologne and her perfume fused into a nauseating mixture.

She turned back to the bed. Sully and Tiffany, wearing shocked expressions and nothing else, just stared at her. "I can see you need more help." She opened Sully's closet and grabbed all of his suits, ties, and dress shirts. When she turned toward the window, Sully finally spoke.

"Don't you dare."

She turned on him, still holding his clothes. "Don't I dare? Are you fucking kidding me?" She was sure the clothes were heavy, but Emily couldn't feel anything. It was as if her entire body shut down; even her leg didn't hurt. She crammed everything out the window.

"Get off," Sully said to Tiffany, who still stared at Emily open-mouthed. She scrambled off and grabbed the sheet to cover herself. "Emily, calm down." He stood. "We need to talk."

Had he really just told her to calm down? Was this some fucked-up dream? Maybe she'd been in a car accident and was in a coma? There was no other explanation. Hatred tore through her, and her blood boiled. "I'll say it slowly this time. Get. The. Fuck. Out. Now."

Sully took one step toward her.

"Now!" Emily screamed so loudly her throat hurt. She

might have just screamed bloody murder because Sully took a step back, and Tiffany looked scared. *Good.*

He put his hands up. "Okay, just let me grab—"

"How have I not been clear? Now."

"You threw our clothes out the window," Tiffany whined. "What are we supposed to do?"

What are they supposed to do? Emily had never experienced such a rush of violence in her life. She wanted to rip Tiffany's face off and cram it down her throat so she'd never have to hear her tinny, whiny voice ever again. Her muscles tightened until she shook. "Now," she said through her teeth. Emily reached for the bat in the closet.

"All right, all right," Sully said. He yanked the top sheet and blanket off the bed. He handed Tiffany the sheet and wrapped the blanket around his waist. "Come on." He stood in front of Tiffany as they backed out of the room and down the hallway.

Emily followed. Every muscle in her body ached with tension. She glared at them as they went down the stairs and out the door. Emily waited until she heard the door close to run down and lock it, sliding the security chain into the housing. A wave of nausea had her rushing up the stairs and into the kitchen, making it to the sink just in time as her lunch reappeared.

She sank to the floor, catching her blouse on the cabinet handle. It ripped, but she didn't care. Tears burned a trail down her cheeks, and her body shook. She couldn't believe what just happened. But she'd seen it with her own two eyes, and the images were seared into her brain.

When her tears finally dried up, she sat on the cold floor, too weakened to move. The muscles in her right leg had locked up, and that pain warred with the pounding in her head.

Emily grabbed onto the counter and pulled herself up. She slipped her engagement ring off her finger and toyed with the idea of dropping it down the drain. Instead, she placed it on the counter and walked out of the kitchen.

April 1st, San Diego, California

"ALL RIGHT, GUYS, THAT'S A WRAP FOR TODAY," THE director said.

Jack stepped back from the microphone and tried to extricate himself from the beautiful blonde model who played his love interest in the video Stone Highway was shooting. She wasn't making it easy. She'd made her interest clear, but Jack just wasn't interested.

Dexter Watts, the band's manager waddled over. "Okay, Shasta, time to go."

"Oh, come on, Jackie, let's have some fun," the blonde model purred into his ear as she trailed her fingertip up his arm.

Jack tensed. He hated being called Jackie. His bandmates, Elliot, Curt, and Buzz, snickered from the side of the stage. He gave them the finger.

Dex led Shasta to the other side of the stage and helped her down the steps. Jack grabbed a towel and wiped the sweat off his face and neck.

"Do you think she knows her parents named her after a brand of soda?" Elliot smirked.

Curt snorted. "Doubt it. She's gorgeous but the attic's empty."

Elliot yanked Curt's ponytail. "Says the blond boy with cobwebs in his attic."

"Fuck you, Black." Curt pulled the band off and left his hair loose.

"Get a haircut, hippie," Buzz said.

Curt flipped Buzz off.

Jack's cell rang. It was an L.A. area code, but he didn't recognize the number, so he let it go to voicemail. He was now that guy with two cell phones, and it pissed him off. After he broke up with Christie, he'd had to change his number because she called every time something went wrong, so pretty much every day. He'd gotten tired of having to explain to his family why he'd changed his number yet again, so Jack broke down and got another cell and only gave the new number to his immediate family, bandmates, Dex, Kevin, and his bodyguard, Jeff.

He still cringed at the thought of having a bodyguard, but ever since he'd received that first letter at his house, Dex had been pushing him to take it seriously. Jeff had been with him for two months now, but Jack still hadn't gotten used to having someone follow him around all the time. With their tour starting next Friday, Jack had to consider everyone else. If there was a real threat, he didn't want anyone in harm's way because of him.

When the voicemail chime alerted him to a message, Jack checked it.

"Jack, it's Amber. I haven't seen Christie in a few days, and I'm worried about her. She was a no-show for a modeling job, and she's not answering her door. Call me."

Jack shoved the phone back in his pocket and ran his hand over the back of his neck.

"Problem?" Buzz asked.

Jack sighed. "That was Christie's friend from across the hall. She missed a job and isn't answering her door. Amber's worried." Jack ran a hand through his hair. *Just fucking great.*

"Why is she calling you?" Elliot asked. "You guys broke up six months ago, and you're no longer obligated to rescue her."

But Jack did feel obligated. They'd been together for three years, and Jack couldn't just shut off his feelings. "Fuck."

Elliot shook his head and sighed. "Why fuck? This isn't your problem. If you're worried, call the police and have them do a wellness check."

"If I call the police and she has drugs in the apartment, she'll go to jail."

Buzz shuffled his feet. "So, then maybe she'll get the help she needs."

Jack winced. Buzz had been sober since last September.

"I'm fine. It's okay to talk about it in front of me," Buzz said.

Jack smiled. "Was I that obvious?"

"We've been friends since we were four. I can read you like a book."

Elliot snorted. "More like a pamphlet."

Jack laughed. Elliot was always good for comic relief. And he was right. Christie needed to figure things out on her own. It wasn't like he could fly to L.A. anyway; they had one more day of shooting. He'd call Amber back tomorrow after they were done for the day.

Chapter Two

E mily bolted upright in bed, her heart slamming against her rib cage. The room was pitch-black, and she was fairly certain the screaming she'd heard had come from her. The air was warm and thick, and she had a hard time breathing past the lump in her throat. The covers were tangled around her legs, she was hot and sweaty, and tears streamed down her cheeks. *That bastard.*

Feeling trapped, Emily kicked the covers away from her. She needed to get out of here. The room she'd shared with Sully; the room they'd made love in. Her fingers curled until her nails dug into her palms. The room he'd screwed Tiffany in. *How could he?*

She knew better than to jump out of bed but did it anyway. Stumbling, Emily caught herself on the dresser. Taking a deep breath, she followed the line of it until she reached the door. She flung it open, and a burst of fresh air billowed around her. The night-light in the bathroom cast a faint yellow glow into the hallway.

The air in the kitchen was cooler because she'd forgotten to close the window over the sink. It was cold, but the brisk breeze helped her body temperature drop a few degrees from inferno. For several minutes, Emily stood barefoot on the cold tiled floor, waiting for her heart rate to return to normal. She closed and locked the window.

The clock in the living room chimed twice. She flopped on the couch. Emily had cried more the last three days than she had since she was seventeen. When she wasn't crying, she was writing scenes of ways to punish them. Her favorite involved covering their naked bodies in plaster and feeding them through a straw so they'd live trapped inside, only able to watch the world and not be part of it—forever locking Sean Sullivan and Tiffany Fake Tits in their own hell.

It was only eleven in California. She could call Vince, but then she'd have to explain why she was calling him on a Sunday night at two in the morning. Eddie and Sheryl had little kids, and Sheryl was pregnant again, so that wasn't an option. Since she'd caught Sully and Tiffany Friday afternoon, Emily hadn't talked to anyone, not even Nicki. But she would have to soon. She'd have to tell everyone.

EMILY CHECKED OFF THE LAST ITEM ON HER LIST AND sat back on the couch. It was done. Her wedding was officially canceled. Nicki had helped her make the phone calls to the guests and pack up and return all her shower gifts. All the vendors had been sympathetic, but they'd signed a contract, and no one had offered to return her money. They would, however, put the money toward a future event if it was held within the next twelve months.

She didn't even have the energy to cry. Like she'd ever get married. All the old and not so old insecurities over her scars had her feeling like no one would ever be able to love her. She was damaged goods, and any man with common sense would see it a mile away and steer clear.

Obviously, Sully hadn't loved her. It had all been a lie.

She'd packed his shit in boxes so she wouldn't have to look at it and stored them in her office. Emily had no idea what he was waiting for. When he'd stopped by last week, she'd expected him to pick up the rest of his stuff, but he'd been in a hurry and just wanted the ring and the tickets for their honeymoon. Said he'd be back to get the rest of his stuff. Seeing him had hurt more than she'd expected, and she wasn't looking forward to seeing him again. At least he'd returned the keys.

Emily dragged herself off the couch. She'd tried to finish her manuscript, but there was no way she could write a happy ending when her life had exploded. She'd obviously been fooling herself all these years; a professional writer would've been able to suck it up and finish.

THE AFTER-PARTY WAS IN FULL SWING, BUT JACK wasn't enjoying himself. The restaurant that Dex had arranged for the party—to celebrate their fourth album, *Hidden Captions*, just being certified double platinum—was packed, and there was no shortage of beautiful women. Most of whom had made it clear they'd like to spend time with him, but Jack wasn't interested. At twenty-nine, he needed more of a connection than his dick getting hard. And ever since waking up with a girl whose name he couldn't remember, Jack had been celibate.

A gorgeous brunette caught his eye across the room. She smiled and sashayed over to him. Everything about her screamed please fuck me: from her painted-on minidress to the jiggle of her too-large-for-her-narrow-frame tits to her stilettos.

Her interest was clear. Four months ago, Jack would've taken her back to his hotel and fucked her crazy all night and then said goodbye in the morning. He wasn't in the mood to evade yet another come-on.

Jack was honest enough to admit that when the band started to garner attention, he'd enjoyed hearing how great he was, but that shit got old quick. He learned to take every compliment with a grain of salt.

"Hey, you're Jack McBride, aren't you?"

Wow. Jack tried not to roll his eyes. "Yup." For fun, he went over in his head his guesses for her name, possibly something with an "i" where a "y" should be and most likely not the name her parents gave her.

"I'm Destiny," the brunette purred. She leaned in and used her arms to squeeze her tits together so they protruded even farther out the top of her dress. "And I think we were destined to meet." She giggled.

Jack couldn't help the groan that escaped. "Hi, Destiny. Are you having a good time?" He wouldn't be rude, but he needed to get the fuck out of here. And soon.

She looked around the room and feigned boredom. "It's okay. But I can think of better ways to have a good time."

The gleam in her eyes and the way she licked her bright pink lips left Jack in no doubt of what she had in mind. Destiny would be disappointed. "Me too, wanna go bowling?" At her puzzled expression, Jack did his best to contain his laughter. "Sorry, just kidding."

Before he could let her down easy, Curt appeared. "Hey, buddy, who's your new friend?" Because Curt stood next to Destiny, she couldn't see him wink at Jack.

Jack was grateful for his friend. "Curt, this is Destiny."

"Destiny, what a lovely name." Curt made a show of looking around. "You are the most gorgeous babe at this party." Then he leveled her with his signature innocent smile.

And just like that, Destiny moved on. She giggled at everything Curt said and took every opportunity to showcase her tits and touch him. Curt had his own bad breakup last summer and was still enjoying all the perks being a musician had to offer.

The party was still young, but Jack was ready to leave. He worked his way over to Elliot, who always stayed on the perimeter of the room. He hated these parties and protested by coming but not participating. Even though he and Siobhan had been separated for the past ten months, Elliot showed no interest in any other woman.

"You ready to blow this party, Black?"

"Hell yeah." Elliot smirked. "You must be exhausted from all that ducking and dodging." He clapped him on the shoulder. "Curt did you a solid." He tilted his chin in the direction of the exit where Curt was leaving with Destiny.

"Yeah. He's not suffering though."

Elliot laughed. "Final count, fourteen dodges with three assists."

"Really? You're keeping track?"

Elliot shrugged. "I was bored."

Jack saw Dex walking toward them, and he pushed Elliot out the door. "Hurry up, I don't feel like listening to Dex's bullshit tonight." Dex was a great manager, but Jack had enough mingling and didn't need Dex's spiel.

Jeff followed them out of the exit as their SUV pulled up. Jack and Elliot climbed in the back, and Jeff got in the passenger seat. "Hotel," Jeff said to Brick. Jeff had handpicked three additional bodyguards to cover the band during the tour. Miller stayed at the hotel with Buzz, who still wasn't comfortable at parties, and Polson left with Curt.

In three days, they'd be back in New York. Since moving to California two years ago, Jack didn't get to see his family as often as he'd like, but he'd be seeing them on Sunday, and he couldn't wait.

I watch Jack and Elliot get into the SUV with the new bodyguards. All brawn, no brains, the lot of them. Do they really think they can keep him from me? Once Jack and I are together, I'll convince him he should lose the dead weight. Jackie doesn't need a band. He's the real star. They'd be nowhere without him.

Elliot looks like he's homeless. Ha! He is since his wife kicked him out, probably for screwing around. Buzz is a loser druggie, and Curt is as dumb as a sack of rocks.

I'll rid Jack of all these hangers-on: no more groupie whores and no more band.

Just the two of us.

Chapter Three

E mily rolled onto her stomach and drew the blanket over her head to block out the daylight. Sleep, when it came, provided the only measure of peace she'd had in the last three weeks. Unless she dreamt of him, then she was out of luck.

Emily opened her eyes. *Sully. Crap.* Those first few blissful moments of peace vanished. Now that her brain had kicked on, the memories rushed in.

She'd hoped to sleep later. Emily glanced at the clock and saw it was 9:11. On a normal day, she'd have been at work for over an hour, but yesterday she'd been ordered to take time off. Emily was no closer to figuring out what went wrong, and until she did, she couldn't move on.

Nicki's ring tone blared out of Emily's cell. She covered her head with a pillow. She never should've told Nicki her bosses forced her to take time off. Emily didn't want to go shopping or talk anymore.

Emily rolled on to her back. Coffee, she needed lots of coffee. Blessedly, the ringing stopped. After a few seconds, it started again. It was too early for this. She threw the covers off, sat up, and rubbed her hands over her face. Coffee.

She climbed out of bed and stood, trying to get her bearings. Lack of sleep made her punchy. She grabbed her cell, and by the time she reached the kitchen, the ringing had stopped.

As she poured herself a cup of coffee, Nicki's ring tone sounded for the third time. *Shit, she only does this when something's really wrong.* With a pained sigh, Emily answered.

EMILY STOOD AT THE OPEN DOORWAY TO HER apartment as she checked her watch. "You're late, as usual."

Nicki gasped for air as she rushed up the stairs. "I'm sorry. It's not my fault this time."

Emily grabbed Nicki's arm as she stumbled through the doorway; her five-inch heels weren't made for running. Neither was the tight pink and black minidress that barely covered her butt and had a V-neck so deep that if she bent over a wardrobe malfunction would no doubt occur.

"No really. Tad called. He wanted his ticket to the concert." Nicki's lips formed a tight line. "Can you believe that? Stone Highway has been my favorite band since their days playing dive bars in the city. He never even listened to them before we met." She stomped up the inside stairs, dropped her designer purse on the coffee table, and plopped on to the couch.

Emily was sure Nicki's purse cost more than her entire living room set. "Are you surprised? The only thing he likes more than flaunting his money is hoarding it. I'd be amazed if he hadn't planned to scalp the ticket to offset his losses." Emily sat next to her friend. Might as well get comfortable because they weren't going anywhere until Nicki had her say.

"Emi, I appreciate you coming with me. None of my other

friends are into Stone Highway, and I didn't want to go by myself." Nicki's pout was unnecessary, since Emily had already agreed to go but was probably just force of habit.

Emily would much rather stay home. "I'm not into them either."

"I know, but you're too nice to say no." She patted Emily's knee.

Her look of pity made Emily's stomach tighten.

Nicki's brows dipped. "Besides, you need to get out of this apartment. You've been holed up for three weeks. I still can't believe Sully—"

Emily put up her hand. They'd spent the last two and a half weeks going over what happened, and Emily didn't want to talk about it anymore. That was the one condition she'd set to going out tonight; no more Sully talk. "I haven't been holed up for three weeks. I've gone to work and gone grocery shopping..." Okay, lame even to her ears. Truth was, she didn't feel like doing anything. She really didn't feel like going to this concert, but she couldn't let Nicki go on her own. After what Tad had done, someone needed to keep an eye on Nicki.

Nicki sniffled. "I still can't believe Tad cheated on me. We'd been talking about moving in together. How do you go from 'let's move in together' to screwing another woman?"

Emily moved closer to Nicki on the couch. "I'm so sorry this happened to you, sweetie, you deserve better."

"Why do guys do this shit?" Nicki's eyes teared up. "He said he loved me, and I believed him."

Emily had no doubt of her friend's broken heart. Nicki really thought Tad was the one. Since Nicki was on a roll, Emily didn't bother to interject.

"I should've known when Tad said he loved me on our third date"—Nicki hiccupped—"he's handsome, rich, successful, a snazzy dresser..."

Emily handed her a tissue as the first tears rolled down her cheeks.

Nicki dabbed her eyes, so as not to disturb the makeup so skillfully applied, and sniffled. "That's it. I'm not shedding another tear over that bastard. He doesn't deserve me."

"No, sweetie, he doesn't." Emily hugged her.

"You never liked him."

"That's not true. I liked him well enough, you know, for the first ten days."

Nicki scrunched up her face. "Yeah. I'm surprised you spent any time with us after that."

"Nic, you're my best friend. Not even you dating a tool could change that." Launching into another rant—about how Nicki should reconsider how she met guys and the correlation to how her relationships collapsed—was pointless. "Besides, he and Sully..." Fuck, there he was again. Emily's head pounded. She got up, went to the bathroom, and got some ibuprofen. Was crying withdrawal a thing? It hurt to breathe. Going to this concert was definitely gonna hurt: too many people and loud rock music.

Only for Nicki.

Emily looked at her reflection in the mirror and sighed. Nicki needed her, so she'd suck it up. She trudged back into the living room. "Sorry."

"Don't apologize. You've been through the wringer the last three weeks. If you'd rather stay home—"

"No. I said I'd go." She looked at her watch. "We should leave, and if we're lucky, we can still grab dinner before the concert."

Nicki's face perked up. "Plus, it's my birthday," she said with a glint in her eye.

That look set off alarm bells. *Shit.* As suspected, Nicki planned on getting into trouble tonight. She'd dressed for it.

Nothing Emily said would prevent trouble, but hopefully she could minimize the damage.

Nicki blew her nose, stood up, and chucked the tissue into the garbage. She grabbed her purse and smiled brightly. "Let's go. I'm determined to have a good time tonight."

Emily locked the door behind them. "That's what worries me."

Chapter Four

Nicki bounced in anticipation of her favorite band taking the stage. The opening band, Xerxes had been great, but she was a die-hard Stone Highway fan.

It was so damn hot in here that Nicki was glad she'd worn her new sleeveless minidress. Smoke from the pyrotechnics used during Xerxes' set still hung heavily in the air. Nicki inhaled deeply; the scent of beer mixing with dozens of colognes and perfumes reminded her of her wild college days. She smiled to herself. She hadn't really been wild back then. It wasn't until she'd moved into the dorms that Nicki realized how small her life had been. Even though she'd traveled all over the world on vacations with her family, her life had been sheltered. Her parents meant well, but once Nicki got a taste of really living life, she never looked back.

The house lights were up enough that she could see Emi. They made such an odd pair; Nicki in her designer dress and five-inch heels and Emi in a burgundy T-shirt, jeans, and flats. Nicki had always envied Emi's dark hair with the natural red and gold highlights complementing her fair skin. Nicki spent a fortune at her salon getting highlights and lowlights in her dull blonde hair.

Looking around, she noticed several guys openly admiring her friend. But Emi didn't notice. Nicki hated seeing her so heartbroken. She was glad she'd been able to cajole Emi into coming. After saying no half a dozen times, she'd left Nicki no choice but to remind her these tickets were her birthday present from Tad. She shook her head. She was moving on, and she wouldn't waste another second of her life on that bastard.

For the past three weeks, Emi hadn't been herself. Who could blame her after what that motherfucker Sully had done? Nicki still fantasized about hogtying him, covering him in honey, and leaving him by an ant hill.

Emi was the calm, cool, and collected one, totally had her shit together since the day they'd met, while Nicki's love life was a mess. Emi had always been there for her, or anyone, if she thought she could help. Well, Nicki would be there for her best friend, and if she didn't snap out of it soon, drastic measures would need to be taken.

She gave Emi a sidelong glance. She looked pale, fragile, almost broken. She'd always been so strong; she'd had to be. If Nicki didn't know better, she could believe this was pod Emi, a duplicate swapped out with the real one, who at this moment could be getting probed, in intimate places, by little green men. *Yuck.*

Time for fun. Her mission was to help Emi, but there was no reason she couldn't enjoy herself at the same time. Lost in her own thoughts, Nicki hadn't realized that Emi was talking to her. Emi could read her like a book. *Play dumb.* "Were you talking to me?"

Emily's face darkened with anger. "You didn't hear a word I said, did you?"

Nicki's smile grew wider. "Sorry, I've been looking

forward to this concert for months. I'm so excited. Aren't these seats awesome?"

"I know you're excited. Yes, these seats are awesome. But, *you* are up to no good." Emily took a deep breath. "I came out with you tonight because you asked me as a favor. I'd rather be home because I'm exhausted. With everything that needed to be done, I haven't had a chance to catch my breath." She paused as the crowd noise intensified. "Instead, I'm here with you in the fifth row at a rock concert." Emily screwed her face up and sighed. "I know that look. Don't."

"Don't what?" Nicki asked, trying to sound innocent.

"Don't what?" Emily mocked. "Don't even think about whatever it was you were thinking about. You promised you'd behave. Come with me to the concert, you begged. We'll have a great time, we'll get dinner, see the best band ever in concert, and call it a night." Emi shouted as the crowd noise went up a few more decibels. "That was your 'I'm looking for fun, a.k.a. trouble look.' I'm begging you, please, let's enjoy the concert and go home."

"I know this great bar where we can stop for a drink and then go dancing. You know, have fun." Nicki shook her ass to simulate dancing.

Someone behind her whistled and Nicki turned. A handsome, tall hottie, wearing a black Stone Highway T-shirt, whistled again. She winked and blew him a kiss. When she turned back, Emi just shook her head.

"Maybe a drink, but we both know what you mean by fun. It involves hooking up. I'm not looking to be your wingwoman." Emily huffed in frustration.

Nicki almost felt sorry for causing her irritation, but Emi needed to break out, have some fun, and as her best friend, it was Nicki's responsibility to help. Nicki was the queen of breakups, and she knew exactly how to help Emi feel better.

"Come on, you could use some fun in your life." Nicki smirked.

"No way. You promised me this morning, if I came with you, we'd keep it low-key. Dinner, concert, home."

Nicki pouted.

Emily put her hand up. "Don't even try that with me. I don't have a penis, so it doesn't work. You promised, and I'm holding you to it." All pleading had left her voice and was replaced by vexation.

Nicki bided her time. "Okay, concert then home." She resisted the urge to cross her fingers behind her back.

AFTER JACK FINISHED HIS VOCAL WARM-UPS, HE stretched out on his yoga mat and took a deep inhale as he leaned forward and wrapped his hands around his feet. Yoga calmed his nerves, and damn, if he wasn't nervous. He'd tinkered with the set list enough. If he changed it again, the guys would kill him.

Elliot slammed his phone on the arm of the chair. He'd been sitting there tapping and then disconnecting a call for the last few minutes. Anger radiated off him.

Jack exchanged glances with Curt and Buzz. Elliot had been a miserable s.o.b. ever since his separation. Jack had hoped that the stalemate that had been ongoing for the past month would end once they got to New York, but it seemed that Elliot wasn't going to be the one to end it. Always one to keep his own council, Elliot had been even more reticent since his last phone call with Siobhan. Jack hated seeing his friend in pain.

Buzz sat closest to the door with drumsticks in hand and eyes closed in meditation as he tapped a beat on the arm of the chair.

A loud knock sounded on the dressing room door. Walt, one of their roadies, opened the door and popped his head in. "Ten minutes, guys," Walt said, his head barely out the door before it closed.

Even though Curt had earbuds in, Walt's voice cut through the music. He removed them, stood, and stretched. He grabbed a bottle of water and downed it.

New York. Madison Square Garden. Jack had seen a dozen concerts here, but tonight would be the first time Stone Highway headlined. Their openers, Xerxes, would travel with them throughout the first leg of the twenty-month tour.

After three singles from their third album, *Traveling Spectacle*, held the top three spots for a week on Billboard's rock streaming chart, their downloads and album sales skyrocketed, elevating them to the next level. Tickets for this tour were sold out everywhere. The Garden gigs had sold out so fast they'd added two nights.

Jack pushed to his feet and stood next to Curt. Elliot and Buzz joined them. Each put in a hand, and for several seconds, no one spoke. "Let's have a great gig," Jack said.

Jack walked to the door and opened it. The dull hum of the audience intensified, and they all paused to listen. From the expression on his bandmates' faces, Jack wasn't the only one who was nervous. Elliot's lips twitched in a reluctant smile. He knew Elliot would be okay, at least until the gig was over.

Outside, Jeff, now head of band security, stood watch. Jeff nodded and strode down the hallway. The band followed along the labyrinth of the backstage area until they reached the side of the stage.

Holden Webb, Jack and Curt's guitar tech, handed Jack his Gibson Les Paul Custom Black. Jack slid the strap over his head. He warmed up by playing the intro to Rush's "La Villa Strangiato." As ready as he'd ever be, Jack looked around;

everyone was ready except for Curt, who argued with Holden.

Jack's body pulsed with nervous energy, so he stepped up to the entrance to the stage and turned his attention to the audience. The dull hum he'd heard from the dressing room was now a rowdy mixture of voices. As he peered into the arena, his whole body tensed as time and air ceased to exist.

Fuck, she's stunning. A beautiful, tall, curvy woman with dark hair stole Jack's attention. He couldn't take his eyes off her. Or breathe. Blinking was out of the question. The sounds from backstage and the audience faded from Jack's consciousness. Movements around him slowed down.

PINKS. In a sea of overdone, stylized women, she stood out like a breath of fresh air. *Breathe, asshole.* She was talking to one of the pinks. He wouldn't have pegged them as friends, but as the burgundy stunner pleaded with the pink, it appeared they were.

Jack heard his name, but it sounded far away; maybe he'd passed out. Elliot waved his hand up and down in front of Jack's face. Jack knocked his hand away, so Elliot stood in front of him. His lips moved but Jack couldn't hear him. He shoved Elliot out of the way. "Fuck off, Black." But as usual, he didn't. Instead, Elliot shook him, and Jack had no choice but to look at him. "Fuck off."

Jack turned his attention back to the audience. *Good, she's still there.* He felt lightheaded, so he took a deep breath.

"Hey, man, what the fuck is wrong with you?" Elliot asked. "We're about to go on, and you're standing here in a fog." Elliot shook him again. "Jack-off, snap out of it."

Grinning and keeping one eye on the stunner, Jack half-turned to him. "That girl is stunning."

Elliot glanced at the audience and shrugged. "Lots of beautiful women, care to be more specific?"

"The one in the burgundy top, fifth row, dead center."

Elliot's lips curled into a smirk. "That one's not gonna fall on her knees for you, buddy." Elliot snickered and smacked Jack on the shoulder. "It's shaping up to be a fun night, Jack. Your celibacy is boring. You know I live vicariously through you." Elliot's smile dipped.

Jack knew his friend was thinking about his wife. Elliot still considered himself very much married. Poor bastard was in love with his wife. Jack sighed. Lucky bastard was in love with his wife. "Brother, you could live my life."

"Go fuck yourself." Elliot's expression darkened.

Jack smirked at him. He took every opportunity to remind Elliot that he wasn't doing enough to get his wife back. He was in sorry shape, so stubborn. Siobhan asked for the trial separation after she'd miscarried. Elliot's only pastime these days was sulking. He needed to act.

"Dude, what the fuck?" Buzz asked, shouldering Jack as he and Curt joined them. "Snap out of it, the show must go on."

The band was ready, so the house lights lowered to near black. Jack's nerves settled down as they always did. When the jumbo screen went on with their intro, they moved into position, the only lighting provided by the screen itself. Jack tried to orient himself; she should be right in front of him. He couldn't wait for the lights to go up.

As Curt launched into the intro to "Secrets," the audience erupted into thunderous cheers and applause.

Jack closed his eyes and inhaled deeply. His fingers rested over the fretboard. Elliot plucked the E on his bass, and Buzz struck the ride cymbal. The stage lights danced before his closed eyes, and Jack felt the volume increase. He exhaled and his mind cleared. The roar of the crowd faded as Jack's fingers glided over the strings. This was his favorite part: the four of them together, guitars and sticks, making music. Opening his eyes, he exhaled, drew a deep breath, and sang. To her.

By the third song of the set, Jack had yet to banter with the audience. Normally, he'd close his eyes, and from the first note, he'd be in the zone. Regardless of the size of the crowd they played to, he'd always been able to connect with them. But tonight, he found it nearly impossible to concentrate on anything other than her. At times, it felt like they were the only two people in the arena. No matter how hard he tried, he couldn't keep his eyes from seeking her out. And his distraction showed. No one ever played a flawless set, but tonight, he felt like an amateur. *Enough. Get your shit together.*

But, he didn't.

After "Dirty Code," during the guitar change, Jack took the '59 Les Paul Flame Top from Holden. It was his current favorite guitar.

"She's not staying in tune," Elliot said to Beth, his bass tech. She shook her head as she placed it back in the rack and grabbed his '67 Gibson EB-3.

When Elliot walked over, Jack said, "I've got to meet that girl."

Elliott's expression was blank for a second and then realization hit. "Do it. Send her a note. Chicks dig that shit."

"A note?"

"Yeah, you know, invite her backstage," Elliot said with an abundance of "duh" in his voice and an eye roll.

Was he really going to do that? She wasn't the type. Her pink friend was, as were most of the girls around her. He needed to get his head back in the gig. He'd screwed up the words to "Rise and Fall." Luckily for him, the crowd sang along.

"I'll cover for you," Elliot said and then walked on stage.

Elliot and Curt bantered back and forth about how great it was to be back in New York. The crowd cheered.

Holden was engaged in an animated conversation with Beth, so Jack said to Walt, "I need paper and a pen."

The guys played an extended intro to "Hurts to Breathe,"

giving Jack time to scribble a note to the stunner. "Here." Jack turned to Walt as he inclined his head toward the audience. "There's a beautiful girl, tall, dark hair, fifth row, dead center, burgundy top." Jack handed the folded note to Walt. "Give this to her."

"Will do." Walt turned and lumbered to the stairs on the side of the stage.

"What the fuck is going on?" Holden asked. He looked at Curt's guitar rack. "First Curt's Archtop was out of tune, don't know how the fuck that happened. I tuned it myself after soundcheck. Now Elliot's bass. Maybe the guitars need security." Holden shook his head as he picked up the next guitar Curt would be using and gave it a once-over.

Jack would ask Holden about that later. He adjusted the Flame Top on his shoulder as he returned to center stage and launched into the song.

He closed his eyes and tried to focus on the lyrics; instead, the image of the stunner flooded his mind. What was wrong with him? Jeez, she was just a girl. He hadn't been this nervous about a girl since he was fifteen and working up the courage to ask Mia Samson to the spring dance. He met hundreds of girls a year. What was it about this girl that had him so on edge? He glanced over to Elliot and saw the large smirk he wasn't trying to hide. *Dick.*

Elliot laughed.

As the song ended, Jack's eyes settled on her. Walt made his way to Section B, and Jack broke out in a sweat. *When did it get so fucking hot in here?* Jack took a swig of water as Walt lumbered past the fans in row five, stopping next to the object of his obsession. Obsession? Damn.

WHEN THE BAND HAD TAKEN THE STAGE, THE volume had gone nuclear. Even so, Emily had heard Nicki's squeal of delight. Of course, she'd heard of Stone Highway, and Nicki played their music all the time, but she knew nothing about the band. Emily had been to several concerts but had never experienced such a reception to a band. She felt like she'd been hiding under a rock. She also had no idea the lead singer was so...deliciously handsome. Like drop dead gorgeous. Totally hot as—

Nicki poked her in the arm. "Hey, you in there?"

Her smirk told Emily that she'd been caught staring. *Shit.* She hoped Nicki wouldn't read too much into it. He was a hot guy, who also happened to be a musician. She had a thing for musicians, but then again, didn't every girl? His voice transitioned from silken to jagged with ease. *So what? Damn. When did it get so hot in here?* No wonder there was a sea of women in the front rows. Nice scenery. Her heart was broken, but the heat that pooled low in her belly reminded her that parts of her were very much alive. Her reaction was more than she'd felt in weeks.

Nicki poked her again.

"Sorry."

"Don't apologize, he's hot."

Emily put her hand on Nicki's shoulder because she bounced like a jackhammer.

The next song sounded familiar, up tempo, and Emily forgot everything, and sank into the sound of Mr. Delicious' voice. Smooth, warm, enticing. He sang about a girl.

Even though it was a love song, it wasn't soft but grinding. Emily was transported into the role of the object of his affections. The singer's voice told the story, but in her mind, she saw it unfold. They were at a crossroads, this couple. They loved each other desperately, but stubbornness was impeding that love. He was trying to find his way back to her; she was trying to move on without him, but she wasn't happy.

Not the welcome home I hoped for, baby
I've traveled so far
Please let me come home

As the last note of the song trailed off in beautiful, haunting reverb, tears filled Emily's eyes. She scrunched them closed. She absolutely wouldn't cry. This wasn't about her. This was about two other lovers. Not her and Sully. There was no her and Sully. He wasn't coming back, and she didn't want him back.

Emily took a tissue out of her purse, wiped under her lashes, and dabbed the corners of her eyes. She needed to keep it together. Looking around, she noticed other women were also dabbing. A young couple in the row in front of her were hugging and swaying back and forth, a solemn, unspoken promise to never let that be them. Everyone had a story like the couple in the song. But it didn't sound like that relationship was over. There was still hope.

Hope. The song was about hope. But Emily had none.

"Elliot," Mr. Delicious said into the microphone. "I think the audience is asleep. I can't hear them, can you?"

Elliot's response was drowned out by the crowd's screams. Emily heard Nicki over everyone else.

Mr. Delicious' laugh was full and warm as the band started the next song. She turned to Nicki, to ask the singer's name, when she felt a tap on her shoulder.

Turning back, Emily had to crane her neck to see the face of a man that stood where a petite woman was before. Between the band playing and the noise of the crowd she couldn't hear what he said, but when he extended his hand with a piece of paper, she took it. He turned and left.

Confused, Emily stared at the note. She looked around but didn't see anyone trying to catch her eye. She opened the folded paper, and even though the light was dim, she could read it.

Come back and say hi.
Jack

"Who's Jack?" Emily asked to no one, since Nicki was talking to a guy two seats down from her, over the guy's girlfriend. She tugged Nicki back to her own space, not missing the nasty look the girlfriend leveled at them. Emily sighed. Impending disaster averted.

Nicki turned to her, saw the note, and snatched it from Emily's hand. Her eyes glazed over as she read it, and she bounced like a small child on a sugar high. "Holy crap. Do you know what this says?" she squealed.

"Yes." Emily swiped the note back from Nicki and repeated, "Who's Jack?"

Nicki shook her head at Emily like she missed the easiest answer ever on *Jeopardy!* and forgot to phrase it in the form of a question. "Jack just invited you backstage," Nicki yelled. She continued to bounce, testing the tensile limits of her dress. Thank goodness, her back was to the guy she'd been talking to. Her dress wasn't designed for bouncing, and his eyes would've popped out of his head. The girlfriend would've definitely lashed out at Nicki.

"Still doesn't answer my question, Nic. Who's Jack?"

"Are you kidding me?" Nicki yelled.

Bounce, bounce, bounce. The song ended just as Nicki yelled, and everyone turned in their direction. Warmth crept up Emily's neck and into her face as Nicki pointed to the stage.

Emily looked up and her eyes met Mr. Delicious'. He smiled. She looked back at Nicki. *Oh, crap.*

"Thank you for coming out tonight. It's so great to be home. This is our first time headlining the Garden." Delicious paused as the audience cheered with deafening volume. "We are so grateful for our success. We wouldn't be here without your unending support. In case you've forgotten or been living under a rock, let me introduce the guys to you."

Mr. Delicious waved his left hand out. "Curt Stevens, guitar and backing vocals."

The guys in the audience woo-hooed and pumped their fists, and the women wolf-whistled.

"Buzz Stewart, drums and percussion."

More shouting, fist bumps, and whistles came from the audience.

"Elliot Black, bass, backing vocals, and occasionally lead vocals."

More whistles and applause echoed from the crowd, and someone yelled out, "We love you, Elliot," which Elliot acknowledged with a nod.

Delicious paused and looked directly at Emily. "And I'm Jack McBride."

The women whooped, shrieked, and bounced. The guys high-fived and yelled "yeah," increasing the volume to almost painful levels.

Jack.

Their eyes locked. This was ridiculous, but Emily couldn't look away. This kind of thing didn't happen to her. This would happen to Nicki. If it had, she would've run up on stage, bouncing in time to the music. She'd love it, but Emily hated being the center of attention and wished the floor would swallow her.

Another song started, a softer one, which helped to calm Emily's heart rate. It was acoustic. She hadn't noticed that Jack changed guitars. Must have been while she'd been trapped in his eyes, like a tractor beam. Was there anything sexier than a guy with an acoustic guitar? Emily moaned.

Nicki stopped bouncing. "Hey"—she put her hand on Emily's arm—"you okay?"

Emily took a deep breath and held it for a few seconds before she exhaled. Yeah. Nicki looked more concerned. Emily realized she might not have answered out loud. "Yeah," she repeated, her voice cracking. Emily nodded and said louder this time, "Yes, I'm fine."

With a sly smile, Nicki said, "Obviously, Jack thinks you're fine."

"Nic, stop it. This has to be a mistake or a joke. He can't be the only Jack here." She could feel her face burning. Even in the low light, she was sure everyone could see she'd turned beet red. Emily looked around and saw disbelieving or nasty looks from the surrounding women. The men looked at the band or at boobs. In their defense, boobs were on display everywhere.

Nicki noticed the nasty looks too and glared at the women who returned their hungry stares back to the stage.

Nicki leaned in and said in Emily's ear, "Jack McHottie, lead singer of Stone Highway, that you've been staring at for the last forty-five minutes, invited you backstage. He's waiting for an answer."

As the song ended, Emily shifted her gaze to see Jack staring at her yet again. She was flabbergasted that this guy, Mr. Delicious, frickin' Rock Star, sent her a note to come back and say hi. What did that even mean? Say hi, like a normal person, and then leave, or was hi a euphemism for a sexual act? Emily looked down at the note. This had to be a joke. "There's no way."

Nicki's mouth dropped open, as if she'd turned down a million dollars or a once in a lifetime chance. Maybe she was.

"Are you insane? Have you lost your mind? He's fucking gorgeous. You have to go."

Emily's stomach roiled, and her heart beat heavy in her chest. She rubbed her palms down her jeans and clamped her mouth shut. People stared. Nicki waited for an answer. So did Jack. *Get a grip.* Emily repeated this mantra over and over in her head. She closed her eyes, and when she opened them, she felt somewhat better. Time to end this.

Nicki rubbed her hand. "Come on, you've got to do this. After everything you've been through, you deserve some fun. Let loose for once."

"I am not going backstage. He should've picked you. You would've sprinted over four rows and scaled the stage without a grappling hook." Emily looked at Nicki's skyscraper heels, and added, "Or a net." Emily glanced at the women around them. Many were dressed similarly to Nicki: tight, low-cut dresses, jeans that were painted on, and barely there tops. One girl wore jeans and just a bra. How had she even gotten in here?

When Emily had dressed tonight, she'd picked out her favorite jeans, T-shirt, and black leather ballerina flats. It never occurred to her to dress up for a rock concert. She thought she looked good, but now she felt underdressed. Five minutes ago, all these women were overdressed.

She avoided looking at Jack because he expected an answer from her. Nicki still talked in her ear going on about how this was the opportunity of a lifetime. He was so hot. Come on, Emi, do this. Live a little. Emily imagined this was the pep talk that Nicki gave herself every time she went trolling for a new guy.

When Emily finally looked up at the stage, Jack stared straight at her. She mouthed no, and inclined her head toward Nicki, as if to say can't leave my friend.

He smiled and nodded.

Nicki screamed so piercingly loud that heads turned, even with the band playing. *The band's playing.* How many songs had she missed?

Nicki barraged her with "Please, please, please, pleeaase? It can be my birthday present. Forever."

"Nic, come on," Emily pleaded. "You promised, concert then home." Emily knew she was running out of arguments, but she wasn't ready to give in.

The band started the next song, "Time is Up," which was another one she recognized. Maybe if she pretended that this was settled...

Nicki pouted. "I've had a bad week too, you know."

Oh, fuck. Emily faced Nicki, put her hands on her shoulders, and looked her straight in the eyes. "You promise me, ten minutes then we leave?"

"Yes," screamed Nicki.

Just. Fucking. Great.

She instantly regretted her decision. Going backstage to meet this guy was insane. Jack McBride was a rock star. It took little imagination to guess what his expectations were, and while Nicki would love to indulge those expectations, Emily sure as hell wasn't going to.

Emily didn't have to wait long for Jack to make eye contact again. She gave him a curt nod that she hoped would convey her reluctance.

The next song was hard rock all the way, and since she didn't want to miss the rest of the concert, she pushed all thoughts of going backstage out of her mind. Maybe he'd forget and move on to someone else. How would they even get backstage, anyway? That settled it. He'd move on to someone else, and this would be fine. He'd want a willing participant, and she was most definitely not willing. She took comfort that rock stars must have fleeting attention spans, and he'd move on to another girl.

Chapter Five

Her acceptance had allowed Jack to keep most of his focus on the rest of the gig. As he sang the last chorus of "Rely," a song he wrote about his dad, he felt triumphant. She was coming backstage. Stunner wasn't happy about it, but it was a start. He had an ally in her friend. Jack would take advantage of that.

Now that the encore was over, Jack handed his guitar to Holden, grabbed a towel, and headed over to the stairs that led to the arena. He sent Walt to get the ladies.

As he dried himself off, Elliot skulked up.

"You stink, buddy," he said with a snarky grin.

"I'm surprised you can smell anything but you," Jack said, waving his hand in front of his nose for emphasis.

"I'm surprised you didn't run for the showers. Don't you want to smell nice for the pretty lady?" Elliot snickered.

"Fuck off." Under his breath, he added, "Pain in the ass."

Elliot smirked and walked away.

But Elliot was right. Jack should've gone to the dressing room to shower, but he wasn't certain the stunner would wait. After her friend begged, she'd reluctantly agreed. Even from a distance, he could tell she regretted it. What could she be afraid of? Jack was a nice guy. Other bands referred to them as the nice guys in rock and roll. He wasn't sure they meant it as a compliment, but that's how he took it—nothing wrong with being nice.

His mom would approve. Jack smiled. He hadn't seen his family since the quick trip at Christmas. Even though he and Christie had broken up in October, her drama had overflowed and cut his trip short.

Buzz walked over and stood next to Jack. Unlike Elliot, who always had a smartass remark, Buzz remained silent. Jack loved them both. "Great job tonight, man," Jack said, turning to his friend. "How you holdin' up?"

Buzz smiled. "Hanging in there."

His nonchalant response didn't fool Jack. He knew Buzz struggled, and it was understandable. He elbowed Buzz in the side. "Don't bullshit me."

"Okay. I'm having a hard time." Buzz lowered his eyes. "I'll call my sponsor when I get back to the hotel."

Jack elbowed him again. "No shame, man, not with us. We're family no matter what." When the guys came out to California to start rehearsal for their tour, Buzz had been excited. He'd been sober for four months, but they'd watched him, looking for any signs that he was using again. They'd have postponed the tour if they'd had to, because nothing was more important than Buzz's health, but he was doing great. Every night when they'd finished rehearsing, Buzz would go to a meeting. He never missed a day. He was in the best shape of his life. Jack and Buzz had worked out together every day since the tour started, and Jack was proud of him.

Buzz nodded and shuffled off toward the dressing room. Watching him leave, Jack wished he could do more.

As Jack turned back, the stunner strode around the corner, and he was struck again. She was even more beautiful up close. The modest V-neck of her fitted burgundy T-shirt provided a tantalizing peek of flawless skin. Her small waist emphasized the flare of her hips. Jack couldn't help but imagine her long, slim thighs wrapped around him. Unlike her friend, she wore flats. Jack's fingers itched to explore every inch of her. His heart pounded in his chest. He'd always enjoyed the chase, and there was no doubt in his mind that the chase was on. Unable to stand still any longer, Jack closed the distance between them.

Before he was able to speak, the pink friend rushed forward. "I'm Nicki and it's my birthday today."

"Happy birthday, Nicki, it's a pleasure to meet you," Jack said, extending his hand. Ignoring it, she grabbed him in a hug and planted a kiss on his lips as her hands trailed down his back. *Whoa.* He was okay with a kiss on the cheek, but anything else would end the meeting. Jack gestured to security to back off.

The stunner smirked.

Oh God, not another one. He sent her a pleading look which she conveniently ignored by looking around as if she were taking in her surroundings.

When their eyes met again, she took pity on him. She tugged Nicki's arm. "Nic, come on, give the guy a break."

Nicki loosened her grip, and Jack disengaged himself from her. Before he could draw a breath, Nicki was talking.

"You guys were great. Best concert ever. I loved that you did 'Pursuit' from your first album." She turned to her friend. "It's about pursuing your dreams, no matter what. I'm a writer and so is Emily. This was the best birthday present in the history of gifting."

As Nicki paused for a breath, Jack's brain tried to catch up. *Emily.* She had the most vibrant hazel eyes. He stared, but he couldn't help it; she was stunning.

"Tad, my ex-boyfriend got the tickets," Nicki said. "He's

my ex-boyfriend because I came home early from a writer's conference and caught him in bed with another woman. We'd been talking about moving in together." Nicki looked up at Jack. "Why do guys do stuff like that?"

Before Jack could register she was asking him, Nicki resumed talking. "Then, he had the nerve to call today, demanding his ticket. Can you believe that? And I told him..."

Jack tuned her out. Nicki should've been here with a boyfriend. Good for Nicki for ending her relationship with a cheater. And for Jack. He'd never have met Emily if not for the asshole ex-boyfriend. *My God, she's still talking.* Jack tried to pick up the thread of conversation. She still rambled on about her ex when she stopped mid-sentence.

The silence was blissful.

Nicki turned to Emily. "But that's not nearly as awful as what Emily's—"

Nicki was cut off as Emily's hand covered her mouth. "Nicki, enough!" Emily shouted. A stunned silence fell over the backstage, and the bustle of activity halted. Emily glared at Nicki, eyes narrowed and lips tight. She was stunning even when totally pissed off. He was surprised to find Nicki had an off button.

"Sounds like your ex is an asshole," Jack said, trying to defuse the situation.

"Emily said he's a tool, but asshole works too."

Noise and movement resumed backstage, but Emily's hand still hovered around Nicki's mouth, as if she didn't quite trust her to stop talking. Emily closed her eyes, and when she opened them, she seemed to have her temper under control and removed her hand.

"Nic, we've talked about this. If you want to share your life story with the whole world, that's fine. It's not okay to share mine." Her tone was that of an understanding parent to an errant child. She looked at her friend with sympathy and smiled.

Her smile lit up her face. Jack felt like he'd missed something, which didn't seem possible, because he was pretty sure he hadn't blinked in the last thirty seconds. This girl probably didn't have a fake bone in her body. "You're better off without him."

"I know. Emily says the same thing."

Jack extended his hand to Emily and smiled. "Hi, I'm Jack."

"Yeah, I got that. Finally."

They shook hands, and all the tension he'd been holding vanished. Her small hand was soft and warm. He didn't want to let go, but she tugged her hand, so he did. "So, you're a writer, too?" Jack asked.

"Yeah. Part-time writer, full-time friend," Emily said with a cute chuckle. "I have a day job."

"Emi, you need to quit that job and focus full-time on writing. You're amazing..." And she was off again.

Emily rolled her eyes and huffed. "Nic, can we leave now? You've met Jack. You used up your ten minutes talking him into a coma. It's time to go."

Nicki's pout was impressive, and Jack had seen his fair share. If pouting were an Olympic sport, Christie would've taken the gold.

"But it's my birthday, and I want to meet the rest of the band." She winked at Jack.

He jumped on the opportunity to not let Emily slip away. He stepped between them and put his arms around their shoulders. "Come on, let's go." Jack guided them through the backstage toward the hallway leading to the band's dressing room. "I'd be happy to introduce you to the guys."

His sideways glance at Emily confirmed she wasn't happy

about it, but he couldn't let her go. He wanted to get to know her, but right now, she was hell-bent on leaving.

ONCE THEY'D CLEARED THE CROWDED BACKSTAGE area, Jack's arms dropped. He was more gentlemanly than expected, and Emily sneaked a sideways peek at him. Damn, he was even better looking up close. His brown hair stuck up in places because he'd used the towel around his neck to dry it. Sparkling deep blue eyes, strong jaw, clean-shaven, athletic build. He was tall, and his low-slung jeans emphasized his height.

Emily noticed a tattoo of sheet music that trailed up his inner left forearm and a Celtic tattoo around his right biceps peeked out from under the short sleeve of his well-fitting black T-shirt. On the inside of his right wrist, he had a tattoo of an infinity symbol with the word family in a fancy script and a shamrock. A few tattoos on a guy were so sexy. No man should be this good-looking. *Whatever.* She wasn't in the market anyway. They'd meet the other band members and leave. After all, Nicki promised. As they turned the corner and walked down a long hallway, Emily had a sinking feeling that she was screwed.

Now that it was quieter, Emily heard Nicki talking to Jack, and she probably had been rambling on the whole time. She chuckled. Served him right. Emily had made her disinterest clear, but if he couldn't take a hint, he was getting what he deserved.

Jack glanced at her with raised brows as she smirked to herself. "What's so funny?"

Her smile widened. "Nothing." *Drop it, rock star, this won't end well for you.*

"I am best friends and on tour with a world-class smirker, okay. That evil chuckle and smirk meant something."

Emily stopped walking and faced Jack. "Okay, yeah, you made a deal with the devil, and now you're paying for it."

Nicki looked around Jack and pouted. "Hey, am I the devil in this scenario?"

"Yes, you are, sweetie."

"What'd I do?" Nicki asked, trying to hide a smile.

"What did you do? Do you really think I missed that wink you gave him? Not to mention you can't even ask that question with a straight face." Emily infused her tone with disapproval, which Nicki ignored, as usual.

"Busted," Jack said, grinning.

Nicki swatted his elbow. "Hey, buddy, a little gratitude, I was trying to help you."

Emily stopped smiling. "Shouldn't you have been helping me? You knew I wasn't interested in coming back here, but you played the 'It's my birthday and this can be my present forever' card," Emily said, mimicking Nicki's voice. Okay, rock star, the gloves were off.

"Emi, don't be mad. I thought you could use a little fun." She wagged her eyebrows up and down a few times and then looked contrite, for Nicki.

Mission accomplished; no one was laughing anymore.

Jack shoved his hands in his jeans pockets and looked down at the floor. When he looked back up at her with a lopsided grin, her heart flipped. "I'm sorry, Emily, I never meant for you to be uncomfortable. I just wanted to meet you."

Emily was surprised by Jack's admission. Nicki always meant well, but, ah, hell. "I'm not really mad, Nicki. I just wish you'd think before you act. Now we're all standing here uncomfortable because you two refused to take a hint. I was trying to be nice about it." Emily sighed. She considered turning and banging her head repeatedly against the wall. It'd be less painful.

Jack and Nicki shared a look. Nicki went to speak, but for once, Jack beat her to it. "Look," he said, meeting her eyes, "I don't want you to be uncomfortable, so if you want to leave, I'll call Walt and have him escort you safely out of the building."

Nicki whimpered but said nothing.

And there it was. *Screwed.* She ignored the fact that his grin and contrite expression caused a tingle low in her belly. She wasn't ready. After what Sully had done, Emily was afraid she'd never be ready. "Can I talk to you over here for a minute, Nic?" Emily stepped a few feet away.

Nicki followed.

"Listen, sweetie, I know you meant no harm, but I'm not like you. This isn't my idea of fun. This is awkward."

Nicki had the grace to look fully contrite. Her brown eyes misted.

Screwed. Emily huffed in defeat. "Remember, you promised, ten minutes, then we leave."

Nicki's piercing squeal broke the relative silence. "Thank you, thank you, thank you." She squeezed Emily in a hug.

"Ow," Emily said, rubbing her arms when Nicki released her from a death grip. She looked over Nicki's shoulder. "That's gonna leave a mark."

Jack rubbed his arms where Nicki had him in her death grip earlier. At five foot three, she was petite but strong.

Jack resumed his position between them, and they continued down the hallway. When they got to the door, Emily gave Nicki a warning look. Jack stepped aside and opened the door. "Ladies."

Nicki burst into the dressing room and said, "Hi, guys, I'm Nicki, and it's my birthday today. Who wants to spank me?"

Curt's blond head perked up. "I'm your guy." He jumped up, grabbed Nicki around the waist, and in a heartbeat, they were gone.

Emily's mouth fell open and a sudden coldness traveled through her. *What the fuck just happened?* Even for Nicki this was outrageous. Her eyes unfocused as her gaze dropped to the floor. She clenched her fists; she simply couldn't believe Nicki had just left. Her. Alone. In the band's dressing room. Her cheeks heated and her heart pounded.

When she looked up, Jack's expression mirrored her own. He'd no idea what he was getting into when he joined forces with Nicki. She should let him off the hook. Everyone stared at her, but no one spoke.

The coldness evaporated as anger took over. Pushing her sleeves up her arms, Emily surveyed the room. It was larger than she expected. The air was warmer than the hallway and smelled a little stale. Bottles of water were on a table in the corner, and a blue bag sat on the floor by the door. The green carpet was faded in spots, but the black couch and matching chairs were relatively new. The only other door led to the bathroom, and there were no windows. A bead of sweat trickled between her breasts.

Freshly showered, his longish black hair curling around his face and not giving a fuck, Elliot sat in a chair with his legs stretched out in front of him. His dark eyes seemed sad. Buzz sat in a chair opposite Elliot. He'd walked out of the bathroom toweling his hair dry when Nicki had burst through the door. He still held the towel in his hands.

She looked back at Jack, his brows drawn together.

The door was still open, and Emily sensed someone there, but unless it was Nicki, she didn't give a fuck who it was. "That's it. I'm finally gonna do it. I'm gonna kill her." The words fell out of Emily's mouth, like she had no control to stop them. "I'll drop a truck on her from a crane. Maybe put her in a giant catapult and shoot her across the planet. Or I could tie her to the frickin' train tracks and watch as she's sliced into itsy-bitsy pieces. Yeah, that's what I'll do." She felt better now that she had a plan.

Jack waved whoever was there away as he hustled past Emily and shut the door.

"Does anyone know if the that company from the cartoon is still in business?" Emily asked, her eyes scrunched closed. "I really need to get my hands on those contraptions. They never worked out well for the coyote, but I'll be smarter. I won't be anywhere near them when setting them off." On a deep exhale, Emily opened her eyes.

Elliot chuckled. "No, I'm fairly certain they went out of business when they stopped making those cartoons. I think he was their only client."

Emily laughed without humor. "I was afraid of that. I'll have to wait for Plan B to pan out."

"What's Plan B?" Buzz asked.

Emily turned to face Buzz, smiled, and said matter-of-factly, "Execute a search on the internet for mad scientists. Check their references, of course, and forge an evil union, so he or she can design and build them for me."

Elliot bit back laughter. "Good plan. How would you be smarter about it than the coyote? He hid behind rocks and trees, and still the catapult backfired and the rock crushed him."

With a smug grin, Emily said, "Remote control."

Jack took a few steps toward Emily. "Come and sit over here." He guided her to the couch opposite the chairs occupied by Elliot and Buzz. His hands felt cool on her too hot skin. "I can't imagine that they'll be gone long."

"Why?"

"Because, Curt has a short attention span for everything except music."

"And I'd imagine his hand would hurt after a while," Elliot snickered.

A knock on the dressing room door had Emily hoping Nicki had returned.

Buzz yelled, "Come in."

The door opened and a tall, muscular man with a buzz cut stood in the doorway. "Is everything okay in here? Viv told me someone was plotting a murder."

Emily raised her hand. "That'd be me."

"You know that murder is a crime, don't you?" He stepped in and closed the door.

Emily smiled. "Only if you get caught. Not to worry, this time it's my fault, anyway."

Jack smiled at Emily. "This is Jeff Monroe...our head of security." Addressing Jeff, he said, "This is Emily. Her friend Nicki just ran off with Curt to get spanked. If they aren't back in half an hour, send out a search team."

Jeff nodded curtly in response and left.

Emily raised a brow. "Wow, for a straitlaced guy, he took that well. I guess working security for a rock band he's used to seeing weird stuff." Emily shifted uncomfortably on the couch. She took out her phone and texted Nicki: *Where the fuck are you?* When no response came, she thrust her phone back into her purse. *Don't overreact.* Elliot had a point about the spanking. Nicki would be back soon and they could leave.

Jack sat next to her. Too close. He must have read her expression because he shifted over to the far end of the couch.

ELLIOT HAD BEEN WORRIED ABOUT JACK SINCE HIS breakup with Christie. He'd never seen Jack so lost. Not even when he'd broken it off with that little bitch Erica when he'd found out she'd been cheating on him. He'd been hurt, but he'd pushed ahead. Jack always pushed forward. But Christie had totally fucked with his head; Elliot was sure Jack didn't even realize how badly. From what he'd witnessed and what Jack had told him, Elliot's dislike of Christie had turned to disdain. He'd never seen a person change so much. She'd been a sweet, somewhat innocent girl but had turned into another piece of self-serving dead weight. His friend deserved better. He knew Jack was better off without her, but Elliot wasn't sure that Jack wouldn't get back with her if she got her shit together.

Until now.

This girl was different. First off, she wasn't exposing herself to get attention. She didn't simper and wasn't a sycophant. And she wasn't handsy. Jack got womanhandled all the time. He was too nice to brush it off harshly; instead he would gently extricate himself. The chicks had never tried that shit with him. Of course, he was married, but that was no guarantee in this business. Even the dumb ones got that Elliot wasn't interested in any woman except his wife. His whole body ached with missing her.

He studied Emily. This girl was strong. Her friend bailed on her, and she wasn't bawling or creating a scene. It obviously wasn't planned, because her shock was genuine, and she was pissed. Elliot chuckled to himself. She was funny too. Her friend was in for it when she returned. It had been clear that Emily only came backstage because Nicki needled her into it. Jack had his work cut out for him.

And what the hell was wrong with Jack? His interest was clear. He'd never been one to wait for things to happen, not even when they were kids. He'd always been easy and confident around people. Elliot always admired that about him. And it meant that he could bow out of a lot of the celebrity bullshit that went along with being famous. Elliot hated it. But he loved Jack, Buzz, and Curt, so he pushed himself to do it, for them.

Jack needed a shove. "Emily, why do you think it's your fault?"

Her attention snapped to Elliot. "What?"

Jack shot Elliot a murderous look, which he ignored. *Ah, that's better.* "After Curt ran off with your friend, you said it was your fault."

"Before we got here, I reminded Nicki that she promised we'd meet you guys and leave. I should've said 'meet the band and leave together.' You have to be specific with Nicki." Emily huffed nervously. "I hope she doesn't break your friend."

He laughed, as did Jack and Buzz.

"I'm not kidding, this could well turn into a rescue or, worse, a recovery mission."

Elliot took in the serious expression on Emily's face. *Fuck.* He'd been trying to lighten the mood, not make it worse. He shot Jack a sorry shrug.

Emily pulled out her phone again and made a call. From the dirty look she gave it when no one answered, Elliot suspected she was trying to call Nicki.

"You okay?" Jack asked.

"Yeah, I'm all right." She checked her watch for the third time.

"Still thinking about ways to off your friend?" Elliot asked.

"No," she sighed. "I'll probably tie her to the PATH train tracks. It'll be the most cost-effective."

"How so?" Buzz asked.

"I only have to buy rope, a black cape, and a fake mustache."

Elliot laughed. He could just picture Emily standing over her friend tied to the tracks and rolling one end of the thin fake mustache between her thumb and forefinger.

"Do your murderous plans include Curt?" Buzz asked.

Emily seemed to consider that. "No, you still need him for the rest of the tour. Although, he volunteered fast enough, and way more information than we needed. You realize that those two will probably get married, and we'll be invited to the wedding. If Nicki thinks I'll be in their wedding after what she pulled here today, she's lost her mind."

Elliot and Buzz laughed. Jack seemed dazed.

She smiled. "Let's agree now to meet at the bar and slam tequila shots. We'll need to wipe the memory of their spank fest from our minds."

Elliot sat up in the chair as fury burned through him. Buzz looked down, and Jack's mouth dropped open.

"What?" Emily asked. After a few seconds of silence, she smiled and said, "Come on, give me a clue."

Buzz cleared his throat. "I'm in recovery."

Emily's smile faded and she winced. She turned to Buzz. "I'm so sorry. If I'd known, I never would've said something so insensitive."

Elliot glowered. "You expect us to believe you didn't know?"

A blush crept along her cheeks. "Nicki only invited me to the concert this morning because the guy she was supposed— never mind. She's a huge fan and it's her birthday. You guys were great, but I really came to keep an eye on her. Something happened yesterday, and I'm worried about her."

Elliot's anger drained away. He was distrusting of most people, but this girl was genuinely worried for her friend. He liked her.

Buzz smiled at Emily. "No harm done. Besides, someone will have to drive your drunken butts home."

Emily let out the breath she'd been holding, and she stood and sat next to Buzz in the chair Curt had vacated. "This must be difficult for you. I understand touring can be grueling, not to mention being away from your family and your support system."

Buzz smiled at her. "I'm not away from my support system. The guys are always there for me. In fact, this whole process would be harder without them." Buzz looked at him and Jack. "I go to meetings every day, and my sponsor and I mapped out the tour."

"That's great, planning is important." She smiled. "How long have you been sober?"

Buzz leaned forward and smiled. "Two hundred and sixteen days."

Emily extended her hand, and Buzz shook it. "Congratulations. That's no small thing. I understand how tough it can be."

"Are you in recovery?" Jack asked.

Emily shook her head. "A dear friend of mine has been in recovery for almost ten years. He still has moments of weakness, although it happens less and less."

"Will you celebrate his tenth anniversary?" Buzz asked.

"Privately. No one knows his history, and he wants to keep it that way. He doesn't want people looking at him differently or, worse, waiting for him to fall off the wagon."

Buzz nodded. "Yeah, I understand. I was lucky I got into rehab when I did. My parents always look so worried when I visit. I don't blame them. My brothers"—he tilted his chin indicating Jack and Elliot—"don't treat me any differently."

Elliot guffawed. "Why would I treat you differently? You're still an ass-hat." Elliot was relieved Buzz had gotten his shit together.

Buzz flipped him off. "Your friend still has urges, even after ten years?"

"Yeah, sometimes. He travels for work, so he prepares in advance and always knows where a meeting is. Traveling complicates matters, but he knows he's responsible for his sobriety. He makes it his number one priority. He loves what he does, but if it ever got to where it put his sobriety in jeopardy, he'd quit. That's how committed he is to himself." Emily smiled at Buzz. "Surround yourself with people who understand and support you, and it'll be you celebrating in ten years."

Buzz nodded. "Thank you for that. It's been a true pleasure to meet you, Emily." He stood. "I'm beat. Black, you coming?"

Elliot ignored Buzz's pointed look. "You go ahead. I'm gonna wait for Curt. I'm dying to see what happens next."

Buzz grabbed his bag and walked out the door.

Chapter Six

J ack leaned back on the couch. He was impressed with
Emily's compassion toward Buzz. Sometimes he felt like a
mother hen; Jack always worried about him. Her face had
been so animated when she spoke of her friend. She was
beautiful, a good friend, funny, and smart. And right now, she
looked upset, and he didn't like it. "Don't worry, a search
party is on standby, remember?" Jack soothed.

Elliot smirked. "Maybe we should upgrade it to a rescue
mission. If the lovely lady here is to be believed, Curt may
need immediate medical attention."

"Not helping, Black-heart." Even though it would cut
their time together, Jack considered having Jeff find Curt now.

"Not trying to, Jack-off." Elliot settled farther into his
chair.

Bastard was enjoying himself. He looked to Elliott for
support, but he gave Jack his signature shrug that said "What
the fuck do you want from me?" Jack scoffed. "Remind me
again why we're friends?"

"I provide comic relief," Elliot deadpanned, no smirk in
sight.

Emily chuckled at that.

"I'm sure they'll be back soon." Jack needed to distract her, but there was no reason they couldn't get to know each other at the same time. Thanks to Nicki's ramblings, he knew exactly what to say. "So, you're a writer. What do you write?"

Emily eyed him suspiciously, but after a few seconds, she said, "Books."

Not the in he hoped for. She fidgeted with her purse strap, but she calmed down, so he held off on calling Jeff. It was just as well Elliot waited around for Curt, as Jack was sure she'd be more comfortable with someone else in the room.

"What type of books?" Jack asked.

"Romance novels," Emily said, lifting her chin.

"I've never met a romance novelist. How many novels have you written?"

Emily's brows drew together. "Eight. Plus, four novellas published with other authors."

"With Nicki?" Elliot asked.

"Ah, no." Emily paused. "Her stories are different."

Elliot leaned forward in his chair. "She doesn't write romances?"

"No, she does, they're just different."

"Different how?" Elliot pushed, his lips curling in a wicked grin.

"She writes contemporary whirlwind romances, set in lavish destinations. Innocent girl meets world-weary tycoon. Mild, two flames tops."

Jack leaned in. "What does that mean?"

Emily smiled. "It's a rating system our publisher uses, like for movies, you know, G, PG, R, except with flames."

"How many flames are there?" Elliot asked.

"Five."

"How many flames do your novels get?" he and Elliot asked simultaneously.

Emily paused, leaned in, looked back and forth between them, and settled her gaze on Jack. "Four." She sat back with a satisfied grin.

Jack swallowed hard. His pulse quickened and his mouth went dry. *Damn.* That was unexpected. He would've pegged Nicki as the one on the hotter end of the scale. Glancing at Elliot, Jack let out a breath. From Elliot's expression, Jack sensed he was thinking the same thing. Jack adjusted his position on the couch to give himself more room.

The wicked gleam in her eyes told him she was enjoying this.

"With no frame of reference, how hot is four flames?" Elliot asked.

"One is low intimacy, kissing, hand holding, nothing graphic. Five is explicit sex scenes, profanity, possibly including BDSM or multiple partners." She smirked and her eyes danced with wicked delight.

For the second time tonight, Jack forgot how to breathe. Elliot was struck with a sudden coughing fit, but he recovered first. "Like those *Fifty Shades* books?"

Jack drew in a ragged breath. He hadn't even kissed her yet, and she left him breathless. He couldn't wait to, but he wasn't about to let Elliot off the hook. "Whoa, you read those books, buddy?"

Elliot flipped him off. "Not me, Jack-ass, Siobhan."

"Siobhan is Black-balls' wife. She's a sweetheart. Don't know what she sees in him."

Elliot snickered. "Buddy, she chose me over you, which proves her refined taste in men."

Jack snorted. "Dude, seriously, she dated me first, but we realized we'd be better off as friends, and I suggested she go out with you, hoped she could teach your lips to smile instead of smirk." Jack turned his attention back to Emily, and the expression on her face was priceless. Her eyes widened, and her lips parted into a soft "O." *I have something that could fill that "O." Shit, not the time.* Unfortunately, his reaction was instantaneous.

"You dated Elliot's wife?" Emily asked in disbelief.

"Yes, when we were sixteen. Siobhan's family had just moved into town. All the guys drooled over her. She's beautiful, red hair, green eyes, classic Irish lass. She was shy, and since she was new, I asked her to the back-to-school dance. She said yes, and we dated for a few weeks, but the chemistry wasn't there, so we became friends." Jack finally had Emily's full attention, and it warmed him in a very pleasant way.

"I felt sorry for Black-balls here," Jack said, tilting his head in Elliot's direction. "Always a stick in the mud, so I suggested to Siobhan that maybe she could ask him out. She didn't vomit at the idea, which was shocking. He wasn't charming, same as now. So, she bit the bullet and asked him out, and the rest is history." Jack shot Elliot a pointed look. "You're welcome."

"Ha." Elliot roared with laughter. "That's not how I remember it. Jack-off has a faulty memory. He was so busy being Mr. Nice Guy that he didn't realize the whole time Siobhan dated him, it was to be around me. We'd get together and jam at Jack's house." Elliot grinned. "We called ourselves McBlack. Siobhan was always over 'cause she and Jack were dating." Elliot air quoted dating.

"Anyhow, she was really there to see me; she always talked to me, and we had a definite chemistry. She did the right thing, dumped his sorry ass, and, as Jack pointed out, asked me out." Elliot leaned back with a triumphant expression on his face.

"Dude, she only talked to you because she was being polite." Jack looked at Emily. "I told you she was sweet. She took pity on this sad sack."

"I'm not a sad sack. I brood. The chicks dig it. They think

I'm deep and shit. I'm just thinking about"—Elliot stopped and cleared his throat—"never mind."

Jack poked the grizzly with a stick. "How's your wife, Black? Talk to her lately?"

EMILY WAS SURPRISED WHEN ELLIOT'S FACE FLUSHED with fury.

"Fuck you, Jack." His dark eyes turned black.

"Why are you pissed at Jack?" Emily asked.

"Yeah, Black, why are you pissed at me?"

Elliot let his middle finger answer for him.

Emily sat forward and drew her left leg under her. *Observing men in their natural habitat, fascinating.* She could use this.

"He hasn't spoken to his wife in weeks."

Emily's brows lifted. Elliot just scowled.

"Elliot and Siobhan are separated. Dumbass here won't call her. She's less than forty miles away. He could go see her, but he's being stubborn."

Elliot exploded. "She doesn't want to talk. Last time I called her, it ended in a fight, said she needed space, so I'm giving her space."

"Almost a month's worth of space, Black? Don't you think she'll be hurt you didn't reach out to her? You know how stubborn she can be. Trying to out stubborn her will end in divorce. Call her."

"Her fingers aren't broken." Elliot grunted. He pushed out of the chair and paced the room.

"Stubborn prick. What did you fight about, anyway?"

Elliot turned on him and said through gritted teeth, "My wife thinks we should date other people."

Shock registered on Jack's face. "Fuck, Elliot. I'm sorry."

"But you're not dating anyone. You're still in love with her," Emily said.

"Yes, always have been, always will be." Elliot's resigned answer was full of hurt.

"That's a long time to be miserable because you're afraid or too angry to pick up the phone," Emily said.

"But..." Elliot drew in a breath.

"How about it, buddy?"

Elliot scoffed. "We've been separated for three hundred days." At Jack's triumphant look, Elliot gave him the finger. "Yeah, that's right, I'm counting."

He flopped into the chair vacated by Buzz. He rubbed the back of his neck and stared at Emily for a minute. With a barely perceptible nod, Elliot continued. "Siobhan had a miscarriage last summer. Instead of being with my pregnant wife, I was in California writing our new album. I rushed home, but the damage was done. We had a huge fight, and she threw me out. Said she didn't want to raise our kids by herself." The muscles in his jaw clenched and unclenched.

Based on Jack's expression, Emily thought Elliot's disclosure was unusual.

Elliot's voice was filled with pain. "We were due in the studio in August to record our album, and that's followed by a twenty-fucking month tour. I would've been home for the birth, but then I'd have to leave again. She can't deal with this lifestyle anymore. Said she's tired of being alone for months at a time. I don't want to miss my kids growing up," Elliot growled and looked down.

The raw pain on Elliot's face made it hard for Emily to breathe past the lump that formed in her throat. "I'm sorry for your loss." Her emotions in turmoil, Emily tried and failed to stop the scenarios from taking over in her head. "Your trip home must've been excruciating. I imagine you were both wishing for the other, both cursing the distance. By the time you got home, I'm sure she'd worked herself up into a frenzy, and that's a bad state to be in, so easy to say things you don't mean. And you must've been out of your mind on the flight home."

Elliot raised his head and nodded.

Emily exhaled deeply. "Definitely one of those times an active imagination is a dreadful thing. No doubt, awful things were said, but do you want to let a"—Emily shifted her eyes to Jack, who held up six fingers—"six-year marriage go down without a fight?"

Elliot shook his head. "She wants me to quit the band, said she can't continue the way things are, that she deserves better. That our children will deserve better."

"She's right," Emily said.

Elliot's head snapped up. "You think I should quit?"

"No," Emily said. "She's right that children deserve the best we can do for them. Sometimes that doesn't fall in line with normal. You quitting the band was the only solution she came up with, but it doesn't mean it's the only one."

Elliot shoulders slumped, and he returned to staring at the floor.

"Do you have a solution?" Jack asked.

Emily tilted her head. "I have an idea."

Elliot leaned in and half-smiled. "I'd consider anything if it can save my marriage."

Emily paused for a long second. She took a deep breath and let it out slowly. "What does she do for a living?"

Elliot laughed wistfully. "She loves kids, always has, she works in a daycare center."

"Well, she may not like the idea, assuming she even wants to hear what a stranger has to suggest, since it's none of my business..." Emily wished she'd kept her mouth shut, but she hated seeing anyone in pain.

"Please, any idea that might help."

With Elliot's pain so visible, Emily had no choice but to continue. Nicki must be rubbing off on her. "Okay, assuming she'd be willing to quit her job, once you have kids, pack 'em up and take 'em on tour with you."

The hope in Elliot's face faded. "Kids need stability, not being dragged all over God's green earth because their dad's in a band."

Emily shook her head. "Kids need their parents, love, nurturing, food, water, shelter, and clothing. The stability comes from being together. Everything else is negotiable."

Elliot started to get up, but Emily stopped him. "My dad was a Marine. My parents married when they were twenty-one. My mom lived with her parents until she finished college, but they were miserable without each other. They'd only see each other when he had leave. Once she graduated and family housing came through, she moved to Camp Lejeune, where my brother was born. I was born in California. When he wasn't deployed, my dad was home for dinner, helped with our homework, played catch with my brother, and had tea parties with me." Emily smiled. "We were happy. We did all the things other kids did. We just moved more often, but that was our normal."

Elliot nodded. "I've thought about maybe bringing the kids along, but it seemed so selfish on my part, you know, having my cake and eating it too. I don't know if Siobhan will go for it, but it's a start, right? Oh." His smile faded. "Siobhan will have to sacrifice more than I will."

"I asked my mom if she ever regretted giving up her life in New York. She said she never gave up anything. She stayed in touch with her friends and family with phone calls and email, and she still loved them dearly but chose to be with my dad."

Elliot relaxed back into his chair. "Siobhan can't hate me anymore than she already does, so I guess it can't make things worse."

The exhaustion that had plagued Emily the last three weeks returned full force. She needed to find Nicki so they could leave.

"Emily," Jack said. "Do your novels have BDSM?"

Emily blinked a few times before she looked at Jack. He was trying to change the subject. Good idea but she wished it hadn't come back on her. "No...well, maybe a little B. One of my characters was tied to a bed with silk stockings during a game of sex truth or dare. It was all in good fun though, just so he wouldn't touch her while she stripped for him. He had a problem keeping his hands to himself, and she didn't appreciate being interrupted."

Jack grunted.

"What does a story have to have to get four flames?" Elliot asked, glancing at Jack with a smirk.

Emily could practically hear Jack call him a dick. "Well, the sex is explicit, there's more of it, and no flowery euphemisms to describe the action. Dick, cock, tits, pussy, fuck. Sex takes place outside, backroom of a bar, executive lounge at an airport under a blanket, anywhere the mood strikes." The room suddenly felt warm, and Emily licked her dry lips.

Chapter Seven

H e was trying not to stare, but Jack couldn't help but notice the way Emily's fitted T-shirt hugged her full breasts. Or the way they rose and fell when she took a breath. Or the flush that crept up her neck. When her pink tongue darted out to moisten her naturally rosy lips, he could practically feel it on his skin. And when she said tits, pussy, and fuck, his brain conjured an image of her naked. Under him. Over him. Up against a wall. *Shit.* He had to shower as he had an urgent need to attend to. A bead of perspiration trickled between his shoulder blades, and he shifted on the couch. As much as he wanted to hear more, he needed to change the subject before he embarrassed himself.

Elliot snickered under his breath, but Jack ignored him. He closed his eyes, in the hope he could clear his mind of the dirty thoughts roving around inside his head.

Big. Fucking. Mistake.

He wanted to fuck her—hard. His dick threatened to burst the seams of his jeans, and it was all he could do not to unzip and rub one off. Good thing there wasn't a bed in this room, or he'd beg her to tie him to it with silk stockings and torture him with a slow striptease.

Jack's mind filled in the blanks; lace bra and panties in the exact color of her burgundy shirt. *Against her fair skin, oh fuck.* The lace barely contained her tits, and her pussy was drenched. Her scent drove him mad.

While tied to the bed, he'd beg her to climb on his face so he could drink up every drop of her juices. Not being able to touch her while feasting on her would drive him crazy, so he'd rip through the stockings and pin her to his face with one hand, while reaching behind her to free her tits from the lacy fabric with the other.

After she came, he'd enter her sweet pussy in one thrust from behind. He'd fuck her hard. With every thrust, she'd scream, "Oh fuck, Jack, yes, harder." So, he'd fuck her harder.

He needed to see her face, look into her beautiful eyes, so he pulled out, flipped her onto her back, and took her again. Her long legs wrapped around his waist. Oh. So. Fucking. Good. She was so wet that his dick glided in and out of her with ease. Their lips met in a brutal kiss. She nipped his bottom lip and moaned. Tearing his lips from hers, Jack trailed kisses down her neck and over to her shoulder, which he bit just hard enough to leave a faint mark.

He took her nipple in his mouth and scraped it with his teeth. She convulsed around his cock, and he came with a shudder. Jack collapsed on her, spent. The smell of their sweat and cum mingled in his nostrils. He could still taste her, and his semi-hard dick was still inside her. Bliss.

When Jack opened his eyes, Emily and Elliot stared at him. *Oh fuck.* He felt every second of his three months of self-imposed celibacy. He wanted to excuse himself to the bathroom, but that would be too obvious, so he had to get his shit together. "Sorry, just got a little light-headed. I haven't eaten dinner yet," Jack said, attempting to explain why he'd zoned out.

"Should I call someone?" Emily asked, her brows pulling together as she stood.

Her concern was apparent. He didn't deserve it, but he was grateful for the out. A quick glance at Elliot confirmed he understood Jack's situation.

"No, I'm fine, really. I need to eat soon." Jack waved her back into her seat. "I eat a small meal about three hours before a gig, then a regular dinner after, but we got held up at the airport and I only grabbed a protein bar. Apparently, it wasn't enough." At least that was the truth.

Elliot grabbed three bottles of water, handing one to Emily and one to Jack. "You're probably dehydrated, too. Drink up."

Jack took a long drink. "Thanks man." He needed to do something with his hands, so he grabbed his bag and fished out a granola bar. He took a bite, trying to remember to chew with his mouth closed.

"Do you have low blood sugar?" she asked, leaning in.

Jack sighed. "No, nothing's wrong with me." He was interrupted by Elliot's snort. *And he's back.* Jack gave him the finger. "No, just bad timing today. This'll help."

Emily's face softened as she sat back and smiled. She had a gorgeous smile. When it reached her eyes, he was a goner. He'd always been a sucker for a great smile, and even though she'd had a rather eventful night, she could still smile. She had the most beautiful hazel eyes. Jack caught himself zoning out again. He searched for a topic besides erotica, sex, silk stockings...

Emily stood. "It's getting late. I don't want to hold you up, you probably have plans—"

"Nope, no plans," Jack said. *What the fuck is wrong with me?* Ask her out already.

JACK'S ZONE OUT SEEMED LIKE SOMETHING ELSE. SHE was normally a confident woman, but catching her fiancé fucking another woman had trashed her self-confidence. Jack could, and probably did, get any woman he wanted. He was intelligent and caring, two things she normally found very appealing, but he had to realize by now he was wasting his time with her. And being in the band's dressing room, backstage at Madison Square Garden, wasn't normal. Not for her anyway. She didn't sleep around, and she was no way near ready to date. Date a rock star? Did they even date? Didn't they just screw random women one after the other?

She knew Vince didn't date, at least not like a regular person. He'd see a girl for a few months, but then he'd be leaving on tour again, and he said it wasn't possible to keep up a relationship like that. Emily knew Vince wasn't lonely on tour. He was handsome, and girls had always flocked to him, including her. One of his bandmates was married, but that didn't stop him from screwing every girl he saw. Even if Jack was like Vince, he was on tour, and that made dating impossible. Not that she was ready. She wasn't. How could she ever trust her judgment again?

Emily grew more uncomfortable by the minute. It wasn't so bad while they'd been talking, but the conversation had stalled, and Jack kept staring at her. And where the hell was Nicki? She'd been gone for twenty-five minutes.

"Are you seeing anyone?" Jack asked.

Emily gaped at him. He was asking her out. Then his zone out... Emily's cheeks heated. She must've given him the wrong idea. Of course, she had with the way she'd stared at him while he was on stage. But then again, he was the singer, everyone stared at him. Had she misled him? Not allowing herself to be a coward, she owned that she was flattered by his obvious interest. Had she allowed herself to enjoy it so much that she'd encouraged him?

When Emily didn't answer, Jack looked at Elliot. "What do you think, Black, boyfriend?"

Elliot leaned forward in his chair and studied her.

She blushed and shifted on the couch but didn't look away. She wished they'd stop staring at her.

"Nope," Elliot said, as verbose as ever. He leaned back and took a drink of water.

Emily ignored them and took back control of the conversation. "How long have you guys been in a band together? I should've done a search, but my main purpose in coming tonight was to keep an eye on Nicki."

Elliot smirked. "How'd that work out?"

Her smile faded, and she looked down at clenched fists. "Epic fail."

"Hey, it's not that bad," Elliot said.

She put up her hand. "Don't. I was supposed to keep her from crashing and burning tonight. Instead I supplied the gasoline and the match." Every emotion she had was so twisted she couldn't trust anything. Rage, frustration, humiliation, hurt, and insecurity all warred against the growing attraction she felt for Jack. It assaulted her fast and furiously, and now confusion mixed with worry for Nicki had her angrily swiping the tears that fell.

Jack moved closer but didn't touch her. "Emily, Curt's a good guy, he'll treat her right. I'll have Jeff find them right now." Jack made a call and issued the order for the search to begin.

As Emily's tears continued to fall, Elliot handed her a tissue. She mentally shook herself. After several deep breaths, she realized her eyes were scrunched closed. More deep breaths. When she opened her eyes, Jack had inched closer, and Elliot crouched down next to her. She smiled weakly at them. A heaviness settled in her chest. She dabbed her eyes with the tissue, much like Nicki had earlier in the day, only her mascara was probably running down her cheeks.

"I know we seem like an odd couple, but Nicki's a good friend, sweet, kind, and nice. Nice is good." Emily excused herself to the bathroom. Not as bad as she'd expected. She splashed her red face with cool water, and she gently dabbed the faint black marks from under her eyes, taking longer than necessary. Her face was red, but there wasn't anything she could do about that. Maybe they'd just leave. Men ran from hysterical women, didn't they?

When she returned to the dressing room, they were still there. Jack was back on his end of the couch and Elliot was in the chair. "Sorry about that." Emily resumed her seat on the couch. Picking up her water bottle, she took a few sips.

Jack smiled. "You never answered my question."

She looked down. "No."

"Bad breakup?"

Emily nodded. She hadn't thought of Sully much tonight, and the break was just what she needed. She was well aware what Nicki thought she needed. In Nicki's own twisted way, she'd probably convinced herself that she was helping by leaving Emily here with Jack. She loved Nicki, but sometimes she wanted to strangle the shit out of her.

"I'm not going to ask you back to my hotel room." Jack's voice drew her out of her head.

Her eyes met his, but she said nothing.

Elliot snorted but Jack ignored him. "I'd like to see you again. I'm in town for the next six nights."

Her mouth fell open, but again, she said nothing.

"Maybe we could go to dinner. What I'd like is your phone number."

Elliot, who was in the middle of taking a drink of water, choked and sputtered loudly.

"Fuck you, Black."

This was worse than she'd imagined it'd be. If he'd been arrogant, expecting she'd fuck him because he was a rock star, she would've told him to go to hell, found Nicki, and left. *Why'd he have to be nice?* Emily looked Jack directly in the eyes. Shit, she had to stop doing that. She swallowed hard and with as light a tone as she could manage, said "Sorry, Jack, but I agree with Elliot on this one, very un-rock star of you."

Elliot erupted into laughter, which quickly turned into coughing.

"Why are you still here, Black?"

"Apparently, I'm not the only one who provides comic relief," Elliot said. "Sorry, buddy, she's right, *very* un-rock star of you." Elliot's face broke into a genuine smile. "I like this girl, Jack."

"Me too."

Jack and Elliot exchanged an odd glance.

She needed to get out of here. What had been uncomfortable was now unbearable. Tonight was a train wreck. Jack smiled when she looked at him. Emily took a deep breath and prepared to let him down easily.

But before she could, Jack asked, "You never liked Nicki's ex?"

"What?"

"Nicki said you never liked her ex."

Where is he going with this? She just wanted to go home. "He seemed okay at first."

"What happened?"

Emily was at a loss. Why was he asking about Nicki's ex? "He invited me to have a three-way with them." She enjoyed Jack's shocked expression. She tilted her head, daring him to ask any more questions.

"Big mistake," Elliot said. "You're not the type. Guy must be an idiot."

That caught Emily off guard, and she was flattered by his observation. "He's an idiot because he kept asking after I declined."

A loud knock on the dressing room door brought a sense of relief to Emily. Good, they could finally leave.

"Come in," Jack said.

Jeff entered alone.

Emily's smile faded.

Jeff looked at Jack. "They're gone."

Chapter Eight

The color drained out of Emily's face so suddenly, Jack feared she might pass out. He needed to fix this. "What do you mean they're gone?" He might have to kill Curt or, at the very least, maim him.

"I mean they're gone. They left. We searched all the usual places," Jeff said. "I called Polson. He took them back to the hotel about thirty minutes ago."

Jack dialed Curt, but the call went straight to voicemail.

Emily shot to her feet, grabbed her purse, and headed to the door. "I have to go." Pulling out her phone she turned to Jeff. "Can you tell me how to get out of here?"

"Ye—"

"I'll take you home." Jack jumped up and crossed the room in three strides.

"Oh," Emily stammered. "You're gonna take me to New Jersey?"

"Sure."

"That isn't necessary. I'll take a cab."

"No. This is my fault. I didn't think they'd leave the building."

"Guess they needed privacy for all that spanking." Elliot snickered.

Jack was pissed at Curt but aimed it at Elliot. "Black, don't be a dick. Can't you see she's upset?"

Elliot's smirk disappeared. "I'm sorry." He stood and put his arm around her. "He's right, I am being a dick."

Emily didn't move away.

Jack glared at Elliot.

He smirked back. In a whisper, he said, "Jack's a good guy. He'll make sure you get home safely." Elliot stepped back, looked at Jack, winked, and left.

Emily stood there, still in shock over her friend's abandonment.

"Let me take a quick shower, and I'll get you home. Jeff, we'll meet you outside in twenty minutes." With Elliot gone, Emily might not feel comfortable alone with him. "On second thought, stand by. If you hear a peep out of her, a hiccup even, rush in and kick my ass, ask questions later."

An unexpected chuckle escaped Emily's lips. He liked the sound of it.

"Sure thing, Jack. I hope you know what you're getting into."

Drawing Emily back to the couch, Jack said, "Jeff's an ex-Marine and—"

"There's no such thing as an ex-Marine," Emily and Jeff said simultaneously.

Jeff looked at Emily with a raised brow.

"My dad was."

Jeff gave a curt nod. "How?"

"Car accident."

Jeff's stern face softened. "I'm so sorry." He looked at Jack. "I'll be outside." He pointed to his eyes with his index and middle fingers and then to Jack. His lips curved up slightly. Jeff turned and left, closing the door. Jack was certain that was the first time he'd seen Jeff smile in the three months since he'd hired him.

Emily chuckled and smiled. Jack wanted it to stay there, so he grabbed her bottle of water off the table and handed it to her. "I really don't want my ass kicked, so in case of hiccups, take a few sips." Smiling, he turned and headed into the bathroom.

Jack peeled off his clothes and stepped into the shower. He considered taking a cold shower, but he was long past that helping. Adjusting the temperature to just under scalding, he grabbed the shampoo and lathered his hair.

Images of Emily filled his mind. The sound and feel of the water raining down on him and the stroke of his hand calmed him. She had a beautiful laugh. And chuckle. Her beauty left him breathless. Her hazel eyes, rimmed in green, were browner when she was pissed. He'd love to find out what shade they turned when she comes. How would it feel to kiss her lips? Taste her? Caress her skin? Jack groaned as he stroked himself.

Hearing his name, Jack opened his eyes to see Emily standing there. Naked. He faced her, his dick at full attention, his hand still stroking. She stepped into the shower, and he tugged her under the spray. Emily's full lips smiled at him as he pulled her close and kissed her. He palmed her ample tits, stroking her nipples with his thumbs, which elicited a shiver from her. Emily's hands went to work on him; one hand stroked his hard cock while the other cupped his balls and gently rolled them.

Oh yeah, that feels so fucking good. He moaned into her mouth, and she responded by nipping his tongue gently with her teeth.

She spread her legs and rubbed his bare cock between her thighs. She was so fucking wet. Emily knelt on the floor and took his slippery cock all the way into her mouth. The sensation was unbelievable. She swirled her tongue around the tip and nipped him lightly with her teeth. If this went on any longer, he'd come.

He pulled out of her mouth and motioned for her to stand. She didn't. Instead she pressed her tits together and leaned closer to his cock. He couldn't resist. He thrust forward, pushing his cock into the valley between her tits. *So close.*

But he needed to be inside her, so he pulled back and helped her to stand. Their lips met in a savage kiss. He trailed his hand down her flat stomach and cupped her pussy, briefly circling her clit, and then slipped his middle finger inside her. Her moan echoed off the shower walls. She was fucking drenched. He stroked her clit with his thumb, and she clenched her muscles around his finger, breaking the kiss to lay her head on his shoulder.

When he withdrew his hand, she whimpered. Raising his fingers to his mouth, he licked her juices. He offered her a finger, and she took it between her full lips.

Jack had to be inside her now.

Turning so her back was up against the shower wall, he lifted her, and her long legs wrapped around his waist. One upward thrust and he was inside her, only a little at first—he wanted her as crazed for him as he was for her. Emily moaned and tried to push down, so he pulled back.

He pumped into her slowly. So fucking good. Emily said his name over and over, which drove him wild. Taking her mouth again, their tongues tangled. He felt the familiar pull in his balls, and he couldn't stop himself from coming. She was coming too, so he kept pumping into her.

"Jack, are you okay?" Emily asked, her voice distant.

Jack's eyes shot open. He was alone. *Shit.*

"Yeah, be out in a minute." He leaned against the shower wall and let the water wash over him for a few seconds before turning it off and stepping out. He quickly dried himself and looked around for his clothes. He must have left his bag in the dressing room. "Emily, can you bring my bag to the door? I forgot my clothes."

"I don't see it."

"It was on the floor next to the couch."

"I'll look around." Seconds ticked by. "Wait," Emily yelled.

Jack tied a towel around his waist, and walking to the doorway, he peered out. *Oh shit.* Emily knelt on the couch, looking over the back. As she reached behind the couch, her delightful ass rose in the air. He should look away but couldn't.

Emily yelled, "Got it." Pulling herself back onto the couch, she turned and saw him.

Now he looked away. Too late, his dick was semi-hard again, and she'd caught him staring at her ass.

"Assuming you didn't put it there, I don't know how it got back there." Emily handed him the bag.

"Neither do I." Jack's mouth was suddenly dry. He stood there wearing only a towel and holding the bag. *Elliot.*

"Why would Elliot put your bag behind..."

Jack must've said Elliot's name out loud. "When you went into the bathroom, I got a text. My phone was in my jacket on the chair. That would've given the bastard time to chuck my bag behind the couch." Emily stared at him. At least he had the bag in front of him, so she couldn't see the towel tenting at his groin.

She looked him up and down. "What? You're standing there in a towel, I'm not supposed to look?"

Now it was his turn to smile. The expression of female appreciation on her face made every day in the gym worth it. Thanks to Elliot, he was sure she was interested. She'd been doing a good job of hiding it. *Patience.* With a wink, Jack turned and strode into the bathroom.

DAMN, THAT MAN HAD THE MOST PERFECT BODY SHE had ever seen: tanned, toned, and wow. Emily took a few steadying breaths. He'd stared at her ass when she was so elegantly draped over the couch trying to retrieve his bag. Why shouldn't she get an eyeful? And what had Elliot been thinking? Jack didn't need help.

Jack in a towel was entirely too intimate. She'd only seen serious boyfriends in such an intimate way. And men in movies, but the effect wasn't the same. An almost naked, living, breathing man in the same room with you was much more potent.

Warmth pooled low in her belly and radiated throughout her body. Damn. Emily fanned herself. She'd gotten a better look at his Celtic band tattoo around his right biceps. He also had "SH" in a fancy script, tattooed on the back of his neck, just below his hairline.

Delicious didn't even begin to describe him. If there was a window, she'd stick her head out it to cool off. Why was she reacting like a schoolgirl? She wiped her damp palms on her jeans. What was wrong with her?

Sully was handsome. He kept his blond hair short, but Emily always wished he'd grow it a little longer so she'd have more to run her hands through or tug. His green eyes had mesmerized her. Not as tall as Jack or as ripped, but he was fit, and he'd looked hot in a suit and tie. He spent more on his wardrobe in six months than Emily did all year. To his credit, he never tried to change her more laid-back, comfortable way of dressing. He'd always said he loved her the way she was, but considering how things ended, that couldn't be true. Emily tore her thoughts off Sully. This emotional roller coaster ride was exhausting. One minute she was eyeballing Jack, and the next she was fighting off memories of Sully. She was in hell.

"Hey, you never answered my question." Jack stood in the doorway pulling on his shirt.

"What question?"

"I asked for your phone number."

Shit, that little ogle was costing her. His swagger was on full display, and he wouldn't let this go easily. "You said that you'd like my phone number, which isn't a question, so no failure to answer on my part." She kept her face neutral, but at Jack's expression, she couldn't help but grin. It was better than crying.

"Fair enough. Emily, may I please have your phone number?"

Jack's cocky grin was breathtaking, but she had to end this now. "No." *Shit*. His stunned expression had her fumbling to explain. "Jack, you seem like a great guy. My breakup was awful, and I'm not ready to date again. I'm not even sure you're asking to date me." Emily shifted her gaze from him. "I don't sleep around, and I'm not into revenge sex, as Nicki calls it." Damn, she was rambling again.

Seeing Jack nearly naked had scrambled her brain. "If you'd singled out any other girl, you'd be balls deep by now. I'm sorry you wasted your time." As flattering as it was to have Jack's interest—he was handsome, talented, and hot as fuck—she wouldn't lead him on.

Jack leveled her with a huge smile. "I haven't wasted my time. It's been a pleasure getting to know you. No reason we can't keep in touch until you are ready."

"Would you stop smiling at me? You are the most exasper—"

A loud knock on the door interrupted her, and it opened before Jack could say anything. Jeff pushed in and said curtly, "There's trouble with Buzz."

Then all hell broke loose.

Jeff's expression told Emily this wasn't just some bullshit rock star drama. Jack rushed for the door.

"Shoes," Emily yelled.

He stopped and looked around.

"They must be in the bathroom," Emily said.

He rushed into the bathroom and returned hopping on one foot while pulling on the other boot.

"What's happened?" he asked.

Jeff looked at Emily.

"It's okay, she's trustworthy."

That was all Jeff needed to launch into a sitrep. "Don't have all the details, but there's been a confrontation with a white male and two of my security guys. Not sure how Buzz figures into this, but since he's there, I thought you'd want to know."

Jack grabbed Emily's hand, and they raced out of the dressing room with Jeff leading the way.

Emily's head spun. She didn't understand why Jack grabbed her hand, but she didn't want to waste time asking. When they reached the area where the commotion was, Jack dropped her hand and yelled to Jeff, "Stay with her."

He ran to where two security guys had a man detained. "What the fuck are you doing here, Dewbury?" Jack asked, addressing the detainee. One of the security guys said something to him, and Jack swung at Dewbury. His punch landed on the guy's jaw, and he fell backward.

Jeff moved Emily behind him, effectively blocking her view of the fight. She spotted Buzz sitting on the floor against the wall. Emily touched Jeff's arm and pointed to Buzz. Jeff nodded, and they walked to where he sat. Jeff stopped two feet in front of Buzz, and Emily sat on the floor next to him.

Buzz stared at a spot on the floor between his knees. When he turned to her, he looked dejected.

"Hey," Emily said.

Buzz nodded and returned to staring.

She glanced over at the melee. Security attempted to get Jack off the white male. It wasn't going well for them. Whoever this guy was, he felt the full weight of Jack's fury.

She let the silence draw out. If Buzz wanted to talk, he would.

"I should've walked away as soon as I saw him. He's bad news."

The security guys were finally able to disengage Jack from Dewbury. Blood trickled out the side of Dewbury's mouth, and he had the beginnings of a nasty black eye. He was doubled over, so two security guys held him in place. And even though security held Jack back, that didn't stop him from kicking the guy.

"That's on me," Buzz said, looking back at Emily.

"Are you okay?" Emily asked.

"Yeah."

What would Vince do? He'd leave it up to Buzz to talk. Emily slid closer and put her arm around his shoulders. When Buzz moved, she was afraid she'd crossed a line, but he pulled a baggie filled with different pills out his jacket and handed it to her. *Oh, fuck.* She shoved the baggie into her jeans pocket.

"He gave me that. I don't know why I kept it," Buzz said weakly.

"Because you were tempted. A guy you used to know handed you a bag with pills in it, and in that instant, you forgot you were sober and took it."

"I've been sober for two hundred and sixteen days. How could I forget that? I worked hard to get here, and it's even harder to stay sober." Buzz shook his head. "He used to be a friend, but we lost touch."

Buzz closed his eyes and rested his head against the wall. "He got in with a bad crowd, petty theft, vandalism. Then he got busted for dealing. Did a few years upstate. I thought he'd cleaned up his act. It was nice seeing a friendly face, we shook hands, and in the process, he left that in my hand."

Emily placed her hand on his.

Buzz exhaled slowly, his voice quivering slightly. "He said 'Great show. Free sample, call me.' One of the security guys saw it and yelled out, and they detained him, but then the baggie was in my pocket. It all happened so fast." Buzz swore under his breath.

"You didn't ask him for drugs."

At Emily's statement, Buzz looked at her. "God, no, of course not."

"You're not responsible for his actions."

"But why didn't I throw them back at him or give them to one of the security guys?"

The anger in his voice sent a shiver down her spine. "That guy is an asshole, okay. You need to focus on what really happened here, Buzz. You didn't ask him for drugs."

"I held onto them. I must have wanted them, right?"

Emily was out of her league here. "Maybe you should call your sponsor."

Jeff's security guys hauled Dewbury away. Jack calmed down, so they released him. He strode over, stopping to have a word with Jeff, and then crouched next to Buzz. "Hey, man, how ya doing?"

Buzz shook his head and looked away.

"Did Dewbury give you anything?"

Buzz nodded.

Emily took the baggie out and handed it to Jack. "Buzz gave this to me." She gave Jack an encouraging smile.

"Jack," Buzz started, "I swear, I didn't ask him for those, and I didn't take any. You have to believe me." He looked down. "You guys have been with me one hundred percent, and I wouldn't let you down like this."

Jack touched his hand. "I know."

"You know what, Buzz?" Emily said. "You were tested, and I say you passed."

"Damn straight," Jack agreed.

"Jack," Jeff said.

Jack stood and turned to Jeff, handing him the baggie.

Buzz took out his phone, so Emily stood and stepped away to give him privacy.

Jack walked over and sagged against the wall.

"He's calling his sponsor," Emily said.

"I can't thank you enough. Buzz should've been my priority, but when I saw that motherfucker, I lost it. If you hadn't—"

"Hey," Emily said, leaning against the wall next to Jack. "You don't have to thank me. Anyone would do the same."

Buzz grunted in frustration and shoved his phone into his pocket.

Jack walked over and Emily followed.

"What's wrong?" Jack asked.

"Voicemail. Fuck!"

Emily checked her watch. Vince might be done for the day. She hated to interrupt when he was in the studio, but this was important. Taking out her phone, she dialed his number.

Vince picked up on the second ring. "Hey, Emi, I'm so glad you finally called. After what happened—"

"I'm not calling to talk about that."

"Okay, what's up?"

"I'm with a friend. He's famous, so I won't tell you his name." Emily looked pointedly at Buzz. "He's in the program, and he can't reach his sponsor. I was hoping you could talk to him?"

Without the slightest hesitation, Vince said, "Sure, put him on."

She handed the phone to Buzz, and she and Jack stepped away.

Several emotions passed over Jack's face. "Thank you." He looked like he wanted to kiss her. Instead he smiled.

She had no idea what else to say to convince him she wasn't interested, so Emily said nothing.

"I'd really like to kiss you."

Emily stepped back. "Jack..."

The moment was so awkward neither of them realized that Buzz stood next to them. He handed Emily the phone.

"Thanks, Vince," she said.

"Emi, don't isolate yourself over that asshole. Eddie said you haven't talked to him either. We're worried about you."

Emily looked at Jack and Buzz, who were listening, so she took a few steps away. "Vince, not now, okay?"

"When?"

"I'll call you over the weekend."

"If you don't, I'm getting on a plane. Understood?"

Emily couldn't help but smile. "Yes. Thanks. This weekend, I promise."

"Later, beautiful."

She disconnected the call and put the phone away.

Buzz smiled for the first time. "Thanks, that helped."

"I'm glad."

Buzz winked at Jack. "You two make a great team. I'm outta here. Emily, may I give you a hug?"

"Of course."

"Jack's a good guy," he whispered before stepping back. "See you at the gym tomorrow, Jack?"

"Absolutely."

They watched Buzz leave. Emily was happy she'd been able to help.

"Ready?" Jeff asked.

"I gotta get my bag. Give me five minutes." Jack took Emily's hand, and they walked back to the dressing room.

Chapter Nine

F*uck. Fuck. Fuck. Okay, bad breakup, must be unbelievably bad.* When Emily talked with Vince, the hollow look in her eyes broke Jack's heart. That fucker had crushed her. Jack wasn't sure why, but he felt like the rest of his life was at stake, which was crazy because he just met her. He'd met thousands of girls and felt immediate sexual attraction many times, but this was different. When he saw her, he'd experienced that instant attraction, but there was something else—something deeper. She was beautiful on the outside but even more so on the inside. The compassion she'd showed to his friends tugged at his soul.

Since his breakup, he'd hooked up with girls, but once the fun ended, he felt empty, and for the past three months, he'd felt nothing more than a slight interest in any woman. He'd been hurting, not ready to embark on a new relationship. Until Emily. Jack glanced at her. She looked tired but not beaten. He needed to ease up; if he kept pressing, she'd tell him to fuck off, and he'd never see her again. When they reached the dressing room, he held the door for her. "I'll just be a minute." Walking into the bathroom, he gathered his stuff.

Emily was beautiful, smart, sexy, honest, sincere, brave, and she had a good heart. Just thinking about her had his heart rate accelerating. When he walked into the dressing room, she waited by the door. "Ready?"

"Yeah." Emily smiled. "I want to thank you. This is very nice of you. It's not necessary, but I appreciate it."

"My pleasure." Her smile was so genuine, so beautiful, that his breath caught. As they walked toward the exit, he tightened his fingers into a fist to keep from touching her.

Backstage was always a bustle of activity, and tonight was no exception. Jack peered at Emily. She was taking it all in. "Hey, Denise, how's Bree?"

"Much better, Jack." Denise smiled. "She's making a full recovery." She gave him a playful punch on the arm as he walked past.

"Her sister got caught in a storm while hiking. She slipped on the wet rocks and sprained her ankle and was missing for two days."

"Thank goodness she's okay."

Jack high-fived Matt, their sound engineer. "Hey, man, sounded great tonight."

"I wish we could take credit for it, Jack. It's the Garden's acoustics."

"Hey, Jack." Jay, one of the sound crew stopped Jack. "Is Curt still here?"

Shit. The last thing he wanted was Emily focusing on Curt and Nicki. "No, man. He left a while ago."

Jay looked dejected. "Oh, okay," he mumbled and shuffled away.

Jack spotted their newest crew member, Bernie, short for Bernadette. She was tiny with a pixie haircut but was incredibly strong. And she didn't take any shit from the rest of the crew. "Hey, Bernie, how ya doing?"

"Running circles around these guys, as usual," she replied with a roll of her eyes.

Jack patted her head because he knew she hated it. She tried to swat his hand away, but he was too quick. He jumped to avoid Bernie's leg sweep. "Too slow."

Bernie gave him the finger. Jack smiled. She'd insisted on being treated like one of the guys. They all did what Bernie wanted because Jack was sure she could kick all their asses without breaking a sweat.

Emily stopped short. Jack turned to her. "What?"

"Nothing, I... Nothing."

"We're an equal opportunity band." Jack looked for Beth and Valerie but didn't see them. "Elliot and Buzz hired two sisters, Beth and Valerie Pearlow. Beth is Elliot's bass tech and Val is Buzz's drum tech. They're amazing musicians in their own right. When the tour's over, we're going to help them get a recording deal."

Outside, Jeff waited with the limo, opening the door as they approached.

"Where to?" Jeff asked.

"New Jersey. Take the Lincoln Tunnel," she said.

Emily sat on the rear-facing seat by the door, so Jack sat opposite her. "What kind of music do you like?" From her surprised expression, Jack could tell he'd caught her off guard and gave her a sincere smile.

Emily relaxed back into the seat, tilting her head to the side, and smiled. "I like a lot of different music. I grew up listening to the Beatles. My dad was a huge fan. He had their movies, and we'd watch them together. He'd get up and sing along to the songs, holding me in his arms and dancing." Her smile widened. "When they thought my brother and I were asleep, he'd sing "I Want to Hold Your Hand" to my mom, and they'd dance around the kitchen. In fact"—she leaned in

—"Paul was my first crush." Smiling, she sat back, her eyes dancing at the memories.

"Well, as it happens, I love the Beatles too." Jack raised his hand. "It's true, I'm not sucking up." At her incredulous expression, Jack said, "When I was eight, my piano teacher introduced me to their music. When I got older, I admired Paul's songwriting and musicianship." He leaned closer and winked. "But I never had a crush on him." Emily's laughter was melodic. Jack needed to hear more of it; he'd seen far too many tears from her tonight. "Go on."

She adjusted in her seat, bringing her left leg under her. "When I'm writing, I listen to classical music, anything instrumental. I love Harry Connick, Jr., Sarah McLachlan, Alchemy Riot, Breaking Benjamin, Dave Matthews Band, Three Doors Down, and Theory of a Deadman."

"That's quite an eclectic taste in music."

"Oh, and you guys," she said, grinning.

"Flattery will get you, well, everywhere," he joked. He didn't understand why that pleased him so much. He heard it all the time, but he knew she was sincere. "You don't have to say that."

Emily scrunched her face up. "I'm sorry, I know how that sounds, but I've heard your songs a lot more than I realized." She flushed and looked away.

She seemed to shake herself. When she looked back at him and their eyes met, he'd swear her breath caught. An expression he didn't understand skittered across her face.

"What about you? What do you listen to?"

Jack never got asked that question except during an interview. Not since he was a teenager had a girl asked him that. "Growing up, my dad played a lot of seventies and eighties music: The Police, Rush, Dire Straits. *There is Nothing Left to Lose* from the Foo Fighters had me begging my folks for a guitar. Foo Fighters led me to Nirvana and nineties grunge and alt rock. Soundgarden, Stone Temple Pilots, Pearl Jam, Alice In Chains. I still remember the day my dad agreed to loan me the money to buy my first guitar."

"Did you pay him back?"

"Absolutely. Elliot and I used to make money by shoveling driveways in winter and cutting grass in the summer." Jack leaned in close again. "We used to sneak into the city to see The Strokes." Winking, he added, "Don't tell my folks, they still think we were hanging out at Elliot's."

Melodic laughter again rang in Jack's ears.

"You said you were happy to be back home. Where were you sneaking into the city from?"

"Pine Hill, in Westchester County, about forty miles away."

The limo hadn't moved for a few minutes, so Jack hit the intercom button. "What's going on?"

Jeff's voice boomed over the intercom. "Traffic, everywhere. Must be an accident or maybe construction."

"Thanks." Jack's stomach rumbled loudly.

Emily raised her brows. "I guess that granola bar wore off."

"It's late, and you're probably exhausted, and you've had a really long day, but would you mind..." Jack hesitated. "Do you think we could stop and grab a quick bite? I'm starving." To emphasize the point, he put his hand on his stomach, and it growled loudly again. The weary look in her eyes returned, and he knew she wanted to say no, but that good heart of hers wouldn't let him down.

With a resigned sigh, Emily nodded. "Nothing fancy, okay?"

"I know the perfect place." Jack hit the intercom and told Jeff their change of plans.

"Do you travel with the same crew or use locals?" Emily asked.

"Both. The sound engineer, guitar and drum techs, and

the lighting and sound crews have been with us for years. It's a good bunch. And this is the second tour we've done with Brian, our tour manager. He and Viv, his assistant, are the best. We have twenty-eight guys and girls that travel with us."

"That's a lot of pieces to move. How do you keep track of it all?"

"That's why having a great tour manager is important. Brian handles all the logistics, makes sure we're on schedule, keeps track of who does what, and gets any replacements if someone gets sick or has a family issue. They handle everything. We just show up."

A look Jack understood well crossed Emily's face. Raising her finger, she grabbed her cell from her purse and typed furiously into the phone for a minute. When she finished, she put the phone away and smiled. "Thanks."

He enjoyed watching her work. It was only a few notes, but he understood. When an idea struck, getting it down before it was lost was essential. Jack inhaled. Her perfume filled the interior of the limo. The warm scent, with just the faintest hint of apple, reminded him of a sunny late summer afternoon. "I like your perfume. What is it?"

"I'm not wearing any."

"Body lotion?"

"Yes, but it's unscented. I don't like strong scents. Most of the body washes and lotions are too smelly for me, but my conditioner is apple scented."

Even better. Just her natural scent. Intoxicating.

I THROW MY KEYS AND SLAM THE DOOR. WHAT THE fuck? Jack has been a good boy lately, not fucking any of those groupie whores. I gave him time to heal and let him have his fun. I thought he was finally ready to settle down. We're perfect

*for each other, and once he sees the real me, he'll realize all he's
ever needed was right in front of him.*

AS THE LIMO PULLED TO A STOP, JACK OPENED THE
door and hopped out. Emily took the hand he extended. It
was unseasonably warm, but Emily shivered as a breeze blew
her hair across her face. She'd left her jacket in Nicki's car.

The trees were budding. Tall brick buildings had
architectural detail that ranged from simple to ornate. The
upper floors were apartments, and even the fire escapes were
works of art. Their beauty reminded her of the French
Quarter in New Orleans where she and Sully had—*Damn.*
Shaking away those memories, she looked at Jack, and he
smiled. "So beautiful," she said.

"I've been thinking that all night." His smile didn't waver.

Emily looked away. *Oh, boy. He's still thinking...shit.* She'd
done a good job of controlling the conversation in the limo,
but he wasn't discouraged.

He'd released her hand after helping her out of the limo,
but now he took it again and led her to the Italian restaurant,
Casa Amici. He held the door open for her. She sighed with
relief as she looked around.

"What?" Jack asked.

"I'm glad you picked a casual place. I didn't want to be
underdressed again."

His gaze washed over her, his blue eyes sparkling. "I think
you look amazing."

"Thanks." T-shirt and jeans were her standard concert
wear. She wasn't surprised Nicki had dressed like she was
going to a party, but a lot of other women were dressed
similarly. "We could've had different ideas of what a casual
restaurant is." She needed to stop rambling.

"I enjoy good food and a comfortable atmosphere, and this place has both. I worked here when we moved to the city. Maya and Antonio are great."

The restaurant was small but inviting with half a dozen tables and four booths along the wall to the right. Nicely lit, not too bright or too dark, so it couldn't be considered romantic. White tablecloths covered the tables, and red cloth napkins were wrapped around the cutlery. Three of the tables were occupied: a couple, a mother and daughter, and one person sitting alone.

A gentleman wearing black pants and a white button-down shirt ambled from the kitchen. When he saw them, he barreled over and grabbed Jack in a bear hug.

"Jack, my boy," he said. "So good to see you. Maya!" the man yelled.

Jack clasped hands with the gentleman. "Antonio, this is Emily," Jack said, as if presenting her.

Frustrating man.

Antonio pulled her into a hug and then lifted and twirled her before setting her down. "Such a lovely girl, Jack, but then you always had an eye for the pretty ones. He's just like me," Antonio said with a wink.

The kitchen door swung open, and a petite, black-haired woman with an angelic face walked out. "What is it, Tonio?" the woman asked, wiping her hands on her apron. "Jack, it's been too long." She strode toward Jack and opened her arms.

Jack leaned down and hugged her, lifting and swaying her. Antonio playfully swatted his arm. Jack returned Maya to her feet and kissed her on the cheek.

Antonio swatted his arm again. "You hitting on my girl, Jack? You have good taste, but she's taken."

"You started it." Jack turned to Maya. "Maya, this is Emily."

Emily smiled and extended her hand but found herself in

WITH YOU   89

Maya's arms.

"Oh." When Emily pulled back, Jack, Antonio, and Maya grinned. "It's nice to meet you both."

Antonio clapped Jack on the back. "Don't forget, if this music thing doesn't pan out, you're always welcome to come back here and work for us." He and Maya laughed.

"Can we get a booth?"

Maya took two menus and led the way to the third booth, placing the menus on the table. "Is this okay?"

"Perfect." He kissed the top of Maya's head.

From across the restaurant, Antonio yelled, "I saw that."

Emily sat facing the back of the restaurant, so Jack sat across from her. Maya waved, and a good-looking, blonde and busty server walked over.

A crash from the kitchen had Maya rolling her eyes. "Antonio, what have you done now?" She smiled at them and left to see what havoc her husband had wreaked.

"Hi, I'm Cindi. I'll be your server." She set two glasses of water on the table. She gaped at Jack, who didn't notice because he was looking at the menu. "Do you need a few minutes?"

Emily rolled her eyes and picked up her menu.

"Hello, Cindi," Jack said glancing up. "Yes, please."

Cindi walked away.

"So, what's good here?"

"When I worked here, I tried everything on the menu. Maya and Antonio let the staff eat free, and for a twenty-year-old starving musician, that was a luxury, so I tried everything at least once. It's all good."

The menu had everything from pizza, lasagna, and salads to burgers and fries. Emily's brows shot up. "Even the escargot?"

Jack's face scrunched and he nodded.

"Did you know what it was before you ate it?"

"Yes. I lost a bet with another server." A look of mock horror crossed Jack's face. His stomach growled again.

"We'd better order soon before an alien bursts out."

Jack's laugh caught the attention of the other patrons. "I'm getting a personal pizza, cheeseburger, and a beer."

"You're gonna eat a pizza and a burger?" *Where does he put it?*

Jack shrugged. "I'm starving. Last real meal I had was breakfast. I'm still a growing boy."

Her mom always said Riley would eat them out of house and home. "I'm getting a burger and fries."

"Would you like a glass of wine?"

"I'll stick with water."

Jack barely nodded before Cindi stood at the ready. She addressed Jack. "What can I get you?"

Jack motioned to Emily, and she gave Cindi her order, who wrote it down while not so casually giving Emily a once-over. With a small snort and a smirk, she turned her attention to Jack.

"I'll have the Luigi pizza, well done. Cheeseburger, medium, with fries and a Brooklyn Lager." After taking Jack's order, Cindi took their menus and turned to leave.

This wouldn't be a quick meal. "I've changed my mind, I will have wine."

Cindi rolled her eyes and handed Emily the menu.

"I'll have a glass of merlot." Emily was sure a few more buttons on the waitress's white blouse were undone. "So, you used to work here?"

"I bussed tables, then graduated to sever, even helped out in the kitchen occasionally."

Jack paused when Cindi approached with their drinks. She beamed at Jack when she placed his beer and a glass down, but her smile faded to neutral when she put Emily's wine on the table.

"Thank you, Cindi," Emily said with a sweet smile.

Jack quirked a brow but said nothing. Ignoring the glass, he took a sip of beer. "What's your favorite color?"

"My favorite color?" *Shit.* He was trying to get to know her. "Purple. What's yours?"

"Green," Jack said. "Purple and green go very well together."

"Jack..."

He didn't let her finish. "Tell me about yourself." He sat back and grinned the cutest lopsided grin. *Fuck.*

Emily's face scrunched in irritation and frustration. She took a deep breath and smiled at him. "Well, I enjoy long walks on the beach, candlelight dinners, champagne, traveling, reading, and yoga. I love spelunking, curling, and tarot card reading. What about you?"

Jack burst out in a deep belly laugh. He laughed so hard he coughed. Jack reached for his beer, but Emily pushed his water glass toward him, and he took a drink. His goofy smile returned, and he raised his beer in a toast. "To friendship."

They clinked glass to bottle.

"Jack," she said, heaving a sigh. "I appreciate you taking me home, but this isn't a date, so I'm paying for my dinner."

Jack's eyes narrowed. "No way I'm letting you pay. It's my fault, and it's the least I can do."

She opened her mouth to argue, but Jack covered her hand with his. "No. I'm buying dinner and taking you home."

Emily picked up her wine and took a big sip. Breaking off a piece of bread she took a bite, taking her frustration out on the bread. Another sip of wine. Jack was infuriating. She'd made it plain she wasn't ready, but he wouldn't let it go. Her head spun; lack of sleep, aggravation, and wine were a bad combination. She wasn't fooled by his friendship toast. Spoiled rock star was used to getting his own way. Well, not this time.

Chapter Ten

Silence hung heavy. Emily stopped asking questions and looked anywhere but at him. She was beautiful when she ignored him. Jack got the distinct impression any more questions would go unanswered, so he tried a different tact. "What can I tell you about myself?" He tapped his chin. "I like playing sports more than watching them on TV, although, I can get into a World Series game, and my dad, brother, and I used to watch football every Sunday. Since I moved to California, I love to hike and surf."

Jack had her attention, but she said nothing.

He sipped his beer. "At my house, I have a studio, so I spend a lot of time working on songs and recording. The guys came out, and we wrote the songs for our new album there."

Emily hiccupped. "Is this homemade wine?"

"Yup, Maya and Antonio make it."

Emily pushed the glass away

"What's wrong? Don't you like it?"

"It's good, but homemade wine has a more potent effect on me. I'm already buzzed."

"Want some of my beer?" Before she could protest, he

took the unused glass, poured half his beer into it and nudged the glass to her.

"Jack..." Her voice broke. She slumped and leaned her elbows on the table.

This is going to be bad.

Staring at a spot on the table, she sighed. "What Nicki started to say backstage, after you got the latest chapter of her life, was that my ex cheated on me too. I'm not over it yet."

Her fists clenched, but then she flattened them on the table. Jack took her hand. She didn't pull away, and her eyes shifted to their entwined hands. Jack waited.

She raised her eyes to meet his. "He was my fiancé."

Oh, fuck.

Pain and humiliation clouded her beautiful eyes. "I know her." Emily closed her eyes, but her face showed her pain. "She works in his office. I've met her at company functions and last summer in the Hamptons." Emily took a sip of beer. "Everyone in his office knew we were engaged. I don't understand."

Jack squeezed her hand. Women cheated, men cheated, he shouldn't be shocked, but he was. Emily was amazing, and he'd only known her a few hours. That fucker was stupid. How could he not know how remarkable she was? Jack had always been faithful to his girlfriends. When he found out that Erica had cheated on him, he'd been devastated. He vowed to never cause that pain to another person. At least now, Jack understood why she resisted the attraction between them.

When Cindi arrived with their food, Emily looked away. Cindi took her time placing the plates on the table and made her interest clear. Jack wished she'd leave.

Emily took another sip of beer. "I know I dodged a bullet here, it would've been so much worse to find out after we got married, but... I'm sorry to lay this on you."

"After all you did tonight, I should thank you. You may

have just helped to save Elliot's marriage, and the compassion you showed to Buzz..."

"You seem like a great guy. If we'd met at a different time, maybe, but now, I just can't." Her voice broke.

So did his heart.

"I had to get tested for STDs. What if I'd been pregnant? I've always been so careful."

That fucker. "If you were careful, why did you think you could've been pregnant?"

"Because that's one way I could've written it, Jack. Bastard cheats, they break up, she finds herself pregnant. Rushed to the doctor the next day to be sure. Still don't have all the STD results. For the next six months, I have to inform any partners I have that I could've been exposed to HIV."

"Did he admit to cheating, I mean before this time?"

"I never asked him."

"Why the hell not?" Jack's voice was louder than he intended. It took effort to uncurl his fist and lay it flat on the table.

"Because, unless the answer was yes, I wouldn't have believed a word he said."

"Yeah." Jack waved Cindi over and ordered another beer. When she returned, he reached for Emily's glass and poured.

Jack brought the bottle to his lips and swigged. "I'm sorry about that." He gestured toward the half-full glass of beer. "Old habit."

Emily tilted her head to the side and quirked a brow.

"My ex, when we first met, we always split a beer, until she...went into rehab the first time. We broke up six months ago." He'd never seen her drink more than a beer, but when he'd come back on a break from tour, she'd been passed out and there were empty bottles everywhere. She looked so pale that Jack had thought she was dead. He'd rushed her to the hospital. She had alcohol poisoning, and she could've died.

Jack begged her to go into rehab, and she had, and from then on, he'd never shared another beer with her.

Emily's eyes softened and she touched his hand.

Jack rubbed the back of his neck. "Christie was in rehab twice, but there was only so much I could do, I couldn't fix this. We went to counseling, that's when I realized that I was enabling her." His eyes closed tightly as he tried to block out her awful words.

"By last fall, I knew she was using again. We had a huge fight, and I told her to pack her stuff and go. I couldn't live with the deceit and the lies. But I couldn't leave her homeless, so I got her an apartment and paid the first year's rent. An actress friend of hers lives next door, so she won't be alone." Jack looked away.

"How awful, Jack."

He felt her compassion. "Nothing compared to what happened to you."

Emily's eyes widened. "Jack, it's hardly comparable. It's been horrible, but nobody was in danger of dying." Emily paused and smiled. "Well, only for a minute. Christie could've died. That's much worse than what happened to me."

They ate in silence for the next few minutes. Jack was humbled. He was hooked on this girl. She was sweet, beautiful, empathetic, sympathetic, and had a kind and generous heart. The list just kept growing.

He understood her pain, and he didn't want to add to it, but he had to pursue this. In spite of the bombshell she'd dropped, there must be a way. He'd find a way. "Emily, I get that you aren't ready to date, but can you honestly tell me you don't feel the connection we have?"

Emily didn't answer, her expression a mixture of frustration and compassion. Jack could tell she was thinking. She could use more spontaneity in her life. Bet that fucker wasn't spontaneous.

When she covered his hand with hers, a tightness settled in his chest. *Screwed.*

"Jack, my messy pile of a breakup aside, even if we met six months from now, I don't see that dating you would be possible." She smiled weakly. "You don't live here, and I'm not interested in a long-distance relationship."

He didn't have to think about it. "Simple. I'm moving back to New York. You live in New Jersey, that's not far."

"That's insane."

"There's nothing left for me in California. We moved there for Christie's acting career. My family's here and my bandmates live here." He waited till she raised her gaze. "You're here."

"Fine, you're just going to move back here on a whim."

Definitely not spontaneous. Luckily, he was. Jack moved his hand out from under hers and placed it on top again.

"I'm not done. How much longer are you going to be on tour?" Emily sat back with a satisfied grin.

She had a point. "Almost twenty months. We'd see each other on the breaks. It's not ideal, but we're perfect together." She was attracted to him, and he was positive she wouldn't lie to boost her arguments, so he'd just keep knocking them down.

"We just met, Jack, you don't know me." Emily huffed. "You could be a serial killer."

Trying to change the topic again. She was fantastic at that. "Really, a serial killer?"

"Sure. They're charming, pillars of the community, always described by stunned neighbors as a nice guy." She smiled. "We've already established that you're a nice guy, Jack."

"Well, thank you, I think. But I'm not a serial killer." He raised his hand. "Yeah, yeah, if I was, I'd deny it."

Cindi interrupted to take their plates. "Can I get you anything else?" she asked Jack.

Emily shook her head.

"What kind of cake do you have?" He wasn't hungry, but once they got to the limo, their night would soon end, and he didn't want it to.

"Chocolate layer, cheesecake, and tiramisu," Cindi said, leaning forward.

Jack averted his gaze. "Chocolate layer, with two forks." Jack looked at Emily. "Everyone loves cake. I'm happy to share."

Cindi and her shocked expression walked away.

Smiling, Jack took a sip of water. "What were we talking about? Ah, yes, whether I'm a serial killer." He couldn't wait to see what she said next. "Go on."

"Well, a musician who travels from city to city is a rather brilliant cover for a serial killer. One kill here, one kill there, it's harder for a pattern to emerge."

"Do you profile as a hobby?"

"Nope, just makes sense. A girl can't be too careful."

"True. Do a search for our band's itinerary and cross-check it with unsolved murders. I'll wait." Sitting back, he stretched his arms along the back of the seat.

"Jack," she said through gritted teeth.

"What else you got?" He smiled and leaned in to take her hand, but she moved away.

"This isn't a date, Jack."

"Are you sure? Dinner and conversation. I know your favorite color and your diverse taste in music. We talked about our exes, even though that rarely comes up on a first date. And"—Jack leaned in—"I'm taking you home. All date-like things."

"Jack McBride, you're infuriating. You don't live here." She twisted her hands together. "Right, you're moving to New York. Fine. I'm not rock star girlfriend material, and if you weighed the pros and cons—"

"That's a great idea." Jack raised his hand, and Maya hurried over.

Emily stared at him with a puzzled expression.

"What can I get you?" Maya asked.

"Pen and paper."

Maya hurried off and returned in a few moments with a child's paper place mat and a pen, handing them to Jack.

"Thanks."

Cindi deposited the cake and two forks on the table with a *thunk* and stormed off. Jack ignored the cake. Drawing a line down the center of the paper, he wrote pro on one side and con on the other. Folding it, he pushed it across the table.

"Pros and cons of what?"

"Me." He crossed his ankles under the table; they could be here awhile.

"You?" She shook her head. "Fine." Emily picked up the pen and started to write.

"Be honest, I can take it."

"Always." She glanced up after a minute and tilted her chin toward him. "Incoming."

"What?" Out of the corner of his eye, he saw two people approaching. He smiled as he turned to them.

A mother and daughter stopped in front of him. The young girl looked to be maybe fifteen, and her smile practically reached her ears.

"We're sorry to interrupt," the mother said. "Ariana and I were at your concert tonight. We had a wonderful time."

Jack stood. "Thank you, I'm always happy when we make our fans happy. I'm glad you had a good time. What's your name?"

"Oh," she said. "Liz."

"Thank you, Liz." He shook her hand. "Well, Ariana, I hope you had as good a time as your mom. What was your favorite song?"

Ariana bounced as she spoke. "All of them." She listed every song they'd played. "My dad is taking me Wednesday to see you again." Her eyes glittered.

Liz put her hand on Ariana's shoulder. "She's been so excited to see you guys. You're her favorite band."

"Ever," Ariana said.

Jack smiled. "How about a picture?

"Please, Mom?" Ariana asked, hopping from foot to foot.

"Ariana, we talked about this. We agreed to just say hello." Ariana stopped hopping and pouted. Liz sighed. "We don't want to put you out."

"I'm happy to."

Ariana squealed.

Jack crouched down next to her. Liz snapped a few pictures with her cell.

"Now mine," said Ariana, handing her mom her phone.

"Liz, why don't you get in the picture?" Emily suggested as she stood.

Liz looked embarrassed but handed Ariana's phone to Emily.

"Smile." She winked at Jack and snapped a few pictures and then handed the phone back to Ariana.

"You're nice. Can I take a picture of you with Jack?"

"Oh, um," Emily stuttered, "Jack and I, we aren't, um what I mean is, we..."

"I think that's a wonderful idea," Jack said as he pulled Emily close. "Smile," he whispered.

"Say cheese," Ariana said and snapped away.

"Okay, Ariana, that's enough."

Jack didn't want to let go, but Emily moved away, so he let his arm drop. She fit him perfectly. He could still feel the heat from her body. "I would love a copy of those." Pulling out his wallet, he took out a business card and handed it to Ariana. "That's our manager's email. If it's okay with your mom, would you email me the pictures? Include your mailing address, and in return, I'll send you a poster signed by the band."

Ariana looked to Liz for approval.

"That would be okay."

"Was there a particular T-shirt you liked?"

Ariana was so giddy she could barely speak. "The black one with the band's name in white, with the red hearts. It sold out in every size."

"Well how about I include one for you and Liz?"

Ariana squealed and jumped.

"Thank you so much." Liz pulled a still bouncing Ariana out of the restaurant.

They sat back in the booth. "Back to the list, Emily."

THE LIST. EMILY LOOKED AT WHAT SHE'D WRITTEN so far.

Amazing friend

Intelligent

Nice

Charming but not in a salesman way

Handsome

Not too many tattoos

Great body

The image of Jack in just a towel warmed her everywhere. Delicious. Better stop thinking about his body before she drooled. His hair wasn't too short, his blue eyes... Damn, still on his body. Focus on the list.

Amazing songwriter

Gentleman

She added *Gracious*

He'd enjoyed talking to Liz and Ariana. And Emily had

been surprised that he'd known so much about the road crew. He knew everyone's names and stopped to talk to several of them, genuinely interested. He'd assumed she was surprised that there were so many women with them, when what had shocked her were her own assumptions. She glanced at Jack. His lips curved in that confident, shit-eating grin of his; even that was adorable. *Fuck.*

Emily turned to the con side. She'd promised to be honest. There was only one con. A huge con. A non-negotiable con. So, she wrote it. *ROCK STAR.*

Folding the paper, she pushed it across the table. She hadn't seen any signs of extreme arrogance. It'd be hard not to be a little arrogant in his position, with people screaming your name and the masses of fans the band had.

His smiled turned into a full-on grin, nearly blinding her with its intensity. She almost felt sorry for Cindi. "Well, according to this, I look damn good on paper." His grin was infectious, and Emily smiled in return. Jack's expression turned serious. "Thanks for that."

"What?"

"For being so nice to Liz and Ariana. Without our fans, we'd be nowhere, so I always try to be nice. She's a sweet kid."

"I just followed your lead."

"Still, I appreciate it. My dad told me 'it won't kill you to be nice,' so I try to remember that. Christie grew to resent it," Jack said, his expression turned sullen.

"You're close to your family?"

"Yes. They've always been there for me, even though my folks weren't happy when I left home at nineteen. But they supported me anyway. They're the best."

Emily nodded and swallowed the sudden lump in her throat. Time to end this. Pointing to the list, she said, "Turn it over."

His smile faded. "Rock star?"

"Yes."

"Care to elaborate?"

"Jack, you live in the spotlight. You're famous, you get recognized wherever you go. I want no part of that."

Jack's mouth fell open, and his head cocked to the side. "You're a novelist, surely you have a spotlight?"

"I use a pen name. I don't do appearances, and the only people who know are people I tell."

"Did the fucker know?"

Emily's brows dipped. "Yes, he didn't—he wasn't... curious about my writing, so we never discussed it." Emily looked down. Maybe that was why he cheated. She shook her head. That didn't even make sense. She *was* losing it.

"He wasn't proud of you?"

Emily's head shot up. No, he hadn't been. Not wanting to explain, she shook her head.

"You told me. Why?"

"Because if you would've laughed..."

"Why would I—Oh." Jack sat back with a disgusted look. "The fucker laughed when you told him, didn't he?"

Emily's eyes stung. She hadn't realized until after they'd broken up how much it had mattered to her. She'd thought that since she couldn't change things... And he'd apologized. He'd been sincere but never once asked to read anything she'd written. Of course, she'd never asked him to either. She'd been so hurt by his reaction; hurt that he'd called romance novels trite. He also said that he thought if she wanted to be a writer, she could do better than romance. She'd known at the time he'd been trying to compliment her. *Wow, maybe I do need to have my head examined.*

Jack didn't push it, and she was grateful for that, but he didn't let things go between them either.

"You don't have to be in the spotlight. We won't advertise our relationship. When I'm not on tour, I like things low-key.

I love spending time in my studio and catching up with family and friends. I love to cook. It's not like we'd be attending parties and getting our picture taken. You want a quiet life, and when I'm home, so do I. See, something else we have in common." Leaning in, he said, "You handled Liz and Ariana like a pro."

"Like I said, I followed your lead, you were gracious, so it was the least I could do. I don't know why Ariana wanted our picture, that was weird." She wanted to get out of here. It was late, and she needed to crash.

"Nicki knows you're a writer. She kept that secret?"

Emily nodded. "She understands. On the outside, she seems ditzy and selfish, but she's not. She's my best friend. Being in the spotlight makes me very uncomfortable."

"Didn't you go to any parties with the fucker?"

"There were company functions we attended, but that's not the same." Emily gritted her teeth. "Jack, you couldn't turn around without finding a woman who'd make a better girlfriend for you than me."

"I'm not interested in anyone else," Jack said through gritted teeth. He slapped his hand on the table. "Why are you being so stubborn? I'll be in town for six days, let's spend time together, we'll take things slow."

Anger, frustration, and sadness battled inside her. Anger won. "Listen Jack, I'm sure you're used to getting your way all the time. I'm guessing few people say no to you. You're a spoiled rock star if you think I'm the one who's being stubborn here." Emily stood and threw a twenty on the table. "Just move on to the next girl, Jack. You'll forget about me in no time."

Emily used more force than necessary to open the restaurant door. She inhaled deeply, the crisp air cooling her. She'd been hot and claustrophobic in the restaurant. Jack had been relentless. Where the hell did he get off, anyway? She wasn't interested. *Jerk.* Even though she was pissed, she knew he wasn't a jerk or an arrogant fuck. He was nice and had been nothing but a gentleman, kind and respectful. Trudging down the street, she had no idea where she was going, but right now she didn't care. She needed to put as much space as possible between her and that rock star.

Why was she being such a bitch? The little voice in her head gave her an answer she didn't like, so she told it to shut the fuck up. Okay, she was officially losing it. No wonder her bosses had insisted she take time off. Emily had been humiliated that she hadn't been able to keep it together at work. Tears streamed down her cheeks. Finding Sully fucking that girl, canceling the wedding, screwing up at work; this breakdown was overdue, just her bad luck it was happening on some street in—*fuck.*

Jack's limo passed, but she kept walking. It screeched to a halt, and then rushed footsteps had her turning.

Jeff strode toward her. "Did Jack hurt you?"

"No," said Emily. "I hurt him." She continued walking. Jeff didn't follow.

Jack called her name, so she turned to see him running toward her. Couldn't he take a hint and just leave her alone? Didn't he understand she was in no shape to start a relationship? She could run, but that seemed dramatic, so she waited for him to catch up.

"Hey, what happened in there? We were having a nice time. If I said or did something to hurt you, I'm sorry. I didn't mean to."

What had he done? Other than constantly trying to hold her hand, he'd been a gentleman. She'd enjoyed his attention. Stupid little voice had been right.

Whatever happened next would be a mistake. Jack wanted more than she had to give; he wanted them. Even though she was wildly attracted to him, Emily wasn't ready for a relationship. He'd made it clear that was what he wanted, but she just couldn't. Anything else would be selfish. Jack was great for her self-esteem, which Sully had totally crushed.

"Emily?" Jack had stepped closer. His pained expression cut deep.

"You didn't do anything wrong. I don't want to hurt you."

"We've both been hurt, but we have something special here."

"We just met."

Jack placed her palm over his heart. "Emily, I'm feeling again." His blue eyes sparkled. "I thought Christie and I would get married. After the breakup, I went crazy. I indulged in—what was offered, until I woke up one morning with a girl next to me, and I didn't remember her name, I'm not even sure that I asked. I didn't like who I'd become." Jack looked away, his breathing erratic and his heart hammering beneath her palm. "I stopped screwing around, stopped the one-night stands. It's been three months since my self-imposed celibacy, and it's been fine. I needed time to heal. But I didn't realize how numb I was until tonight. When I saw you, something inside me roared back to life. I know you need time, but there has to be a way for us to be together."

The limo pulled up, and Jeff got out.

"It's better if we don't see each other again." Emily choked on a sob.

Jack guided her over to the limo. "Please let me take you home."

"No, I'll get a cab."

He tipped her chin up until her gaze locked on his. "I lied."

His eyes were sincere and lust filled, and her heart skipped a beat and then pounded. "About what?"

"Come back to the hotel, spend the night with me."

"Jack, we don't even know if there's any real chemistry."
She knew they had something.

"I know what I feel, Emily. Nothing has felt this real to me
in years."

Her back pressed up against the door, and Jack leaned in,
their lips only inches apart.

Emily should look away but didn't want to. "We haven't
even kissed."

"We can remedy that right now." He moved closer but
didn't kiss her.

Emily blinked slowly. This was a bad idea, but she wanted
to kiss him. *Just one kiss.*

"I need a yes or no, Em."

"Yes."

Jack closed the distance, their bodies touching from thighs
to almost lips. Bracing himself with one hand on the
doorframe, he snaked the other around her waist. He smiled as
his lips touched hers. She closed her eyes but didn't open her
mouth.

Jack pulled back. "Em, please..."

"I don't French on a first date."

"It's not a date, remember?"

She had no resistance left. "Oh, well, in that case."

Parting her lips, Jack gently kissed her. He traced his
tongue along her bottom lip before dipping in. Someone
moaned.

His tongue tangled with hers. He cupped her face, and she
tilted her head to get better access to him. Her arms encircled
his waist. She was lost. Time ceased.

Chapter Eleven

J ack moaned when she sank into his body; all coherent thought evaporated. Lifting her up, he pinned her against the car. He no longer felt the chill in the air. There was only Emily's warmth. Emily kissed him back, and their tongues tangled and withdrew, only to tangle again. She tasted of the beer they'd shared.

Jack was in heaven as Emily's body pressed up against his in all the right places. His dick throbbed. Her lips were soft. He wished she'd wrap her legs around his waist. Outside be damned. Chemistry didn't even describe what was happening between them. They both heaved in air. His thumb rubbed her wet, slightly parted lips.

"Jack."

Their lips met again.

"Jack!" Jeff shouted.

He pulled his lips off Emily's. "Fuck off, Jeff." She tasted so damn sweet.

"Paparazzi."

The only word that would stop him. "Fuck." Jack's eyes opened, and he rested his forehead against Emily's. Her eyes opened but were still dazed. "Em, get in the car." He tried to pull away, but she tightened her arms around him. He groaned. "Baby, if you don't want to be photographed looking like we just..." Jack swallowed hard. "You need to get in the car. Now."

She didn't move, so he lifted her, stepped back, and opened the door. He turned and gently pushed her head down so she wouldn't smack it on the doorframe, closing the door just in time.

Flashes.

Jack turned and smiled. There were five or six photographers. He accepted this as part of his career, but tonight he wasn't in the mood to be gracious. These assholes had interrupted the best kiss of his life. Jack had to protect her. His body should've blocked their view, so even if they got a couple pictures, Emily should be obscured. Jack wished he could tell her he planned it that way, but the truth was, he couldn't get close enough to her; he wanted to be inside her.

"Jack, over here."

Jack turned toward the voice and smiled. He'd told Jeff to fuck off. He'd apologize for that later. He focused on the photographers. The sooner he gave them a pound of flesh, the sooner they'd leave. How had they known where to find him? These city guys rarely made a fuss over him; there were always real celebrities to stalk.

"Jack, who's the new girl?" the one closest to him asked.

"What's her name? How long have you two been together?" another asked.

"Does Christie know you're dating again?" someone asked from the back.

Jack forced a smile. "Guys, there's no new girl. I stopped to have a meal at Casa Amici's. Best food in the city."

"We saw her Jack. You two were in a lip-lock."

"No, you've got it wrong. My friend had something in her eye. I was helping her." Still smiling.

When the photographers were done, he told Jeff to drive. Emily was back in her seat, so he sat across from her. He hoped she didn't regret what happened between them.

She didn't acknowledge him and just stared at the floor. The limo turned a corner and Emily lifted her gaze to him, finally reaching his eyes. Lust. Jack's reaction was instantaneous, so he shifted, trying to ease the discomfort.

He hadn't given up on dating Emily, but if he could get her in his bed, or up against a wall, she wouldn't be able to deny that there was something special between them. The sex would be epic. Jack would give her all the time she needed, but the universe dropped this opportunity in his lap, and he wasn't about to waste it.

"One night."

"One night?" Jack asked.

"We spend one night together, explore whatever this is between us, but tomorrow morning I'm leaving."

"Okay."

Emily launched herself into his lap, and her hand went for his belt.

"Whoa, what's the rush?" Jack stopped her before she got the end out of the buckle.

"Clock's ticking, Jack." Pulling her hands free, she flattened them on his chest. "Take this off. I want you. Now."

He groaned as his head dropped back against the seat; he never expected her to be so aggressive, and he loved it. As much as he'd love to fuck her right here, they had to make it into the hotel, and he couldn't guarantee they wouldn't be seen.

Straddling his hips, she kissed him. Jack let his control go and devoured her. His dick was so hard it hurt. He cupped her full breasts in his hands, and her nipples hardened.

He had to put the brakes on this before he took his cock out and begged her to suck it. His dick jerked in response. Fuck. Yes, he wanted to fuck. Her. Repeatedly. If this kept up much longer, he'd come in his pants. Tearing his lips from hers, he gulped air. "Hold up, baby, I have to tell Jeff our change of plans." He helped Emily on to the seat. As Jack reached for the intercom, she palmed his dick, and she wasn't being gentle about it either. Damn, it felt good. Taking a deep breath, he pushed the intercom. "Jeff, take us to the hotel."

Two could play this game.

Jack trailed his fingers up her firm thigh. He couldn't wait to find out what she had on under that shirt. If it was lace, he'd lose it. If it was burgundy lace. *Shit. Stop thinking about it.* He kissed her lips as his hand cupped her pussy, her warmth an invitation. Their lips met again, and this time she thrust her tongue first. He wasn't sure how Emily ended up on his lap again. His head spun.

She ran her palms up and down his chest. Breaking the kiss, she nibbled his jaw up to his ear. "Let me take care of that for you," she whispered.

Oh fuck.

When he didn't answer, she leaned back, shrugged, and reached for his belt. Again, he stopped her.

"Jack, are you a tease?" Emily slid to the floor and knelt, licking her lips.

"You don't play fair," Jack managed. *Jeez, what's wrong with me?* He was single. Emily was different. This wasn't how he wanted to come with her. He needed to be inside her. "Em, you're killing me here. I want you more than I've ever wanted any woman. I've ached for you since the moment I laid eyes on you. Baby, it'll happen, just, not like this."

"What's wrong with this?" she asked sitting back on her heels and assessing the inside of the limo. "Nicki says limo sex is second only to airplane sex."

"How would Nicki know about either of those things?" The words tumbled out of Jack's mouth. Nicki? *Oh, shit, that Nicki.* Curt and Nicki.

Emily smiled, patted his knee, and sat next to him. "Either you're being really sweet, or your lower brain is in complete control and you forgot who Nicki is."

Damn, she was quick. He liked that about her, and her pro list continued to grow. One night wouldn't be enough. Like he would've even considered saying no, but he never promised to stop trying to change her mind. "Sorry."

"Don't be, I'm desperately trying to hold on to what's left of coherent thought. So, limo sex, not all it's cracked up to be?"

"We'll need way more privacy and space than this metal box can afford us. There isn't enough head room, and I would hate for you to get rug burns on your beautiful fair skin."

Her hand went to the bulge in his lap. "I'm not as concerned about head room so much as I am about mouth room."

Jack groaned. "I appreciate that you want to relieve my suffering, but I haven't been with a woman in three months, and when I come, I want to be inside your pussy."

She smiled, but it faded. She looked down at her hands. When she looked up, sadness filled her eyes. "We need to talk."

Shit. If she changed her mind...he'd deal. "About?" His blood raced through his veins.

"STDs, last blood tests, condoms."

Jack snagged a couple bottles of water that were stashed in the door and handed one to Emily. He opened his and drank. Emily turned the bottle in her hands, and her expression was a mixture of anger, sadness, and fear.

Shit, she had to be thinking about the fucker. At least she wasn't pining for him; she deserved better and knew it. Jack planned on being that better man.

"Okay, let's talk." Jack finished his water. "When I'm single, I have blood tests every three months. I get tested for everything. All blood work has come back negative. No STDs ever. I've never had unprotected sex, always used condoms, every time. Only exception is when I'm in a committed relationship, and the girl and I agree it's time to lose them, and she's on birth control."

Emily sighed. "I wish I could give you the same guarantee, Jack, but I can't. I'm on the pill, and I never forget to take it, and carry it with me at all times, so tomorrow won't be a problem. All the guys I've slept with used condoms every time. When Sully and I got engaged, we stopped using them." She swallowed hard. "I assume you have plenty of condoms?"

"Yup, a new box in my suitcase and one in my bag."

"Nothing in your pants?" She chuckled. "I thought guys always carried one in their wallet."

"Baby, I've got plenty in my pants, right here." Jack grabbed his crotch. "The wallet is a bad place to keep a condom." He slipped out the one he'd put in his front pocket earlier and waved it at her, whisking it away when she made a grab for it.

"Tease," she said.

"Just you wait until I get you alone." He kissed her but pulled back before things got out of hand. Again.

"Where's your hotel, anyway?"

Jack leaned over her and hit the intercom. "How much longer?"

"Keep your pants on," Jeff barked back. "ETA five minutes."

Emily's laughter filled the limo. "Keep your pants on," Emily repeated while struggling to breathe.

When she settled down, he asked, "You okay?"

"Yeah." Emily rested her head on his shoulder, still

giggling. "You're a responsible fellow. Never once forgot to rubber up?"

"No. Never." At her raised brow, Jack said, "My dad sat me down before I moved out. He said 'Jack, you need to be responsible, that means using a condom every time, no matter if the girl says she's on birth control. I know sometimes it can seem like a hassle, but it's important. You don't want to catch anything, and you don't want a kid walking up to you in eighteen years saying "Hi, Dad, nice to meet you."' I've been safe every time."

"Wow."

"Yeah, my dad doesn't mince words. I want kids someday, but ideally after I'm married. I don't want a child of mine growing up without me. If it ever happened, I'd take full responsibility."

EMILY TRIED TO SETTLE HER MIND, BUT SHE STILL saw the flashbulbs going off in rapid succession when they were caught kissing. How did he live like that? Those photographers descended on them like vultures. If Jack hadn't had the frame of mind to get her into the limo—a shudder tore through her—they would've gotten her picture. With Jack McBride. Her brain had been so clouded with lust she hadn't realized what was happening.

It was flattering that Jack, hot as fuck musician, wanted her. Emily hoped they did it up against a wall. One night, of what promised to be the best sex she ever had, would have to be enough. Her breasts felt heavy, and a deep need curled low in her belly. Jack smelled of soap and his own musky scent, no cologne. She'd always had a thing for guys in bands, they were so—fuckable. Not that she'd ever slept with any, but it was the stuff of fantasies. Emily wasn't tired anymore, but she was more aroused than she'd ever been.

As soon as the limo slowed to a stop, Jack opened the door and helped her out. Emily's heart thumped in her chest, and her stomach fluttered. Jack's eyes glittered with lust. With that one look, he undid some of the damage to her self-esteem.

"Just a sec. I need a word with Jeff." Jack walked to the driver's side door as Jeff got out. Jeff nodded curtly, got back in, and pulled away.

"Hey, Jack, do you have time to sign a few pictures?"

The muscles in Jack's neck bunched, and he uttered a silent curse. "Can you give me a minute?"

Emily nodded.

Jack smiled and pointed toward the vestibule that housed the elevators. "Wait in there. Sorry." He smiled, shrugged helplessly, and turned to the voice. "Hey, Anne, I wasn't expecting to see you so soon."

Emily walked to the double doors and went inside. Leaning against the wall opposite the elevators, she inhaled deeply and focused on how she was feeling. Calm. Sometimes, the first time could be awkward. Her skin tingled all over in anticipation of Jack's touch. She checked her reflection in the high-polished steel of the elevator doors: her lips were swollen, eyes glazed, cheeks flushed. For the first time in weeks, she felt beautiful.

She glanced out the glass doors. Anne was in an animated conversation with Jack. He didn't appear the least bit uncomfortable. He'd said he loved meeting fans. Needing to be anonymous, Emily didn't do meet and greets. After that one guy turned creepy, she'd shut down that email account, but she interacted with her readers on her website and through social media.

Jack handed Anne back the pictures, but they were still talking. Jeez. Come on already. They'd be naked and sweaty by now if she hadn't interrupted. Interrupted. She'd bet that happened to him a lot. Good thing this was only one night; she definitely couldn't deal with this. A rush of sadness washed over her. *Whoa, stop that.* She was about to embark on a wild night of uninhibited sex with the hottest fucking rock star on the planet. Emily groaned. She bet her idea of uninhibited sex was way more inhibited than his.

The woman handed Jack a piece of paper, and he gave her a brief hug. He turned and jogged toward Emily.

She pushed away from the wall and hit the up button as Jack opened the door.

"Sorry about that. Anne's the president of our unofficial fan club. She and her friends started it almost ten years ago when we were still playing bars in the city. She'll raffle off those pictures to raise money for the local ASPCA."

Jack enfolded her in his arms. His erection pressed into her, so she leaned back and wiggled her butt.

"Hey, I'm in enough discomfort here." Jack kissed behind her ear, sending a shudder through her.

"Sorry." She wasn't, so she smiled. "Why don't you get her better stuff?"

Jack nipped her earlobe. "Get who, what?"

"Anne, better stuff, you know, like a—signed jacket or guitar…" Warmth crept up her neck. Jack's hands hovered on her rib cage.

He lifted his head. "Hmm, why didn't I think of that? Oh right, because ninety percent of the blood in my body is in my groin. I thought I was going to pass out."

The elevator dinged, and the doors opened. Jack ushered her in and hit the button for the thirty-seventh floor.

He leaned against the back wall. She stayed by the door. *Didn't this thing have air conditioning?*

"Nervous?" Jack asked.

"What?" Emily met his eyes in the mirrored wall.

"Are you nervous?" Jack waved his hand between them. "You're way over there."

"No." Emily stepped back and leaned against the wall next to him.

"Tell me what you're thinking."

She turned to face him. "Well, it occurred to me that we may have very different ideas of what wild, uninhibited sex entails."

Jack faced her. "Hey, nothing will happen that you aren't okay with, I promise." His arms closed around her, and his chin rested on her head. "Since you brought it up, a wild night of uninhibited sex is just what I need."

"Agreed." Emily went up on tiptoes and gave him a quick kiss. Only it didn't stop there. In a heartbeat she was up against the mirrored wall.

The elevator dinged, and Jack let her go as the doors opened. No one entered, and Emily sighed in relief. The fewer people that saw them together, the better. Jack adjusted himself and leaned back against the wall.

Emily looked at their progress: ten floors to go. "Why couldn't you be on the first floor? Is this a rock star ego thing?" Her voice was strained.

"First floor is all hotel stuff, check in, boutique, bar, restaurant. It's not like I'm in the penthouse." Jack said, his voice equally strained.

The elevator dinged, and the doors opened. Finally.

Chapter Twelve

Jack ushered her out of the elevator and down the hallway to his room. In a matter of seconds, they were inside, the door slammed shut, and he had her up against it.

Desperate lips crashed together. Hands scrambled to touch bare skin. He grabbed the bottom of her T-shirt and lifted while her hands lifted the hem of his T-shirt. "Please," he begged.

Emily let go and raised her arms, the shirt followed, and he tossed it away. Needing to see her, he fumbled around for the light switch. The soft light of a table lamp cast a warm glow. Holy fuck, black lace and satin. His heart skipped a beat.

Reaching around, she unclasped her bra and slid the straps off, revealing her perfect breasts. His dick returned to its painfully hard state. He didn't want to rush this, but he might not have a choice.

"Your turn."

Grabbing a fistful of shirt, he whipped it up and off. Her hands were on him before the shirt hit the floor. She rained kisses over his chest as her hands moved over his abs and down to his belt. This time he didn't protest.

Their lips met again. He cupped her breasts, gently kneading her flesh. When his hands hit the button of her jeans, Emily pulled back. "What?" Jack said, gasping for breath.

She looked down. "Nothing special on, I wasn't planning on this."

Tipping her chin up until their eyes locked, he smiled and kissed her on the side of the mouth. "I don't care."

"You looked like you care. I thought you'd swallow your tongue."

"I've been imagining what you had on under your clothes all night. Now, I just want you naked." Popping the button and unzipping her jeans, he mentally prepared himself for granny panties. He wasn't sure what they were, but he'd heard they were awful.

Dropping to his knees, he tugged the jeans down. Pink cotton bikini panties with a crocheted edge and a small bow. "I don't know why you were worried. These are cute." Hooking his thumbs in the waist, he pulled them down. She gripped his shoulders as she stepped out of them.

Her scent had been driving him wild all night. "I have to taste you." Jack leaned in, parting her lips, and his tongue dipped in. Her musky taste intoxicated him. His tongue swirled around her clit before sucking it into his mouth.

"Jaaack," she whispered as her fingers tangled through his hair, tugging it. "Yes."

She tasted like honey and cream, and he couldn't get enough. His hands caressed her thighs, but as soon as he felt the raised skin, she tensed and tried to move away. *Shit.* He rested his forehead on her belly, giving her a gentle kiss. She took a shuddering breath and relaxed her body.

That was all the invitation he needed. He'd never wanted a woman more. Standing, he kissed her hard as his hands resumed their rightful place on her breasts. Her hands fumbled with the zipper of his jeans. Reluctantly, he broke the kiss, kicked his boots off, and pushed his jeans and boxer briefs down and stepped out of them, toeing off his socks at the same time.

His cock jutted upward, the tip glistening. Her eyes widened, and with a wicked grin, she swiped the bead of fluid off with her thumb. Not breaking eye contact, she raised it to her lips and licked.

Enough games. Grabbing his jeans off the floor, he fished out the condom, tore it open, and rolled it on. He pushed her up against the door and kissed her roughly. Then she moaned the five sweetest words he'd ever heard.

"Jack, please fuck me now."

He lifted her up, her legs wrapping around his waist and her arms around his neck. In one fluid movement, he thrust into her. "So fucking tight, so wet, baby." Taking several deep breaths to calm down, he moved her away from the door, settling her back against the wall. He gave her a minute to adjust to him, then withdrew, and thrust into her. Oh damn, she felt so good. She kissed him, biting his lip, which amped up his need. He pounded into her.

Their tongues thrust to the rhythm of his cock driving into her. He wouldn't last long at this rate, so he forced himself to slow down. Pulling back, he looked into her eyes. Deep green. "So fucking beautiful."

"Jaaack," she whimpered.

The way she drew out his name excited him further, and his dick hardened even more. "I know, baby." She needed this as much as he did. She smiled when he thrust faster. He'd spend the rest of his life a happy man making her smile. Trailing kisses to her neck, he whispered, "I can't hold off much longer."

"So close."

Needing her to come first, he thrust hard, as he nipped her

shoulder. His balls tingled as they pulled up into his sac. She tightened around him, and she cried out as she came. Jack followed, coming in long, hard spurts. *Fuck, that was amazing.*

Her legs loosened around his waist.

"No." Jack turned so his back was against the wall. He slid down, extending his legs out as his butt hit the floor. Emily straddled him.

Jack held her as he recovered from the most intense orgasm he'd ever experienced. *Bliss.*

Emily kissed him on the shoulder, neck, jaw, and finally on the lips. Her mouth was warm and inviting, and his dick jerked back to life.

Her hum of satisfaction had his heart skipping a beat. She fit against him perfectly. Jack was more convinced than ever that they belonged together. As soon as his brain functioned again, he'd figure it out, but for now, he rested against the wall and enjoyed his post sex stupor.

Emily shifted. "How tall are you?"

"Six two." Jack turned his head away to yawn, his arms too comfortable around her to cover his mouth. "Why?"

Emily leaned back, and his arms tightened around her, not wanting her to move away.

"Why do you have a"—Emily paused and moved her hand over to an object and tapped her nail on it—"six-foot, acrylic penis filled with condoms in your hotel room?"

His eyes shot open. "A six-foot what?" Jack tilted his head to the side so he could get a better look. "Elliot. Fucking bastard."

"Elliot?" Emily looked at him, eyes sparkling. "Are you saying this is a mold of Elliot's penis, because no way he could walk around if it was life-sized." She chuckled. "I know they make kits so guys can make a mold of their junk, but this is ridiculous." Her body shook as her chuckle turned to full-on laughter.

"It's a running joke. Elliot thought it was hysterical when I decided to give up sex temporarily. It started three months ago with a few boxes of condoms on my bed. Then, bigger boxes. Then open boxes with condoms strewn all over. Then he acquired a humongous glass vase and filled it with rubbers. Glass doesn't travel well, so he's moved on to acrylics."

"Why did you tell him?" Her laughter bubbled out, so she sucked her lips in to stop laughing.

"I didn't. Elliot doesn't miss much. He noticed I wasn't indulging, and after a week of 'does it burn when you piss' jokes, he figured it out. Smartass has been busting my balls ever since. I've no idea how he got that in here."

"Probably charmed housekeeping," Emily said, resting her head back on his shoulder.

"Black, charming? Ha!"

"He can be. When we hugged, he was charming, in an 'I've been an asshole but not afraid to admit it and apologize' kind of way. I thought he was sincere."

"Jeez, you sound like Siobhan. That wasn't here earlier when I dropped my stuff off, or I would've had it removed to Elliot's room to remind him he's not getting any."

"He's an evil genius."

"Not a genius, just evil," Jack said. "I'm glad you think it's funny."

"It's hysterical."

"Wait a minute, they have kits to make a mold of your penis? Why would anyone do that?"

"So your girlfriend or wife can pleasure herself with a replica of your dick. I think it's called phallic memories."

Jack burst out laughing at the same time his dick hardened at the idea of her using a vibrator molded from his junk.

EMILY PULLED BACK AND KISSED HIS LIPS. HE TASTED faintly of beer and pizza, and he was a good kisser, not too sloppy or overbearing, and happy to let her kiss him. Probably because he got a lot of practice. She shoved that thought aside because she didn't want to think of him with anyone else.

The sex had been amazing. He'd lifted her like she weighed nothing, and, oh, wall fuck, even better than she'd imagined. Where had he been all her life? *Whoa.* This was no time for feelings. Her leg ached, and she needed to move, but she was so comfortable and sleepy. She shuddered.

Jack's arms tightened around her, and he stroked her back. "Cold?"

"A little."

Jack looked down and smiled. Her eyes followed. Her breasts were squished up against the firm wall of his chest. She quirked a brow as their eyes met.

"They're perfect." He grinned.

"And they're real." She grinned back.

Grinning turned into kissing, but she didn't know who made the first move. Didn't care.

Still kissing, Jack said, "I need to use the bathroom, and you're cold, so we should—"

Emily nibbled his bottom lip gently. Her lips left the warm haven of Jack's mouth and trailed to his jaw. He was sweet; he could be done now and want her to leave, but instead he was concerned. Oh, right, he had to use the bathroom. "We better get up before..."

With Jack's hands on her hips for support, she stood and stretched. She offered her hand to him, and when he folded his large hand around hers, she leaned back and helped him stand.

As he stood, he pulled her into his arms again and tilted her chin so their eyes met. "Em, that was amazing."

Jack was—her brain couldn't settle on one word—he was all of them. Hot, sexy, nice, handsome, and perfect.

He lifted her and carried her into the bedroom.

Inexplicably, her eyes filled with tears. She wasn't normally a crier, but after everything that happened the last three weeks, it seemed her tears had a mind of their own. Emily needed to keep it together. Jack would love to play knight in shining armor, but that would only make it worse when she left. And she was leaving.

"Do you need to use the bathroom?" Jack asked.

"You go first."

Jack went into the bathroom but didn't shut the door, returning in a few seconds carrying a robe. He held it open. "You're cold." He dropped a quick kiss on the top of her head and walked into the bathroom, closing the door.

The thick robe warmed her, but her feet were cold. Socks would be good, but she didn't want to root around in his drawers because that'd be rude. Probably terrible one-night stand etiquette. His slippers were next to the bed, so she slipped them on.

The sex had been amazing. Jack got a lot of practice. Sometimes she wished she could turn her brain off.

"Hey." Jack strode to her. "I thought only I had what it took to put that look of ecstasy on your face. Apparently, a pair of slippers has the same effect on you."

"Never underestimate the value of warm, fuzzy slippers." Grabbing his cock, she stroked him. "That in no way means *this* is of any less value."

Jack kissed her as his hands went to the belt of the robe and tugged it free. As Emily shrugged out of it, a loud knock broke the silence. Pulling back, her foot came out of one slipper and she stumbled. Jack's hands steadied her.

"It's Jeff. I'll be right back." Giving her a quick kiss on the forehead, he strode into the living room.

Emily wished she'd brought her clothes into the bedroom. She closed the robe, and went into the bathroom, locking the door. Flipping on the light, Emily sighed. Well, it'd been fun while it lasted. God, she hoped it wasn't another girl. *Whoa.* Why would she assume that? Writer's brain strikes again.

The bathroom was huge, much like the rest of Jack's suite. Neutral beige tones were accented with chocolate-brown polished tiles that bordered the wall. The ceramic tiles on the floor alternated between cream and brown. The granite vanity was varying shades of brown, gold, and cream, and the cabinets had a dark cherry finish. She'd never stayed in a hotel so extravagant.

She forced herself to calm down by taking several deep breaths. Jack was a nice guy, so she wouldn't allow her imagination to run wild. *Okay, benefit of the doubt.* Emily used the toilet, washed her hands, and splashed her face. Damn, she didn't have cleanser, and wetting her face would only make a mess of her makeup.

She never wore a lot of makeup, so there wasn't much to disturb. Using a tissue, she dabbed under her lash line. Her cheeks were still flushed. She could do with a little powder, but since her purse was in the living room, she used another tissue to blot.

A single knock sounded on the door. "Em, you okay?"

Crap, she'd locked the door, and now she felt bad. Maybe he wouldn't notice. Turning the lock, she opened the door.

"You okay?" His voice was full of concern.

She nodded.

"Why'd you lock the door? Did you think I wouldn't give you privacy?"

Emily stepped aside, and he entered and placed a white bag on the counter. He'd slipped into jeans, the button undone. *Delicious.* Turning to face her, he leaned up against the counter.

Emily shook her head, but she was hedging. She knew he

wasn't the rock star ripper, serial killing from coast to coast, but maybe he wasn't all he seemed.

"Hey," Jack said, waving his hand up and down in front of her face. "Have I fucked you into deafness, or are you ignoring me on purpose?"

"Neither. When you said it was Jeff, I thought..." Emily stammered. *Holy hell, what is wrong with me? Just say it.* "If the itch has been scratched, just say so. I don't know the protocol here. It's been fun, but I don't want things to get weird." *Too late.*

Jack didn't smile. Confusion turned to comprehension and then to annoyance. She wanted to look down, or over his shoulder, but she'd never been a coward and wouldn't start now.

He closed the distance between them and put his arms around her. "Baby, I'm sorry. I'm such a jerk. I should've told you Jeff was coming by. He ran an errand for me."

Emily rested her head on his bare chest, a sigh of relief escaping her lips. "I don't understand. Why do you think you're the jerk in this scenario?"

"Because I should've known you might misunderstand. Be honest, you thought Jeff was here to take you home?"

Allowing herself a little cowardice, Emily nodded. Jack's arms tightened around her, and she nestled in closer.

"See, jerk. I'm sorry."

"Jack." Emily forced herself to meet his eyes. "You asked me to spend the night with you, and while we could argue when the night ends and day begins, it certainly isn't now. You've been open and honest, and it's just that sometimes, my brain, in writer's mode, indulges thoughts that if I'd been thinking clearly, I wouldn't have been thinking. It got the better of me for a minute. I'm sorry."

"How far off the cliff did you get?"

"Well, my first thought was that, yes, Jeff was here to take me home now that you've had your fun. The second, I hoped he wasn't making a delivery."

"Well, he did make a delivery." Jack grinned and pointed to the bag. "Go on, open it."

"Well, I know it isn't condoms, because, courtesy of Elliot, you have a lifetime supply." Opening the bag, she looked inside and pulled out bottles of moisturizer, face wash, body wash, and lotion. All unscented. She looked at Jack's reflection in the mirror. His blue eyes watched her intently.

"I don't know if these are brands you like, but they're unscented. The hotel supplies all that stuff, but it's all very smelly. I wanted you to feel right at home in the morning," he said, with a shy smile.

Oh, hell on a stick. She'd known he was a nice guy, but this was so far out of the realm of nice; it was so incredibly, amazingly, wonderfully nice. Fuck. Why couldn't he be a prick? Speaking of pricks, her gaze dropped to his crotch. *Stop it, right now, young lady.* Lady? Yeah, like she'd still qualify as a lady.

Chapter Thirteen

"What did you think Jeff was delivering?" Jack asked as they walked into the bedroom.

"A girl," Emily said, stifling a yawn.

Jack yawned too. "Already have one." Jack pulled the covers down. Unzipping his jeans, he pushed them down and stepped on the bottoms to pull them off. He stretched, plopped on the bed, and patted the spot next to him. Seeing her all sleepy and mussed up had his body responding.

Emily walked to the free side of the bed while slipping out of the robe, and with her back to him, he had a great view of her fine ass. She sat and swung her legs onto the bed, grabbing for the covers at the same time.

Jack needed to hold her, feel her body against his. He leaned over and kissed her on the forehead and then flicked off the bedside lamp. She'd had a rough few weeks and probably wasn't sleeping well. He turned to face her. Emily lay on her back, her breathing even and steady. Maybe she thought cuddling would be too intimate, but he needed it, so he gently burrowed his arm between her neck and the bed, cradling her with his hand resting on her arm. Not ideal, but it would do.

She'd be a challenge. All the circumstances that led to her being at the concert tonight: catching her fiancé cheating and subsequent broken engagement, and Nicki's asshole boyfriend cheating on her. So much pain. He wouldn't wish that on anyone. Ever. But, he wouldn't waste this opportunity. Jack would make her understand what they had was special. She must feel it, too. Definitely a challenge, but one he was up for.

Jack woke with a start. He was cold and Emily was no longer next to him. She lay on her side on the far edge of the bed. Glancing at the clock, he saw it was almost two, and he hadn't been asleep long. At least with her on her side he could spoon her, but before he could move, she rolled onto her back.

Her lips moved, and she made small sounds, but he couldn't make out any words. She made a swatting gesture as she bolted upright and screamed, "Jack, don't."

What the fuck does that mean? He sat up but didn't touch her. She was looking around, probably trying to get her bearings. Jack smiled. She'd never woken up in the middle of the night in an unfamiliar bed with a man she wasn't dating. He hadn't given up on changing that. "Hey, you okay?" He scooted closer, placing his hand on her shoulder. The sheet pooled at her waist, but she didn't cover up, just leaned back into him. "Did you have a nightmare?"

"No, just a dream." Too soon, she pulled away. "I have to use the bathroom." Not bothering with the robe, she walked to the bathroom. The door clicked shut, but she didn't lock it.

Jack rubbed the back of his neck. That was bullshit. Did she really expect him to believe it was just a dream? She woke up swinging and screaming "Jack, don't."

Had the sex been too rough? Had he hurt her? He'd held back as much as he could, considering he was out of his fucking mind with need for her. The drive to possess a woman had never been so strong, urgent, and scary. Shit, maybe he wasn't ready for a relationship. He cast that thought aside; he was ready. For her anyway.

His breakup with Christie had really fucked with his head. This time last year, he'd planned to propose. They'd bought the house in California and he'd bought a ring. He'd known for some time he wanted to marry her. After her first stint in rehab two years ago, things had been good. She'd been newly sober, and her career had blossomed. She'd gotten that supporting role in what turned out to be a huge blockbuster, and her reviews had been stellar.

But by last June, she was drinking and taking uppers. He'd begged her to go back into rehab, even flying her folks out to talk to her. She'd resented that, big time. Turned out, that was only the tip of her resentment. During her rehab, they'd gone to counseling. According to her, he was a self-centered prick who only cared about his own success. He'd done everything possible to help her. They'd moved to California to further her acting career, for fuck's sake. He'd supported her financially and emotionally, but it was never enough.

That was the day he'd realized that the woman he'd considered the love of his life didn't love him so much as the idea of him. The supposed rock star. The fame. The money. The power couple. *What the fuck does that even mean?*

Jack was a simple guy, and he didn't need a lot of stuff. Guitars, food, shelter, clothes. Christie used to be that way too. A career in music was hard work, and Jack and the band worked hard. There might be a bigger payoff, but it wasn't an easy life, like that Bachman Turner Overdrive song would have people believe. Writing and recording music was a small part of their life; touring ate up most of their time. Time away from their families and friends, missed birthdays and family celebrations. He'd missed his sister's college graduation because he'd been on tour in Europe, but his family had understood. Their support meant everything, and he wouldn't be where he was today without it.

They loved what they did, and they were the luckiest fucks on the planet since they got to do it for a living. He loved performing and meeting their fans, but touring was grueling, a life of extremes, busy or boring. There was always promotion to be done, radio stations, interviews, and fan meet and greets. To combat the boredom, they found things to fill their time— working out, video games, girls.

Speaking of girls... Jack got up and walked to the bathroom. Emily had been in there a while. The dream must've been bad.

Jack was about to knock when the door opened. The light from the bathroom illuminated her gorgeous body. Breathtaking.

"I want to brush my teeth, but I didn't want to go through your stuff. Toothpaste?"

"Oh yeah, sorry." Jack walked into the bathroom and opened a drawer, pulling out a tube of toothpaste and his toothbrush and a new one for Emily. "Here." Their fingers skimmed as he handed it to her.

She opened the toothbrush, ran it under hot water for a minute, then put the paste on it, and brushed her teeth. They were both naked and brushing their teeth. Every time she made eye contact with him in the mirror, he smiled and toothpaste threatened to spill out.

Emily rinsed her mouth and laid the toothbrush on the counter. She picked up the body lotion and used some on her hands. "Thanks for this."

"My pleasure." Jack rinsed his mouth. "Ready?"

She nodded, and they walked into the bedroom and back to bed. He lay on his back and waited for her to snuggle closer, but she didn't. Instead, she lay next him and held his hand. Jack turned, coming up on his elbow, and waited. He could just make out her outline. "What's wrong?"

She sighed and faced him. "Nothing."

"Something has to be wrong. You're all the way over there, and you woke up screaming 'Jack, don't,' which has me concerned. Did I hurt you in your dream?"

"God, no. It was a nice dream, I guess, just a little weird. You did nothing to hurt me."

"Then why are you all the way over there?" He couldn't keep the hurt out of his voice.

"I get hot in my sleep, no big deal. As for the dream, it's nothing."

"Tell me," he demanded.

"It was just a dream, okay? I've dreamt plots to my books. Sometimes I wake up in the morning with the perfect solution to a part where I was stuck. Don't make too much out of it okay?"

Jack settled onto his back and laced his fingers behind his head. He wanted to pull her into his arms but didn't. "Em, tell me a story."

Emily sighed. "Fine. We're on a double date with Curt and Nicki—"

That was all Emily said before he sat up, turned the light on, and faced her with a shit-eating grin. "Officially, the best dream ever."

"Jack, it was just a dream," Emily repeated, as her earlier frustration returned. "I don't have to continue."

He lay back and pulled her to him so she was flush up against his body with her head on his shoulder. "I'm sorry for interrupting, won't happen again. Please continue." He couldn't stop smiling.

"Okay, we're at my apartment. From the front door, there are six stairs to the walkway. We start down, you have your arm around me, and I'm on your left side. Curt and Nicki are behind us. The fourth stair down has a chunk missing on the left side, from all the snow this past winter. The heel of my shoe caught on the broken edge, and I slipped. You tightened your arm around me and said 'Don't worry, baby, I've got you. I won't let you fall.'"

Under his breath he whispered, "Yup, best dream ever."

He felt her head shake and imagined she rolled her eyes. He also felt her smile. "Wait, you didn't say 'Jack, don't.'"

Lifting her head, she narrowed her eyes. "You interrupted, I didn't get to that part yet. We make it down the stairs without further incident as do Nicki and Curt. We're walking across the parking lot, when I see Sean coming toward us. He's talking, and I can't understand him at first, but as he gets closer, he's saying we have to talk." Emily took a steadying breath.

"Who's Sean?"

"You refer to him as the fucker. That's Sully's first name."

"Why do you call him Sully?"

"Everyone calls him Sully, even his bosses." She sneered. "Tiffany. Everyone, except his parents. I only called him Sean when I was angry at him. Can I finish this story now, Mr. I Won't Interrupt Again?"

"Oh, I can't wait."

"I tell him we have nothing to talk about, it's over, leave me alone. He won't take no for an answer, as usual, and he grabs my arm, pulling me toward him. Again, he says we need to talk, and I tell him he has nothing to say that I want to hear." She paused giving him a look. When he didn't interrupt again, she continued. "He's pulling me harder, and you let go. I turn to see you raising your arm to punch him. That's when I yelled 'Jack, don't.'"

"Damn right, I'll punch him, he grabs my girl—"

Emily sat up and put her fingers over his lips. "I'm not your girl, Jack."

"Well, your subconscious thinks you are or soon will be. It's trying to break it to you slowly. It's telling you that you like me, and you should listen."

"Jack, it's not my subconscious doing any of those things. It's taking bits and pieces and weaving them together in a nice little story."

"Are you saying you don't like me?" Jack asked, grinning stupidly.

"If I didn't like you, no amount of good looks or charm would've tempted me to sleep with you. A girl has to have standards, even for a one-night stand. And this is a one-night thing." Her tone was gruff, but she looked down.

Jack ignored that and smiled as he turned out the light. "Definitely, the best dream ever." He had no doubt that she'd be his girl. He also had no doubt that the fucker would be back.

EMILY COULDN'T SLEEP BECAUSE HER MIND REFUSED to shut down.

Jack cleared his throat. "Can I ask you a question?"

Oh crap, here it comes. "If I say no, would that stop you?" Emily asked.

"Yes."

Talking to Jack was so easy, like they'd known each other for a long time. She'd known the moment he realized what he'd felt when he'd touched her leg. She'd been so caught up in the moment, in wanting him, that it never occurred to her that this conversation was inevitable. No way someone like Jack didn't ask. "Go ahead."

"Were you in the car when your dad died?"

Emily's breath caught. Even though she'd known what he wanted to ask, she blurted out the full truth. "My parents, brother, and me." She could barely breathe past the lump in her throat, and swallowing didn't help. "They didn't make it."

"I'm so sorry." He nudged closer and tightened his arm around her.

"Drunk driver." Emily inhaled deeply and slowly exhaled, like she learned to do in therapy when her emotions overwhelmed her.

The last person she'd told was Sully and only after they'd dated for several months. Heat crept into her body. Turning away from Jack, she rolled onto her other side and tucked her legs up into her chest. She rubbed the scar that ran down most of her right leg. Jack turned on his side and settled behind her, but their bodies didn't touch.

"After I woke up in the hospital, they told me my parents had been killed instantly, but Riley held on for a few days." Way too much reality for a one-nighter, but she couldn't stop herself.

He kissed the back of her head. "I'm sorry, baby."

"It was a ten years ago. I get through most days okay. I can think of them now without it hurting so bad that I can't breathe. Planning my wedding was hard—" Emily choked back a sob.

"I'm so sorry that happened. I couldn't imagine my life without my family." He snuggled in closer and gave her a gentle kiss. "Get some sleep."

Emily stirred in her sleep. A familiar voice sang softly, and she wanted to wrap it around her like a blanket; it warmed her from the inside out.

The room was dark except for the light from Jack's cell phone that was propped up on the nightstand. Jack sat on the edge of the bed, gently strumming his guitar and singing. He stopped and wrote something in a notebook.

Closing her eyes, she focused on the lyrics. It was a love song. He stopped again to write something down and then crossed something out. Picking up his cell and tapping a few times, he laid it on the bed. Adjusting the guitar, he strummed and sang. Beautiful words. Emily squeezed her eyes shut and fisted her hands so she wouldn't touch him. She wanted to hear every word. His voice had such a beautiful, silky quality that it calmed her.

He implored the girl to believe they belonged together. If the world disappeared, they'd have each other, and that was all they needed.

Shit. Jack was too attached. This had been a huge mistake. She'd been selfish. Jack wanted more, but she didn't have more to give; she'd been running on empty the last three weeks.

She'd never had any doubts about Sully. He'd been into her from the first date, but it had taken her longer, way longer. It always did.

This time yesterday, she'd felt like shit. She hadn't been able to sleep, couldn't write, TV pissed her off, forget about reading. Until she was tired enough to pass out, every time she closed her eyes, the images of Sully and that little bitch waited. Except for tonight. Emily hadn't thought of Sully or weddings that much. Just Jack. She was sure that meant something. Probably the hot sex. Damn, she missed the end of the song.

As the last note faded away, Jack didn't move and his breaths came in hard bursts. His head dropped to his chest, and he rolled his shoulders.

No longer able to not touch him, her hand stroked his back. He didn't startle. His head came up, and he looked over his shoulder and smiled.

"That's beautiful." She felt almost guilty for intruding on his creative space; his beautiful song still hummed through her mind.

"It's about us," he said.

Emily had known that in her heart. How could he be so open? Why couldn't he just... What? Hide from his emotions?

Something her therapist had said from ten years ago tried to fight its way to the surface, but she wasn't in any shape to analyze right now. The last three weeks, she had felt like a walking raw nerve. Emily pushed all thoughts of the past away before they pulled her under. She wasn't sure she'd be able to surface again.

Jack stood and put the guitar in the case. He crawled onto the bed next to her. She lay on her side with her head on the pillow, the sheet no longer covering her. Emily rolled onto her back to give him a better view. He leaned down and kissed her, not the full-on invasion of his earlier kisses but gentle, the way he might kiss a longtime lover. Her nipples tightened to near painful as he palmed her breasts.

He broke the kiss and trailed kisses down her jaw, neck, and chest until reaching her nipple. Reverently, his tongue laved her until she thought she might pass out. With a final flick of his tongue, he sucked her nipple into his mouth.

She moaned and threaded her fingers into his hair. His hand caressed her other breast, stroking the nipple with his thumb. When he groaned and looked up at her, a shiver tore through her. He licked the underside of her breast, and his hand traveled down her belly until it rested at the apex of her thighs. He dipped two fingers inside as he kissed his way down her rib cage and across her hip until his mouth joined his fingers. Gently, he sucked her clit into his mouth, and she moaned.

"Jaaack."

He returned to her lips, and she wrapped her hand around his erection and stroked. Now it was his moan that echoed through her ears.

"I want to make love with you," Jack whispered.

Emily stopped kissing him. His eyes were filled with raw emotion. *Shit.* "Let's keep it fun," she said, not breaking eye contact.

"I want to do everything with you, Em. You're limiting me to one night." His lopsided smile undid her. "Please."

"I don't want to hurt you. That was never my intention." She tried to look away, but his hand cupped her face, forcing her to keep eye contact.

"Em, you've generously given me one night to make a lifetime of memories. I want making love to be one of them."

She must be the rottenest person alive to agree to this. In the morning, she would leave, but right now, being with him felt so good. "Okay."

She moved her hands to his shoulders and guided him onto his back. When he hesitated, she said, "You said make love with you. Lie back and enjoy."

Jack reached over and turned on the light. Emily scooted to the bottom of the bed while Jack adjusted the pillows behind his head. She'd been wanting to touch him all over since she'd had that eyeful of him in the towel. She placed her hands on the tops of his feet and gently massaged. Moving to his legs, she caressed the tops and sides of each leg, the hair tickling her palms.

Glancing up, Jack appeared to be struggling to keep his eyes open. "Just enjoy the sensations."

"But, I want to see you."

Cupping his balls in one hand, she stroked his erection with the other. When she moved to his hips, he grunted in disapproval.

"Patience." Emily continued her exploration, kissing and stroking him everywhere she could reach. His moans egged her on, and his chest heaved as he drew breath. She licked his abs and then trailed kisses up to his nipple, which she licked and then tugged.

"Oh fuck." Jack's lips went slack.

She kissed her way across his chest and up to his neck. Jack's eyes were half closed, but his grin was full. She kissed his lips, and his grin faded into her. His hands pulled her so she was on top of him, full body contact. When her nipples brushed against his chest hair, jolts of pleasure shot through her.

Emily nibbled his earlobe and whispered, "I need you inside me soon."

Jack groaned. "Can it be my turn now?"

Chapter Fourteen

Jack burned to touch her, to taste her, to be inside her.
Emily nodded, and in a flash, he switched their positions.
She deserved as good as she gave, so he had to get himself
under control. He kissed her lips, dipping his tongue in,
tangling with hers for only a few moments before
withdrawing. He tried to slow things down, but his dick
jerked; he wanted to go for a dip, too.

Reluctantly, Jack climbed off, as he needed a few minutes
to regain some control. The temptation to just take her
overwhelmed him. If he gave into it, he'd come like a clumsy
teenager. Emily's beautiful hazel eyes sparkled for him. "Roll
onto your stomach." His tone was tight, but Emily did as he
asked. "Get comfortable."

Jack couldn't remember a woman ever touching him so
thoroughly. Sure, his junk got plenty of attention, and so did
his chest and abs, but never the way Emily had touched him.
After a few deep breaths, he massaged her shoulders and back.
Her skin was so soft. Jack couldn't just use his hands.
Straddling her body, he caressed her shoulders while kissing

her neck. Her moan of approval ratcheted up his own arousal. He shifted down so he could touch more of her.

When he looked down and saw his dick nestled between her cheeks, his temperature rose several degrees. A few strokes and he'd come on her back. Jack forced himself to keep moving, kneading her ass firmly but gently. Leaning down, he kissed each cheek. As much as he'd like to linger, he wasn't doing himself any favors. He slipped his hand between her thighs and stroked her a few times. She was so warm, wet, and inviting. She clenched her muscles around his fingers, which drew a groan from him.

He kept moving, kissing her thighs and lingering at the dip behind her knees. When his hands wandered around her calf, his fingers grazed over her scar, and she gasped and lifted her head, so Jack quickly moved his hand. After a few seconds, she settled back down, but her legs were still tense. Sweeping his hands up her body, he lay next to her on his side, and Emily adjusted to face him.

She had the most gorgeous flush. He watched her as her gaze trailed down his body to his hard cock. She wrapped her fingers around him and stroked as her eyes locked on his. Damn, the girl knew how to handle the equipment—a firm grip and the perfect pace.

"Jack, please," she moaned.

Without breaking eye contact, he reached over to the nightstand and grabbed a condom. Within seconds he was over her, his dick resting between her lips. He kissed her while coating himself in her juices. He was about to claim her when she smiled into the kiss and giggled.

"What?" Jack asked.

Her eyes glittered. "Is Jack your real first name?"

Had she just asked him his name? "What?"

Emily repeated, "Is Jack your real first name?"

"Yes, Jack William McBride. It says so on my birth certificate. Why?"

Her lips broke into a huge, wicked grin. "You're about to be a real-life Jack-in-the-box."

It took a few seconds for his lust-clouded brain to register what she'd said. His laugh started deep in his belly. He loved that dirty mouth of hers. He fucking loved...her.

The realization hit him so hard he couldn't breathe. As soon as the thought registered in his brain, he knew the truth of it; he was falling in love with her. Something tight in his chest loosened, and a warmth spread throughout his body. The dull ache he'd grown accustomed to vanished.

Oh fuck. He couldn't tell her because she'd think him certifiable. Emily was far too practical to understand. Besides, she was in no condition to accept or return love. He'd do well to remember that.

"Jack, is everything okay?"

His eyes shot open. Her eyes were filled with concern. Jack forced a neutral smile and pushed fully inside her. "Yeah, I'm fine. Sorry, holding you feels so fucking good. I got caught up in the sensations." It wasn't a lie; it just wasn't the reason he hadn't been moving.

Certain his eyes would give him away, he closed them. He took her lips in a soft, hungry kiss as he moved inside her, and they both moaned.

Her nails bit into his back, and her legs hooked around his calves.

He buried his face in the crook of her neck, kissing and licking. With every thrust, she tightened around him. She panted, trying to get enough air. He cupped her face as he kissed her lips. If he'd more time... His eyes flew open. He had to change her mind. Jack couldn't let her walk out of here, out of his life, in a few hours.

"Jack, something has to be wrong. First, you're squeezing

your eyes closed so tightly you looked like you were in pain, and now they flew open in a panic. Am I doing something wrong?"

He stopped moving and rested his forehead against hers. "No, Em. You're doing everything right."

"Then what? Do you have a cramp or something?"

"No. Everything's great." Jack smiled like an idiot. *Come on, man, dial it down, or she won't believe you.* He tried to stop smiling, but couldn't, so he moved to her shoulder and nipped at it gently with his teeth. *Mine.* She arched into him.

"Jack, please tell me what's wrong. Now you're smiling like a crazy person. You're scaring me."

Emily's pleading tone was his undoing, and before he could think of anything else to say, he blurted out the truth. "Em, I'm falling in love with you."

Shit.

♪ ♫ ♪

IF EMILY HAD BEEN THINKING STRAIGHT, OR AT ALL, she wouldn't have asked. Why couldn't she keep her big mouth shut? Now it was out there, and she had to say something, but she had no idea what. He didn't expect her to feel the same, did he?

She'd spent the last three weeks going over every detail of her relationship with Sully. She'd come to resent all the compromises she'd made and all the allowances she gave trying to see the best in him. Not that she was perfect by any means, but it was one of his shortcomings. Things he didn't understand—like her need to write stories—were dismissed. Why had she put up with that? How did she get back on this topic? She was having the best night of her life. Oh, right, Jack said he was falling in love with her. A frustrated groan escaped her lips.

"You probably think I'm nuts."

Emily's eyes focused on him. She smiled and touched her lips to his. "I think you're impulsive, relentless, and spoiled. Let's finish what we started. Oh, and Jack"—Emily paused for effect—"seriously, missionary?"

"It's more intimate this way, baby." His blue eyes, darker than normal, shimmered with emotion.

Emily swallowed the lump in her throat.

Keeping his gaze locked on hers, he moved, pulling out and then slowly sliding back in until he filled her. With each thrust, her muscles gripped him. With their bodies locked together, she felt his heart pounding in his chest. Or was it hers? Emily closed her eyes. She had to; she couldn't keep looking at the raw emotion in his.

He ducked his head and took her nipple in his mouth, suckling her, while his hand reached between them, and he stroked her clit. Every muscle in her body tightened as she arched off the bed, and as she screamed out her climax, Jack kissed her, swallowing her cries, as he growled out his own release. He collapsed on her, but only for a moment, before he rolled off, disposed of the condom, and pulled her on top of him. Emily felt his heartbeat beating in time with hers.

"You think I'm spoiled?"

"You're clearly used to getting your own way. Does any woman ever say no to you?" She tried to raise her head but couldn't; her mind and body were exhausted.

"As a matter of fact, I met this amazing girl last night. Beautiful, sexy, intelligent, funny as hell, with a dirty mouth that drives me wild. She said no, repeatedly."

"Mmm. Sounds like a head case, Jack. You should move on to the next girl." She yawned and snuggled into him.

"Maybe she's just hurting so bad she can't tell a good guy when she meets him."

Emily mustered her strength and lifted her head to meet

Jack's eyes. "I see a good guy right now. You're all the things on the pro list and more. Under different circumstances, at a different time, if you had a different life..." Emily didn't finish the sentence. What was the point? None of those things were.

"You're still leaving even though you know we're good together?"

"I needed to cut loose tonight, although I didn't know that's what I needed until I met you. You've been fun." Emily wasn't a no strings kind of girl, but for the first time in her life, she wished she was.

"Not all guys cheat."

"I know." She tried to move off him, but Jack tightened his hold.

"Since I left home ten years ago, I've had three serious relationships, that's six and a half years in monogamy. At least, I was. My first serious girlfriend cheated on me. Of the remaining three and a half years, I've slept alone plenty of nights. I'm having the best time I've ever had, and I don't want it to end. I want to see you again."

Emily sighed, wanting to just pass out. "Jack, you agreed to one night, and I'm leaving in the morning. That was our deal. I needed to bust out tonight, but I'm not the girl you think I am, and you don't really know me at all."

"That's bullshit."

"Maybe if I had been wilder in bed..."

"That fucker cheating on you wasn't your fault. That's on him."

Emily rolled off him and onto her back, covering her eyes with her arm. "I hate that this is making me crazy, and I know it's not my fault. But I also don't understand what happened. We were happy. If his feelings changed, why didn't he break up with me? Something must've happened."

"Nothing you could've done is justification for cheating."

"I know that, but—"

"But nothing." Jack turned on his side. "Spend time with me this week."

"No."

"You won't even consider it?"

"There's nothing to consider. We agreed."

He growled, "I lied. You shut me down at every turn. Did you expect me to walk away from the offer of a lifetime? And I think you knew I was lying. You wanted me as much as I wanted you. Why can't you admit we have something special? It's okay to admit you don't want this to end in the morning."

"Jack, it has to end."

"Why?"

"Because three weeks ago, I was supposed to get married" —Emily choked on a sob—"and now I'm not. Please drop it."

Jack's anger bubbled over. "Or what, you'll leave now?"

"I don't want to leave now. Please, can't we enjoy the time that's left?"

Jack heaved a sigh. Kissing the top of her head, he whispered, "Em, I'm not giving up."

"I know."

Chapter Fifteen

J ack awoke to Emily cursing softly as she moved about the room. *Bet she stubbed her toe. That had to hurt.* The room was mostly shadows since it wasn't even six a.m. yet. Jack sat up and adjusted the pillows behind him and leaned back. "Sneaking out?" he asked, as she walked back into the bedroom.

"Oh shit! You scared me." Emily clutched her clothes to her chest. Dropping them on the foot of the bed, she stepped into her panties and pulled them up.

"You didn't answer my question." Jack flicked on the lamp.

She squinted as her eyes adjusted to the light. "Not sneaking, just trying not to wake you." Emily slipped on her black satin and lace bra. The sheet tented at his groin. Usually, with these one-nighters—what was the phrase Emily had used? Once the itch had been scratched—Jack chuckled at that—he was ready for it to end, but he wasn't a dick about it or anything. He always bought breakfast and made sure they had a safe way home. If not, he paid for a cab. Everyone left happy. But with Emily, the itch had only gotten worse. "Were you going to leave a note?"

"Yes."

"Maybe we should have that debate over what time night ends and day begins. It's still dark out. That has night written all over it."

"Jack, the sun is rising."

"So am I." He gestured to the tent. "Guess you're right, it's morning." Laughing, he threw the covers back and stood. Walking over to her, he took the shirt she'd been holding for the last minute and dropped it on the bed.

"It's only six o'clock, you don't have to leave so early. Let's go back to bed, have sex, get a little sleep, then repeat. Then we'll have breakfast."

Emily faced him. "I'm sure in rock star, six in the morning is bedtime, but for the non-rock star community, it's time to get up and get ready for work."

"I thought you were off?" Jack kissed her neck. He leaned his erection into her, so she could feel up close and personal the effect she was having on him.

"I'm off from my day job, as Nicki calls it." Emily moaned and tried to pull away, so Jack let her. "I have a meeting with my editor."

Her eyes were dazed, and it wouldn't take much to get her back into bed. "What time is your meeting?" Jack sat on the edge of the bed, his dick at attention.

"Ten. Gotta get going," Emily said, as though she needed the reminder.

"You need four hours to get ready?"

"No, and yes. Gotta get home, shower, get dressed, then drive back into the city, find parking, get up to the forty-third floor, and not be late."

Pulling Emily into his arms, Jack kissed her. Her arms wrapped around him. "Stay," he said between kisses. He was getting dizzy, whether from not breathing or from her kisses, he wasn't sure.

"You agreed," she said, still kissing him.

"Fuck that, I lied and you know it. You're lying now if you say you want to leave." Jack's dick throbbed.

Emily sighed. "I don't want to leave, and I don't want to go to this meeting and get chewed out."

He stroked the inside of her thigh, just bumping her with the top of his hand. Her panties were wet; he inhaled deeply, relishing her amazing, unique scent. "Stay." He pulled back to look at her. His brows dipped "Why do you think you're getting chewed out?"

Emily slumped against him, so he tightened his hold and waited.

"Because, Jack, I missed my deadline. Monday came and went, and no manuscript. And it's not going to be finished. I trashed it."

Rage surged through him. If Jack ever met the fucker, he'd take him apart. "Doesn't your editor know what happened? Can't they cut you some slack?" He knew missing a deadline was a big deal. If publishing was anything like the music business, there were a lot of moving parts after the band finished recording. Even small delays screwed up the works, and that equaled loss of money.

"Of course, she knows. Meg is a hard-ass on a good day. Part of her job is keeping her writers on schedule. She can't edit something I haven't submitted, so she can't do her job. Which was how she began the conversation on Monday, as if I didn't feel bad enough."

He rested his cheek on her chest. Everything with her felt good. No strings fun, with any other girl, would be ideal. But with Emily, he wanted the strings. Jack wanted it all.

"I've never missed a deadline. When Monday rolled around, and I had nothing to submit, I hated it. I hated that

WITH YOU 149

he screwed me up so bad I couldn't write. I've had writing to lean on since the accident, but now it's gone."

"Why did you trash your book?" Jack stroked her back. "Was it so bad? Can't you rework it?"

Emily's eyes met his, and they held unshed tears. He'd bet she'd suck it up rather than cry. Two deep breaths later, she blinked and the tears were gone.

"It was good. The main characters were engaged and planning their wedding. Dealing with discordant in-laws to be, a maid of honor who wants everyone to wear pink, including the groom, a groom who green-lights everything the bride wants, including having the ceremony at a haunted castle." Emily heaved a sigh. "Then, my life blew up, and I couldn't write, I couldn't suck it up and finish it. How was I supposed to write a happy ending?" She tensed and pulled back. "Sorry."

"Don't be." Jack got the impression she wasn't used to sharing. Rubbing her cheek with his thumb, he whispered, "Don't go. The last thing you need right now is more grief. Spend the day with me."

"I can't just not go."

"Call and cancel, of course." Jack kissed the tip of her nose. "Stay. I want to show you something."

Emily leaned back and looked down at his still hard penis. "I've seen it."

Jack rolled his eyes. "Jeez, all you women think about is sex. Something outside the room." His hands skimmed down her back and into the waistband of her panties, cupping her bare cheeks.

Emily let out a long moan.

His hands caressed down her legs, taking her panties with them. Emily put her hands on his shoulders and stepped out of them. *One down, one to go.* Jack stroked her back and unclasped her bra. He hugged her to him, and when she pulled back, he slid the straps down her arms. She lifted her hands from his shoulders as he pulled her bra off and tossed it aside. He was ready to go again, and from the look in her eyes, so was she.

"Jack." Emily's fingers snapped by his head.

Mouth open, he stared at her glorious tits. "Sorry, what did you say?" he asked, as his gaze snapped up to hers.

"I said I can't. It's not right. I'm using you."

It was cute that she thought that. "I volunteer." Jack grabbed his cock. "Reporting for duty." Kissing her lips, he whispered, "Stay."

Emily sighed. "Have you ever been on vacation and wished you could stay a few more days? That's how I feel. For the first night in almost a month, I got a good night's sleep."

"A good reason to continue your vacation."

"I closed my eyes last night and for the first time in weeks, I didn't see the man I was going to marry inside another woman. I ate a meal that I didn't want to immediately throw up. And I laughed."

Her smile made his heart flip over.

"My job all but forced me to take time off because I've been messing up."

"Then stay." Jack gave her his most sincere smile.

THE BEAUTIFUL HEAT THAT PASSED BETWEEN THEM ignited once again, and Emily kissed him hard. Minutes passed, and they only stopped to come up for air.

"Em, spend the day with me, extend your vacation."

"I got so lost in my rant that I forgot my point. I don't want to hurt you. Last night, if I'd been stronger, been able to resist you, you wouldn't be in this mess. If I stay, it'll only make it worse later when I leave." She placed her palms on either side of his face and looked him dead in the eyes. "And I am leaving."

When Jack smiled as if he knew better, she sighed in frustration. "Don't you have any sense of self-preservation?"

"First off, you aren't using me, I already volunteered. Secondly, this doesn't have to end today. Spend the rest of the week with me. Let's get to know each other, enjoy each other, and see where we go from here." Jack tilted her chin until their eyes met. "I don't need self-preservation around you. You're more concerned about me than you are for yourself right now. Considering everything you've been through, that's extraordinary."

Staying was the wrong thing to do, but she just couldn't seem to force herself to leave. Emily felt alive for the first time in weeks. "If I stay, I will leave at the end of the afternoon. If you can't accept that, then I have no choice but to leave now."

Again, he smiled. "I accept that, right now, you know you're leaving. Doesn't mean you won't change your mind. Again."

"You're infuriating." Emily huffed. "I'm not playing hard to get."

"Look, I get it, okay. You're going. Doesn't mean I'll stop trying to convince you to stay. Share your day with me."

The last of her pathetic resolve to leave crumbled. She needed a few more hours where she didn't have to think about — "Okay."

"Great. Since you've chosen wisely, I have a reward." Taking her in his arms, he kissed her. This was no ordinary kiss but filled with emotion and passion that sparked something inside her. Deep in her belly, a warmth spread throughout her body. She held onto Jack, curling her fingers into his flesh. When they broke apart, Emily was more turned on than she could ever remember. From a kiss.

Jack was hard, and she wanted to take him in her mouth.

He must have realized her intention, because as she dropped to her knees, he stopped her.

With a brief kiss on her lips, he muttered, "Wait here." He went to the window and opened the curtains, the sunrise casting a gentle light into the room.

What's he doing?

"Not to worry, we're thirty-seven floors up, no one can see in."

He flipped on the bathroom light, which added a soft yellow glow. He stretched out his hand to her, and Emily padded to him, taking his hand. As their fingers entwined, Jack smiled and drew her in for another knee-melting kiss. Jack moved until he stood behind her, and his erection nestled in the small of her back. His large hands started at her hips and teasingly moved up her body until he cupped her breasts. When his thumbs stroked her already tight nipples, she gasped at the sensation and leaned back on him for support.

"You're perfect," he whispered.

He trailed kisses on her neck as his fingers pinched her nipples. Emily didn't need any more foreplay; she was ready for whatever he planned. She wiggled her bottom, and Jack groaned.

His hands stilled. "Not yet, baby, this is for you."

Emily turned to look up at him. He tipped his chin forward and her gaze followed. Their reflection in the mirror startled her, and she tried to step away, but Jack pinned her to him with his left arm as his right hand traveled down her rib cage, coming to rest on her hip.

"No."

"Relax, baby, see how beautiful you are?"

But she didn't look, so Jack tilted her chin. When their eyes locked in the mirror, she was lost.

"You're so beautiful when you come. Haven't you ever watched in a mirror or recorded yourself during sex?"

Her mouth suddenly dry, she shook her head. Obviously, Jack had. An unexpected shyness overtook her, and Emily wanted to look away, but Jack's hands resumed their teasing of her nipples. She'd never understood why people filmed themselves having sex. "What do you have in mind?"

"Well, I want to fuck you with my hand, while watching your reactions in the mirror. Then, I want to kneel before you and eat your sweet pussy until you come, while you watch me. Finally, I want to fuck you. Hard." Jack pressed his erection into her back.

Her imagination kicked in, and the mental pictures overwhelmed her. A moan escaped her lips.

"Nothing will happen that isn't okay with you."

She squirmed, trying to ease the throbbing between her thighs. "Do I have to watch?"

"Your choice, but I'll be watching." He swiveled his hips back and forth against her back. Turning her head to the side, he kissed her.

"Okay."

Not wasting any time, his right hand slid over her mound. "Spread your legs."

Emily widened her stance to grant him access. He teased her swollen lips, dipping his finger in well below her clit. She thrust her hips back, trying to get him where she needed him.

"Patience." He looked straight ahead. "So wet already, and I haven't even begun."

She looked in the mirror, but Jack's gaze was fixed lower, and his lips were parted. She saw herself. Naked. Wanting. Wanton. The sight of his hand buried between her legs was so erotic she almost came from the image.

"Beautiful isn't it?" Jack said, his voice deeper than usual. "You're stunning. Your body is fucking incredible. Soft, yet strong. I want to look at your ass, but I can't tear my eyes off the stunning view before me."

She shifted her hips, trying to force his hand, but he moved with her.

He moaned, and his cock moved on her back. Maybe he'd come from looking at them. *Oh, that's fucking hot.*

He finally fingered her clit.

"Oh yes," she moaned.

"I can't wait to taste you. That little taste earlier wasn't enough." He dipped two fingers inside as his thumb worked her clit.

Emily heaved a breath, trying to fill her lungs. She was going to come soon, too soon. She rocked against his hand. His thumb eased off as he hooked his middle finger inside and pinched her nipple at the same time. The sensations from top and bottom met in her belly, and she felt faint. "Oh, that..." Her whole body was warm and coiled. Needing to do something with her hands, she grabbed his hips.

He chuckled as he nipped her earlobe. "I'm not going anywhere, baby." He ground his cock into her back as his thumb circled her again, so close. She wanted to watch, but her eyes fluttered closed.

"Not yet, baby," Jack whispered. Raising his hand, he inhaled and then licked his fingers. Jack stepped back but didn't let go. "Can you stand?"

She nodded.

Slowly, he released her and came to stand in front of her. Emily peered past him and into the mirror. "Love the view, Jack."

"Front or back?" he asked, shaking his ass.

"Both," Emily said, as she shifted her gaze to his front, licking her lips.

"Stop that now, young lady. I'm not done with you yet."

Emily grabbed his shoulders, stood on tiptoes, and took his mouth. She needed to come. Reaching down, she stroked his cock, swiping the bead of fluid off the head. Slowly, she raised her fingers to her lips, and locking her eyes on Jack's, she took her finger in her mouth. "Mmm."

Jack's eyes glazed over. He licked his lips, dropped to his knees, grabbed her hips, and pulled her to him. Starting at her belly, he kissed his way down to her pussy. Glancing up at her, he smiled as he spread her open. He circled her with his thumb. When his tongue grazed her clit, sensations burst throughout her body.

Jack moaned and pulled back, licking his lips and ending with a loud smack. "Lean forward and use my shoulders to support yourself. Don't bother begging for mercy. I'm not stopping until you come." Then he pulled her hips to his waiting mouth.

"Oh, yes. Jack—" Her voice was loud, and she was already so close. Within seconds of Jack's mouth on her, her climax broke. He didn't stop until the last shudders of her orgasm faded away.

As her knees buckled, Jack leaned forward taking her onto his shoulder as he stood. "I've got you, baby, I won't let you fall." By the bed, he set her on her feet, sat, and pulled her onto his lap, cradling her in his arms.

Emily felt warm, protected, and sated.

Chapter Sixteen

God, she was beautiful. Jack stroked her hair as her breathing returned to normal. He didn't know how she'd stayed on her feet; even with leaning on him, her thighs had trembled.

Her cheek rested on his shoulder. He kissed her lips. His dick throbbed with need, but she was exhausted.

"Jack?"

"Yeah?"

"How do you want me, baby?"

Six sweetest words ever. "Anything?" His heart slammed in his chest. He wanted her so badly, but that would be...

"Within reason."

He had to fuck her now. Setting her on her feet, he stood and crooked a finger at her to follow him. Once in the bathroom, he stood behind her and wrapped his arms around her. Her skin had the most gorgeous flush. The little vixen wiggled her ass against his groin. He didn't need the added stimulation, but he didn't shift. She teased him, and he liked it.

"You liked watching us in the mirror, didn't you?" Jack asked as he nuzzled her neck. "Turn your head."

A slow smile spread across her face as she saw their reflection in the mirrored wall. "Another fine view, Jack." Turning to face him, she put her arms around his neck. "I believe you said something about fucking me hard?"

Jack moaned. *My turn.* "Turn around and bend over." His voice shook with pent-up desire.

"About time." She turned and faced the mirror.

He reached around her and grabbed the rubber he'd placed on the counter earlier. After tearing it open, he rolled it down his length. Grabbing her hips, he walked them back a few steps. "Hold on to the counter."

Bending at the waist, Emily curled her fingers around the edge of the sink. She wiggled her ass at him.

Jack had to get inside her now. Rubbing his cock between her thighs, coating himself, he was practically out of his mind but somehow remembered to warn her. "I need to know during, not after, if it's too much for you." He slid into her hot, wet pussy up to his balls. *So good.*

"Jaaack."

He gave her a second to adjust, and then he pulled out and pounded back into her. Her gasp excited him further. Again. And again.

"Oh, fuck."

He turned his head to the mirrored wall. Emily watched too, and her lips parted as she uttered another "Yes." Her voice was husky, and she panted for breath.

He slowed the pace so they could get a better view of his taking her. Oh shit. He turned away because watching drove him wild. He pounded her so hard his balls slapped against her. She liked that. So did he. Fuck, so good. He tightened his grip on her hips. Shifting his gaze to the vanity mirror, he was treated to the stunning view of her tits bouncing.

Their eyes met in the mirror. It was the best of both worlds; he fucked her from behind and still saw her lovely face. He leaned forward and kissed the back of her neck. "So beautiful." He wanted to say more, but speech was impossible. Dropping kisses over to her shoulder, he nipped her. *Mine.*

He slowed down as her muscles contracted around him because he didn't want to come yet.

She looked over her shoulder. "Come on, Jack. Fuck me like you mean it."

A primal grunt tore from him, and he didn't hold back. She wanted more, so he obliged. This time he didn't slow down when he felt her muscles grip him.

"Fuck, Jack, don't stop," she screamed.

A sudden pounding echoed on the bathroom wall. "Jack, please fucking stop. Some of us have to work today," a man's voice yelled from the other side.

Jack paused for a second as their eyes met in the mirror. Emily's flush deepened. He pumped into her twice more and exploded inside her, biting his tongue to keep from screaming out.

Unable to stand, he grabbed Em around the waist, leaned up against the mirrored wall, and slid down to the floor. The tile was cold on his ass, but he didn't give a shit since he was still inside her. She moved to climb off him. "Not yet."

"One sec." She crawled forward and grabbed the bath mat. "Up." Jack lifted his butt, and she slipped the rug underneath him. Facing him, she settled back on his lap. Much better.

Sated beyond belief, Jack felt the lust cloud slowly lifting. "Fuck me like you mean it?"

"Worked, didn't it?" She grinned at him. Then her smile faded. "Do you think he heard us all night?" She was cute when she was embarrassed.

"Sounds like it." At her contrite expression, he chuckled. "Don't worry, I'll make it up to him."

"How?" Emily asked, nestling into his embrace.

"I'll figure that out later. But now"—he paused as a yawn overtook him—"we should get some sleep."

"Here?" She didn't move a muscle.

"Tempting, but the bed will be more comfortable."

She leaned back, and her eyes were filled with emotion. When she smiled, his heart flipped in his chest, and he was a goner.

She stood gracefully, and he clumsily got to his feet. Before she turned to leave, he pulled her into his arms. "That was amazing, Em."

"Yeah."

"Do you need to use the bathroom?"

"I went first last time," she said, closing the door behind her.

He was in serious fucking trouble here.

When Jack opened the bathroom door, Emily sat on the edge of the bed wearing his T-shirt. He liked that. A lot. She smiled and sauntered into the bathroom. His dick stirred.

He busied himself with straightening up the bed and retrieving the rest of his clothes he'd left in a pile by the door. They could get a few hours of sleep before she had to call her editor. Jack glanced toward the bathroom. She'd been in there a while. As if on cue, the door opened and Emily came out. She smiled at him and went up on tiptoes and kissed him. Before he could deepen the kiss, she moved past him, whipping off his T-shirt and climbing into bed. He joined her. Picking up his cell, he asked, "Is nine thirty okay?"

"That's fine." Emily stretched and yawned. "Thanks."

"My pleasure." Taking care of her would be his greatest pleasure.

EMILY TURNED ON HER SIDE, AND JACK CUDDLED UP next to her. Damn, she should've lain on her back. Hopefully he'd fall asleep soon, and she could move away. For now, she tried to enjoy how good it felt to have him up against her.

When she was in the bathroom, she'd barely recognized herself. The reflection she'd seen in the mirror for the last three weeks was gone. Sad eyes and that lost look were replaced by confidence. Damn. Maybe she needed a dose of Jack more often. *Why not? Friends with benefits.* People did it all the time. Why couldn't they hook up whenever he was in town? But he'd said he was falling in love with her. *Stupid love.* It complicated everything. When it was great, there was nothing better, but when it went bad, nothing was worse.

Until Sully, she'd thought she'd had her heart broken before, but those were just dents. No real damage done. Nothing a few drinks, several pints of ice cream, a good old-fashioned bitch fest, and time couldn't fix. Emily had been twenty-three when she'd met Sully, and she'd thought she'd recovered from the accident, at least as much as she ever would. Her body had taken over a year. Her heart, soul, mind, and spirit had taken much longer. A piece here and there until all the pieces were restored. A little worse for wear but complete.

Sully had been her first serious relationship. Colby, Don, and Bill had all been great in their own way, but she hadn't fallen in love with any of them, not really. Sully had been different from the beginning; at twenty-seven, he'd been a man and fully established in his career. He'd pursued her relentlessly, which had both excited and scared her. She realized now, that at the time, she'd still been afraid to allow herself to care about someone again. Not that she'd withheld her love from Sully, but it developed slowly.

When she'd caught him cheating, all the love she'd had for him had evaporated. She was terrified of what else might be gone. She'd already rebuilt her life from the ground up once, and Emily didn't know if she could do it again.

Jack's breathing leveled out, and she shifted, half on her back, half on her side. Jack didn't stir, so after a few seconds, Emily turned on her back. His arm was still draped over her torso, but she wasn't trapped.

Still, Emily couldn't fall asleep. Something niggled at her. Nicki. She'd meant to text Nicki last night to make sure she was okay. Emily's purse was on the table by the window. She inched toward the edge of the bed, but even in his sleep, Jack couldn't keep his hands off her. His hand cupped her breast, and her nipple hardened. After enjoying Jack's touch for a minute, she tried again to extricate herself without waking him. She had one leg on the floor before Jack turned onto his back.

Sliding out of bed, she grabbed her purse and walked into the living room. She sent Nicki a quick text. Emily waited several minutes but got no response. Nicki slept with her phone, so if she'd been awake she'd have texted her back.

She crawled back in bed and lay on her back. Pulling the covers up, she drifted off to sleep.

Chapter Seventeen

Jack opened his eyes. Bright sunshine cascaded through the windows. Emily was next to him but not in the spooning position they'd started in. He was on his back, and she was tucked into his side with her head nestled against his shoulder. It was nine o'clock.

He canceled his alarm and dialed room service and ordered breakfast. Then he left a message for Anthony, the concierge.

Emily stirred in her sleep, making little sounds, but didn't wake. This felt so right, so normal. Usually after a one-nighter, the mornings started with sex, a quick shower, breakfast, and depending on the band's schedule, maybe hang out for a bit, and then goodbye. Not this morning. Sex would be great. Maybe she'd offer that blowjob she'd been so intent on giving him in the limo. A long shower, a nice breakfast, but definitely not goodbye.

They needed to get a move on if he was going to take her to The Rock House. Jack hadn't seen Sid, the owner, in over a year, so he was looking forward to it. The Rock House held a special place in the band's hearts. Sid Levinson was the first guy to tell them they had a real chance at making it as professional musicians. He'd taught them so much about the industry and told them the steps needed to move forward and not just play local gigs. His help had been invaluable, and the band owed him a huge debt.

Emily moaned in her sleep, and now it was Jack who stirred. Maybe she was having a sex dream about him. Totally plausible since she'd already had one dream about him. Best dream ever.

Emily's hand slid down from his chest until she reached his dick and stroked.

"Mmm, that feels so good."

"Good morning." Her warm breath tickled the sensitive skin on his neck.

"Fantastic morning." Jack's stomach growled. Food better get here soon or he might have to eat her. *Excellent idea.*

Before he could flip her over, she lifted her head and said, "Don't even think about it, McBride."

"Already did." He shot her a wicked smile.

"No, enough screwing around. For now. Gotta call my editor." Emily turned her face into him and sighed, still stroking.

Since her hand was occupied, he offered, "Want me to dial the phone for you?"

"No." She kissed his chest as she leaned up.

If she kept this up much longer... Jack moaned again. He removed her hand. Before she could guess what Jack was up to, he pinned her to the bed and kissed her. Their tongues danced. Kissing her was unbelievable. Jack kissed down her body. He settled between her thighs and gently rubbed his beard stubble against her inner thigh. A knock at the door broke the silence. They both groaned.

Jack kissed her soft thigh and smiled. "Rain check." One he couldn't wait to collect.

Emily grabbed Jack's shirt and slipped it over her head. "What?" she asked at his incredulous expression.

"Why bother? It's only coming off again."

"I'm not talking to my editor naked."

Another knock, this time louder. Jack picked up his jeans and stepped into them. "Why?" Tucking himself in, he carefully zipped up. He didn't bother with the button or a shirt since Emily wore it.

"Because I need to concentrate." Emily swallowed hard. "Aren't you going to get the door?" She looked away.

Jack smirked and walked into the living room. Opening the door, Anthony, The Yorkshire Hotel's finest concierge, greeted him.

"So good to have you back, Mister—" Anthony stopped at Jack's raised brows. "Jack."

They shook hands. "Great to be back. How's your lovely wife?"

"Much better, sir. Her treatments are over, and her last round of blood work was perfect. She has one more scan coming up, but the doctor thinks he got it all."

"That's great news."

"I understand last night's concert was a smashing success."

As one of the top concierges in the city, it didn't surprise Jack that Anthony had the scoop on last night's gig. He had connections all over the city—from restaurant reservations and Broadway shows to emergency pet grooming—Anthony could get it done. "Yeah." Jack paused as he looked over his shoulder. "I need a favor."

"Anything."

"What's the laundry's turnaround?"

"Four hours."

Jack frowned. He hated to ask, but it was for Em. "Any chance we can get it done in two?" He hoped they could be on their way before noon.

"I'll see what I can do."

He needed a backup plan. "What about the boutique? What time do they open?"

"There was a leak in the stockroom. They should reopen by tomorrow." Anthony leaned in and winked. "The manager, Belinda, owes me a favor. What do you need?"

"Not me, the young lady who's with me. We're spending the day together, and I don't want her walking around in yesterday's clothes. I don't want to cause a problem for the laundry, so if they can't do two hours, do you think Belinda could help me out?"

"I don't see that being a problem," Anthony said. "Tell me what you need, and I'll make it happen."

"You're a lifesaver." Jack hurried into the bedroom, but Em was in the bathroom. He scooped her clothes off the bed and grabbed a laundry bag from the closet. Jack wrote down her sizes, put the clothes in the laundry bag, returned to the living room, and handed the bag to Anthony.

"She's a jeans and T-shirt kind of girl. Let's stick with that. Also, bra and panties." Jack handed Anthony the paper with Emily's sizes.

"Any color preferences?"

"Yes, burgundy top, and the bra and panties too, something pretty, but nothing too sexy, or we'll never make it out of the room." The idea of staying in the room all day appealed to him, but he wanted to show her where the band got their start. "What's the weather like today?"

"It'll be cooler today, only about fifty."

Emily didn't have a jacket last night. "She'll need a jacket, too."

"Not a problem, Jack. I'll take care of everything. Glad to be of service." They shook hands, and Anthony left.

When he walked into the bedroom, Emily was just coming out of the bathroom. She had that wild night of sex look about her. Her face was flushed, hair messed up, and she wore his shirt, and he couldn't resist grabbing her and kissing her. Her arms went around his waist, and he hoisted her left leg up so he could touch her soft skin. By the time he let go, they both gasped for air.

"Stop, Jack." Her palms stroked his bare chest before pushing him away. "Meg can sense sex over the phone. She has this creepy sixth sense. I don't want to answer questions. I want to get off the phone as quickly as possible. I also don't want to hear another person tell me I need to have revenge sex."

Emily picked up the room phone but put it back down. Grabbing her cell from her purse, she sat on the bed.

"Can I listen in?"

"Sure, I guess. No touching."

Jack reached for her. Of course, he'd touch her.

Emily shot him a stern look. "I'm not kidding about Meg. If she hears the slightest difference in my voice, her barrage of questions won't end until she gets answers."

Emily thumbed through her contacts and tapped Meg's number, but she disconnected the call before it rang. She looked up at him. "What the hell do I say to her?"

He crawled on the bed and sat behind her, pulling her up against his chest. Her body heat warmed him. "Tell her the truth."

"That I spent the night with hot rock star Jack McBride? She won't let up until she has all the details."

"Not that truth. So, you think I'm hot?" His smile spread into what he was sure was a goofy grin. Emily tried to pull away, but he wasn't having that. "I'll behave, I promise."

ANOTHER KNOCK INTERRUPTED THEM. JACK dropped a kiss on her head and scooted off the bed to answer the door.

Emily stood and paced the room. This was ridiculous. She looked out the window. Procrastination only made things worse, and as her dad used to say, "suck it up." Heaving a sigh, she sat on the bed.

"Breakfast is served." Jack crawled across the bed and resumed his seat behind her, resting his chin on her shoulder and wrapping both arms around her. "Did I miss it?"

"You will if you don't cut it out, mister. I'm serious, no talking and no touching. Meg will know." Emily tried to scoot forward to put some distance between them.

Jack didn't loosen his hold. "How could she know?"

"I can't explain it, but maybe after all these years as an editor for romance novels, she's developed a sex sense." She allowed herself to relax into Jack's body, no point in wasting it.

Emily tapped Meg's number. Teanna, Meg's assistant, answered. "Hey, Tea. It's Emily Prescott. How are you?"

"Meg's on a rampage," Teanna said, chuckling.

"Sorry." Her conversation with Meg wouldn't improve things.

"Why are you sorry?"

She took a deep breath and exhaled on a sigh. "I'm not coming."

"That is so not funny. Oh crap. Are you running late?"

"No, I told you, I'm not coming."

Emily winced at Tea's uttered expletive. "Meg is going—"

"I'll deal with her. Just tell Meg I'm on the phone," Emily said, not wanting Meg's wrath taken out on Teanna.

"Emily, about your wedding... I'm so sorry," Teanna said before putting Emily on hold.

Barely two seconds passed before Meg's voice bellowed through the phone. "Emily, don't tell me you'll be late. I expect you to walk through my office door in fifteen minutes. Hold on."

Emily had already moved the phone away from her ear, so her eardrums were safe. Jack tensed, so she turned to look at him. "I told you she's a hard-ass, and she likes me." She squelched the urge to kiss his stunned lips. She couldn't kiss him when she'd forbidden him to kiss her.

They overheard Meg's conversation, not really a conversation, as she unloaded a series of curses that made a rock star blush. Apparently, her dress for an industry dinner wouldn't be ready. Meg didn't even try to cover the phone, so they could hear every fuck Meg uttered, which was in the double digits in less than two minutes.

"Can you believe that shit?" Meg announced she was back on the phone with Emily.

"You just can't find reliable help these days," Emily said.

That had Jack pulling back from her and turning her face so he could see her. She gave him a reassuring wink. "Imagine the gall of Al's sister-in-law breaking her leg when you have a dress that needs altering. It's not like you have twenty other dresses in your closet that would be perfect. To leave you in the lurch like this is"—Emily paused for dramatic effect—"unacceptable."

"Where are you?"

"I'm not coming."

"I expect you here in"—Meg paused—"twelve minutes."

Emily let the silence draw out. She'd already said she wasn't coming. Seconds ticked by.

Meg blinked first. "Listen, Emily, you missed a deadline. Your book is overdue, and we need to talk."

"There is no book, Meg. I trashed the whole thing. I have to start over, and it'll be a while before I have anything for you."

"You what?" She huffed out a breath. "I never expected

this kind of behavior from you, Emily." Meg launched into a second profanity-laden attack, this time aimed at her.

And Emily had enough. "Meg!" she shouted into the phone. When Meg stopped talking, she lowered her voice and continued. "Look outside your window."

Stunned into silence, Meg recovered quickly. "What? Why?" The squeak of Meg's chair and the clicking of her heels assured her that Meg was going to the window.

"Because I want to confirm that where you are the world is not only still turning but that the sun is up and people are going about their day. My missing a deadline hasn't changed that. I understand the severity of the situation, but you calling me into your office to yell and curse at me won't change the fact that I have to start over. I know I don't have to remind you what happened."

"Well, it's about fucking time." Meg's voice was filled with relief.

Surprised, Emily mumbled, "About time for what?"

"You can ask Tea. I was taking you to the Hamptons today if you didn't snap out of it." The sound of Meg plopping into her chair had an image popping into Emily's head. Meg with her feet up on the desk, smoking a cigar. Which was crazy, because Meg would never risk her Manolo's like that. "You really had me scared, kiddo."

"What do you mean?"

"Kidnapping, of course," Meg said, in such a way that implied Emily had gone dense. "As soon as you got here, I was sending Tea out to your place to pack a bag." She took a sip of something, and knowing Meg, it could be whiskey. "Emily, in the four plus years you've been writing for us, I've never needed to get on your case about deadlines. You understand, it's my job. But when you said you'd be here today, and you didn't even argue with me, that scared me. I expected you to tell me to go to hell, that after what that bastard did you needed time. You had me scared shitless." Meg sighed. "You didn't even sound like yourself on the phone."

"You wanted me to tell you to go to hell?"

"Emily, you're one of my best authors, not just because you write some of the best books I've had the privilege of editing, but the readers love you. They would love to see more books from you. We get emails all the time asking when your next book is coming. Not to mention the nominations—"

"I'll get to work on a new outline soon. I know I put you in a bad spot, and I appreciate your concern. But, I'll be okay, eventually." She'd said it so many times in the last three weeks, but for the first time, Emily believed it.

Jack hugged her to his chest. She turned to tell him to stop, but before she could speak, he kissed her.

Meg was talking again, so Emily tore her lips away from Jack's.

"Emily, where are you?"

Shit, shit, shit, shit. "Out."

"Out where?"

Emily elbowed Jack in the side and mouthed, "This is your fault." Bastard just smiled. Needing to change the subject, Emily returned her attention to her phone. "Why were you going to kidnap me to the Hamptons?"

"To screw hot guys, you know, have tons of revenge sex."

And there it was. "Meg, how's having sex with random guys getting revenge on my ex, who, for all intents and purposes, dumped me? I know he doesn't care who I sleep with." Emily sniffled.

"Emily, I'm sorry. Look, whatever you're doing, keep doing it. You sound more like your old self."

Jack leaned in and whispered, "I think that's excellent advice. Get off the phone so we can get back to doing what we're doing that makes you more like your old self."

"Who was that?" Meg asked, her tone smug.

Emily elbowed him again, but not too hard as she didn't want to damage the goods. She wasn't done with him. "Bye, Meg." Emily disconnected the call and stood.

"Let's eat," Jack said as he hopped up.

Before dropping her phone on the bed, Emily checked her texts. Still nothing from Nicki. Maybe she should call her. No. If Emily could just get through the day...

As they walked into the living room, Emily stopped short and Jack plowed into her. She turned, hugged him, and rested her head on his chest.

"Hey, what's wrong?" he asked.

"Nothing." Emily lifted her head so she could look him in the eyes. "I need you to know that spending the night with you had nothing to do with revenge."

"No? Why then?"

"I wanted you." Emily turned but looked back over her shoulder. "Still do."

Jack groaned and tried to grab her, but Emily anticipated his reaction and darted away.

His stomach growled. "Okay, this is just a small reprieve, eat first then we reconvene here, where I will undoubtedly catch you, and then I'll have my way with you."

"Okeydokey," Emily said as she sashayed to the table, wearing only Jack's T-shirt and a sexy attitude.

"That's not going to work."

Without turning around, Emily grinned to herself. "Of course, it's working." She shook her ass at him for effect.

"That's just mean. You're a cock tease." He pulled out a chair for her.

"I'm only a cock tease if I don't plan on fucking you again. Which I do." Tucking his shirt beneath her butt, Emily sat. "Jeez, how many people are joining us for breakfast?" There were five trays of food, coffee, orange juice, fresh fruit, and croissants.

"Just us. I didn't know what you'd like, so I ordered a bunch of stuff."

Jack sat across from her. Damn, he looked good. If she weren't so hungry, she'd skip breakfast and go right to dessert. Her stomach growled.

They spent the next few minutes uncovering the trays and filling their plates. Spying the coffee pot, Emily poured herself a cup, added cream, and sipped. "Mmm, delicious. Coffee?"

"Please."

She poured and handed him the cup. He added two teaspoons of sugar and cream.

She sipped her coffee and then dug into her food. They ate in a companionable silence. Emily poured herself orange juice and offered some to Jack.

Jack helped himself to a second plate of food. Emily sat back and sipped her second cup of coffee.

"You're not done?" Jack asked. "You had one pancake, one piece of French toast, eggs, and two strips of bacon. You'll need to keep your energy up, so eat." He took a bite of croissant as he waggled his brows.

"That's what the coffee's for." She helped herself to two sausages along with another piece of French toast and syrup.

She took a bite of the French toast. It melted in her mouth. "Mmm." Jack watched her every time she lifted the fork to her mouth. "Do I have something on my face?" Emily asked, trying not to smirk.

"No. Why?"

"You're staring. I thought maybe I had a glob of butter on my chin or something."

Jack looked down at his plate and resumed eating. "Your face is perfect."

Chapter Eighteen

J ack stifled a groan. *Shit, caught staring.* She was so damn beautiful. Every time she brought the fork to her mouth, her pink tongue peeked out from behind naturally rosy lips. He wanted to feel her lips and tongue on him. He broke out in a sweat. *Abort this line of thinking.* Jack tried to adjust himself without calling attention to it.

"Everything okay over there?" Emily asked, smirking.

"Fine." *Stop looking at her, she's just eating breakfast.*

Emily picked up a sausage and brought it to her lips. Her mouth opened, but she didn't take a bite. Instead, her tongue darted out and licked the tip. Her eyes met his. "There was a tiny bead of syrup on the end." She smirked as she bit off a piece of sausage and smiled as she chewed. "Delicious."

He was sure she was trying to elicit a reaction, so he obliged. Pushing back from the table, his fingers went to his zipper and lowered it.

She stood, grabbed a pillow off the couch, and knelt in front of him.

He needed to get these jeans off before they'd have to be cut off. Lifting his butt, he slid them over his hips. Emily grabbed them and pulled them off. Better. His cock was at full attention. Spreading his knees, Emily moved in closer.

She was about to take him in her mouth when she paused and looked up. "Wouldn't you be more comfortable on the bed?"

"I'll be more comfortable when I'm in your mouth." He lifted his hips. *So close.*

She took his cock in her mouth all the way to the base, and it felt fucking incredible. She placed one hand on his thigh as the other cupped his nuts. She withdrew and blew on him, immediately taking him back into her warm, moist mouth. A jolt of electricity shot throughout his body. "So good, baby." She hummed. If she kept doing that...

Suddenly, she sat back. She looked to be admiring his erect cock that glistened with her saliva. He was. Her smile was both wicked and innocent. Needing to touch her, he stroked the back of her head. Jack shifted, trying to get more comfortable. They should've gone into the bedroom.

Emily stood, extended her hand, and smiled. "The floor is hard even with the pillow. Why don't we go to the bed?"

Taking her soft hand in his, he stood. "Excellent idea."

"I heard a song at Nicki's once, thought it'd be great to fuck to." Emily tapped her pointer finger on her chin. "I think it was called 'Tempers Flare.' Do you know it?"

Jack's brain wasn't fully functioning since most of the blood in his body resided in his dick. He heard "song," "fuck to," and "Tempers Flare." Of course, he knew it; he'd written it. She wanted to fuck him to it—quite possibly the hottest thing ever. He grunted and pointed to the nightstand. Emily picked up his cell and handed it to him. Jack queued up the song.

She walked to the foot of the bed. He was naked and spread-eagled. If she didn't finish what she started soon, he might fucking die.

She crawled up the bed and settled between his thighs. "One more thing, shirt on or off?"

Jack nodded.

"Is that a yes to shirt on or off? Hmm, well, if I take the shirt off, you have a nice view of my tits as I suck you off, but if I leave it on, then you can remember this the next time you wear this shirt."

Grabbing his cock, he shook it.

"Okay, okay, I'll decide. Shirt on." Then her mouth was on him.

Holy fuck. Emily swirled her tongue around the head before slowly taking his full length into her mouth. One hand grasped the base of his cock while the other cupped his balls. He tangled his hands in her hair. "Em..."

She eased up, releasing him, and then licked upward like an ice cream cone. She took his left nut in her mouth and massaged it with her tongue, all the while stroking his cock. As his balls tightened, he fisted her hair, but he was careful not to direct her movements. She didn't need help. She took him into her mouth and hummed.

The vibrations were his undoing, and he managed to groan, "Gonna come."

She didn't let up, and he exploded in her mouth as his hips bucked wildly. As the last shudders of his orgasm racked through him, his head dropped back on the pillow.

His eyes shot open. He was pretty sure he'd passed out when he'd come.

She sat up and moved to get off the bed, but he needed her warm body next to his. He reached in the air for her, and she lay next to him, snuggling into his side. Still unable to speak, he kissed the top of her head but managed, "Mmm." When he finally had command of his body again, he pulled her closer. Holy. Fucking. Shit. Best blowjob ever.

His eyes drifted closed. Emily was amazing, and he had a

hard time believing any guy could be so stupid as to cheat on her. She was the type of girl you grabbed on to and never let go. *Whoa.* Jack was getting ahead of himself here. *So what?* He was crazy about her. So she wasn't ready to be all in in this relationship, but that wouldn't stop him from trying to stay connected to her until she was.

The blowjob coma slowly faded.

Emily lifted her head and smiled, and his heart thudded in his chest. He lifted his arm to touch the top of his head.

"Something wrong?" Her smile grew.

"Just making sure."

"Of what?"

"I was concerned that when I came I blew the top of my head off and my brains splattered everywhere." Jack rested his arm over his still intact head.

She reached up to the top of his head. "No, you're good. No brains."

"Funny." He kissed her, tasting himself.

She rubbed her hand up his chest, and he covered it with his other hand.

"You okay?" Emily asked.

"Mmm."

"Verbal skills still impaired. My work here is done."

She tried to sit up, but he didn't let go. "Don't leave."

"Relax, I just need a shower."

"Give me ten minutes, and we can shower together."

"If we shower together, we'll never get out of here. You still want to show me something, don't you?"

Jack scowled but released her. She dropped a quick kiss on his lips and was gone. *Temptress.* They'd have an amazing day together. He drifted to sleep, just a catnap.

EMILY SMILED AT HER REFLECTION IN THE MIRROR. She looked thoroughly fucked: hair messed up, no makeup, and wearing Jack's T-shirt. She brushed her teeth and stripped out of his shirt, folding it and placing it on the vanity.

After she stepped into the shower, the warm water surged down on her. Her leg ached; she hadn't done yoga in over three weeks, and now she was paying for it, but no sense in looking backward.

Emily grabbed Jack's shampoo and lathered her hair. Damn, she forgot the unscented body wash. Emily's heart flipped. Was this guy for real? Who did that? A genuinely nice guy. He was normal, not very rock star at all. He cringed whenever she called him that. Better she kept some distance between them for his sake. He looked out for everyone else, but he needed someone to look out for him.

Emily needed to focus on moving forward, starting with today. She fell back on one of her mantras as she rinsed her hair. Focus. *Mmm, Jack.* Damn. What the hell, a little rewind was okay.

When Jack opened the door to the shower, she jumped. Emily had been so lost in her thoughts she hadn't heard him enter the bathroom.

"Didn't mean to startle you." He held the bottle of unscented body wash. He soaked a washcloth and squirted it with body wash. Moving her hair over one shoulder, he washed her back.

Emily braced her hands on the wall in front of her as Jack washed her arms and legs. He paused on her right leg, adjusting the cloth and using less pressure.

When he turned her, she was treated to the sight of semi-hard, naked Jack. He dropped a quick kiss on her lips but didn't linger.

When he'd finished, she took the washcloth from him. Adding more body wash, she took her time washing him. He was fit, his muscles sculpted, and she loved the contrast of the firm muscles under his soft skin. Jack washed his hair while she washed him. She suspected it was so he wouldn't touch her.

He caught her smile and shook his head. "You're not helping." He tried for a stern tone but failed.

She rinsed and stepped out of the shower while Jack finished. Toweling off, she used the lotion and slipped into the luxury robe The Yorkshire provided. Jack must've hung it back up. Emily hoped he wasn't a neat freak, but it didn't matter, because after today, she'd never see him again.

Inside the vanity, she found the complimentary hair dryer. She finger-combed her hair and used the dryer. Better to get out of the bathroom before Jack finished his shower. She didn't trust herself or him, and it wouldn't take much to spend the rest of the day in bed together. Why were they going out, anyway? Right, Jack wanted to show her something.

The shower shut off, and Jack stepped out, grabbing a towel. He rubbed his hair and then worked down his body. His eyes were closed, so she indulged in the show. Her head spun with the possibilities. When Jack cleared his throat, her head snapped up. She'd been staring at his groin. She shrugged and returned to drying her hair.

Emily went into the bedroom, but her clothes were gone. She was sure she'd retrieved them from where they'd discarded them last night. She turned to see Jack pulling on black boxer briefs. She cocked her head.

"I sent your clothes to the laundry. I didn't want you walking around in rumpled clothing." His lopsided smile was adorable.

"That was very thoughtful of you. When will they be ready?"

"Anthony was going to try to work his magic and get them back in two hours." Jack glanced at his watch. "Best-case scenario in about thirty minutes."

A knock on the door had her head turning. "Wow, even faster than magically possible." Good timing. She could read Jack's lewd thoughts on how to pass the time. Maybe it was bad timing.

"Probably not, four hours is the usual turnaround time. More likely, Plan B." He pulled on black jeans and a gray T-shirt.

"What's Plan B?" She followed Jack into the living room.

Jack paused before opening the door. "Don't be mad."

An older gentleman greeted Jack warmly. He carried two bags from The Yorkshire's Amused Boutique, and stopping in front of Emily, he handed her the bags. "Miss." She looked at the bags and then at Jack.

"Sorry, Jack. Laundry's backed up, so I followed your instructions." He smiled and left without further explanation.

Jack did that aw-shucks thing again, this time with his hands in his pockets. "Plan B. If the laundry couldn't do two hours, I asked Anthony to pick up clothes from the hotel's boutique."

Emily took two boxes out of the first bag. The first box held a beautiful burgundy V-neck sweater, and the second box contained a pair of jeans. Nice.

The second bag held a smaller gold box wrapped with burgundy ribbon and a much larger red box. She opened the gold box. A note was on top of the folded tissue paper with the boutique's name emblazoned across it.

Miss,

The gentleman requested "Nothing too sexy, or we'll never get out of the room." We do not carry anything less than "too sexy." May I suggest this be your secret?
Belinda

Emily smiled and quickly replaced the lid.

"What did the note say?"

"None of your business, Mr. Nosy." Emily picked up the bag and carried the boxes into the bathroom to dress. When she turned to shut the door, Jack had followed her, his eyes glittering.

"Come on, let me see."

She stuck out her tongue, closed the door, and locked it for effect.

Jack's laugh cut through the door. "Don't stick out that lovely tongue of yours unless you plan on using it."

Emily opened the gold box, and her breath caught at the matching bra and panties. The bra was burgundy lace and a fine mesh with a bit of extra push-up. The panties were satin and mesh in the front with lace in the back. She dropped the robe and slipped them on.

Emily studied her reflection. Her butt looked amazing. These must have cost a small fortune. She pulled on the jeans, another perfect fit. The sweater was so soft. She looked at the label, cashmere. Jack had officially lost his damn mind. She carefully pulled the sweater on. Stalking to the door, she flung it open.

Jack sat on the bed tying his boot laces. When he looked at her, his mouth dropped open, and he blinked a few times. "Wow, you look"—Jack swallowed hard—"amazing."

Emily blushed. *Okay, mouth shut.* It was his money. The raw heat in his eyes warmed her, and she felt the flush as it crept up her neck. If he didn't stop soon, she might spontaneously combust. She smiled to herself. Good thing she didn't flash him her underwear, or they'd both go up in flames. He stood, pulled her into his arms, and kissed her.

When the room phone rang, Jack cursed and stalked over to the offending phone and snatched it up. "What?" he barked into the phone. "Sorry. Thanks for letting me know."

"Everything okay?" Emily asked, knowing full well he was

pissed for being interrupted. She tried to hide her smile but failed.

"Go on, smile now, young lady, but when we get back after our outing, a ringing phone will not save you." Jack's wicked intent was clear.

Emily smiled wider. "Can't wait."

"It's chilly today. You'll need a jacket." Jack slipped on a cream crew neck sweater. A black leather jacket lay on the bed.

Emily remembered the other box and retrieved it from the bathroom. She pulled out a soft brown distressed leather motorcycle jacket. Slipping her ballet flats on, she picked up the jacket.

"Not ready to leave yet. Give me a couple of minutes," Jack said.

Emily grabbed her purse and followed him into the living room. He opened the door, looked out, and then stepped back, leaving the door half open.

DREAMING OF JACK MAKES ME HORNY AND WET. MY body still hums with desire; a desire only Jack can quench. I slip my hand between my thighs. I picture his blue eyes as I stroke my clit. I can't wait to feel him inside me.

I grab the photo I'd taken of him swimming in the backyard pool last June. The day had been oddly hot for L.A. The temperature hovered near ninety. Water sluiced down his naked body as he'd just hoisted himself out of the water.

I could spend an entire week on my knees sucking his cock. The image of his face locked in ecstasy as he comes in my mouth sends me over the edge. "Yes!"

Today will be our day.

Chapter Nineteen

Todd pushed the button for the elevator. The doors opened within seconds, and two women stepped out. He walked in, smiling. This was the first thing to go right all morning. His meeting didn't go as well as he'd expected. He didn't get much sleep last night because of those two assholes in the next room fucking their brains out all night. He'd expected a better clientele at a hotel of this caliber, and he toyed with the idea of complaining.

The elevator doors opened on the thirty-seventh floor, and Todd walked out and down the hallway. As soon as he got to his room, he'd call Cassie. God, he missed her and Evan. This was his first business trip away since the birth, and it sucked. He'd never regretted starting his own software development company, but now that he had a baby at home, leaving had been ridiculously hard. Then, hopefully, he'd get some sleep before his dinner meeting.

As he approached his room, he could see the door was open to the room next to his. Great, he hoped housekeeping was cleaning up because they'd checked out. As he rifled through his jacket for the key card, he dropped his briefcase. *Shit.*

He bent to pick it up, but it was already off the floor. Someone in this Godforsaken city was doing something nice. As he looked up, he nearly choked. *Holy shit, Jack McBride.* Cassie would never believe this.

"Hey, I'm sorry about last night, man. My girl and I didn't realize we were so loud," Jack said. "We've only been together a short while, and you know how it is."

Todd had no idea what Jack McBride was going to say to him, but he didn't expect an apology. Maybe tell him what a dick he'd been for yelling at them. Jack Fucking McBride. As far as knowing how it was, he could barely remember.

He realized his mouth was hanging open, so he snapped it shut. "Don't worry about it." *Totally lame.* Stone Highway was one of their favorite bands. He planned to surprise Cassie with tickets when the band hit Chicago in few months. Tickets had sold out in a matter of minutes, but he had a connection.

"Listen," Jack said. "We want to make it up to you, so I'm paying for your room."

Todd nearly choked but managed to say, "That's not necessary."

"Sure it is. You're in town on business, and we were rude. These rooms aren't cheap." Before Todd could assure him it wasn't necessary, Jack raised his hand. "It's already done."

Wow. What a nice guy. "Well, thank you. Sorry for interrupting you this morning." Todd laughed. "I'm just jealous." At Jack's raised eyebrows, he lowered his voice. "Since my wife had our son four months ago, our sex life has been...sparse." He wouldn't tell Jack McBride he wasn't getting any. He wasn't sure why he said anything, must be his exhausted brain.

EMILY HEARD VOICES IN THE HALLWAY, SO SHE
poked her head out the door. Jack was talking to the guy in the
room next to them. She'd forgotten all about that. Poor guy
looked exhausted.

Jack told the guy he'd already paid for his room. That was
nice of him. She'd be pissed if she spent her hard-earned
money on a hotel and was up all night because her neighbors
couldn't keep it down. Even though she was alone in the
room, her cheeks flushed. The guy said something like he
wasn't getting any because his wife had a baby. Without even
thinking, Emily walked out the door and stood next to Jack.

"Maybe she feels fat and ugly?" Emily said.

"Who?" Todd asked.

"Your wife." Emily's chin dipped as she looked down. "I
overheard your conversation. Sorry."

"My wife is not fat or ugly." He reached into his suit
jacket, pulled out his phone, and held it out for them to see.

"Your boy is beautiful. What's his name?" Emily asked.

Todd smiled, his eyes softened, and his voice cracked when
he spoke. "Evan."

"I'm Emily. Your wife and Evan are both beautiful."

"Emily, this is Todd. I'm Jack."

"I know," Todd said, with a guilty smile. "Cassie and I love
your band. We've got tickets when you guys finally come back
to Chicago."

Emily's brows pinched. "I'm sorry. I didn't mean to imply
your wife was fat and ugly, only that may be how she feels."

"I'm the one who's sorry. I've been short with everyone
today."

Emily's cheeks warmed. "That's our fault."

"Hey, don't sweat it." He gave her a brilliant smile. "Wait,
why do you think she feels fat and ugly? Because she had a

baby? She was so beautiful her entire pregnancy. She looks amazing."

Emily shook her head. "On a bad day, I feel fat and ugly, doesn't mean I am, but that's how I'm feeling. I imagine after having a baby, if her body isn't back to pre-baby weight or shape, with all those extra hormones swimming around inside her knocking down her self-esteem, she doesn't always feel beautiful. Or thin."

Jack and Todd stared at her. Perhaps she'd grown a second evil head? Emily glanced at both shoulders. Nope, no second evil head. Just her big mouth. *Damn.*

Jack shuffled his feet. "How do you know how a woman feels after giving birth?"

"I don't, but I do listen when people talk. I was at a conference, and a few attendees were first-time moms. They were all insecure. The pressure to be perfect at something you have no idea how to do is overwhelming. And I know how I feel. Hormones fluctuate during the month, and when that coincides with a bad hair day, or a pimple, or a bad day at work, women experience self-inflicted emotional shaming."

"Huh?" Jack and Todd said in unison.

"Internal dialogue sounds something like this. I feel fat, so I must look fat. Pants are snug, and not in a good way. Great, blouse gap. They don't make a tape strong enough to combat that. What's up with my hair? It looks like I stuck my finger in a socket."

"Babe, what are your talking about, you're beautiful. Your hair isn't frizzy, your skin is clear, and very soft, I might add. You don't need makeup."

Emily smiled at Jack. "Thanks." He was good for her ego. "I was telling you how I feel some days. Doesn't mean it's true, but it feels that way sometimes."

"So, you're saying that even though I tell my wife every day how beautiful she is, she has this voice in her head that says stuff like that?"

"She's a woman, so probably."

Todd brows dipped. "She thinks I'm lying?"

"No, not lying, trying to make her feel better—exaggerating the truth."

"What can I do to make it better?" Todd asked, his expression desperate.

Foot meet mouth. Too late to keep it shut now. "Well, she's probably at the bottom of her list if she's on it at all. Have you guys had any dates since Evan was born?"

"No. She's not comfortable leaving him alone with anyone, including me. She says I've no idea what it's like being alone with him." Todd rubbed the back of his neck. "How am I supposed to know? It's like she doesn't trust me."

"That's an excellent point. Have you told her how you feel?"

"No. She has so much on her plate she doesn't need grief from me."

"It's not grief. You need to tell her how you're feeling." Emily touched Todd's arm. "You need to talk to your wife."

"It's not just that. I mean, we haven't been intimate since Evan. She said she's not ready, that she wants to be perfect for me. I told her she's already perfect. I feel like a pig for even thinking of sex. It's not just me either, my buddies who have kids are in the same boat. Their wives put all their energy into the kids and they get left holding—" He closed his eyes. "I'm sorry."

Emily grit her teeth. "I can probably help with the sex part."

Todd's head snapped up, and Jack's mouth dropped open.

Pigs. "Not like that." Emily rolled her eyes at them.

Jack and Todd both looked down.

Yeah, pigs. "Convince your wife she needs a spa day. Better yet, book one for her. Tell her you're concerned about her, and you need time to bond with your son. Get a car service to drive her, that way she can relax, have a glass of wine, and enjoy being pampered. No worries." At Todd's look of terror, Emily stopped. "You haven't spent time alone with your son?"

"Sure, nights and weekends, the three of us are together, and Cassie will nap, but a whole day?"

"Then ask your mom to help."

Todd relaxed.

"She'll have this great relaxing day. Send her pictures of Evan while she's out to keep her mind at ease. Let her know you think she's doing an amazing job."

"I tell her that every day. Just like I tell her she's beautiful and the sexiest woman on the planet. She laughs at me and says 'yeah right.' I never seem to say the right thing."

Jack chuckled but said nothing. *Wise man.* "Maybe she needs a little reminder." Emily thought for a few seconds. "I understand the boutique downstairs has very alluring lingerie. What's her favorite color?"

Todd grinned. "Blue. She has the most beautiful aquamarine eyes."

"Great, buy her something elegant in blue, with a cover up or robe, something that will make her feel beautiful wearing it. Have the shop gift wrap it for you. The wrapping is the first thing she'll see, so it'll make her curious as to what's inside. Ask the shop for an extra set of wrapping."

"Go on," Todd said.

"Then go shopping for you. Get something that turns you on." Emily smiled as Todd looked away. "Have them wrap it up in the extra wrapping."

Todd gave her an encouraging nod.

"Get some nice card stock. Print 'Nice' on the first sheet and 'Naughty' on the other. On the back of both, write 'When you're ready, sweetheart.' If you use the computer, pick an elaborate font. Put them on the appropriate boxes and leave them on your bed. Get dinner from your favorite restaurant, set out the good china and the nice crystal, light a couple candles, and get flowers."

Emily paused, hoping Todd would get the idea. Both men waited, brows raised. She sighed. "When she comes home from her spa day, all smooth and pampered, she has this lovely dinner already prepared. Afterward, leave the dishes and snuggle on the couch. When you sense she's tired, tell her to go up, you'll put Evan to bed and take care of the dishes." Emily stopped and wagged her finger at Todd. "Make sure you take care of the dishes before you go upstairs, you don't want to forget or fall asleep."

Jack and Todd laughed. Emily playfully elbowed Jack in the ribs. He playfully pretended that she'd hurt him.

"Meanwhile, she's feeling all warm and fuzzy, thinking what a wonderful husband she has for taking care of everything, so she can just go upstairs and go to sleep. But wait, what's this? Two lovely packages. She picks up the first box with 'Nice' and wonders what's inside, then picks up the other box with 'Naughty,' and perhaps she can guess what's inside. She turns both cards over and sees 'When you're ready, sweetheart' and knows you want her but it doesn't have to be tonight." Emily exhaled, pleased with herself.

Both men stared. *Jeez, do I have to spell it out?*

Jack looked at Todd then back at her. "How does it end?"

"Yeah, how does it end?" Todd repeated.

"Seriously?" Emily heaved an exaggerated sigh. "Your wife decides that."

"That's it?" asked Todd.

"You've done everything you can to let her know you appreciate all her hard work, that you love her, and that you're attracted to her. Maybe you get lucky, maybe you don't. But now, she realizes that she doesn't have to do it all on her own, and that you want and need to be involved. Maybe she's not ready, but knowing you're interested goes a long way to getting her ready."

"Wow." Todd's eyes misted. "Are you a therapist?"

"No."

"You could be, you'd make a mint. What do you do?" Todd asked.

"I'm a copywriter."

"She's a writer," Jack answered at the same time she did. He turned to her puzzled. "Copywriter?"

Emily scrunched her nose. "Day job."

"You should do your own podcast," Todd said. "My friends and I would definitely listen. I learned more about women in the last ten minutes than the six years I've been married. Don't get me wrong, Cassie and I have a great marriage, it's just sometimes I feel like I'm supposed to be a mind reader."

"Now I feel like I need to add a disclaimer. I'm not a doctor, a wife, or a mother, I listen when people talk and make up stories."

"Thank you so much, Emily. You've really helped me. Would you mind if I pass that lingerie idea on to my buddies?"

"No. You know, none of what I said might be the problem, but I hope it helps," Emily said, shaking his hand.

Jack shook Todd's hand. "How about a picture?" Jack asked.

"I don't want to be a bother, you've already been so cool." Todd hesitated but pulled out his phone.

"He's happy to do it." Emily took Todd's phone and snapped a few pics.

Jack coughed. "Leave out the part about..."

"Oh, absolutely," Todd said.

Jack and Emily turned to go.

"Hey, you guys make a great team. Thanks again for

everything," Todd said, using the key card. He disappeared into his room with a wave.

Jack's smile said it all. Emily just made things worse for him. Would she ever learn to keep her big mouth shut? He wasn't gonna let that team comment go, but she had to set him straight. She should leave now but didn't want to. Just a few more hours of peace before—*Fuck.*

Chapter Twenty

J ack felt like his whole body smiled. Knowing her made his life better. He had to convince her they belonged together. His life depended on it, at least, the life he wanted. A life with her.

Emily wanted to talk, but his head was full of ideas he needed to get down. He felt more connected writing with pen and paper. Before she said anything, Jack gestured to the couch. "I need a few minutes." Grabbing his notebook and pen, he sat next to her. Opening to a clean page, he let the words flow. He'd look at it later. Right now, he needed to get the ideas on the page.

When he closed the notebook, he looked up, and Emily stared at him, her expression a mix of curiosity and awe. Jack angled his body toward her, and she smiled. He'd be a lucky man to see that smile every day of his life. Even luckier if he put it there. When her smile faded, Jack settled back. *Here it comes.*

"Your girl, Jack?"

"Would you have preferred I told him we met last night at the gig? That you came backstage, and despite your protestations to the opposite, you came back to my room and fucked my brains out?"

Emily winced but only for a second. "Good point. Thank you, that was very considerate of you."

Jack moved closer. She lifted her chin. He loved that about her. She wouldn't make this easy. He cupped her face in his hand, caressing her chin with his thumb. "See, we make a great team." He kissed her slightly parted lips. Within seconds, she was on his lap, their lips and hands working each other into a frenzy. She tasted like mint and spice. Emily pulled back and climbed off.

As she paced in front of the couch, he settled back onto the cushions and laced his fingers behind his head.

"Jack, how do you see things going between us?" Her brows pinched together, and her voice was filled with concern.

She was sweet. "We fall madly in love, get married, make lots of babies, raise 'em, and grow old together. We have dozens of grandchildren, great-grandchildren, and great-great-grandchildren."

She threw her hands up in the air, giving physical release to her pent-up exasperation with him.

Jack smiled.

"Ahh," Emily growled in frustration. She gaped at him for a few seconds and then sat next to him on the couch. "Jack, listen, you're a nice guy, we've had tons of fun. But—"

He took her hand. "Em, we make a great team. Everyone thinks so. We deserve a chance. You see that, don't you?"

"Everyone?"

Jack ticked off on his fingers. "Buzz, Elliot, Todd."

"That's three people, hardly everyone."

Jack moved closer. "Does my opinion count?"

He knew she wanted to say no. He saw her struggle and then she said, "Yes."

"We make a great team, and what's more, I think you

know it. You aren't ready for this, but the opportunity is here now, and we have to grab it." He locked his jaw. *Patience.*

"This makes for a great story, Jack, but that's all it is, a story, all it can ever be."

His pulse hammered through his veins. "Why are you being so stubborn?"

"Why are you?" Her face flushed, and she stood and moved away. "We had a deal. A nice guy lives up to his promises." Emily plodded into the bedroom.

Jack followed her, not about to let her go. But if he didn't want to blow this, he needed to ease up.

Emily stood looking out the window. He stepped up behind her and loosely put his arms around her. She didn't move.

"I don't want to hurt you," Emily said on a sigh.

He rested his chin on her head. She fit him perfectly.

Emily leaned back against him. She'd been through so much, and he never meant to add to her pain. He'd back off, but he couldn't let her go. Jack needed a plan. This full-frontal assault was too much.

She was no closer to accepting that they were meant to be together. He considered making a joke about this being their first fight, with makeup sex as the punch line, but that wasn't what she needed. Em needed time and understanding. Now, more than ever, he needed to show her where the band started. She'd see that he was a normal guy, even if his life wasn't. Turning her to face him, he smiled. "Let's go see my friend Sid."

"Okay."

He dropped a quick kiss on her lips and grabbed his jacket. They walked into the living room, and he helped Emily into her jacket.

She turned to him, her face shining with sincerity. "Thank you, for...everything."

He took her hand as they walked to the elevator.

The elevator dinged. When the doors opened, Buzz walked out wearing his gym clothes.

"Oh shit, Buzz, I'm sorry. I totally forgot."

"Don't sweat it. I needed a day off from getting my ass kicked." Buzz smiled at Emily. "So nice to see you again."

"Nice to see you, too. How are you doing today?"

"I'm okay, much better than last night."

Jack breathed a sigh of relief. "Hey, we were just on our way to see Sid. Wanna come?"

"Nah, three's a crowd. Say 'hi' for me."

They stepped onto the elevator, and Buzz hit the button for his floor. "Garage?"

"Lobby." Jack said, hoping Buzz wouldn't say anything.

Buzz shrugged and hit the button.

"Did you get off on the wrong floor?" Emily asked.

"No, just checking up on our boy here. He hasn't missed a workout since the tour started. Wanted to make sure he was okay." Buzz looked at Jack. "Relaxed posture, goofy-ass grin. Yeah, looks okay."

"Way better than okay." He took Emily's hand.

Emily shook her head. "Would you girls like to be alone to gossip?"

"Can't, got a haircut and color at noon." Buzz made a kissy face at Jack. "We'll catch up later."

The doors opened on the thirty-fifth floor, and Buzz stepped out. "See you two later," Buzz said with a wave.

As soon as the doors to the elevator closed, Jack pulled Emily to him and kissed her. By the time they reached the lobby, they were both out of breath and flushed. They pulled apart just before the doors opened. Luckily no one was there. He moved a stray strand of hair from her face before taking her hand and exiting.

Once outside, he hailed a cab. As it pulled up to the curb,

a flock of paparazzi across the street caught his eye. He quickly opened the door, and they got in. "Sixty Lincoln Center Plaza, please."

As the cab pulled away from the curb, Jack resisted the urge to look out the window. Hopefully she hadn't noticed them. Emily leaned into him as the cab swerved to miss a stray pedestrian. Once they were underway for a few minutes, and thoroughly ensconced in a sea of yellow, Jack gave the cabbie a new address.

Emily looked at him with wide eyes. "You gave the driver the wrong address on purpose."

"Yup."

"Clever. Mind if I use that in a book someday?"

"Sure. Just so long as it has a happy ending."

"All my books have a happily ever after."

"Is that why you became a writer? So you could control the endings?"

Emily didn't answer right away. "I never really thought about it like that. Life has enough tragedy. I don't need to add to it in the fictional realm." She rested her head on Jack's shoulder but, almost at once, withdrew.

He let that go. "Did you always want to be a writer?"

Emily shrugged. "I always enjoyed writing assignments in school, but I never wrote for fun, only what was necessary. The first story I ever wrote wasn't fun, but it had a happy ending."

"Why would you write a story if it wasn't fun?"

"Therapist in the hospital insisted. Only did it to shut her up."

Jack didn't know what to say to that. He hadn't meant to remind her of her family. "Sorry."

"They're never far from my thoughts," Emily whispered.

"If you don't mind my asking, why did your therapist want you to write a story about..."

Emily looked out the window. "Because I wouldn't talk to her about my feelings. I just wanted to be left alone. Since I was trapped in bed and couldn't walk away, I had to listen to her psychobabble for forty-five minutes every session."

Jack rested his hand on his thigh, face up, hoping she'd take it. "Didn't you like the therapist?"

"She seemed okay at first. Loads of empathy. Loads of empathy. Her brother had died of leukemia when he was ten, so she said she could understand what I was going through. I didn't like being forced to talk, and I told her that. She explained she was only there to help me deal with my loss."

Emily laughed bitterly. "Truth was, I didn't know how I felt. In the blink of an eye, my family was dead, my leg looked like it had gone through a meat grinder, and I was stuck in a hospital bed instead of starting my senior year. I'd already had two surgeries and there'd be more."

Jack winced. Her scars were ten years old but still very visible. The thick raised skin must be sensitive because she'd tensed every time he touched her leg.

"Anyway, during the third session, I told her that my life ended the day my family died, that my body just hadn't caught up yet."

Jack gasped. That didn't sound like Emily, at least not the Emily he knew.

She rested her hand in his. "Meadow wanted to know how I felt, and that was how I felt."

"Holy shit, Em."

"No, holy shit is still coming. Meadow was a new age hippie hybrid. When I said this, she jumped up, grabbed my hand, and congratulated me on my new life." Emily shuddered. "My mouth dropped open, but no words came out. Finally, when I could speak, I asked her what she meant. She said 'Now you can reinvent yourself, be anyone you want to be.'"

She gripped his hand tighter. "I lost it. I screamed that I didn't want to reinvent myself, I wanted my life and my family back. I wasn't some drugged-up kid who'd OD'd and got a second chance. I was still on my first chance. I lost everything that mattered because someone else fucked up, not me." She relaxed her hold on his hand but didn't move away.

Jack's mind reeled. Didn't she have anyone to deal with this stuff? She hadn't mentioned any other family. Was she alone in the world? Jack couldn't even imagine. He was so close to his family. Both his parents came from large families, so he had aunts, uncles, and cousins galore. "I'm so sorry, baby."

"I didn't mean to unload my baggage on you. Guess I have a raging case of Nickiitis. I'm not sure if it's contagious, so you may want to get a penicillin shot just to be safe."

Jack laughed. She had a great sense of humor, another thing he loved about her.

Queen's "Another One Bites the Dust" blared out of Jack's cell interrupting his laughter. Crap. It was their manager. Begrudgingly, he answered. "Hey, Dex."

"Jack, listen, I've rescheduled the interview with Jeremy Rennert from *The Beat Goes On* for this afternoon at three. I've arranged to use the hotel's ballroom for the photos and interview." Dex finally took a breath. "I've already talked to Brian, and he'll make sure everything is ready on their end. If the interview goes over, the techs will do soundcheck."

"Three o'clock today?" Jack repeated. He'd planned to spend the rest of the afternoon in bed with Emily. Shit. "We're here for five more days, can't we make it another time?"

"Sorry, they want to get the interview in the next issue, and the deadline is today. He wants to interview the band, so make sure Buzz is there, please."

"We'll *all* be there, Dexter," Jack said, as he disconnected.

Dex was a good guy, but he could be a dick sometimes. "Fuck."

"Me?" Emily asked, with a naughty smile.

"Temptress." Jack kissed her hard on the lips. "We have an interview at three, and soundcheck is at five. I had other more pleasurable plans for this afternoon." Shit, she hadn't agreed to stay yet, and now he had to leave earlier than planned.

"It's okay, Jack, I have to leave anyway."

She looked away when she spoke. A burning sensation settled in the pit of his stomach. Something had changed. She was still determined, but she barely whispered the words.

THEY'D BEEN IN THE CAB FOR FIFTEEN MINUTES. Emily fidgeted with her purse strap. "Where are we going?"

"It's a secret."

"Okay. Will we be arriving at this secret destination soon?"

Jack looked out the cab window. "In this traffic, probably another ten minutes. You okay?"

"Yeah." Normally she didn't run on, but something about Jack had her feeling very comfortable confiding in him. This was a one-time thing, so no use pretending that there could be more. Of course, that didn't explain her extended conversation with Todd. What had gotten into her, butting in like that? So not like her, at least not since the accident. Not wanting to remember the life she lost, she pulled out her phone.

Nicki still hadn't responded. As much as she didn't want to talk to her, she needed to be sure she was okay, so Emily sent her another quick text: *Hope you are okay.*

She retyped it twice since her fingers didn't seem to want to work properly today.

"You know, most people just type letter 'u' and letter 'r'

for you are. I've never seen anyone correct a typo in a text message."

Emily chuckled. "Can't help it, a text is no excuse for poor grammar or typos. It makes me nuts." She needed to direct the conversation away from her.

"You've written eight novels, that's impressive."

Crap. "Not really, that's only two a year. Nicki writes four to five a year. Of course, she writes full-time."

"It's still impressive. Do you have a favorite?"

"My first story will always be my favorite, but I'll never publish it."

Her phone dinged, and she yanked it out. Shit, Eddie, not Nicki. He was sweet to check up on her, but she didn't want to talk. She'd be lucky if she made it through the weekend without him and Vince ganging up on her. Her lips curled into a warm smile. She would never have survived without them. She sent a quick reply and put the phone away.

"The one you wrote while recovering in the hospital?"

"Yes."

"What's it about?" When she tensed, he added, "I'm sorry. I don't mean to pry."

She'd only shared that story with Vince and Eddie. Her leg ached, and her body heated. Emily wanted to tell him but didn't want to examine why.

"I'm sorry, Em, I didn't mean to make you uncomfortable. Forget I asked."

Emily rubbed her thigh. "In an alternate reality, I was the one who died. One day a man visits me, he seems familiar, but I don't recognize him. He says my family is alive in a parallel universe and that they're trying to find me." Emily lurched forward as the cab braked hard.

"Sorry," the cab driver said. "Damn jaywalkers."

Emily's heart pounded. An unpleasant memory tried to push its way to the surface. She took a few deep breaths.

"Hey, you okay?"

Emily nodded. Then she realized that her entire body was so tense that it hurt. Jack touched her cheek, wiping away a tear she hadn't realized she shed. She forced herself to relax back into the seat. "Sorry." Emily took a few deep breaths. "He could bring them to me, but it was up to me to decide. Finding me would alter things in both universes with unintended consequences. My initial reaction was to be selfish and have my family back. He said that's how people usually react but suggested I take a few days to think about it. Once it's done, it can't be undone and the collateral damage wouldn't be fixable in either reality."

Jack watched her intently. "Wow."

"It's not as easy as it sounds. I started thinking of all the possibilities. On the one hand, I'd have my mom, dad, and brother back. It's what I prayed for every day laying in my hospital bed. It was better than torturing myself with the what-if game."

"The what-if game?"

"Yeah, you know, what if we hadn't left late because I was on the phone with this boy I liked, saying our thousandth goodbye. What if I hadn't been such a brat? What if..."

"Hey, no way the accident was your fault." Jack squeezed her hand. "You were just a kid."

"I know that now. But then, I wanted an explanation. My brother was going into his senior year at UCONN. I was going to be a senior in high school. In a heartbeat it was gone. I couldn't accept it. I guess that's why I wrote the story, it was my way of pretending I could somehow affect the outcome." In his eyes, she saw compassion and empathy but no pity. She hated pity.

"So, what did you decide?"

"I realized that it wasn't a decision I wanted to make. How do you choose happiness for yourself at the cost of pain for others? I wouldn't wish what happened to me on anyone, so when the man came back, I told him things had to be left as they were."

Jack's genuine smile warmed her. "I love that story. Did you ever figure out who the man was?"

"It was my grandfather. He died when my dad was seventeen. My dad kept his parents' wedding picture on the desk in his office. That part came to me in a dream."

The cab slowed to a stop. "We're here." Jack paid the driver and helped her out. Across the street was a red brick building with a huge sign. The Rock House.

Wind blew her hair, and Emily shivered, zipping up her jacket. She'd been hot when they left the hotel. Jack had ushered her into the cab so quickly that she hadn't noticed the wind or that the sun was shining. Just the photographers. Their movement caught her eye as soon as they'd stepped out of the hotel.

God, how did he live like that, with every movement recorded? Luckily, the photographers had been across the street, so they'd escaped before they'd been mobbed. Why hadn't Jeff driven them? They could've gotten in the limo in the garage and avoided that. But Jack had been prepared, and he'd protected her. He'd pulled her close, and she'd tucked her head into his shoulder.

The light changed, and they crossed the street. The large sign in block letters, when lit at night, would be impossible to miss. The red brick façade was cracking, and a few bricks were missing.

Jack stopped at the ornate wooden door. "Sid owns this place. He gave us our first break." Jack's eyes shone as he talked. "He's discovered a ton of talented musicians. We've toured with a few bands that got the break they needed because of Sid. He never wanted anything in return, which is

rare in an industry where everyone wants a piece of you."
There was no bitterness in his voice, only truth.

The sudden realization of what Jack was showing her hit.
Not just the band's history but someone he respected and
loved. Emily reached out and touched Jack's cheek. He closed
his eyes at her gentle touch and pulled her into his arms.

"I haven't seen Sid in over a year, so this is long overdue."
Jack dropped his arms to his side and opened the door for her.
"It doesn't look like much now, but at night, fans line up
down the block."

Emily walked through the door into a dark vestibule.
Another larger door leading into the club was propped open.
Even in the dim light, she could make out the flyers of bands
that had played here, protected behind large sheets of
Plexiglass. Several of the flyers were thirty years old. She
recognized a few of the bands, Alchemy Riot for one. Then
she saw it.

A yellow flyer, featuring a picture of the band. *Stone
Highway, November twenty-first, 2007, Debut Appearance at
The Rock House. Doors open at nine.* All the other flyers were
stapled haphazardly to the wall, but this one was set straight at
eye level.

Emily snapped a few pictures with her phone. She'd text
Vince the picture of his flyer later. She looked up at Jack, who
watched her intently. "Wow, that's amazing, Jack. Thank you
for bringing me here." She was honored. This place obviously
meant a lot to him, and he wanted her to see it. Instead of
analyzing why, she enjoyed the moment. "That's so cool." She
touched the glass in front of the flyer. "It's great that this is
still here."

"Sid's great." Jack smiled back at her. "He told us if we
didn't give up, we'd make it. No one had ever said that to us
before." Jack swallowed hard and broke eye contact. "Let's go
in," he said, taking her hand.

The stage lights lit up a good portion of the room. The inside was bigger than she'd expected. Two long bars, one on each side of the room, were fully stocked. Jack stopped in the middle of the room and pulled her into his arms. He danced them around in a circle, never missing a step. She stepped on his foot twice. Before the accident, she'd loved to dance, but now it was more of a requirement at a gathering than something she enjoyed. Sully loved to dance, so she always obliged. "You should've asked Jack. I would've told you I'm a terrible dancer," Emily said, stepping on his foot a third time.

"Stick with me, baby, I'll give you lessons." Jack dipped her, kissing her in the process.

"Jack McBride," someone said from across the room.

With a quick kiss, he righted them, keeping her tucked into his side as he extended his hand. "Hey, Eric, right?"

"Yeah," Eric said, taking Jack's hand. "I figured you'd be stopping by."

"Is your dad here?"

Eric's hand fell away. "Dad passed away two months ago."

Jack's arm tightened around her and his face grew pale. "I'm so sorry, I hadn't heard. He was a great man." Jack's body tensed. "Was he sick?"

"No, not that we knew. Locked up for the night and had a heart attack in the parking lot. When he didn't come home, Mom called the police, and they found him in his car," Eric said, his voice cracking.

"How awful, I'm so sorry. He always seemed invincible."

Emily put her arm around Jack.

Eric swallowed hard. "I have something for you. Be right back."

As soon as Eric was out of earshot, Emily turned to him. "I'm so sorry." He opened his arms, and she stepped into them, resting her cheek on his chest and wrapping her arms around him. "Poor man, dying alone in his car like that."

"At least he didn't suffer."

Eric returned, so Emily moved to Jack's side. Eric handed Jack a framed original of the same flyer hanging in the vestibule. "Dad was going through some old papers and came across that. He thought you'd like to have it."

"Thank you. Wow, that's great." He cleared his throat. "What's going to happen to this place?"

"Dad was this place. He loved it. I thought about trying to keep it open, but, as you can see, it needs work," Eric said, waving his hand around. "The bathrooms need to be redone, the stage needs reinforcing, and the electrical is outdated. Dad was going to get a loan, but with him gone, I don't know if I could secure one. Not even sure I want to."

"This place is a landmark. I'd be sad to see it close." Jack shook his head, then a slight smile crossed his lips. "Listen, man, if you're serious about trying to make a go of this place, I'd be interested in investing. Do you have a proposal?"

Eric's eyes lit up. "Are you serious?"

"Why not? I'd like to give something back. Places like this are essential in helping musicians launch careers. Hell, who knows where we'd be if your dad hadn't helped us." He reached into his wallet and pulled out a card. "Fax your proposal to Kevin. He handles my investments. Let's see what he thinks."

"I don't know what to say," Eric said, taking the card from Jack. "This is unbelievable."

"It's not a done deal, but this is the first step." Jack shook Eric's hand.

"Thanks, man."

Jack turned and led Emily to the vestibule. He stopped and looked at the flyers on the wall.

"You okay?" she asked.

Jack released a heavy sigh. "It's a shock."

Emily pushed open the outside door and stepped into the

sunlight. Even though she squinted at the brightness, when she looked across the street, she swore she saw Jeff. But when she blinked to get a better look, whoever it was disappeared. At least there were no photographers; Jack needed a minute.

She led him down the street to the corner and turned. As soon as they were out of view of the main street, she stopped, turned to Jack, and put her arms around him.

"We'd been in the city for over a year before we met Sid. We were playing at this crappy bar, to maybe fifteen people. Not our best gig. After our set, Sid came up to us as we're packing up. He said he owned The Rock House, and he wanted us to play there." A melancholy expression shrouded his handsome face. "That changed everything for us."

Emily stood on tiptoes and kissed him.

Jack looked at her questioningly. "What?"

"About that rock star thing?"

"Yeah?"

"Well, I've been thinking about it, and the thing is, as far as I can tell"—Emily met his intent gaze—"the rock star can't hold a candle to the man." Emily urged his head down as she turned her lips to him. Suddenly, the world fell away.

When they finally broke apart, panting for air, Jack smiled at her. "That's the nicest thing anyone has ever said to me."

I ALMOST MISSED JACK LEAVING THE HOTEL THIS morning, since I'd expected that muscled idiot to be driving him, but as soon as I saw those damn paparazzi moving, I ran to the front of the hotel. Jack was still with that groupie whore. He ushered that little bitch into the cab so fast they were gone before I could regroup.

Anger still coils throughout my body. I'd planned on bumping into him today. I'd taken extra care dressing this morning: tight low-cut black sweater, pink miniskirt, thigh-high boots. I lined my gorgeous blue eyes in thick black liner, added three coats of mascara, and painted my full lips red. I'd even taken the time to straighten my hair, since Jack prefers it that way.

All for nothing. Fuck.

It shouldn't be too hard to find him since he is the biggest rock star on the planet.

Chapter Twenty-One

How did he get so damn lucky? Em blew him away at every turn, and he'd known her less than a day. Jack smiled. He was glad she'd been with him when he'd found out about Sid. He'd gotten more comfort from her touch than any words could've provided. She'd understood what this place meant to him, without him having to explain. When he'd last seen Sid, Christie had been with him. They'd been together for over two years, but she hadn't understood. She'd been bored and wanted to go shopping. New York wasn't L.A., she'd said, but it'd do.

For the first time, Jack acknowledged in his head what his heart had hoped when the tour started, that they'd get back together. It had been foolish because he'd known it wasn't possible, not after all the things she'd said in a rage when he told her she had to leave. He'd known he couldn't fix this for her, but he'd wanted to help her fix it. She blamed him for everything. But still, he'd loved her. Jack hoped Christie would clean up, but he no longer wanted to spend his life with her. That realization hit hard. He still had the three-carat Harry Winston engagement ring locked up in the safe at home.

As the wind whipped past, Emily shivered, but her hazel eyes sparkled. He looked around and blinked slowly. Until that gust of wind, he forgot they were standing on a street in New York City, outside The Rock House. He thought it was paradise.

"Why don't we walk for a while?" Emily asked, as another shiver tore through her.

He should've gotten her a warmer jacket.

Emily slipped her hands in her jacket pockets as she shivered again. "It's a beautiful day, and we'll warm up as we walk."

"Are you sure?" Jack asked, looking around as they walked toward the front of the club. "We might be better off in a cab." Between the wind and the paparazzi, a cab sounded better.

"They're hard to miss. If we see a gaggle of people with cameras, we'll make a break for it."

He scanned up and down the street. No paparazzi. "Walking sounds great." They walked arm in arm for several blocks. This felt so right, so normal. She had to be feeling it, too. He'd have five days to convince her they had something worth pursuing. She was having a good time with him, and not just in bed. Their chemistry went beyond sexual. Never before had he experienced such intensity. The sex was unbelievable, but being around her made him feel so alive. Maybe because she'd been through so much and it hadn't broken her. Em looked distracted. "Looking for something?" he asked.

"What? No. Nothing." She smiled and resumed looking at nothing. Jack didn't buy that. He knew Jeff was following them, but Jack hadn't seen him. They'd argued over his going out alone with Emily today, but since he hadn't gotten a letter since the tour started, Jack was confident this ridiculous business was over. Since Emily was a writer, she was probably soaking up the neighborhood.

He had to tell the guys about Sid. They'd dedicate a song to him at their gig tonight. Jack remembered the song he'd written last night and couldn't wait to play it for them. It was a rare bit of inspiration that came together so easily. The lyrics flowed, and the music followed; he'd hardly made a change. When he read it over this morning, he was amazed at how good it was.

Elliot would bust his balls over this, but he didn't care. He and Emily fit together so well, in so many ways. Jack was happy.

Emily looked over her shoulder again. Shit, she knew something. He didn't want to alarm her, so he kept quiet, but he had to distract her. "Wow."

"What?" she asked, her attention snapping back to him. "What?"

"You said 'wow.' Sounded like a revelation."

Jack smiled. "It was. It's about us. Wanna hear it?"

Emily stiffened "No."

"Not at all curious?"

Emily stopped walking and turned to face him. "Jack, there is no us. There's you, Jack Rock Star McBride, and me, Emily Grace Prescott, not interested."

"Grace is a beautiful name." Jack hugged her close. "It suits you." He chuckled. "My middle name is William, not Rock Star. But you already knew that."

"Jack…" Emily's voice was laced with frustration.

He tried to usher her forward, but she didn't move, so he turned and walked backward.

Scrunching her eyes closed she let out a low growl. "I can't believe I didn't see it earlier. You're insane. Certifiable."

She didn't catch up, so Jack slowed down.

They crossed the street and Emily stopped in front of a jewelry store window. Shaking her head, she leaned her forehead against the glass.

"You okay?" Jack asked. Maybe her leg ached.

She turned and looked at him. "Yeah, I just remembered something."

"What?"

She pointed to a purple pendant. "See that?"

Jack nodded.

"I've always wanted a piece of Tanzanite jewelry, a pendant or earrings. I promised myself after my first novel got published that I'd buy a piece. I looked around but didn't find exactly what I wanted. Then I met Sully, and I wanted to write more, so I cut my hours back at work. Once we got engaged, I had a wedding to pay for."

"Why not tell the fucker you wanted it for your birthday or Christmas? Or was he cheap?" Jack couldn't help the smirk from curling his lips.

"Sorry to disappoint you, but Sully wasn't cheap. He makes good money. He would've gotten it if I'd asked him to. I never told him because I wanted to buy it."

"Really? What does golden fucker boy do for a living?"

"Investments. He's brilliant at it, makes tons of money for the firm and his clients."

"If the fucker is so well off, why wasn't he paying for the wedding?" It wasn't any of his business, but he was pissed on her behalf.

Emily shot him a back off look. "I don't expect you to understand. None of my friends did."

"I'm sorry, I didn't mean to upset you, but I don't like the fucker."

"I don't like him right now either." Emily wrapped her arms around her waist.

"What do you mean right now? Are you thinking of getting back with him?" He hadn't meant to blurt that out, but he needed to know.

"No, of course not, but I have to forgive him, someday.

What's done cannot be undone. I don't want him back," she said in a flat tone.

Jack's audible sigh of relief had Emily looking up to meet his eyes. "Leaving, Jack."

His cell rang. He pulled it out of his pocket. Shit. Eric hadn't wasted any time. "It's my financial guy. I should take this."

"Of course." She pointed to a street vendor. "I'm going to get water. You?"

Jack nodded as he connected the call with one hand and took his wallet out with the other. Her indignant expression had him putting the wallet away and smiling. "Hey, Eric." He watched as she sauntered away.

"Jack, I received a proposal from Eric Levinson, about a night club."

"Yeah, I told him to fax it to you." A car horn honked incessantly, making it impossible to hear. "Hold on." Jack turned and went into the jewelry store. "Sorry about that, I had to get inside."

"Jack, you know night clubs, bars, and restaurants are all risky."

"Yes, but this place is special, we got our first big break there, the place is a landmark."

Kevin sighed. "Okay, I'll take a look." He paused for a second. "I have to recommend what's best for you, not taking nostalgia into consideration."

"Got it. Thanks, man, appreciate it. How's the family?"

"Linda and the kids are great. They miss Uncle Jack though." Kevin chuckled. "My sister-in-law's single again—"

"Gotta go." Jack ended the call. He didn't need a fix up. He'd already met the girl for him. Jack looked around, and his eyes landed on an older gentleman standing in front of the engagement rings showcase.

"Can I help you?"

Jack walked over to the man. "Mind if I just look?"

"Surely. Let me know if you'd like to see anything. I'm Albert." He smiled and resumed wiping the clean glass on the case.

Without meaning to, Jack glanced at the rings. *Holy crap. It's perfect.* Em would love it. Jack took a step back. Maybe he should get his head checked. Maybe that shot Buzz gave him when they'd sparred yesterday knocked his brain around. If Emily came in and caught him looking at rings, she'd lose it. He smiled. No way he'd charm his way out of this, so he better not get caught.

He crouched to get a better look. He scanned the case but came back to the same ring. A simple square cut diamond with three smaller round stones on either side. Jack's heart thudded against his rib cage. *Someday.* "Albert, I'd like to see that one." He placed the framed flyer on the counter top.

Albert smiled, took a ring of keys out, selected a key, and opened the case. "Here you go." He handed Jack the ring. "It's a one and three-quarter carat princess cut center stone, VVS2, with three round cut diamonds on each side weighing approximately .20 carat each, set in platinum."

This is it. Jack handed the ring back to Albert, and as he took out his wallet, the door to the store jiggled from a huge gust of wind. Jack jumped and swallowed hard. *Better not get caught.* "I'll take it." He slid his credit card onto the counter. "If a stunningly beautiful brunette walks in, pretend like I didn't buy this."

"No problem. We offer free sizing. What size is she?" Albert asked as he wrote up the sales receipt.

Shit, he should know this. "I don't know."

"No problem, just come back after you pop the question, and we'll get it taken care of." Albert grinned.

Jack grinned back; he was so ready for this adventure with

her. It wouldn't be easy, but he'd be patient, give her time to heal, and then they'd be together.

"You're Jack McBride, aren't you?" Albert asked.

"Yes," Jack said, smiling his friendliest smile. He hadn't expected to get recognized by this guy, but then it still caught him off guard whenever it happened.

"My granddaughter is a huge fan."

"How old is she?"

Albert's face lit up with pride. "Fifteen."

"Would she would like an autograph?"

Albert smiled so wide Jack feared he might tear something. "I hate to bother you."

"It's no bother at all. I'm glad to do it."

"We have tickets for Monday night." Albert beamed as he placed paper and pen on the counter.

Jack picked up the pen. "I bet you're the cool Grandpa. What's her name?"

"Jemma."

Jack wrote a few lines and signed it. Signing autographs was still so weird. He handed the paper to Albert, who shook Jack's hand.

"I can't wait to tell her when she gets home from school. She won't believe it."

"Would she believe a picture?" Jack asked. "I can send you one."

"I have my cell," Albert said as he walked to the back of the store.

Jack looked around. Mother's Day was fast approaching. He walked to the case that held earrings. The shop door opened, and he turned. Emily carried two bottles of water in the crook of her arm and was eating an ice cream cone.

Even from across the store, he saw the flash of anger in her eyes.

EMILY FIGURED JACK WOULD BE ON THE PHONE, NOT shopping. She suppressed the urge to throw the water bottles at him. She'd spent the whole time on line wondering what else she could say to make him understand.

This was her fault. She'd known last night what an epic mistake this was. He was used to getting his way. Emily had shared more with Jack in a few hours than she'd shared with Sully in the first five months. It had been one of the things she liked best about Sully. He never pushed her to share emotional stuff. Jack did nothing but push, even when he was trying not to. He couldn't help himself, but he meant well. But she would give him no purchase here. She had to make a clean break; otherwise, he'd have hope, and he'd never let her go.

Nicki had told her to just move on, but she couldn't. Emily didn't want to make the same mistakes again. She'd almost married Sully. How could she have been so wrong? And why the fuck didn't Sully talk to her if he was unhappy? And why did the asshole have to bring Tiffany back to their place? He could've fucked her in the city, and Emily wouldn't have been the wiser. Okay, better she found out before. Oh God, how many others were there? *Bastard.*

The drip of the cold ice cream on her hand snapped her out of her internal hell.

"Just in time." Jack strode over, giving her a quick kiss on the lips as he took the water bottles. "Is that for me?" He eyed the ice cream cone.

"Nope, I ate yours waiting on line for the water because it was melting. This one's mine." She took an exaggerated lick.

"Why can't this one be mine?" Jack crossed his arms and leaned up against the counter.

"Because, this is vanilla chocolate swirl, my favorite." She licked the cone again. "I got you a chocolate vanilla swirl."

"Did you ask the guy for a vanilla chocolate swirl and a chocolate vanilla swirl, or did you say two vanilla chocolate swirls?" Jack pushed away from the counter and stood before her.

Emily backed up slowly, all the while licking the cone. "I don't remember."

He stalked toward her. "Emily, I want that cone."

"What'll ya give me for it?"

"What do you want for it?"

She bumped up against the counter.

"Ahem."

Emily peered around Jack. An older gentleman stood a few feet away holding his cell phone. Jack had the weirdest effect on her. It felt like they were the only two people in the room. The sooner she left, the better. She handed the cone to Jack. "I reserve the right to ask for a favor."

"Done." He took the cone and licked. "Albert, this is Emily."

"Hello, Albert, nice to meet you," Emily said, shaking his hand.

"What a lovely girl, Jack."

"Em, would you mind taking a picture of Albert and me? It's for his granddaughter."

Emily took the phone. "It's okay, Albert," Emily teased, "you can admit the photo is for you."

Albert laughed.

"Hold on." In five bites, Jack polished off the cone.

Emily dug a napkin from her pocket and handed it to Jack.

"Thanks, baby."

Emily took three pictures and handed the phone to Albert. "How are those?"

He swiped the pictures to view them. "Great. Thank you. My granddaughter will be so excited."

Seeing Jack's credit card on the counter, Emily looked at Albert. "Did he buy anything from you?" Emily's face heated. "A piece of Tanzanite jewelry, perhaps?"

"No, he didn't."

"Okay then." She pointed to the counter. "Jack, you shouldn't leave your credit card lying around." She sighed. "Silly rock star," she said under her breath.

Jack picked up his credit card and walked over to the earring case. "Mother's Day is coming up. I was thinking earrings." He scanned the case. "How about those?"

Albert opened the case and handed the earrings to Jack.

Emily stood behind him, feeling awkward, until she saw his choice. *Holy crap, they're so huge they could be seen from space.* From Jack's grin, she could tell he was proud of his choice. It wasn't her business, anyway.

"What do you think of these, Em?" Jack held the earrings out to her.

Crap. "They're nice."

"You don't like them?"

"No, they're beautiful."

"What, then?"

"They're kind of...big?"

"They'll go nicely with a pendant I got her for her birthday."

"Is the pendant that big?" Emily asked. Still none of her business. Why did he want her opinion, anyway? *Buy the damn earrings and leave me out of it.*

"No, bigger," Jack said with pride.

Emily rolled her eyes.

"What?" Jack held them out to her.

Damn. Why hadn't his ex-girlfriend explained it to him? *Bad girlfriend.* "Is your mom a princess?"

"Huh?" Jack's puzzled expression was so cute.

"Or a game show hostess? Beauty pageant winner?"

"No, she's an English teacher."

"They're beautiful, Jack. But..."

"What?"

"I don't know your mom. Maybe she'll like them."

"Tell me the truth."

The floodgates burst. "They're huge. I can't imagine that the woman who raised you would wear those that much, maybe on holidays and special occasions. I'm sure she loves whatever you get her, but these aren't everyday earrings. I think she'd wear something smaller all the time."

"Oh. Christie used to help me. She said when it comes to jewelry, especially diamonds, bigger was better."

Emily kept her face neutral. "They're not practical."

Jack nodded. "Practical is better?"

"Yes, to me." Emily shrugged. *What the hell.* "Sully got me this huge elaborate engagement ring, which was beautiful, but not practical. The marquise cut snagged on everything. I'd take it off as soon as I got home, and sometimes I'd forget to put it on and leave the house without it, which he hated." They'd had more than a few fights over that. Sully had accused her of doing it on purpose.

"What do you suggest?" Jack asked as he turned to the display case.

Emily walked over and scanned the case. She pointed to a more modest pair, also round cut. "Those are a decent size, the kind she'd wear every day."

Albert handed Jack her choice. "These are half carat each, set in fourteen karat yellow gold. I also have them in white gold."

"Yellow or white?" Jack asked.

"Do you know what metal your mom's wedding set is?"

Jack scrunched his face up. "No, why?"

"Well, I think it's nice to match, but you can't see the metal once they are in, so it doesn't matter."

"I'll call my dad." Jack took his phone out and called. "Voicemail."

"How about your sister?"

He leaned in and kissed her lightly on the lips. "Thanks." He dialed and this time the call connected.

"Hey, big brother," came a thrilled voice from Jack's phone.

"Hey, Trish. How are you?"

"I'm doing well." They both chuckled.

So did Emily. Their mom *was* an English teacher.

"You're still coming to dinner on Sunday?" Trish asked.

"Wouldn't miss it," Jack said, smiling. "Hey, is Mom's wedding band yellow or white gold?"

"White gold. Why?"

"I was thinking of getting her earrings for Mother's Day."

"Oh."

Jack frowned at the phone. "Oh, what?"

Emily pointed to her earlobes.

"She has pierced ears, doesn't she?"

"Yes."

"What then?"

"Jack, it's just—never mind. She'll love whatever you get her."

"Does she wear any of the jewelry I buy her when I'm not there?" Jack glanced at Emily; she could tell he hoped she was wrong.

"Sometimes." Trish's voice wavered.

"Trish?" Jack used his older brother voice.

Riley used to do that to her all the time, to remind her he was older. She smiled.

"No. It's not that she doesn't like what you buy her, Jack, it's, just…"

"It's gaudy, isn't it?"

"Not gaudy, too big. You know Mom's not into flash."

"Well, you'll be happy to know the first pair I picked out was vetoed. Another more practical pair is up for consideration."

Emily blushed. Why? Not wanting to consider the possibilities, she looked away.

"Practical is good, Jack," Trish said. "Are you seeing someone?"

"As a matter of fact"—Jack stopped when he looked at her —"Um, Trish, I have to go. I'll see you Sunday. Love you." Jack quickly disconnected the call, cutting his sister off. "Sorry about that. Little sister is a psych major. Very nosy."

"Jack—"

"I know, I know. You don't have to say it." He put his hands up palms facing out. He turned to Albert. "White gold."

Albert pulled another pair of earrings out in white gold and handed them to Jack.

"Perfect, I'll take them."

"Wonderful choice," Albert said. "Would you like them gift wrapped?"

"That'd be great." Jack handed his credit card to Albert.

Albert ran Jack's card and handed it back. "I'll just be a minute."

"Thanks for your help." Jack took her hand.

Emily pulled free and walked over to the other side of the store, feigning interest in the contents of the display case. This was silly. She couldn't even be in a jewelry store without getting teary-eyed. Maybe they made a pill for this. Duh, of course, they did. They made a pill for everything these days. She took a long calming breath.

Jack walked up behind her. "Are you in the market for a man's watch?"

Emily sniffled and wiped under her eyes with a napkin. "No." She turned to face him. For once, he said nothing.

Albert came back and handed a bag to Jack. "It's been a pleasure. You and Emily make a lovely couple. Good luck."

Jack said nothing, but the smile that spread across his face said it all. She was screwed. She was going to hurt him. *Well, fuck.*

After they left the store, they walked for several minutes in silence. Exhaustion overtook her. What'd she been thinking? She never should've gone back to his hotel, not after he said he wanted to date her. He would never settle for less.

"I'm hungry," Jack said. "Do you want to go back to the hotel to eat or stop somewhere along the way?"

"It's so nice out, why don't we keep walking and see what comes along?" She needed time to figure a way out of this mess, hopefully without causing him too much pain.

"Sounds good."

They fell back into silence, which was fine by her. The longer she knew him, the longer the pro side of the list grew. But even if her life wasn't in shambles, the con side remained. Rock star. She wanted no part of that attention.

She'd been shocked that Albert recognized Jack. The man had to be in his sixties. What grandfather took an interest in his granddaughter's music? Not hers. She'd grown up with one set of grandparents, and they'd never recovered from the loss of their only daughter. No! Get off the accident because she couldn't handle those thoughts on top of everything else. Her pulse was already racing. She took a few deep breaths and cleared her mind. She focused on Jack's hand holding hers. Okay. Better.

Across the street, she saw a café. "How about there?" Emily pointed. Bella Luna Café.

"Sure." Jack brought her hand to his lips and kissed it.

They crossed the street, swept along by the sheer volume of people. Jack tightened his grip on her hand.

The door opened just as they were coming to it, and Nicki and Curt walked out.

What the fuck? Shit. Emily was screwed.

Nicki's face broke into a satisfied grin. "Well, well, well, what do we have here?" Curt's arm was around her, and he carried two bags from a boutique they'd passed.

"Nicki," Emily said.

Curt and Jack exchanged a simple "Hey."

"Hello, Jack. So nice to see you again," Nicki purred. "Did you have a pleasant evening?" She cocked her hip out and rested her hand on it.

"How's your hand, Curt? Will you be able to play guitar tonight?" Emily asked.

Curt and Jack both snickered.

Another couple was trying to leave the café, so the four of them moved out of the doorway.

"Curt, don't Jack and Emily make a beautiful couple?"

Curt nodded but wisely said nothing.

"It's nice to see you again, Nicki." Jack grabbed Emily's elbow and maneuvered her closer to the door.

Curt did the same with Nicki, but away from the door. "Emily, a pleasure to see you again." At the curb, he hailed a cab and they were gone.

SNUGGLED NEXT TO CURT IN THE CAB, NICKI would've patted herself on the back if she could've. There'd be hell to pay for helping Jack last night, but it'd be worth it. Emi had needed to cut loose, and she was glowing.

She glanced at Curt. He'd taken the bags when they'd walked out of the café. Tad never would've done that. Curt was tall, handsome, with soulful crystal blue eyes, and had long blond hair. She wasn't usually attracted to guys with ponytails, but Curt pulled it off. At least he didn't do the man-bun. That was one trend that needed to die. Now.

He also had a very innocent way of viewing the world. Things were simple with him. He was a sweetie, not at all her usual type. Emily would say her usual type was the problem. She was right, of course.

Curt asked her to spend the next week with him. He saw past her defenses just like Emi did. She didn't feel the same way about breakups as Emi; if the attraction was there, she was all in. Maybe she got her heart broken more that way, but one of these days, she'd risk it all, and it would be the right guy.

Jack had that same look that all the guys did when they were into Emi. She didn't realize the attention she got. It was like she only noticed when she was interested, and Emi was definitely interested.

Chapter Twenty-Two

L unch passed in near silence. She'd been distant since they'd run into Curt and Nicki, but Jack hadn't a clue why. A melancholy had settled over her, and she avoided looking at him. Em answered all his questions with one-word answers, polite but detached, not like earlier. Her smiles were all forced. Jack knew something bigger was going on, and it was sparked by seeing Nicki. No matter what he said, the playful banter they'd shared was gone. When their server Trent asked for a picture, Emily obliged, snapping a few pictures. It was obvious she didn't want to talk, so he occupied his mind by reciting the lyrics to the song he'd written last night. Maybe she just needed time. Jack hoped that was all it was.

She only ate half her sandwich and offered Jack her pickle.

"You okay?"

When she finally looked at him, he could see the effort she put into collecting herself. She forced a smile. "That was unprecedented."

"What?"

"I cannot believe Nicki's still with Curt. That's a break in her behavior. Maybe it's a rock star thing. That has to mean more than an average"—Emily leaned in closer, lowering her voice—"revenge lay, right?"

"I don't know how to answer that."

Emily tilted her head. "Normally she would've skulked out in the middle of the night, the way she says guys do. She sleeps with a bunch of random guys, and the last one is her next boyfriend. It's foolproof, really."

Okay, she was concerned for her friend. Earlier, she'd checked her phone several times.

But Jack had his own concerns. Curt had been taken advantage of before. They'd been shopping, and Jack recognized the store they'd been to, as it was one of Christie's favorites. He couldn't imagine Emily being friends with a rapacious female, but Nicki had expensive tastes. "I don't know quite how to put this, but Curt's been generous in the past, overly generous…"

Emily's eyes met his. "Nicki doesn't need Curt's money."

She didn't elaborate, but he felt she was being honest, so he dropped it.

Honesty was a rarity in this business. The farther up the ladder the band climbed, the more lies they heard. Jack was honest enough to admit he liked his ego stroked but not with lies. When people began telling them what they thought they wanted to hear, they'd relied on each other to be honest.

Even Dex. When he'd suggested Jack make a solo album, he'd lost it and told Dex to fuck off. He'd no desire to record music without the guys, and Dex wouldn't bring that topic up again.

Someone was always looking for a piece. One of the first things Sid told them was "Give away enough pieces of yourself, and you'll be left with nothing." They'd been young and stupid and had no idea what he was talking about, but his words stuck with Jack. Em would give him her honest opinion, always tell him the truth. She seemed to have shaken off whatever was bothering her.

As soon as they stepped outside the café, Emily shivered and looked around. Thick, gray clouds rolled in. When her eyes locked onto his, their green depths told him all he needed to know. Jack hailed a cab. She'd been so amazing this afternoon. He needed to get her back to the hotel so he could show her again how she made him feel.

EMILY COULDN'T SHAKE THE CREEPY FEELING THAT she was being watched. The hairs on the back of her neck stood up as soon as they'd stepped out of the café. Just like earlier, when Jack had taken that phone call. She'd surreptitiously looked around, catching a quick movement out of the corner of her eye. When she turned, the door to the ice cream shop was closing. She'd followed but only the employees were there. The distinctive bells on the door hadn't rung a second time.

She'd considered asking the girl behind the counter if anyone had come in before her, but she'd felt paranoid, so she'd dropped it. Now she wished she'd asked. Her dad always told her to follow her instincts. God, she missed him.

Once they were safely inside the cab, Emily tried to relax. Her leg ached, and she rubbed her thigh to try and loosen the muscles.

"Your leg hurts?" Jack asked.

"A little."

Jack's face was shadowed with concern. "We shouldn't have walked so far."

"It's my fault. I haven't been doing yoga lately. I didn't

think we did that much walking." She needed to start taking better care of herself. But right now, she was more concerned about Jack. She *had* to leave. Remembering the phone call from his manager earlier, she relaxed. The band had an interview this afternoon. They'd enjoy each other one last time and then leave together and part as friends. She'd told him enough times today she was leaving. He couldn't still think he would change her mind.

When they neared The Yorkshire, Jack told the driver to stop a block before the hotel. He paid and helped her out. Jack pulled her down a side street, and they crossed to the underground parking entrance of the hotel.

They walked hand in hand to the elevators. So normal. *Stop that.* Nothing normal about having to enter through the garage instead of the front of the building. Nothing normal about photographers stalking you or strangers asking to have their picture taken with you. The only thing normal about today was...Jack. But she wasn't doing him any favors with this line of thought. It just couldn't happen.

The elevator arrived and an older couple exited.

Jack hit the button for the thirty-seventh floor, but as he reached for her, the ding alerted them to an impending stop on the main level. Two men dressed in business suits stepped on and smiled at her. Emily shifted closer to Jack. The younger guy kept looking at her over his shoulder. Jack tightened his grip on her hand until he pulled her into his arms and kissed her.

She kissed him back. If she wasn't going to be with Jack, she'd no interest in anyone else. Not now. She needed time.

Message received, the guy stopped looking back at her, but Jack didn't let up until the doors opened on their floor. Jack shouldered between them and pulled her with him. She couldn't help the smile that crossed her face. Being with Jack felt good. And Emily needed to stock up on feeling good, because in a few hours...

Jack fumbled in his pocket for the key card and unlocked the door.

Chapter Twenty-Three

J ack placed the bags on the floor, and the second the door closed, he pounced. Lips and tongues and hands and tugging clothing. Jackets came off and landed in a pile on the floor.

His hands found the hem of Emily's sweater, and he caressed his way up to her breasts. He was already hard, but his dick jerked when his hand cupped her breasts. *Lace*. Emily's lips curled in a wicked smile. *Holy shit*. His heart hammered in his chest, and the blood ran hot in his veins. "What's under this sweater?"

"What does it feel like?"

Lifting the hem up and over her breasts, Jack's breath caught at the sight of burgundy lace and mesh. "You've been walking around in this all day?" A trickle of sweat rolled from his temple.

"Uh huh."

He blinked a few times and stepped back, needing to regroup. "What about the panties?" So much for regrouping. Jack wiped his brow on his sleeve.

"What about them?"

"Do they match?" He choked out the words. It was hard to breathe, or he was breathing too much.

"Why don't you unwrap me and find out."

Jack didn't waste another second. He moved in and grabbed her sweater where it rested and tugged it up and off. *Stunningly beautiful.*

Their tongues met and clashed. Her arms curled around his neck as he hauled her closer. His fingers undid the button of her jeans, but it took a few tries. Lowering the zipper, his hand slipped in until he hit the waistband of her panties. He pulled back from the kiss and gulped for air.

Seeing Em's eyes glittering with lust and her lips swollen caused Jack's heart to skip a beat. He'd been in love many times, but it had never been like this. He was drowning but didn't want to be saved.

The fabric was soft, like satin. He cupped her mound and her breath caught. Their eyes locked, and they were the only two people in the world. His other hand slid around her waist and down the back of her jeans, more lace. He needed to see all of her.

Emily swayed, even though she leaned against the door. "You okay?" he asked.

"I left okay three minutes ago. I'm headlong into sheer ecstasy."

Kneeling, he slid the jeans over her hips, down, and off. He sat back on his heels and looked her up and down. Gorgeous. Jack leaned in and inhaled, and his hands caressed her cheeks under the lace. Emily made a small sound, her lips moved, but no words came out.

Emily cleared her throat. "When you look at me like that, I feel like the sexiest woman on earth."

"You are."

The burgundy against her fair skin was sublime. Her scent beckoned him. His phone vibrated in his pocket. Reluctantly he removed one hand from Emily's fine ass and grabbed the phone but didn't take his eyes off her. Her smile reflected the knowledge of the effect she had on him. When he finally looked at the phone, it was a text from Jeff: *Ballroom 2:45.* Shit, just over an hour. He was about to toss his phone aside but stopped. He looked up at Emily.

"Don't even think about it, McBride."

"Come on, baby, just one. No one else will ever see it. I promise," Jack begged as he crossed his heart. He stood and took in the sight of her in just the bra and panties. He needed to get his pants off before he injured himself.

"Famous last words, until you lose your phone and nearly naked pictures of me end up on the internet." Emily's hip jutted out, and her fist rested on it.

Jack tossed the phone aside.

Slowly, Em turned to face the door. She looked over her shoulder at him, her tongue slipping between her rosy lips to moisten them. He knew what she wanted—a good hard fuck against the wall. Then she'd ride him on the bed, or he'd bend her over the couch. All the possibilities flooded his mind, until he remembered he had to leave in an hour. *Fuck.*

"How long do we have?"

"Hour." Lifting her into his arms, he carried her into the bedroom. "Depending how long the interview takes, we may have to leave right after for soundcheck." Setting her down next to the bed, in a matter of seconds, he undid all of housekeeping's hard work. He reached for his sweater but Emily stopped him.

"Let me."

Within seconds, he was naked. Her palms spread over his chest, and she licked his nipple, gently scraping it with her teeth. The sensations vibrated down his spine and ended in his nuts. "Em…"

Her hands trailed down his abs until she grasped his

engorged cock. She stroked him a few times before dropping to her knees and taking him into her mouth.

Jack moaned as she covered his dick with her beautiful lips. Her tongue swirled around the tip while she cupped his balls. He filled her sweet mouth. She was still in her bra and panties, and the view almost made him come.

Jack leaned back, pulling his dick out of her mouth with a popping sound. Em licked her lips. Helping her to stand, he removed the last of her clothing, and at the sight of her, his hand pumped his wet cock. Her saliva provided just enough lubrication. *Holy shit.*

She gasped and her eyes widened, so he did it again, and this time she bit her lip. He placed a finger under her chin, and as he raised it, her eyes lowered farther. He stroked again, and a bead of fluid emerged from the tip. Em's breath caught. "You like that, baby? You like watching me stroke my cock?" His breath caught at the sight of her.

Emily nodded, meeting his eyes. "Fisting your cock."

"Fisting my cock?" Jack repeated.

"Yeah, that's how I'd write it."

Pulling her in for a kiss, he never wanted it to end. "Em"— Jack drew in a ragged breath—"I have that damned interview, we don't have long. Less than an hour. Please..."

Kissing him hard on the lips, her tongue delved into his mouth, taking what she wanted. He loved it. He held back as long as possible before picking her up and laying her on the bed and stretching out next to her. Their lips never parted. Jack let his hands wander over her luscious curves, breasts to hips, then settling on her ass.

Emily's hands wandered down his torso and up his arms until they cupped his face. The way she touched and explored him drove him wild, but he tamped down on the urge to take her. They caressed each other as if they had all the time in the world. When Jack couldn't stand it any longer, he reached into the nightstand drawer and grabbed a condom, quickly rolling it on.

Emily was sprawled out on his bed, hair in a halo, eyes bright and sparkling, and lips swollen. A warmth spread from his chest throughout his entire body and down to his toes. Love had never felt like this.

Her eyes trailed up and down his body, and when she reached for him, his heart stuttered. Settling between her thighs, he silently vowed to not rush this. He focused on her, showering soft kisses on her breasts and neck. His hand caressed down the hollow of her belly, over her hip, and between her legs.

Her hands brushed up his sides and around to his back, dragging her short nails over his skin. The commingled scent of their arousal was more potent than any perfume, alcohol, or drug.

"Jaaack," Emily whispered, parting her legs wider. Jack used her warm, fragrant juices to coat himself. It drove him wild when she said his name like that, wanton, singular. No one else existed.

Inch by inch, he slid in until he settled himself fully inside her warmth.

She caressed his face, and her eyes drifted closed as she kissed him. For what seemed like an eternity, he just stayed there, buried inside her, as she nibbled along his jaw. When their lips met again, he moved. *So good.* The gentle pace intensified his feelings until he thought his heart would explode.

Emily didn't rush him, and her hands never left his body. She kissed him back with such fervor he knew in his heart she had feelings for him. It was enough, for now. He'd ease up on pushing her to move forward. He'd be happy to stay right where they were. For now.

They were covered in a fine sheen of perspiration. Her

muscles clenched around him, and the tingling sensation of his orgasm exploded. "I love you, Em," he said as the world crashed around them.

Emily's gaze pierced his. "Jack..." Her muscles tightened as she convulsed around him.

He collapsed on her, his heart hammering in his chest. Emily's did too, their heartbeats in sync. That had been the most intense orgasm he'd ever experienced.

Jack mustered the strength to roll them so she lay atop him. Her sigh of contentment told him it had been the same for her.

Bliss.

As Emily's pulse settled, coherent thought returned. *Shit.* That just made things so much worse. They should've just fucked. That had been her plan until Jack got all gooey eyed. He romanticized this whole affair, and he'd blow this out of proportion. He'd ask her to stay. He almost did before she distracted him. Distracted herself too—that was when the whole fuck hard plan vanished. Which was his fault since he was an excellent kisser. But now what?

Jack stroked her hair. Now that the perspiration was drying, she broke out in goose bumps. If he hadn't gone all caveman and thrown the comforter, blankets, and top sheet off the bed, she'd cover them.

Jack lifted his head. "Shit, that's my cell."

"Aren't you going to answer it?"

"It's Elliot."

"So, no?" Emily paused. "That's 'Welcome Home.' It's about him and Siobhan, isn't it?"

Jack nodded, groaned, and threw an arm over his head.

Emily looked at the clock and groaned. "It's two forty-seven."

"I'm never late."

His cell stopped ringing, but the room phone rang.

"Shit," Jack said as he dropped the receiver on the table.

A loud curse came through the phone.

"Sorry," Jack said.

"Jack, stop screwing around and get the fuck down here." Elliot's voice boomed through the earpiece.

"I'll be there in five minutes."

Emily rolled off so Jack could sit up.

"Hurry the fuck up," Elliot said.

"Did he slam the phone down?"

"Yeah."

"Why is he so angry? I thought you didn't have to be there until three."

"He enjoys a good phone slam, can't do that with a cell phone." Jack grinned. "Baby, I'm sorry. I need a quick shower, then I have to leave."

"It's okay." *This might work out yet.*

He went into the living room and returned a moment later with their clothes and his bags. He went to the safe and put the earrings he'd bought for his mom in.

Jack walked over, kissed her, and then walked to the bathroom. Pausing at the bathroom door, he turned to her, smiling. "Stay."

Fuck. Fuck. Fuckity, fuck, fuck, fuck.

"Please." He looked so damned happy. "Come to the gig tonight. We need to talk." A few seconds later, the shower turned on.

Emily could only guess at her expression, deer caught in headlights, because that was how she felt. This was all her fault. She should've left this morning or never come back here at all. A heaviness settled in her stomach. It wasn't like her to play with someone's emotions, but that was what she'd done here.

The shower shut off, and she was out of time. What else could she say? Jack had been so nice, sweet even. She didn't want to hurt him, but she was going to because she was leaving.

He walked out of the bathroom, a towel slung around his hips, another drying his hair.

"How about it, Em?" Jack said with a cocky smile.

Shit. He was convinced she'd stay. She swallowed the lump in her throat and did something she'd hate herself for, for a long time

She nodded.

"Excellent." Jack pumped his fist in the air. He dropped the towel on the bed and kissed her. Another soul-crushing kiss.

"Welcome Home" sounded from the living room again.

"Fuck off, Elliot," Jack muttered, as he grabbed a pair of boxer briefs, socks, jeans, and a T-shirt. He dressed in under a minute.

Emily refused to close her eyes. A tightness had settled in her chest to join the nausea. She deserved to feel like shit.

He combed his fingers through his damp hair and sat on the bed to put on his boots.

She held the sheet around her like armor, but it wouldn't protect her from her awful, lying self.

Jack leaned in for another kiss, so she grabbed the back of his head and kissed him hard. When his cell rang again, Jack pulled away.

"We'll be in the ballroom. Soundcheck is at five thirty, gotta leave by five. Grab a shower and rest, tonight will be great." With a quick kiss, he strode into the living room.

Emily jumped off the bed and grabbed the towel he'd dropped and wrapped it around herself. She shuffled into the living room and leaned against the sofa. When he looked at her, she forced a smile. "Goodbye, Jack."

"See ya later, baby." Jack winked, opened the door, and, with one last look over his shoulder, walked out.

As the door closed, she sank to the floor. The lump in her throat wouldn't be swallowed. As much as she'd like to give in to the tears, she forced herself to stand. Emily went into the bedroom and looked around. Where were her clothes? Oh, right, Jack sent them to the laundry. The tears spilled over. She looked around for the outrageously expensive underwear. Through the blur of her tears, she spotted them at the foot of the bed. Grabbing them, she yanked them on and then dressed in the rest of the clothes Jack had purchased.

In the bathroom, she splashed her face with cold water. She ran a washcloth under the tap and held the cold cloth over her swollen eyelids. Jack's beautiful face filled her mind, and she thought she'd throw up. She cupped her hands under the faucet and drank. Emily had to calm down because she couldn't walk out of the hotel like this. Damn, walk out of the hotel and then what? If Nicki was still with Curt...scratch that. Emily had been lucky this afternoon. Nicki hadn't remembered. And Emily needed to be alone tonight.

She'd have to call a cab. Just as she picked up the hotel phone, there was a knock at the door. Replacing the receiver, she walked over and peered out the peephole and saw Anthony. She rested her head against the door for a second before opening it.

"Hello, Miss, I have your clothes from the laundry."

Emily smiled and took the package from him. "Thank you. Anthony, I need a cab, one that will take me to New Jersey."

"Miss, are you all right?" Anthony asked with genuine concern.

"Nothing fatal." *For me.*

"I can arrange a cab for you."

"Thank you, Anthony."

"When would you like to leave?"

When? Now. She should never have come here. "As soon as possible." She needed to be long gone before Jack returned.

"Very good." Anthony smiled cheerily again. "I'll call when the cab is here." He turned and walked with purpose down the hallway.

Shutting the door, Emily leaned against it. She was being a coward and hated it. Pushing off the door, she walked to the desk and found the complimentary hotel stationery and a pen.

What the hell was she going to say? Jack had gone out of his way to be—no, not out of his way. That was his way. He was genuinely nice, caring, and an all-around great guy. But she wasn't in any shape to start a relationship, not after everything that happened with Sully. *Fucking bastard.*

Maybe if they met in six months—No. Vacation was over. It was more than great while it lasted, but Emily needed to return to reality. Her shitty, miserable, gut-wrenchingly awful reality.

She picked up the pen.

Dear Jack,

I'm sorry, I have no excuse for lying. I needed to leave, and you wouldn't take no for an answer. I never wanted or meant to hurt you. But I know that I have. The road to hell and all...

I know you have feelings for me, feelings I'm unable to return. You deserve the best, Jack. I know you'll find what you're looking for. Someday, probably sooner than later, I'll regret that it wasn't me.

I won't lead you on. I can't make promises now, even though it would be easy enough to do so. You've been honest and forthright with me, and being so to you in return is the least I can do.

I had a wonderful time last night, as well as today. You helped me reestablish my self-esteem and confidence, and for that I will always be grateful.

Please let this be the end. For both our sakes.

Best wishes,

Emily

That didn't seem like enough, or was it too much? She couldn't just leave without a note, but was it for his sake or hers?

She stood and looked around the room. Folding the note, she placed it in an envelope and wrote his name in block letters. She laid the envelope on the table next to the six-foot-tall phallus. *Elliot.* She liked him, too. When the room phone rang, she jumped. She hoped it wasn't Jack. "Hello?"

"Miss, your cab is here."

"Thank you. I'll be right down." The sick feeling in the pit of her stomach intensified.

She considered changing and leaving the clothes Jack bought, but that would piss him off. He'd meant it as a gift. Emily put on the jacket and grabbed her purse and the package with her laundered clothes.

She plodded to the door but hesitated before her hand reached the doorknob. No, this was the right thing to do. The only thing to do. She turned the knob, opened the door, and left.

I BLEND INTO THE BACKGROUND OF THE LOBBY AS *I'm waiting for Jack to be done in the ballroom. I'd only caught a glimpse of him before the doors closed. It's been months, and waiting for this moment has frayed my nerves, but Jack is finally going to see what he's been missing out on. I take a few deep breaths to calm myself. Jackie needs a strong woman in his life. Calm, cool, and collected.*

I can't contain my smile when I see that little groupie whore rush out of the hotel. Good, one less thing to worry about. As soon as I find out what Jack's plans are for tomorrow, I'll plan our meeting.

It's a cheap trick, but Jackie can't resist a damsel in distress.

Chapter Twenty-Four

J eremy was cool because he'd kept the interview professional, about the band. His only personal question was to Buzz, about his sobriety, which he was okay with talking about it. The fans worried.

None of them liked talking about their private lives, although since Christie was an actress, Jack didn't get as much privacy as he would've liked. He tried to keep it business, limiting his answers to her professional career, but sometimes these guys asked far more personal questions. First and last interview.

"Thanks a lot, guys," Jeremy said, as he shook Jack's hand. "Sorry for the short notice, but we wanted to get this in the next issue."

"Not a problem." Jack checked his phone again, but Em couldn't text him because they hadn't exchanged numbers. He'd rectify that when he got back to the room.

"Sebastian, you ready?" Jeremy asked.

"Yeppers."

Jeremy and his photographer, Sebastian, were setting up by the time he'd arrived. Curt was even later. Elliot wouldn't let that go. He was still in a pissy mood because he hadn't talked to Siobhan yet.

Yesterday, they'd all been pissed. The flight delay and the bumpy ride had only worsened their mood. He'd been miserable, lonely, and hurting. Since meeting Emily, his world changed. Today he felt like a new man. Jack wasn't a fool, so he knew she wouldn't make this easy. He didn't blame her, not after what she'd been through. That fucker. Every time Jack thought of what he'd done, he wanted to break something, preferably him.

If he'd met her six months ago, after his final breakup with Christie, he wouldn't have been in any shape to start a new relationship either. They couldn't un-ring any bells here, but they'd slow things down. Now that he'd convinced her to stay, they could get to know each other better. If they also happened to have sex, then so be it. Shit, just thinking about her made him hard. He couldn't imagine being around her for a week without being able to touch her, but if that was what she needed, he'd damn well do it.

As Sebastian adjusted the lighting, Elliot nudged Curt in the ribs.

"Hey, why the fuck did you do that?"

"You were late."

"What are you, the time police?" Curt said, giving Elliot the finger. Sebastian's camera flashed.

Buzz smacked Curt upside the head. "Knock it off. What are you guys, ten?" Curt was the youngest, and they never let him forget it.

Curt pulled his hair back and fastened it with an elastic into a ponytail.

"Hey, dickhead, you call your wife yet?" Jack asked. Nothing made Elliot pissier than the situation with Siobhan.

"None of your fucking business, Jack-off," Elliot sneered through his smile.

Another set of camera flashes.

Jack, Curt, and Buzz shared a look. "That's a no."

"I called you like six times, Curt. Even Jack picked up his phone and pried himself away from his new piece—" Elliot winced. "Sorry, man. Emily isn't any man's piece, she's a lady." Elliot lowered his voice. "From your shit-eating grin, I can tell you had a nice day together."

"How'd you know we spent the day together?"

"I have my ways."

"Would that be the same way you got a six-foot-tall, acrylic cock filled with rubbers into my room?"

Curt spit out the water he'd been drinking. They all broke out into juvenile laughter, and Buzz high-fived Elliot.

Elliot gasped for air. "I would've loved to have seen your face when you saw it." He coughed and laughed some more. "Oh, shit," he said stifling his laughter. "How did Emily take it?"

"We were kinda busy, so we didn't notice it at first. She pointed it out to me, and lucky for you buddy, she has a sense of humor."

"What did she say?" Elliot asked.

"She laughed so hard she couldn't breathe and said you're an evil genius. I told her you're just evil." Jack took a swig of his water.

Elliot's laugher filled the ballroom. "I knew I liked her."

"Then why haven't you called your wife. Change your mind about Emily's idea?"

Elliot stopped laughing. "No." He ran his hand through his hair. He glanced over at Sebastian, who was making more adjustments. "I'm...scared. What if it's too late? Or if she met someone else?"

"Dude," Curt said. "It's better to know where you stand than not. Besides, say she is seeing someone"—Curt stopped at Elliot's growl—"hear me out. Maybe it's because she thinks you don't care, since you haven't been speaking. Maybe she needs to hear you still love her."

Curt wasn't known for his sage advice, so Jack was impressed.

"What idea?" Curt asked. Sebastian moved into position. "Never mind. Nicki said Emily gives great advice, so I'm sure it's good."

"Where's Nicki?" Jack asked.

Buzz and Elliot groaned and said, "Why?"

"For shits and giggles," Jack said.

"She's tied to my bed. Wanna see?" Curt grinned as he pulled out his phone.

Buzz pushed Curt's phone away. "Way more information than we needed."

"Like I'd show you buttheads." Curt shoved his phone back into his pocket.

They'd learned a long time ago not to share too much information about any girl they saw for more than a few hours. Never knew who might end up as the next girlfriend.

"Shit," Curt said.

"What?" Elliot asked.

"I hope I put the do not disturb sign on the door." He grinned from ear to ear.

Elliot smacked him upside the head.

Rubbing his head, Curt turned to face Elliot. "Call her."

"I will," Elliot whispered.

Jack threw him a disbelieving glance.

"I will," Elliot repeated.

After fifteen minutes, Sebastian packed up his gear.

"Hold up. Listen to this." Jack tapped the recorder app on his phone and turned up the volume. "I wrote this last night, needs work, but I... You'll tell me what you think."

They listened in silence. Not the best quality, but Jack was still pleased with the song.

"Holy shit, brother." Elliot said as the song ended. "That's fucking awesome."

"Jack, damn." Curt rubbed his beard growth. "Maybe two acoustics, keep it simple."

"That's beautiful." Buzz tapped on his thighs. "Drums?"

"Absolutely. It'll add strength." Jack thought it was brilliant, but there was always a chance that since he was still high on the best sex of his life, the song was really a piece of shit. Wouldn't be the first time.

"Let's work on it after soundcheck," Buzz said.

"Great idea," Curt agreed.

Elliot scoffed. "Harmony will want to put that out ASAP."

"How about after we work the kinks out, adding it to the encore as a special thank you to all the fans who come out and support us," Jack said. "Release it after the tour ends."

"I love that idea." Elliot clapped him on the back.

"Are we agreed?" Jack asked.

Yups all around.

Jack checked the time on his phone as he waited for the elevator. They'd have time to talk before the band had to leave for soundcheck. He'd tell Em he'd be as patient as she needed him to be. Dating was normal. She wanted normal, and he was a normal guy who happened to be somewhat famous. They'd keep their relationship private, but it would come out, eventually. Hopefully by then she'd realize they were perfect for each other. It'd be tough at first, but the paparazzi would move onto someone else. Normal was boring.

He'd been so caught up in his thoughts Jack hadn't realized Curt stood next to him. He had a goofy grin on his face, much like the one reflected back at Jack this morning while shaving.

Curt pushed the up button several times. "Nicki's great."

"Emily thinks highly of her, so I'm sure she is."

The elevator doors opened, and they entered. Jack pushed the buttons for their floors.

"Is Emily coming tonight?" Curt asked.

Jack smiled. "Yeah." He couldn't wait to see her. "Is Nicki coming?"

"Depends."

"On what?"

"If she's been a good girl." Curt wagged his brows.

The elevator doors opened on the thirty-fifth floor, and Curt stepped off with a wave. "Later."

When the elevator stopped on thirty-seven, he dashed out, almost colliding with an elderly couple. "I'm so sorry. Are you okay?"

The couple smiled and nodded. Jack apologized again and ran down the hallway. Skidding to a stop in front of his room, he dug the key card out, and opened the door. Something was wrong; it was too quiet, empty. He couldn't breathe.

Jack still stood there when Jeff walked down the hallway. His room was two down from Jack's.

"Everything okay, man?" Jeff asked.

"She's gone," Jack managed.

"Have you been inside?"

"No."

"Then how do you know?" Jeff peered into the room. "She's probably in the bathroom."

It was too quiet. Jack leaned against the wall and slid to the floor. "Gone."

Jeff jerked his head toward the open door. Jack nodded and Jeff entered. A minute later, he walked out with an envelope in his hand. He handed it to Jack. "Sorry, man," Jeff said and walked to his own room.

She'd used large block letters to write his name. He didn't need to read it; he knew what it said. He'd been a stubborn fuck. She'd told him repeatedly she'd leave, but he'd been so arrogant. Jack opened it and read it anyway. She was nice about it, taking most of the blame on herself. She ended with asking him to leave her alone. How could he? He was in love with her.

How could he not? It was what she needed.

Getting up, he walked into the room and gently closed the door. Empty. The room and his heart. Jack went to the mini bar. Grabbing a bottle, he cracked it open and downed it. Then another. And another.

Chapter Twenty-Five

Once the cab cleared the congestion of the city, the hum of the tires was a welcome relief. Emily tried to clear her mind, but thoughts of deep blue eyes, a lopsided smile, and tousled brown hair kept invading. Emily repeated her mantra, but nothing helped. She couldn't get Jack out of her head. Did she really want to? The alternative was worse. Sean. *Bastard*.

She let her thoughts drift back to Jack. He'd been very attentive to her needs in bed and out. He was handsome, talented, funny, considerate—*Shit*.

As far as the cons, rock star was what he did for a living not who he was as a man. Not really a con. He was humble. Not a con. Damn. He looked out for people. When they'd left the Garden, he talked with many of the crew, genuinely interested in their lives. Also, not a con. Crap. But he lived in the spotlight, a definite con.

Elliot, Buzz, and that lovely couple from the restaurant all vouched for him. Elliot and Buzz might have been wingmen, and Antonio and Maya knew him a long time ago, but Jack had Jeff's respect. Marine. That may not mean much to most people, but to Emily, it meant honor, faithfulness, and loyalty. The only tattoo her dad had was Semper Fi.

Had she made a mistake leaving Jack? He was a great guy. What was wrong with her? And she knew it was something wrong with her.

Until three weeks ago, she'd thought Sean was a great guy, too. But it was hard to remember anything good; her love vanished when she'd caught him. Why not just break up? Say he changed his mind, wasn't ready, made a mistake, anything. Maybe she should've talked to him. Had he tried to talk to her? She only remembered the horrible picture of him inside that little bitch.

Sean said he'd be back to pick up the rest of his shit. He must have a new place by now. What the fuck was he waiting for? She'd call him and tell him to pick up his shit tonight or she'd throw it away. Not tonight. It'd have to wait three weeks. Maybe she'd just throw it all out anyway. That would serve him right. Too bad she wasn't like that.

As the cab slowed to a stop in front of her apartment building, Emily took her wallet out and pulled out her credit card. She paid and gave the driver a nice tip. She plodded up the walkway, pausing at the bottom of the stairs. The broken stair had been there since the heavy snow last winter. She'd seen it several times a day for months. Now every time she walked up these stairs, she'd remember Jack. *Stupid dream.*

It would've made for a great story, but in reality, it'd just remind her of one of the worst things she'd ever done to another person. Maybe after some time had passed, she'd only remember the good times they had. Maybe in another lifetime.

Emily closed the door to her apartment and leaned against it. After three weeks, how was it possible the apartment still smelled like Sean? She pushed off the door, trudged up the stairs, and got the scented candle that Gail gave her for her birthday. She hated scented candles, and everyone who knew her knew that. Everyone, except her future mother-in-law. Ex-future mother-in-law.

Edward and Gail Sullivan. Sean and his parents weren't close, but she'd always hoped that after they married that would change. Emily got the impression they thought Sean could do better. Not that they ever said anything, they wouldn't, bad manners and all that. Sean was well-mannered, never raised his voice, or used foul language around them. They were all very respectful but distant. Conversations never flowed easily.

When they'd first dated, he'd mentioned his family only once when he told her he was an only child. He didn't talk about his parents because they weren't close. She hadn't talked about hers because they were gone.

The only fight he'd ever had with his parents happened when they'd insisted Emily sign a pre-nup. Sean had yelled and dropped two F-bombs. Said the last thing Emily was interested in was his money or theirs. He'd accused his parents of trying to sabotage their marriage. Did they think it wouldn't last? Edward had raised his voice back. Not to the level that Sean had, but still. Having their lawyer draw up the agreement had been the last straw. He'd told them where they could shove it and stormed out, dragging her with him. He'd actually slammed the front door.

Emily had never seen him so angry. Until she'd said she would sign the papers. She hadn't had a problem with it. She'd told Sean his parents were looking out for him, but he'd accused her of thinking their marriage wouldn't last. He didn't talk to her for two days after that, and he always talked to her. How did a man go from furious over a pre-nup to cheating in two weeks? Or just getting caught. He could have been cheating for a while or the whole time.

She sniffed the Lavender Seafoam Beach Escapade Bliss candle. It stunk worse than the three-week-old stale vapor trail of Sean's cologne. She replaced the lid and chucked it in the trash.

Emily dragged herself to the bathroom, stripping out of her clothes and turning on the shower. For the first time in her life, she couldn't look at herself in the mirror. As she stood under the hot water, her cheeks burned; whether from her tears or the hot spray, she didn't know. She cried in the shower till the water ran cold. If Emily didn't have such a pounding headache from crying, she'd drink that expensive bottle of wine he'd left in the fridge. Getting drunk appealed but dealing with a hangover didn't.

Emily sat at the computer and looked through ideas she had for stories, but nothing excited her. It was hard to write with a headache; unless her character had a headache, then it could be useful.

She should eat something, but she still felt the nausea in the pit of her stomach. Jack would've read the letter by now. She'd half-expected him to be banging on the door. Guess he decided to honor her wishes. A rush of disappointment ran through her. The sex had been amazing, and she'd miss it, that was all. That was why she felt disappointed. Not for any other reason. A little voice in her head said *liar*.

Wasn't she entitled to a few white lies? She couldn't have written a worse story than the last three weeks of her life. Sometimes it sucked to be a writer. Maybe she'd write a murder mystery. First victim, Sean Sullivan, age thirty-one, investments. Death by choking on his own dick. Second victim, Tiffany Fake Tits, age twenty-two, assistant at an investment firm. Death by drowning in the toilet. Suspect, Emily Prescott, age twenty-seven, copywriter by day, novelist by night. Jilted by victim number one with victim number two. They were both number two, all right. Not much of a whodunit.

Jack would've laughed at that story.

She'd gone three minutes without thinking about Jack. What was wrong with her? She'd made her decision. Why was she second-guessing herself?

Even if she had agreed to see him, where would that leave her? They'd have a great time, maybe even leave the hotel room. Then what? Off he'd go to other cities for almost two years. How could they have a relationship like that? They couldn't. Even if she was ready to have one, which she most definitely wasn't. She wanted a quiet, anonymous life. Life with Jack would be anything but. It was better this way. He'd find someone who'd give him what he needed, what he deserved.

Sleep, that was what she needed. Emily crawled into bed and hauled the covers over her head. The new mattress smell further nauseated her, so she uncovered her head. How could she be so tired yet unable to sleep? All she'd wanted to do for the past three weeks was go to sleep and wake up when the nightmare ended. Just like ten years ago.

She could call Vince or Eddie. Emily had promised them both a call, but she didn't want to talk. She wanted to cry, scream, and swear at the unfairness of it all. Oh fuck, now she was feeling sorry for herself. She should call Nicki. She'd do most of the talking. It would be better than this silence, but since Nicki hadn't shown up on her doorstep, she was probably still with Curt.

She wandered into her office and turned on the laptop. She needed to hear Jack's voice. She typed Stone Highway into the search bar and, within a few minutes, purchased their catalog and downloaded the songs. She connected her cell and transferred the music. She queued up the four albums, put them on shuffle, and hit play.

Jack's voice sang to her, a love song. Skip. Second song was better, hard rock, a little raunchy. Emily smiled. She liked this one.

Pulling out a bottle of Maker's Mark from the pantry, she grabbed a glass and poured a generous portion. She sniffed the amber liquid and her stomach rolled. *Bad idea.* She poured it down the drain and rinsed the glass.

She wandered back into her bedroom and crawled under the covers. "Rely" came on. Nicki had told her she'd read in an interview that Jack wrote that song about his dad. He could've been writing about himself. The words washed over her, comforting her. Not that she deserved comforting, especially not from Jack after what she'd done to him.

She wished her parents were here. She'd wished that a million times in the past ten years. Maybe her dad would've seen through Sean, known he wasn't trustworthy. Riley would've beaten the shit out of him. She smiled. He was a good older brother and always looked out for her. No one ever picked on Riley's little sister. They'd all been so close. Growing up on military bases, families came and went, but her family was always a constant.

No one understood what it was like not having her family. They knew it was awful, but they couldn't really comprehend. A hole that never closed resided in her heart, although it had gotten smaller. In some ways she felt like she was stuck at seventeen. Forever that scarred girl, trapped in a hospital bed, people coming and going as they pleased, issuing orders and commands. *"We've scheduled your next surgery; go to physical therapy; work hard and maybe walk again."* Not that they weren't compassionate, they were, and they were looking out for her. But they were all strangers. They'd go home to their families, but she'd never see hers again.

If her parents were alive, she could've gone to their house and cried on her mom's shoulder. Her mom had a way of comforting that didn't need words. There was that hand thing they did when other people were around, like their own secret language. Three squeezes meant I love you. Four squeezes meant I love you, too. They all did it. Even her and Riley. Her parents had always been demonstrative about their love for each other. It never embarrassed Emily; she'd thought it was sweet.

Not that her mom wasn't happy to listen to all her teenage babble, and babble she had. Usually about a boy she was infatuated with. She'd thought it was love. Dad and Riley would make fun of her. Every time she danced around the house, it was love with a new boy. "Who is it this week?" he'd ask. Or "How's Terry?" Her answer was often "That was last month, Dad." Emily missed them.

She thought she'd gotten used to it, until Sully proposed, and she had to plan her wedding alone. Who'd walk her down the aisle? She shouldn't have had to make that decision. It should've been her dad. In the end, Nicki and Trina, her only other friend from rehab besides Vince, helped her plan. They went dress shopping with her and helped her pick flowers and color schemes. She'd asked Eddie and Vince to walk her down the aisle together and they'd agreed. They were the foundation on which she'd built her new life. She couldn't imagine getting married without them.

She awoke to Jack's voice still singing to her. She had to stop thinking about him.

Maybe she'd get dressed, go out to a bar, and hook up with the first guy she saw. No guy would turn down an offer of no strings sex. Except Vince.

They'd both been through something awful, which was why they'd bonded. After the hurt of his rejection wore off, she understood just how screwed up she was. Vince had let her down gently, said he'd loved her, but... It had never hurt their friendship. Since he ended up in a band, that was almost as popular as Stone Highway, it was just as well. Emily loved Vince but didn't want any part of that life. Not even for him, and he'd understood.

Maybe Nicki had it right. Love 'em and leave 'em. She should've done that with Jack. Lesson learned. According to Nicki, no matter how gorgeous the guy or how hot the sex, leave. Guys fell asleep right after sex anyway, so it was easy. Except, Jack hadn't fallen asleep. He was a cuddler. Definitely a con. Emily hated to cuddle. Although, it wasn't so bad with him; he wasn't a crowder. *Enough about Jack.*

Emily laughed. Nicki had broken her own rule; she'd stayed with Curt. Emily would've been concerned if Jack hadn't vouched for him.

Nicki. Thank God, she'd forgotten about today. She had explaining to do though. She'd promised not to go off the deep end. "Who wants to spank me?" Seriously? Only Nicki could walk into a room and say such a thing. It was kind of hard to stay pissed considering—No. Nicki would have to pay.

Emily dozed off again, pondering ways to maim Nicki.

Chapter Twenty-Six

A faint vibrating and a muffled song jarred Jack from sleep. It was annoying and he wished it would stop. It did, but not for long. Music played louder now. *Fuck.* Cell phone. Jack rolled over. Why was the bed so hard? Opening his eyes, he saw dismal, dark clouds outside the window. What time was it? He sat up and realized he was on the floor. The room spun, so he didn't try to stand.

Music and vibrating again. He didn't have the energy to get it out of his pocket. It was still daytime, judging by the light outside, but dark, heavy clouds hung in the sky, taking away all the sunshine of earlier in the day.

Emily left. His eyes focused on the note on the floor and several empty bottles from the mini bar. Resting his back against the wall, Jack had never been so tired. Ringing and vibrating again. Fuck. Not good. He dug his phone from his pocket but not in time. The light from his cell hurt his eyes. It was after five; no wonder his phone rang incessantly since they were late. Thumbing through the call list, he saw Elliot, Buzz, Curt, and Jeff. The last call was from Brian. Really fucking bad.

His eyes closed. Jack should get up, get moving, but his body wouldn't cooperate. A sudden and persistent knocking on the door startled him. He tried to stand, but the room spun again, so he crawled toward the door. Jack tried to yell out that he was coming, but his mouth was so dry it hurt to swallow. Knocking turned into pounding. Just as he got to the door, it opened, smacking him in the head. "Fuck."

"What the fuck was that?" Elliot said.

"My head," Jack yelled. He rolled away from the door and sat up against the wall. "Asshole."

The door opened, and the light switch flicked on, flooding the room with sun-intensity brightness.

Elliot, Buzz, Curt, and Jeff stood in the doorway.

"Hey, man, you okay?" Jeff asked.

Buzz walked over to Emily's letter and read it. "Damn."

He handed the letter to Elliot, and they exchanged a glance. "Jack, I'm sorry. I know you really liked this girl."

Jack let his head fall forward between his bent knees.

"This is bad," Curt said. "Really fucking bad."

"What the fuck do we do? We have a gig in three hours. Any chance we can sober him up by then?" Elliot asked.

"Jeez, man, it's not like I'm the expert," Buzz said.

"I didn't mean it like that."

Buzz huffed in disbelief.

"Okay, I did a little, but you've been in this situation, what did you do?" Elliot asked.

"Uppers. Not an option."

Someone picked up the bottles and tossed them in the trash can. The shrill clanking had Jack covering his ears.

"Should we call Dex?" Buzz asked. "I mean, what did you guys do?"

"We took care of things in-house, only called Dex if we needed damage control." Elliot paused. "Look man, that's ancient history. We have no doubts about you, so you don't get to doubt either. Dumbass."

"Better a live dumbass than a dead fucker," Buzz said.

"I'll call Brian. The techs can do soundcheck. Gonna need to stall, too," Elliot said.

Jack should be pissed with himself, but he only felt an ache in his chest where his heart used to be.

"Motherfucker," Elliot said into the phone and then kicked something metallic.

Jack's stomach rolled. As quickly as possible, he stood and ran for the bathroom. Just in time. *Oh fuck.* After throwing up what felt like everything he'd ever eaten, he sat on the cool tile of the bathroom floor. His knees hurt, his throat burned, and his eyes felt like they were coming out of their sockets. Someone handed him a wet washcloth. He wiped his face and neck.

"Here, drink this but just take sips," Buzz said, handing him a bottle of water.

Jack swished the water around his mouth and spit in the toilet. Resting the cool washcloth over his hot face, he took a few sips of water.

If he hadn't been such an arrogant fuckhead, he'd have realized that, after assuring him all day she'd leave, she'd agreed too easily to stay. What choice had he given her? He'd pushed too hard; she was brave but fragile after her breakup. She'd lied, and he felt like shit because he'd driven her to it. Emily never wanted to see him again. His head pounded, but that was nothing compared to the crushing ache that resided throughout his body. She'd called him spoiled.

"Am I spoiled?" Jack asked, his voice loud in the tiled bathroom.

"Fuck yeah," Elliot said. "We all are. Glad you're still with us."

"You say that like it's a bad thing," Curt said.

"Says the only child," Buzz taunted.

Jack opened his eyes in time to see Curt give Buzz the finger. "She left, and she's not coming back." Saying it out loud had such a final ring to it. Tears pricked the backs of his eyes. He wasn't one of those macho assholes who thought only pussies cried, but now wasn't the time.

"Man, I'm sorry," Curt said.

"Where's Nicki?" Jack asked.

"Still tied to your bed?" Elliot snorted.

"Hey, it's what she wanted," Curt said. "She said the anticipation was half the fun. I made sure she was comfortable."

"Now that Jack's somewhat coherent, what are we going to do?" Buzz asked.

How could he have forgotten that they had a gig tonight? *Fuck.* Grabbing hold of the side of the counter and the front of the toilet, he attempted to stand, making it halfway before two sets of hands helped him the rest of the way.

"Thanks," Jack said, trying to get his bearings. He took one step and then another. Okay, moving was doable. "I fucked up. I'm sorry."

The most he ever drank before a gig was one beer. He'd never been this fucked up before. The only time in his life he drank to the point of puking was senior year in high school at a year-end party. He'd gotten so drunk that he had to call his dad to come get him. His folks were angry but happy he'd called for a ride. They'd been disappointed in him, and he'd felt like shit for letting them down. They'd made him promise before his first party; if he ever drank, no driving. No excuse then, and none now. How could he have been so irresponsible? The band, the crew, the fans, all counted on him.

"Don't sweat it, brother. We've all been there. Remember that time on our first tour? Siobhan and I had a huge fight, and she hung up on me, then wouldn't answer my calls. We were in Virginia at some shit-hole college bar, and I got so drunk you did the entire set without me."

"Yeah, and when Shauna dumped me by stealing most of my stuff and moving out. We lost two days in the studio because I got so shit-faced. You guys covered for me," Curt said.

"I wish it was only once you guys covered for me," Buzz said. "That's what friends do for each other. Jack, you fucked up, no worse than we have over the years. If anything, it's long overdue."

"Thanks."

"Sip the water, you need to hydrate," Elliot said.

"What about coffee?" Curt asked.

"That doesn't help," Buzz said. "You should eat something, it'll help settle your stomach."

Jack grunted. "The thought of food makes me want to puke."

"I'll call room service and ask them to send up crackers and ginger ale," Elliot said. "What? It helped Siobhan when she had morning sickness," Elliot said, flipping them off as he left to make the call.

"Isn't there a song about how the fans will forgive us no matter what?" Curt asked.

"At least one," Jack said.

After eating the crackers and sipping the ginger ale, his stomach felt less like the Atlantic Ocean at high tide. His throat burned less, so he hoped singing wouldn't be a problem. They'd already missed soundcheck. No way they wouldn't play tonight. "I'm gonna grab a quick shower."

He stood under the hot shower spray, letting the water warm him, at least on the outside. A chill took up residence in his body that had nothing to do with the outside temperature. Needing to get a move on, he grabbed for the shampoo but lost his footing and landed on his ass. "Fuck." Part of him wanted to stay there, but too many people depended on him for him to wallow in his own misery right now. He'd have the rest of his life to do that. He got his feet under him and leaned forward, but the wall was closer than he realized, and he smacked his head on the tile. "Fuck!" Jack yelled. "That's going to leave a mark." His voice echoed off the bathroom walls.

The bathroom door crashed open. "Jack, you dead?" Elliot asked.

"Not yet."

"Good." The bathroom door closed.

He finished showering without further injury and in a few minutes joined everyone in the living room.

"Damn, Jack, you sure you're okay?" Buzz asked.

"What?"

"That's some bump," Curt said. "What happened?"

"I slipped and fell on my ass, then trying to get up, smacked my head against the wall. In case you care, I also squashed my nuts when I landed."

Jeff examined Jack's forehead. "Are you nauseous?"

"No more than I was before I fell. Why?"

"You might have a concussion." Ever to the point, Jeff asked Jack a series of questions. Blurred vision, double vision, did he lose consciousness? No, no, no. Dizziness, confusion, memory loss. No, no, and Emily's gone. After a few more questions, Jeff led him through physical tests of balance, which Jack assumed he passed since Jeff grunted.

"If any of those symptoms occur, we're going to the hospital," Jeff said. It wasn't an offer.

"All right, enough about Jack and his now bigger oversized head due to that goose egg. The show must go on. That is, if you girls are ready?" Elliot said.

Six middle fingers and they were out the door.

They reached the Garden in record time. As they entered, the crew looked worried. Jack couldn't blame them. He looked and felt like shit. Brian and Viv waited just inside the entrance.

Brian took one look at him and asked, "Are you okay? What the fuck happened?"

"I'm fine, I fell in the shower and hit my head." He touched the bump that seemed to have gotten bigger. "Ow, fuck."

"And he squashed his nuts," Elliot said.

Brian leaned closer. "I thought you were...drunk."

"That too," Jack said.

"What do we do about Ken Clarke?" Brian asked. "What's the plan?"

"Who the fuck is Ken Clarke?" Buzz and Curt asked at the same time.

"Fucking shit," Elliot said. "I was so worried about Jack choking on his puke, I forgot to tell you. He's from Harmony, here to check up on us or some shit."

Jack moaned. *Nice going, asshole.* The timing couldn't be worse. Next year their deal was up, and Dex would renegotiate. He told them they needed to keep their shit together. *Hidden Captions* was headed to triple platinum, and they'd sold out shows all over the country, and the European sales were way up.

A rather smug-looking guy dressed in a gray three-piece suit with purple tie and pocket square made his way through the crowded backstage. The crew wasn't cooperating with him.

"That's him," said Brian under his breath as the guy approached. "Ken, I thought you were taking your seat?"

"I'd rather see the show from here. Everything okay? You guys are late," Ken said.

Without skipping a beat, Jeff stepped next to Jack. "Jack hit his head. We're taking things slow. You understand, right?"

Ken reached out and tried to touch Jack's head. "Back off, man," Jack said knocking his arm away and stepping back. The room spun, and he lost his balance but didn't go down. Elliot put his hand on Jack's back to steady him.

Jeff stepped in front of Jack. When Ken tried to maneuver around him, Jeff growled, "Stay."

It seemed Mr. Ken Clarke didn't like to be ordered around. He tried to muscle closer, but this time when Jeff turned on him, he stopped.

Turning back to Jack, Jeff ushered them to the dressing room and closed the door. He put Jack through another round of concussion protocol. Even though he passed, Jeff said, "I think you need to—"

Jack raised his hand. He sat on the couch where last night he'd sat with Emily. In less than twenty-four hours, his life turned upside down twice, first when they met, the second... *Gotta stop thinking about her.* It was over. He'd respect her wishes. "I'm okay. You know, as okay as I can be for getting drunk and falling before a gig. Mostly the drinking though, pretty sure that caused the falling."

After a single loud knock, Brian opened the door and entered. "That guy is an asshole. He's grilling the crew to see what really happened."

Jack's head pounded. He knew everyone stared at the ever-expanding bump, so he brushed his hair forward to cover it.

Elliot stifled a laugh.

"What?" Jack asked.

He shook his head. "Now it looks like a second head, it has...hair."

Jack brushed his hair back.

"It's getting bigger," Curt said. "Maybe we should cancel, you fell, it's a valid excuse."

"Because I was drunk."

"We'll leave that part out," Brian said. "The crew won't tell that guy anything. They love you guys, and they're loyal."

"It's not right to lie. I fucked up, I should own up to it," Jack said running his hand carefully through his hair.

"It's not just about you, Jack," Elliot said in a low voice. "If it was one of us, you'd be all over covering it up. Let's vote, show of hands, who thinks we should cover Jack's ass and say he fell and hit his head, leaving out the details of any other dumbass behavior?"

Five hands shot into the air.

"Thanks, guys. What about the gig?"

"That's up to you," Buzz said. "Do you have it?"

"I hate to disappoint the fans." Jack stood and walked around the room. "I seem to be steady, better than I deserve. My throat's a little raw, from, well, you know." He sang a few lines from the opening song. Not great but not terrible. "What about it, Black, can you sing lead on a few songs tonight?"

"I got you covered, brother," Elliot said, without hesitation.

"I'm stopping the show if I see any signs you're in trouble Jack," Jeff said. As he opened the door, he slammed into Ken Clarke—who'd been listening at the door—knocking him on his ass. Jeff stepped around him and the band followed. He nodded to Brick, Miller, and Polson. "No one gets near them tonight." They nodded and followed the band to the stage.

Chapter Twenty-Seven

All things considered, the gig wasn't a train wreck. Jack's voice was off, and Elliot sang more than a few songs. Viv kept a constant supply of water so Jack would stay hydrated. He'd fucked up the middle to "Welcome Home," but Curt covered for him. He had to walk off stage at one point and didn't return for several minutes. Elliot let the audience know Jack was under the weather but wanted to finish the gig. The audience responded with cheers and applause, and when Jack returned, they erupted even louder.

Curt suggested they skip the encore, but Jack refused to hear it. The fans had been great, and they wouldn't short change them. He suggested they do "Tempers Flare." They hadn't done it live in a while, but they were all good to go with it, so they went back on stage and killed it.

As the song ended, Elliot wandered over to Buzz. Curt and Jack joined them. "How about doing the new song you wrote? Can you remember it?" Elliot asked.

"We haven't worked on it yet," Jack said. Now that Emily was gone, he wasn't sure he wanted to share it. Ever.

"Just you and the acoustic, man, like you played it for us."

Elliot looked at Curt, who gave them a thumbs-up, and Buzz nodded in approval.

"All right," Jack said. He walked to the side of the stage and handed Holden his guitar. "Give me the Martin." Acoustic in hand, Jack walked back on stage. Buzz, Elliot, and Curt were still there. That settled his nerves more than alcohol ever could. He put the guitar strap over his shoulder and walked up to the microphone.

"Thank you, guys, for coming out tonight. We hope we lived up to—" Before Jack could continue, the audience showed them the love. He waited for them to settle down before continuing. "We have a new song we'd like to play for you tonight." Closing his eyes, Emily's beautiful face appeared. "It's called 'With You.'"

He played the intro, and the audience fell silent. Not even a whistle. All the emotions he'd felt while writing it flooded back. His voice reflecting his love, he sounded way better than he deserved. His heart pounded in his chest. He remembered her kisses and the tender way she'd made love to him. He'd respect her wishes, but he was in love with her. Before he knew it, he played the last chord. Jack's heartbeat pounded in his ears. *Shit, did I just bomb?* Jack opened his eyes.

The audience exploded with cheers, whistles, and woo-hoos. The volume was deafening.

Elliot pushed him off stage, with Curt and Buzz in front of them. They didn't stop until they reached the safety of the dressing room. They all had tears in their eyes.

"Hey, man, you gonna be okay?" Curt asked.

Jack just nodded.

Curt promised Nicki he'd come right back after the gig, and he couldn't wait to see her, but he'd never seen Jack like this before. Breakups sucked, but Jack looked beaten. Jack was a force of nature; nothing kept him down. And he was always looking out for everyone else. "Anything I can do?"

Jack raised his head, and the sadness in his eyes was so deep, Curt had to look away.

"Nothing to do, man, she's gone, doesn't want anything to do with me."

"Maybe in a few days..." Curt knew from Nicki that once Emily made up her mind, she was set.

"Yeah, Jack. Give it a few days, she just needs some time," Buzz said.

"Her fiancé cheated on her, she needs time, but there's more to it than that." Jack dropped his head on the back of the couch.

Wow, Nicki hadn't told him that, but Curt understood. Since Shauna pulverized his heart nine months ago, he'd been having fun, not interested in being attached again. Until Nicki. She hid behind a layer of makeup and clothes, but on the inside, she was sweet. Curt suspected that was her way of keeping the world at bay. Everyone had their defenses, but Nicki's were just more outrageous than most. He missed her.

"If you want to talk..." Curt said. "I'm outta here." With one last look at his best friends, Curt rushed back to Nicki with a smile.

Buzz stuck around because he was concerned about Jack. He was brooding. Jack never brooded. Elliot brooded. He wished he knew what to do for his friend. Ever since they were little kids, Jack had been there for him. The best thing Buzz could do for both of them was keep his shit together. Jack needed to focus on himself right now, even if he didn't want to.

Buzz thought about Sally. That breakup had pushed him off the cliff. He'd loved her, but she'd blamed him for all her shit. Better not to go there. He needed to be strong. He'd call his sponsor as soon as he got back to the hotel. No way Buzz would let the guys and his family down. He'd put them through enough.

Emily had been so compassionate, and he couldn't thank her enough for hooking him up with her friend Vince. Sobriety was a journey, he'd said. He understood the extra burden of traveling, and if this guy could do it, so could Buzz.

"I'm going, you guys coming," he asked.

Jack just waved.

Elliot shrugged. "Something I gotta do first," he said, looking at Jack.

Buzz eyed Elliot. He was up to something. "Later."

ELLIOT WATCHED JACK. HE KNEW JACK WAS thinking about Emily. Not that he was a mind reader. This was Jack; he always thought of others, never putting himself first.

Jack hadn't hesitated to get on a plane with him when Siobhan had miscarried. He'd never been more terrified in his life, but Jack kept reassuring him that Siobhan was okay. Jack was one of the few who knew the struggles he and Siobhan had gone through.

God, he loved her. He would do whatever it took to get her back.

Elliot smiled as the plan formed in his mind. He knew how to get Jack to act. He'd give Jack a few more minutes to stew and then the plan would be afoot.

EMILY. SHE WAS ALL JACK COULD THINK ABOUT. Last night, in this room, she'd offered compassion to his friends, and then this morning with Todd and him when he'd found out Sid died. He missed her, but he'd made his decision. He'd leave her alone like she asked. She'd been through so much. The last thing he wanted to do was cause her more pain. He felt like his heart was pumping cut glass. But it would pass.

Jack dragged himself off the couch. The sooner he got back to his room, the sooner he'd be left alone with his misery. Elliot had his own shit to deal with.

He hadn't seen the record company guy, so hopefully he'd get back to the hotel without having to deal with Ken.

As he opened the door, Elliot's hand rested on his shoulder. "Hey, man, let's get a drink."

"No way. I've had enough," Jack said.

"Okay, then come with me while I get a drink," Elliot said. "You know it's bad to drink alone."

"I need to go back to the hotel and sleep it off. I don't want to be around people."

Jeff waited outside the dressing room and got them to the exit without incident.

"Listen, man." Elliot paused as they got in the SUV. "I need liquid courage, I'm calling Siobhan. One drink?"

Jack sighed. Elliot wanted his help. How could he refuse? "Okay."

"Great. I know just the place."

Elliot gave Jeff the address of Quivers Irish Pub.

Jack rested his head on the back of the seat. "What are you up to?"

"Nothing."

Tabitha still worked at Quivers.

Chapter Twenty-Eight

A s they walked in, Elliot looked around but didn't see Tabitha. It was after eleven on a Friday night and Quivers was packed. The hook-up competition had been in full swing for a while. Jack and Elliot wove their way up to the bar.

"One drink," Jack reminded Elliot. "You want courage, not drunk, when you call Siobhan."

Elliot smirked. "No problem, I've already seen what overindulgence can do to a man."

"Fuck you."

They waited several minutes before a tall, dark-haired bartender made his way down the line of bar patrons. "What'll ya have?" he asked in a faint brogue.

"Seltzer," Jack said.

Elliot had no intention of getting Jack a drink. Yet. The bartender eyed Jack suspiciously. No one ever ordered just a seltzer at Quivers. Jack pointed to Elliot.

"Pint of Guinness," Elliot said.

The bartender placed their drinks on the bar, still eyeballing Jack.

Elliot threw a twenty on the bar. "Keep the change." The bartender went away happy. He watched as Jack glanced around the bar. He was looking for *her*. Good.

Elliot turned and smirked as he spotted a tall dark-haired, blue-eyed beauty walk up to the bar and accidentally on purpose bump into Jack while trying to get the bartender's attention. Jack shifted to give her more room but didn't notice her.

The beauty didn't give up that easily. "Sorry." A confident smile spread across her face. "It's so hard to move around in here on a Friday night. Even harder to get a drink. I should've stayed home." Her full, red lips formed a pout.

Jack raised his hand, and the bartender walked over. "This young lady would like to order a drink," he said without looking at said lady.

The beauty didn't appreciate being ignored. Shunned fury covered her face. She ordered a drink and pulled the bump routine on the guy on the other side of her, who paid for her drink. She cast Jack a "your loss" look over her shoulder and turned back to her second choice. The entire scene was lost on Jack; he hadn't seen any of it because he stared at his seltzer as if the bubbles held the key to the universe.

Elliot was sure this was the right way to go. Jack needed a nudge. Elliot looked up and smiled, as the nudge entered behind the bar, coming toward them. *Excellent.*

"Hi, hot stuff, long time no see." Tabitha greeted Jack with a kiss on the cheek.

"Tabs, gorgeous as always," Jack said.

Hands planted on her hips, she turned to him. "Elliot, you still taken?"

"'Fraid so, my dear," Elliot said, showing her his wedding band. He never took it off and never would. "Looks like you're stuck with sour puss here."

Tabitha cocked a brow. "Jack, tell your bartender what the

problem is." When she leaned on the bar, the deep V of her black shirt revealed more than just a peek at her fine tits.

Elliot smiled when Jack sat up. *Outstanding.*

WHEN JACK WAS SINGLE, JUST SEEING TABITHA would turn him on. Of course, he only sought her out when he was single. She was a classic Irish beauty: long red hair, almond-shaped green eyes, fair skin, dusting of freckles, tight body, nice tits, fun personality, and an excellent listener. They'd been friends for ten years. With benefits for almost as long. That worked for them both but only when he was single.

Tabitha was only single because she had one focus. Graduate from grad school and then get her dream job. She was getting her PhD in psychology, and she had to be getting close. "How's school?" Jack asked, setting aside his problems to talk to an old friend.

"One year to go," Tabitha said, straightening up at the sound of her name. She ran down the bar filling orders.

Jack eyed Elliot. "Did you know she was working tonight?"

"Yeah," Elliot said with a grin. "You looked like you could use cheering up. Who better than your friendly bartender with benefits? You are single, after all, aren't ya?"

Jack sneered at Elliot. "Yes."

"So what's the problem?" Elliot took a sip of his beer.

Jack glanced at Tabitha. They always had a good time, but they weren't in love. She didn't have time for a relationship, and Jack respected her drive in pursuing her dreams. Nothing got in her way. They were happy with their arrangement, neither giving nor asking for more than an occasional fuck.

But only when he was single.

Tabitha's hand waved in front of his face. "Sorry, what?" Jack asked, trying to focus on her.

"What happened to your head?" she asked, touching his bump.

"Long story."

"The doctor is in, sweetie."

A sad little laugh escaped Jack's lips. "Met a girl, lost the girl, got drunk, slipped in the shower, hit my head."

"There'll always be another girl, Jack." Putting up her finger, she walked to the other side of the bar to help a customer.

"Not like this one," Jack whispered.

Not wanting to talk anymore, Jack turned to Elliot, who had hardly touched his beer. "Dude, how late do you plan on calling your wife? Drink up, already."

"Hey, not everyone's in your league downing six mini bar bottles of vodka before a gig," Elliot sniped back.

"Fuck me. Sorry, man."

"Jack, you need to stop thinking about Emily. She's gone. Tabitha is right here, ready, willing, and able. You said you're not going after Emily, so you're moving on, right?"

"Right." Maybe if he told himself that often enough, he'd be able to. Jack's eyes met Tabitha's across the bar, and she winked and licked her lips. Jack nodded.

"I gotta take a piss." Jack walked to the back of the bar to the men's room. He took care of business, washed up, and when he opened the door, Tabs waited.

Taking his hand, she led him to the storage room. Unlocking the door, she pulled him in and flicked on the light switch. As soon as the door closed, she had him up against it, her hand cupping his dick through his jeans.

Jack groped her tits. Using his teeth, he lowered the V of her tight T-shirt until he could suck her nipple through the lace of her bra. Tabs moaned. She unbuttoned his jeans, slid the zipper down, and then curled her fingers around his cock. Her warm hand stroked his dick as her other hand ran through his hair, holding his head in place as she kissed him.

Jack turned them so her back was up against the door. He lifted her slightly and took her other nipple in his mouth, grazing it lightly with his teeth.

"Oh, yeah," Tabs said.

Jack kissed his way up her neck and took her mouth in a fierce kiss, attacking her tongue with his. He nipped her lip, and his cock throbbed in anticipation. He couldn't wait until Em took him in her mouth.

Except he wasn't with Em. He was with Tabs. "I can't do this." Jack lowered her to the floor. He turned away and zipped up his jeans. "I'm sorry." He ran his hand through his hair, and when he hit the bump, pain shot through his head. Jack deserved it. He should never have come here. When had he become such an asshole? His stomach burned and he was glad this room didn't have a mirror. He was in love with Emily, and he wouldn't be getting over that any time soon, if ever.

Jack had to end things with Tabs.

Before he could turn, her hand was on his shoulder. "She must be some girl, Jack." Tabitha rested her cheek on his back.

Jack reached up and covered her hand. "She is." He turned to face her. "I'm sorr—"

Tabs covered his lips with her finger. "I'm not." She kissed his cheek. "I always knew this day would come, Jack. Remember what I told you when we hatched our friends with benefits arrangement?"

Jack nodded. "No regrets." He sighed and looked down.

"I have none. It was great while it lasted."

He looked at her then, and she smiled at him. A genuine smile, one he didn't deserve. He nodded. With a quick hug, she left, closing the door behind her.

Standing there, in the cold, concrete room, the single naked bulb casted eerie shadows. It *had* been great while it lasted, but it was over. He was in love with Emily. Jack would give her the time she needed. He'd move back to New York, and by then, maybe, Em would ready. He could only hope.

Chapter Twenty-Nine

E lliot sipped his beer as he watched Tabitha return from the back of the bar alone. Jack emerged several minutes later looking more miserable than ever. *Good, it worked.*

Jack slumped on the bar stool. "What the fuck is this?" A whiskey sat next to Jack's untouched seltzer.

Elliot shrugged. "You look like you could use a drink."

Jack picked up the whiskey and downed it. As soon as the glass hit the bar, the dark-haired bartender filled it without asking.

Jack downed it and placed the glass on the bar upside down.

Elliot turned to face Jack. "What the fuck are you going to do?"

Jack's head dropped into his hands. "About what?"

"About Emily," Elliot said.

"Nothing. She asked me to leave her alone."

"So, you're just giving up?"

"It's what she wants." Jack ran his hand over the back of his neck.

Elliot shook his head. "Never thought I'd see the day when

Jack McBride gave up. The whole reason we stayed together long enough to be a success in this business was because you refused to give up. One time or another the three of us wanted to quit, admit defeat, and go running home to mommy and daddy. But not you. You were always the one to rally us. You never thought of giving up."

Jack scoffed. "Sure I did, many times."

"Then why didn't you?"

Jack rubbed a hand over his face. "Ever since I was a kid, I knew I wanted to be a musician. It was all I ever wanted, and nothing else came close. Remember when my folks insisted I go to college for at least a year before deciding if music was the best choice for me?"

Elliot nodded.

"I felt sick. College had nothing to offer me." Jack laughed. "Even if we were still touring cross-country in that old battered van, pulling our gear in a trailer, I would've been happy"—Jack paused—"of course, this is better."

"And how do you feel knowing you'll never see Emily again?"

"Sick."

"Then why are you giving up on her? Giving up on what you could have with her?" Elliot asked. "And don't say because she asked you to. Why else?"

Jack turned to him. "I don't know." He shrugged. "What else can I do?"

"Find a way," Elliot said in a low voice, pushing his beer away. He took out forty dollars, left it on the bar, and sent Jeff a text.

"That sounds familiar," Jack said.

"It should, brother. It's what you said to me the night I got hammered because Siobhan broke up with me while we were on the road. She wanted to get married and said it wouldn't work long distance." Elliot remembered all too well how he'd felt without Siobhan. Miserable. Just like Jack was now.

"What is this, payback?" Jack stood and wobbled.

"No, a reminder."

"Of what?"

Elliot smirked. "That if you want something badly enough, you'll find a way. Which, I'd forgotten myself until a lovely brunette with a smart mind and a smart mouth reminded me last night. I just love her."

"So do I."

Elliot pushed away from the bar. "Then let's get the fuck out of here and go get your girl."

"I don't know where she lives."

"No, but someone who's tied up in Curt's room sure as hell does." Elliot rolled his eyes. *Do I have to think of everything?*

"Why didn't I think of that?"

"Because you get all sappy when you drink. What would you do without me?" Elliot clapped him on the shoulder.

Jack turned and strode out the door.

Jeff waited at the curb. "Where to, gentlemen?"

Jack dialed Curt's cell phone and hung up. Next, he dialed the hotel and asked for Curt's room. "Bastard isn't answering."

"To the hotel," Elliot said, with a smug grin. "Then to get Jack's girl."

Jeff hit the accelerator and they were off.

JACK BARELY WAITED FOR THE SUV TO STOP BEFORE he had the door open. Last night—No more reminiscing. He'd see her again, tonight.

"How do you plan on getting Nicki to tell you?" Elliot asked as they got in the elevator.

"Don't need a plan. Nicki will just tell me."

"Why, because you're *so* good-looking?" Elliot mocked.

"Why thank you, but no." Jack paused as Elliot flipped him off. "Because she's a talker."

"Ah, always a good source of information."

The elevator opened on Curt's floor. He ran down the hallway to Curt's room but paused before knocking.

"What are you waiting for?" Elliot asked, as he knocked.

When Curt didn't answer, Jack knocked again, harder. It was late, and he didn't want to wake up anyone else, but he needed that address. Now.

Elliot banged on the door. "Curt, open up."

They heard voices but the door didn't open.

"Fuck off. I'm busy," Curt yelled from the behind the door.

"I need to talk to Nicki. Now."

Elliot pounded again. "Curt, open the fucking door."

"Hey," Buzz said, jogging toward them. "What are you doing? I can hear you all the way down the hall."

"Jack's going to get Emily. Nicki knows where she lives. Jack needs that address."

Buzz's fist hit the door. "Curtis Stevens, open the damn door." At Jack and Elliot's raised brows, he said, "Always worked for his mom."

The door flew open. Curt's face was covered in shaving cream, and he was pissed. "What the fuck are you guys doing? Fuck off, we're busy," he said, trying to close the door, but Jack's boot blocked the door.

"Really?" Curt said. "What?"

"I need Emily's address."

Curt still blocked the door, but Nicki said "Can't do it,

Jack. If she wanted you to have it, she would've given it to you. Emi would kill me."

"Enough of this shit." Elliot pushed into Curt's room. Jack and Buzz followed. Elliot stopped short, and they smacked into him. Curt closed the door behind them.

"Oh jeez," Elliot said, looking away.

In the middle of the living room, Nicki stood half naked, her breasts covered in whipped cream.

Curt walked around his friends. "Babe, what the fuck are you doing?" He rushed over to her and wrapped the towel that had been around his waist around her.

"I'm not shy."

"Nic, they're my friends."

Nicki clutched the towel around her body and blushed. "I'm sorry, babe, it won't happen again."

It would've been a very touching moment except Curt was now naked.

"Dude, put some clothes on," Buzz said.

Curt faced them before walking into the bedroom, returning a minute later wearing a pair of sweat pants and carrying a robe. He tenderly put the robe around his girl.

"That's not shaving cream, is it?" Elliot asked, trying to hide his smile.

"Hey, you guys barged in here. Don't like what you see, get the fuck out," Curt said.

Jack walked over to Nicki. "We'll get out of your way in a minute."

"What happened to your head?" she asked.

"Jack got drunk, fell, hit his head, and crushed his nuts," Elliot said. "But that's not why we're here."

"Why do I tell you anything?" Jack asked, looking over his shoulder at Elliot.

"Jack... I can't, she'll never speak to me again."

"I understand, but I'm in love with her. I know it's crazy,

but it's true. She asked me to leave her alone, but I can't. I need to talk to her, convince her to give us a chance."

NICKI PLOPPED ON THE COUCH. *WHAT SHOULD I DO?* Emi would know what to do. Jack seemed so sincere, and Emi had looked happy when she and Curt had run into them earlier today. Ever since Emi caught that lying bucket of shit cheating she'd been so distressed, understandably, but Emi was strong, and it scared Nicki to see her so beaten down. Then having to dismantle her wedding. *Oh, fuck.* Tears welled and spilled down Nicki's cheeks, but she didn't wipe them away.

Curt rushed to her. "Babe, what's wrong?"

She could barely swallow. Curt put his arm around her, but it didn't help. "I'm the worst friend ever."

"I'm sure that's not true," Jack said.

Curt grabbed a tissue, and Nicki swiped at her tears. Blowing her nose, she looked up, and four handsome men stared dumbfounded at her.

Curt whispered soothing words to her, but she didn't deserve to be soothed.

Nicki took a few breaths trying to calm herself, then raised her eyes to meet Jack's. "Emily was supposed to get married, Jack."

"She told me about it. That fucker cheated on her. She kicked him out."

Wow. "She told you that?"

Jack nodded.

Nicki considered that for a moment. So very unlike Emi to be so open about her pain, especially to a stranger. But earlier, she'd looked like her old self. Nicki inhaled deeply, slowly letting it out. "Today, Jack. She was supposed to get married today." Nicki lowered her eyes as fresh tears formed and fell. *Worst. Friend. Ever.*

Jack sat on the couch next to her, looking like he'd been kicked in the gut.

"Why didn't she tell me?" he asked.

"I'm still shocked she told you about that asshole. Emi isn't a great sharer, Jack. She's not like us." Nicki patted his knee. "Did she tell you how she threw them out?"

"No."

Nicki gave a humorless laugh. "It would've made a great story. She looks all nice and sweet, but don't piss her off, she's got a real evil genius streak in her."

Elliot and Buzz laughed. They tried to stifle their smiles, but it didn't work.

"What's so funny?" Jack asked.

Elliot and Buzz exchanged glances.

"Maybe you were too busy mooning over her yesterday, buddy, because she went on this epic rant of all the ways she was going to"—Elliot looked at Nicki—"facilitate your demise for ducking out on her after you promised you wouldn't."

"Did she include me?" Curt asked.

"No. She was worried about you," Buzz said.

"Oh, that's nice." Curt smiled.

"How did she throw them out?" Elliot asked.

"Okay, so long story short, she got home from work early and walked into her bedroom and caught her scumbag fiancé being—cheating with a tramp from his office. She opened the window, scooped up their clothing, her purse, his wallet and keys, and dumped the whole shebang out the window. They must've been in shock, because they didn't get up, so Emi went to the closet and, in one armful, grabbed all his two-thousand-dollar suits, custom dress shirts, and silk ties and crammed them out the window, too." Nicki smiled. "Then she told them to get out of her apartment."

"Wow," Jack said.

"That's not even the best part. The bedroom windows are in the back overlooking the parking lot. They had to walk around the front of the building to retrieve them, and it was a chilly, sunny day."

"Babe, I don't get it," Curt said.

"That bastard and Tiffany Fake Tits had to walk out wearing nothing but the bedsheets. A whole new twist on the walk of shame." Nicki's lips curled into a wicked smile.

"Wow," Elliot said. "Evil genius."

Jack implored her, "Nicki, please."

"I can't, okay, I've already been a bad friend. Ever since it happened, she's been beating herself up over it." Nicki burned with fury. "I was supposed to take her out tonight, so she wouldn't sit home alone. She's done enough of that the last three weeks. This gutted her." Nicki took a deep breath. "Jack, you don't know what she's been through besides this. Not that everyone doesn't deserve happiness, but Emi, well, she deserves it more than most."

Jack heaved a sigh. "She told me about her family."

Nicki jumped up and paced. *Holy shit.* She'd known Emi two years before she'd told her the whole story. The accident, her rehab, her grandparents abandoning her. She knew that Emi hadn't told Sully about it until they'd been dating for several months.

She walked to Curt, who opened his arms to her, and she rested her head on his chest. Would Emi really never talk to her again? It was a possibility. She had her reasons for not staying in touch with Jack, and Nicki wished she knew what they were.

She shrugged out of Curt's embrace, picked up her cell, and dialed Emily, but it went straight to voicemail.

Jack stood and looked her in the eyes. They shone with love. For Emi. How was she supposed to resist?

She grabbed Curt's notebook off the table and wrote her friend's address and phone number. She said a silent prayer that Emi would forgive her as she handed Jack the paper. When he hugged her, she whispered, "Don't you fucking hurt her."

Jack pulled back and looked her in the eyes. "I won't."

Chapter Thirty

J ack texted Jeff Em's address and then ran to his room,
showered, and was on his way to see her in fifteen
minutes.

It was almost one, but he needed to talk to Em now. It was
selfish, but he couldn't wait. To see her, talk to her, beg her, to
give them a chance. He considered calling, but what he had to
say needed to be said in person. And she couldn't hang up on
him. But she could slam the door in his face.

He closed his eyes and rested his head against the seat.
He'd give her all the time she needed, but she needed to
understand he'd be waiting. The SUV pulled up outside her
apartment complex. Jack broke out into a sweat, and his pulse
hammered through his veins. *Don't fuck this up.*

The cool night air breezed past him as he stood at the
bottom of the stairs that led up to her door. He took a
steadying breath, exhaled, and started up the stairs but
stopped. It was just like she'd described it. *Their stair.* Taking
out his phone, he snapped a picture.

Feeling inspired, he jogged up the stairs. His mouth was
dry as his finger hovered over the doorbell.

EMILY TOSSED AND TURNED, BUT SHE COULDN'T sleep because she couldn't get comfortable. At least, that was what she told herself. It was almost one, and she needed to sleep, needed the escape.

She'd sat at the computer and written a smoking hot sex scene. It didn't take long, because she broke her one rule. She wrote about her own sex life—Jack and her in front of the mirror in his hotel room. She'd never use it in a book, but she needed to get it out of her head. She'd been sure after her failed attempt at self-pleasuring that writing out the scene would allow her to either get off or fall asleep. Neither had happened.

Turning on the light, she picked up Nicki's manuscript. She was on the second chapter and made a few notes but couldn't concentrate.

The doorbell rang.

Looking at the clock, she saw it was ten minutes later than the last time she'd looked. Only one person would ring her doorbell this late. *Nicki. Good. Let the murdering begin.*

She threw the manuscript on the bed and got up. After her shower, she'd put on her favorite oversized college T-shirt that ended well below her knees. She didn't bother with a robe and slipped her feet into slippers. This wouldn't take long. If Nicki was smart, she'd just run. She should know better than to come here when Emily was freshly pissed off.

She walked down the hall into the living room and stomped down the stairs. Not bothering to look in the peephole, she undid the security chain, turned the deadbolt, and flung the door open with such force it hit the wall.

It wasn't Nicki.

"Jack?" Emily choked out. "What are you doing here?" She tried to kill the smile that crossed her lips. There was no use in encouraging him. After he was gone, she'd examine why she was so happy to see him.

"I forgot to give you this." Jack handed her a twenty-dollar bill.

Emily looked at the money. "What's this?"

He smiled that lopsided grin of his. "The money you left for dinner Thursday night. I told you I was paying."

"So, you came all this way to give me twenty bucks?"

"Yup."

Not what she'd expected him to say. Why did he have to be so damn good-looking? The man had no business looking so good at one in the morning, especially when she looked a mess. Old T-shirt, hair falling out of her ponytail holder, eyes still puffy, and she had no makeup on. Whenever she cried, her skin got blotchy, and it took hours to go away. She tucked the twenty into the pocket of her shirt. "What happened?" Her fingers gently touched the bump on Jack's forehead. He flinched so Emily withdrew her hand.

Jack looked down. "Fell."

He looked embarrassed and contrite. Emily's heart flipped. She closed her eyes because she had to get the wild torrent of her emotions under control. She resisted the urge to ask him in so she could take care of him. That would only end one way, in bed. Now it was something deep in her belly that flipped, sending a warmth throughout her body. The oversized T-shirt would do nothing to hide her hardening nipples. *Shit.* She crossed her arms and tried for humor. "On what? Concrete? That's a huge bump."

"No. Slipped and fell in the shower and hit my head on the wall trying to get up." Jack shuffled his feet as he raised his eyes to meet hers.

Fuck. His eyes sparkled, and she resisted the urge to fan herself. It was another brisk spring night—Emily should be cold—but sweat formed between her shoulders. Hadn't she gotten enough of a Jack McBride fix? This was ridiculous. He was just a guy. A really hot, sexy, kind, caring, thoughtful —*STOP*. "Were you dizzy?" She stepped closer and her nose was assaulted by the stench of alcohol. "You smell like a distillery."

"Yeah." Jack took a step back. "I'm pretty sure the falling was due to the drinking." Jack looked down again.

Emily couldn't help but feel like this was her fault. "Jack—"

"I'm a grown man, Em, this is on me."

"When?"

Jack looked away.

"So this *is* my fault because I lied to you."

"I didn't leave you much choice, did I?" Wind whipped a few strands of hair in front of her eyes, and Jack tucked them behind her ear, his fingers lingering for a few seconds.

Emily suppressed the urge to lean her cheek into his palm and was sorry as soon as his hand dropped back to his side. What was wrong with her? The full implication of Jack's actions hit her. "Before your gig?"

Jack nodded.

Heat flooded her body and not the good kind. She'd known he was attached, knew he'd be hurt, but never considered he'd drown his pain in alcohol. She stepped out and closed the door behind her. The landing outside, that she shared with the first-floor apartment, had built-in benches on either side. Tucking the T-shirt under her, she sat. The bench was cold but did nothing to cool off the guilt she felt.

Jack shrugged off his black leather jacket and placed it around her shoulders before sitting next to her. "Em, I forced you to lie. You told me all day that you were leaving, and I was an arrogant fuck thinking I'd convince you to stay." He took her hand. "I was irresponsible for getting drunk before a gig, totally my own fault."

Emily stared at their joined hands. She swallowed the lump in her throat. She'd expected to live with the consequences of her lie, but since Jack had no idea where she lived, she'd never thought she'd see him again. The guilt threatened to overwhelm her. How had he found her? "Nicki." Emily's jaw tightened.

"It's not her fault. I made her tell me."

Emily's anger rose, and she grabbed on to it. She stood and paced. Nicki had betrayed her. Emily shrugged off Jack's jacket because her skin felt like it was on fire. *How could she?* Her best friend. She seethed with anger, and it seeped from her pores. She opened her mouth so she could breathe because she couldn't seem to get enough oxygen in her lungs.

She stood at the railing for several seconds before she realized that Jack stood next to her. "How exactly does one make a grown woman tell?" She didn't try to keep the anger and sarcasm out of her voice, but she'd hoped it covered the hurt. When Jack didn't answer, she turned toward him. "Cat got your tongue? You can't save her."

"She didn't want to tell me. She told me you'd be pissed and never forgive her." Jack brushed a tear off her cheek with his thumb.

"And yet, here you are."

"Because I told her I was in love with you."

Emily groaned. Yeah, that'd do it. No matter how many times her heart had been broken, Nicki was a hopeless romantic; no way she could've resisted spilling. Emily's anger drained away, and she slumped against the railing. Anger had been a blessing, taking over for the confusion she'd been feeling since she'd gotten home. The confusion returned, and having Jack here only made it worse. As far as she was concerned, there wasn't anything left to say. She knew how he felt, and he knew how she didn't feel.

Stalemate.

Chapter Thirty-One

J ack tried and failed to not think of her naked. The T-shirt covered her completely, but she wasn't wearing a bra. He'd seen her, and his mind went there. Emily naked in the shower, on his bed, in his bed. Under him, over him, up against the wall. Damn. His heart thudded in his chest, and he started to sweat. God, she was beautiful. All his good intentions vanished. He didn't want to wait. He wanted to be with her now. Not just sexually but in every way. He wanted to fall asleep with her in his arms every night and wake up with her every morning. And spend every minute together in between.

She'd been crying; he knew that was his fault. Jack wanted to ease her guilt, but he didn't think she'd let him. She was stubborn that way. Other ways too. As the silence drew out between them, Jack knew he'd have to stick with the plan he'd formed on the ride over here. He'd give her time. It might kill him, but he'd do it. Just seeing her filled the hole in his chest, and his heart resumed beating. He also knew he'd need to confess what happened with Tabitha. Hopefully, Em would forgive him, but he couldn't have that hanging over his head.

Emily sighed. "So, Nicki's still with Curt?"

"Yeah." Jack scrunched his eyes at the memory. "If it's any consolation, I saw more of Curt and Nicki than I'd ever want to."

"You busted in on them?"

"Sort of. Wouldn't have been necessary if Curt would've answered the phone, but Elliot insisted we had to get your address tonight."

"Elliot was there, too?"

"And Buzz."

"Wow, you guys are really close."

Jack laughed. "Being on the road together for the last eight years, you see way more than you want to. Let's just say we were all happy when we could afford privacy."

Emily scrunched her face.

Her tension had eased, so Jack continued. "Our first tour consisted of us in a Chevy van pulling our gear in a trailer, driving from bar to bar down the East Coast. We didn't have the money to stay in even the most questionable establishments."

Emily turned from the railing and sat. "What about showering?"

"Lots of sink washing in gas station bathrooms, and a few times a week, well, those rent by the hour motels come in handy." Jack laughed. Those places would charge for another hour even if you were a minute over, and they hadn't had any money to spare. The one time they'd gone over, they hadn't eaten the rest of the day.

"Where did you sleep?"

"In the van, in sleeping bags."

"But you were getting paid."

"Yeah, but most of the money we earned went to gas, insurance, instrument repair that we couldn't do ourselves, a fund if the van broke down, then whatever money was leftover we spent on food. We'd all worked while we lived in the city and saved as much as we could. Luckily, Curt had a cell phone and a GPS that his folks had insisted we take. Our folks chipped in and bought the van and we rented the trailer. It took us months to plan our first tour."

Emily leaned back on the bench.

Jack was sweating and his palms were damp. "Em, I came here to…" He had to give her time. "I know you're not ready, so let's keep in touch until you are." *Wow, that was eloquent.*

"You know that's not the only problem." Emily stood, and her hands gripped the railing.

That again. "You don't have to be in the spotlight." Jack stood next to her, and when she turned to look at him, he was a goner. Again. He wanted to pull her into his arms and kiss her until she gave in.

Emily sighed. "You can't go anywhere without being recognized. And you're on tour for twenty months. It would never work."

Jack wasn't giving up. "It worked for your parents."

She nodded. "Yeah, but they had a solid relationship and a plan when my dad joined the Marines." Emily faced him. "Other than sexually, we don't know if we're even compatible."

Jack shrugged. "You'd have to give us a chance to find out." Before he went any further, he needed to come clean. "I…fooled around with another woman tonight." He closed his eyes; he couldn't bear to see the hatred in hers. After a few grueling seconds, he opened his eyes.

Emily turned to him. "Jeez, Jack, way more information than I needed." A small smile played across her lips.

Was she laughing at him? This wasn't funny. He'd almost cheated. He was an almost cheater, and he hated himself. Maybe she had no feelings for him at all. "You're not mad?"

"Jack, we aren't together. You're free to fool around with whoever you want."

"But I want us to be together. I don't want any other woman. You're it for me."

Emily huffed. She was exasperated with him again, but Jack refused to let what he did for a living prevent them from being together. He didn't understand why that was such a problem for her, but he'd find out, then he'd fix it, and she'd have no more reasons why they couldn't be together.

She turned to look at him, ready for battle.

He faced her, smiling.

EMILY'S FACE HEATED AND RAGE RETURNED. *WHY IS he being so stubborn?* As much as she hurt after what Sully had done, she understood now, in a way she hadn't two days ago, that she would recover. It would take time, but she'd get over it. Get over him. Get over what she'd thought they'd have together, and the life they'd planned. But that day wasn't today.

She couldn't make him promises. And the thought of a relationship with anyone made her stomach turn. Emily took a deep breath to keep from retching. She would get over Sully, but would she ever be able to trust so completely again?

Jack's smile blinded her. Oh, fuck. Her anger melted away for the second time tonight, abandoning her. She clutched at it, reminding herself that he'd come here, when she asked him not to, begged him to leave her alone. But it was gone and with it the righteous indignation she needed to pull off sending him away. The iron fist that had gripped her heart, squeezing every last ounce of good will from her for the past three weeks, melted. Despite herself, she laughed.

"What's so funny?" Jack's smile widened and his eyes sparkled.

Emily shook her head, trying to catch her breath. "All the women of Oakdale will wake up tomorrow, pantyless, since that smile just melted them all off."

Jack stepped closer. "I'm only concerned with one woman's panties." He brushed another stray hair off her face. "Yours." He looked down at her feet, then slowly returned his gaze to her face. "Did yours melt?"

Emily cleared her throat. "I'm sure they would've...if I'd been wearing any."

Jack swallowed hard. His fingers went to her thigh and bunched the T-shirt up until he reached the hem and then his hand trekked until he reached bare hip. He licked his lips. He seemed to have trouble breathing.

"Em, why aren't you wearing panties?"

Emily closed her eyes at his touch. His hand caressed her hip in small circles. She had a smartass remark, but it vanished as soon as he touched her. "Um..."

"Yes?"

"Well, I'd tried to..."

"Tried to?" Jack's hand continued circling, and lust shone in his eyes.

Damn him, he knew. "Get off."

"Only tried?" He smirked.

Bastard. "Tried and failed." Two could play this game. He was hard. She licked her lips slowly.

He groaned.

Ha.

Jack stepped closer, hand still circling, but making no attempt to move. He smelled good, clean, no cologne. He looked even better. She was out of her league here, in more ways than one. She wanted to step back, run inside her apartment, lock the door, and hide under the covers. But her legs refused to move. Refused. *How dare they?* She was in control here not them. Except the part of her that was in control had no intention of moving. Her lips were swollen, and her juices moistened the inside of her thighs. Her nipples were painfully hard. Emily wanted his mouth on her.

Jack dropped to his knees. She put her hands on his head, stopping him. She shook her head. This was crazy, they were outside, in front of her apartment, and there was more than enough light from the fixture for anyone to see what he was doing. Then she noticed the SUV. *Oh shit.* Jeff must be here. She stepped back.

"Don't worry, he won't watch. Jeff's very discreet." Jack leaned in and inhaled.

"Jack, anyone looking out their windows would see..."

"Nuh-uh, it's like one thirty in the morning. All the good people of Oakdale are fast asleep. I need to taste you. Please?" He looked up at her, and the heat in his eyes threatened to ignite her.

A moan escaped Emily's lips. Jack's hands caressed both hips before moving back to cup her bare butt. *Shit.* "Stop." Emily blinked and tried to clear her lust-clouded brain. She couldn't believe she'd been about to let him go down on her outside, in front of her building. What was she thinking? Truth was, she wasn't thinking, she was feeling. Pure lustful bliss. And that was the problem. Feeling, that's how she got in this mess with him. Being with him felt so fucking good. Normal. Her mind was at peace. She didn't think of Sully, or weddings, or honeymoons, just Jack. And right now, he was on his knees, wanting to taste her, to pleasure her. She'd definitely lost her fucking mind. How could she make any decision in the state she was in?

Jack stood and smiled at her. Emily took a deep breath. Being with him was wrong. Walking away yesterday had been the right thing to do. Her knees felt weak, and she barely made it to the bench before she collapsed.

When he crouched down beside her, she tried to look away, but he held her chin, his thumb lightly brushing her lips. She tried to speak, but he stopped her with a gentle kiss that ended too soon.

For the first time in three weeks, Emily said in her head what she'd been trying to avoid. She was supposed to get married yesterday. They should be getting up in a few hours to board the True Love for their three-week European honeymoon cruise.

"Your wedding would've been yesterday. I think you should cut yourself a break."

Jack's voice cut through the awful thoughts in her head. It took a second to process what he said. "How did you know?" Her head throbbed. She preferred the other part of her body throbbing, but that was gone now, and she felt broken again.

Jack raised a brow at her.

"Nicki." Every part of her body ached with exhaustion, and she couldn't even muster the strength to get mad at her.

"She remembered after we'd busted in on them. She was inconsolable. Said she was the worst friend ever." Jack tilted her chin up, so she had no choice but to look into his eyes. "Why didn't you tell me? I would've understood."

Fresh tears filled her eyes, streaming down her cheeks, leaving wet streaks on her T-shirt. Jack hugged her as the first sobs wracked her body. She didn't deserve to be comforted by him, but since she felt like she'd explode if he let go, she let him. She cried on his shoulder as he stroked her back, whispering in her ear that everything would be okay.

Nothing was okay. Taking comfort from him wasn't okay, so she pulled back, and he let her go. "I couldn't say it out loud. I couldn't even think about it without my brain feeling like it would burst. Nothing has hurt this bad since—" She couldn't say it, couldn't deal with those memories on top of this; it was too much. "I can't trust what I think anymore. I thought Sully loved me, thought we were happy. I thought we were getting married and we'd grow old together. Everything I've thought for the past four years has been a lie."

Chapter Thirty-Two

J ack hated seeing her so torn up. His body filled with rage. He wasn't a violent guy, but he wanted to tear that fucker apart. Jack pushed to his feet and paced; he'd deal with his feelings later. Right now, he had to help her. He took a few deep breaths, and the cold air burned his lungs. She needed him to support her right now.

"Is everything okay here?" Jeff's voice cut into Jack's thoughts.

Jeff stood at the bottom of the stairs, his tall, heavily muscled body tensed.

"Yes," Emily said and hiccupped.

Jeff nodded curtly and went back to the SUV.

"Did he think I'd hit you?" Emily asked.

Jack turned back to her. Her beautiful face was tear stained and her eyes still teary. Heat started in his chest and radiated outward until it reached his toes. "He's worried about you. He would've kicked my ass if you said I made you cry."

"You didn't make me cry." Emily chuckled. "Shouldn't he be looking out for you? I mean, you pay him to protect you right?"

Jack shifted. He trusted Jeff implicitly. "I pay him to protect me, but he likes you. If I did anything to hurt you, he'd kill me in heartbeat." Jack liked that about Jeff. And when he and Em moved ahead, there was no one he'd trust more to keep her safe while he was away.

Emily smiled up at him. "I wouldn't let him kill you, maybe just hurt you a little.

Her smile warmed him further. His body reacted to being so close to her, but he resisted the urge to pull her into his arms and kiss the daylights out of her. Then carry her upstairs and—now was not the time. She needed to decide to move forward with him with a clear head.

"Em, there has to be a way for us to be together. I know it's not ideal. In three months, I have a month-long break before we head to Europe. We could spend time together, go out to dinner, catch a movie. It can be casual, I just want to keep in touch." He was pushing her again and trying to lock her into a commitment. Despite his best intentions, he couldn't stop himself.

Emily heaved a sigh. "Jack, I'm exhausted. I can't make any decisions right now. I'm afraid that anything I say will be the wrong answer. I..."

He knew what she didn't say. She didn't want to hurt him again. If he was smart, he'd take the hint and leave and never look back. But he couldn't. He'd tried that tonight, and he'd felt like he was dying. He was normally a patient guy, but despite constantly reminding himself he needed to be patient, he kept pushing. Maybe because in his heart he knew two things. He was head over heels, completely and utterly in love with her, and the fucker would be back. He believed her when she said there was no way she would get back with her ex, but Jack was also concerned with every other male in a hundred-mile radius. A lot could happen in three months. She wasn't looking to meet anyone, which was exactly when someone new dropped into the picture. Like she'd done to him.

"Will you call me in the morning, to let me know you're okay?" Jack asked.

EMILY SIGHED AGAIN. SHE COULD BARELY STAND. IF he'd asked to stay, she'd have said yes, they'd have sex, and it'd be the temporary relief she needed. But she wouldn't do that to him again. She'd feel the repercussions of her actions the last two days for months. Surely a phone call would be okay? His voice calmed her. As confused as she felt, his being here somehow made her feel better.

"Okay." Emily waited for her brain to scream at her that she should make a clean break, not lead Jack on, or give him hope. Silence. She exhaled the breath she'd been holding. "I don't have your number."

"Get your phone and I'll give it to you."

She went inside and grabbed her phone, half-expecting Jack to follow, but he didn't.

She handed him her phone, and he added his contact information. When he handed the phone back, their fingers touched and neither pulled away. They stood there, staring at each other, with that slightest of touches connecting them. She'd never felt more connected to a person than she did at that moment. That should've had her yanking her hand away, but instead, she stared into his eyes. It was a mistake, but she just couldn't break the contact. She'd been wafting through the ether for the past three weeks, scared she'd never feel the ground beneath her feet again.

Jack pulled his hand back and kissed her briefly before walking down the stairs and getting into the SUV. She watched as it pulled away until the taillights faded in the distance.

After a small pep talk, her legs obeyed and walked her inside, up the stairs, down the hall, and into her bedroom. She fell face first onto the mattress and was asleep before she hit it.

Emily awoke to a crash of thunder. She rolled onto her back. She couldn't tell if it was dark out because it was early or because it was raining. Memories danced on the edge of her consciousness. She was supposed to do something. When the clock in the living room chimed, she forced herself to ignore it. She didn't want to know what time it was. She wanted to go back to sleep and stay there. Stupid clock chimed a lot. It had to be at least eight. Damn.

Jack. Her heart rate sped up just thinking his name.

She'd promised to call him when she woke up, so she grabbed her phone off the nightstand and turned it on. Three missed calls. Two from Nicki and a text, but Emily wasn't ready to deal with her yet.

The other call was from Vince. She'd promised she'd call this weekend, but it was only Saturday. It was only five in California, so it was too early to call him. Vince wouldn't care what time it was if she needed him. She grabbed her note pad and pen and wrote call Vince in block letters. She figured she had the rest of the day before he got on a plane. She didn't want him coming, yet another reminder of what yesterday should've been.

Instead of calling Jack, she stalled by using the bathroom. Emily didn't know what to say to him. Did he even expect her to say anything? Or did he just want to know she'd survived the night? With Jack she couldn't tell. He had this maddening way of drawing her into conversations she didn't want to have. Sully had always respected her space that way. He never pushed her to share when he knew she was upset, and she'd appreciated it.

Even though she'd passed out after Jack left, exhaustion still plagued her. Emily's body felt leaden, and her eyes kept fluttering shut. The tug of sleep beckoned, but she'd promised Jack. *Crap.* She thumbed through her contacts and tapped on his name. Maybe she'd luck out and get his voicemail.

"Good morning, baby."

His voice was rich and soft, and it made her stomach flip-flop. What was she, twelve?

"How'd you sleep?"

"I passed out as soon as I hit the bed, but I'm still so tired." She meant to simply say thanks for asking and be off the phone. Damn him.

"It's no wonder, since you haven't been sleeping well, you're mentally and emotionally drained. You need to take it easy today."

She had her out. "I plan to. I just wanted to call and let you know I was okay. I'm going to go back to sleep now. Good—"

"You really should eat something."

She had no food in her apartment. Her fridge looked like a bachelor's: a couple bottles of condiments, milk that was most likely sour, and half and half. She'd run out of cereal on Thursday but couldn't drag herself to the store before Nicki had arrived to leave for the concert. But she wouldn't tell Jack that.

"I'm not hungry."

"Did you eat last night?"

She'd had no appetite after what she'd done to him, but Emily wouldn't tell him that either.

"I'll take your silence as a no. You need to eat. Do you have any food in the house?"

"Yes." It wasn't a lie; she had stuff in the freezer. She'd order a pizza. Later.

"What food?"

"Jack—"

"Em. Glad we got the names straight. After my breakup with Christie, I don't think I ate a real meal for at least a couple of days. I'm guessing you have no food in the house."

She didn't want to lie. Damn him. "I have plenty of frozen stuff."

"I'll be there in an hour with breakfast." Jack hung up.

"Wait, what?"

He was gone. *Fuck.*

Chapter Thirty-Three

J ack hated hanging up on her, but he knew she'd protest, and he didn't want to give her the chance to say no. He wanted to take care of her, but he'd bet his '59 Flame Top that she'd rather deal on her own.

He'd woken early; he'd had a lovely dream about her. Jack could practically taste her on his lips, and since his morning erection ached for release, he'd obliged with images of her: Em riding him, her head thrown back as she came, Em on all fours. That had done it. Even jerking off to her felt great. He'd gotten up and showered. That led to memories of showering with her, how the water cascaded over her naked body, the shampoo dripping down her back, and over her perfect ass as he'd washed her. That made him hard, so he jerked it again.

Jack arranged with Anthony to have breakfast to go in thirty minutes.

He dialed Jeff, who picked up on the first ring. "What's up?"

"Leaving for Emily's in thirty-five minutes." He kept it short because that's how Jeff liked it.

Jeff cleared his throat. "Is that wise?"

The only other time Jeff questioned him was when he'd wanted to escort Emily on Friday without security. Jeff had followed them at a discreet distance.

"We're bringing breakfast. Emily has no food in the house, and she didn't eat last night. I'm worried about her."

"I'll be waiting in thirty." Jeff hung up.

It had taken Jack a little time to get used to Jeff's curtness. He didn't chitchat and was always on guard. But Jeff had a soft spot for Emily. On the ride back to the hotel this morning, Jeff questioned him further about Em's tears. Since he was still breathing, Jack must've convinced him that he hadn't been the cause. Now there were two men who wanted to tear the fucker limb from limb. Jeff would have to incapacitate him to beat Jack to it though. Em was his girl, and she was his responsibility to protect.

Fuck. So much for patience. He'd fuck this up if he didn't dial it down, but no matter how many times he reminded himself of that, the primal need to protect her, to be with her, overwhelmed him. Jack's patience was shot to shit. He had never felt this strongly for a woman.

Anthony met Jack in the garage with thermal bags to keep their food warm.

The clouds and rain dissipated, and the sun shone brightly in a now cloudless sky. It was just after ten when they arrived. Jack grabbed the box that held the coffee, orange juice, and cream. As he walked up the stairs, he remembered their conversation, her lack of undergarments, and how he'd almost gotten to taste her. Damn. Taking a few deep breaths as he reached her door, he rang the bell.

After a minute, he rang again. Maybe she'd decided not to let him in. Setting the box on the bench, he took out his cell and tapped her number. It rang three times before she answered.

"Hello." Her voice was raspy.

"Hi. Breakfast is served." Jack decided on levity, keep it easy, no pressure. He heard her shuffling the covers aside.

"Sorry, fell back to sleep."

Jeff stood behind him with the thermal bags. Jack heard the lock turn and the chain clank against the doorframe. When she opened the door, the sight of her made his heart palpitate. She was still wearing the ugly, white oversized T-shirt, her hair was mostly out of the ponytail holder, and her eyes were still sleepy. Jeff cleared his throat. The sun highlighted the fact that she was naked beneath the T-shirt. Jack stepped in front of her to block Jeff's view.

Her eyes widened when she saw Jeff, and a blush crept up her face. She tugged the shirt down. "I'm sorry, I didn't realize Jack wouldn't be alone. Give me a sec." Emily closed the door over, returning a few moments later wearing a long sweater coat that went to her calves. "Come in."

She led them up a flight of stairs to her cozy living room. A well-used blue- and white-striped couch sat in front of the picture window with light oak end tables on either side. A matching rectangular oak coffee table was in front of the couch, and a darker oak entertainment center took up most of one wall. There was also a large black leather recliner that was much newer and seemed out of place. While there was no clutter, the place could use a good dusting.

They followed Emily past a small table and chairs and into the kitchen. Jeff placed the bags on the counter, and Em took the box from Jack and unpacked it. "Jeff, are you joining us?"

"Thank you, but I've eaten."

"Still get up at five?"

"Habit."

"My dad always kept that habit, too."

"What time do you want me to pick you up?" Jeff asked.

"Uh..." Jack hadn't thought that far ahead. He didn't want to assume he was spending the afternoon, but dammit he wanted to spend the afternoon. He wanted to spend forever.

"I have a buddy in the area," Jeff said, with an almost imperceptible nod.

"Great. I'll call you." Jack suspected that was Jeff speak for he had no intention of going back into the city, and he'd be close by.

"Emily, a pleasure to see you again." With a quick smile, Jeff turned, and in a few seconds, the front door opened and closed and then opened again. "Lock it," he yelled.

Emily complied and when she returned to the kitchen, she'd dressed in a pair of faded jeans and a black pullover sweater. Her hair was still a mess. She looked beautiful.

Damn. She'd probably put on underwear. Jack needed to get his mind out of the gutter, but the image of her in just the T-shirt, with the sun streaming into her apartment, made him hard again.

Emily took out plates, cups, and cutlery and laid them on the dining room table. Jack held out her chair, and with a small smile, she sat. He sat opposite her because the view was better and there was less chance he'd touch her. He was fairly certain touching was off the table right now.

They filled their plates, poured the coffee and juice, and ate in a comfortable silence. She looked tired. After they finished eating, Em stood and picked up her plate.

"I've got it," Jack said, standing and piling her plate onto his. "You're exhausted. Go lie down. I'll take care of everything."

"Jack..."

"It's okay, go lie down, I'll clean up, and then if you want me to leave, I will." He smiled to reassure her.

Her beautiful face was weary, but she forced a smile. "Thank you for breakfast. It was thoughtful." She turned and walked down the hallway.

Jack put the remaining food in the refrigerator. She didn't have a dishwasher, so he rolled up his sleeves and washed the dishes, laying a towel on the counter to let them air dry. It didn't take much to remember how he'd felt after Christie moved out. Every room had memories.

He walked down the hallway and stopped at the first door on the right. It was her office. Em had a nice little setup: a large wood desk, office chair, and bookshelves on two walls. He'd love to read her books, but she hadn't told him her pen name, and he didn't feel right about snooping.

He walked down the hall and stood in the doorway to her bedroom. Em sat on the edge of her bed, rubbing her right thigh. "Does it still hurt?"

"Always on rainy days and more when I don't keep up with yoga and strength training."

The thought of Em having even a small amount of physical pain all the time, made his heart ache. She looked so worn down. Jack knew he should go, but he didn't want to leave her like this. Or at all. But that was selfish. If he stayed, they'd end up in bed. Sex was a great distraction from emotional pain, and Em had that in spades right now. If all he wanted from her was sex, he'd convince her to let him stay, but he wanted more. Jack wanted it all.

And that would take time.

LEG PAIN WAS THE LEAST OF EMILY'S PROBLEMS. Jack had said last night that they could keep in touch until she was ready to date again, but right now, she didn't feel like she'd ever be ready. The irony of meeting Jack now, when she was still licking her wounds from her breakup, wasn't lost on her. She envied Nicki's ability to move on so fast. Of course, her relationship with Tad had only been four months old, but that didn't lessen the hurt of his cheating. She'd been with Sean for four years, and they'd made plans for their future. She'd thought that once her wedding day had passed, she would feel better, but if anything, she felt worse. Even though he'd only moved in with her after they got engaged, he'd imprinted himself on every part of her home. She swallowed past the lump that formed in her throat.

"I'm gonna go." Jack took out his phone and called Jeff.

Emily nodded and exhaled. She was glad he didn't make her ask him to leave, because she'd spent the entire time he'd been here going back and forth between wanting to have sex with him and asking him to leave. If he'd offered to stay, she wouldn't have refused. But that would've been selfish. She'd already hurt him once, and she didn't want to hurt him again. Her brain felt like swiss cheese, and she just couldn't make any more decisions right now. Emily had always been able to figure out the right thing to do, and once her mind was made up, she never vacillated. Until Jack.

"Jeff will be here in fifteen minutes."

Emily pushed to her feet. "Okay." Jack followed her into the living room. "Thanks again for breakfast."

Jack smiled that lopsided grin that caused her heart to flip. "My pleasure. Maybe we could have dinner while I'm here?"

Emily opened her mouth but nothing came out. He must be a glutton for punishment. Couldn't he see she was in no shape for this?

Jack looked down. "Em, I meant what I said. We can go as slowly as you need to. Is it okay if I call you later?"

She closed her eyes and tried to muster the strength to cut him off. "Jack—"

"It's okay. How about you call me, to let me know how you're doing so I don't worry."

His beautiful blue eyes held hope, and she just couldn't

bring herself to crush it. "Okay." There was probably a circle in hell for people like her.

After Jack left, she texted Eddie, Vince, and Nicki that she was okay. Eddie and Vince's responses were identical: *LIAR*. Nicki's response was to please call her. But Emily couldn't talk now, not without having a complete breakdown, and she didn't want to cry anymore.

A second text from Eddie read "Call or else." She'd already promised to call Vince this weekend, and she had no doubt he'd get on a plane if she didn't. Now she had Eddie threatening to drive up. She tapped Eddie's picture, and he answered on the first ring.

"Talk to me," Eddie demanded.

Emily smiled. Eddie wouldn't tolerate any of the pat answers that she'd been giving people these last three weeks. He'd only accept complete honesty from her, or he'd be on her doorstep. "I'm...confused."

"Totally understandable. What else?"

"I hurt." Tears welled in her eyes, and it was hard to breathe. "I still don't know what happened."

"With fuckhead? That's what Vince and I are calling him now."

"Yes"—Emily smiled in spite of her tears—"I don't know what happened with fuckhead."

"Did he even try to explain?"

Emily's breakfast threatened to come up, so she swallowed hard. "I've only seen him once when he came to pick up the ring and tickets and drop off his keys the Tuesday after... I couldn't even look at him. He said he'd be back to pick up the rest of his stuff." *Shit.* She hadn't told Eddie or Vince about that.

"His shit is still there?"

Fuck. "Yeah."

"Not for long, I'll be up later and we'll clear it out. Call him and tell him to come get his shit today or—"

"I can't."

Eddie ground his teeth together. "Can't or won't?"

"Can't. He's not here."

"Where the fuck is he?"

"Cruise."

Eddie growled. "Are you fucking telling me that motherfucking fuckhead is on your goddamned honeymoon cruise?"

"It's not my honeymoon anymore."

"Emily Grace Prescott." Eddie took a deep breath, and his voice softened. "Why didn't you tell me?"

Tears rolled down her cheeks. "I couldn't..."

"Shit." Eddie swore again. "He took *her*, didn't he?"

"Yeah. I don't know why I care."

"You care because you loved him, and it's an exceptionally shitty thing for him to do," Eddie said. "Want me to beat him up?"

"No... Yes... No."

Eddie laughed. "Okay, for now I won't, but I cannot promise that Vince will be so easily swayed. You know he's a hothead."

Emily laughed. Vince was one of the most laid-back people she'd ever met. "Yeah, Eddie, he's the hothead."

"Want me to come get you? You can spend the weekend. The boys will keep you busy."

Eddie's sons, Teddy, Michael, and Nicholas, had been practicing for weeks to be her ring bearers. "No. I'd be terrible company."

Eddie scoffed. "What company? You are family, and your nephews miss you. Sheryl and I miss you too, it's been too long, and the worst thing you can do right now is isolate yourself."

"I need time."

"Emi, you've been down this road before. Too much time alone isn't good for you."

"I just can't."

Eddie sighed. "Okay. But promise me you'll call. You know I fucking hate texting. It's a bullshit cop-out for real conversation."

"I'll call you later in the week." Emily's heart felt a little less heavy knowing she had such wonderful friends. They'd give her the time she needed, but not so much that she'd drown herself in isolation. "Love you."

"Love you too, beautiful. Bye."

Emily hadn't felt this lost since she'd woken up in the hospital with no memory. The doctor had told her she'd been in an auto accident. During the surgery on her leg, she'd gone into cardiac arrest, and she'd been in a coma for a week. He said her memory would most likely come back and not to worry. Those first hours had been so weird. She'd felt like she was inside a bubble where the world around her turned but she stayed still. The way the doctors and nurses spoke to her, she'd known something awful was coming and that everyone around her knew what it was. Then she started asking questions. When the doctor told her that her parents had been killed instantly and Riley had died three days later, Emily stopped asking questions.

Emily had thought she'd put the accident and everything that followed behind her. It had taken three surgeries and months of physical therapy before she could get around without the wheelchair. Once she'd moved in with the Boyers, Eddie had driven up every weekend to continue her physical therapy. Eddie had refused to give up on her, even when she'd given up on herself. For two years, she'd only left the house for doctor visits. She never thought she'd have a normal life again.

When she'd fallen in love with Sean, for the first time she

felt like she could have a normal life and a family of her own. When she'd caught him cheating, everything she'd planned for her future vaporized. Again. She knew time would heal her pain, and she wasn't starting from scratch this time.

Emily liked Jack, but it wasn't enough. There would be no slow with him and she wasn't ready. He said he understood that she needed time, but it wasn't just that. He was famous, and his career depended on visibility, and life with Jack would never be normal. He'd be on tour for twenty months which made dating impossible. Seeing him this week would only give him hope that at some point she'd be able to be with him. He couldn't give her what she needed. And she doubted she could give him what he deserved.

Emily had already used Jack once to get through her wedding day. She wouldn't do that to him again.

She was a certifiable mess.

Chapter Thirty-Four

Motherfucker! By the time I got to his hotel this morning, Jack was gone. It's been too long. He needs a reminder.

It's my time, and nothing will keep us apart. That stupid whore was an unexpected kink in my plans but that didn't last. How could it? I'm the woman for Jackie. No one will ever be more devoted to him than I am. I'm scheduling my life around his, and if that's not devotion, I don't know what is.

I lay the magazines on the table next to the scissors, glue, and plain white paper. Grabbing the first one, I tear out all the pages with pretty blonde models and cut their heads off.

Enough fun, I need to focus. I do enjoy working on my love letters.

DURING SOUNDCHECK, THE BAND WORKED ON "With You." The guys from Xerxes and the crew applauded. He ran through his vocal warm-ups and did yoga, as the deep breathing really helped his breath control while singing. Last night he'd fucked up. But tonight, with Em maybe giving them a chance, he felt great.

When Curt began his pre-gig rituals, Nicki walked over to Jack and sat. "Does she hate me?"

"No." He'd hoped to hear from Em by now. "You haven't heard from her?"

"She texted me earlier that she was okay. I asked her to call me, but she replied that she didn't want to talk anymore. I spoke to Eddie, he talked to Emi, but he's worried."

"Eddie?" Em hadn't mentioned him, only Vince. Then again, he'd known her less than two days.

Nicki smiled. "He was her physical therapist. Emi said she wouldn't have made it without him and Vince. They're all still really close."

"She met Vince in the hospital, too?

"Yeah, they'd both been transferred to the facility where Eddie worked. Vince wrapped his car around a tree and was hurt pretty badly from what Emi told me. I've talked to him, but he moved to California before Emi and I met." Nicki scoffed. "I was finally going to meet the elusive Vince at the wedding."

Jack nodded.

Nicki's smile faded. "Emi's so damn stubborn, she's beating herself up for what that fucking bastard did." She stood and paced. "I still can't believe it. I never saw it coming. None of us did. She'll obsess over this until she makes herself nuts."

"I wish I knew how to help her." Jack stood, grabbed a bottle of water, and downed it. An uneasy feeling settled in the pit of his stomach.

A brisk knock sounded, and Walt opened the door. "Ten minutes, guys."

Jack's muscles were tight, so he stretched to try to loosen up. He couldn't wait for the gig to start so he could concentrate on something other than the unease that had settled inside.

Another brisk knock and Jeff entered. "It's time."

The guys formed a circle, all hands in. "Let's have a great gig," Curt said. Jeff led as security escorted them to backstage.

Holden handed Jack his black Gibson Les Paul Axcess, then handed Curt his Gibson Snow Falcon Flying V.

Curt strummed his guitar. "What the fuck, Holden?"

Holden hurried back to Curt, and both men looked at the guitar dumbfounded.

Jack shook his head. All the strings were slack. Curt hadn't used that guitar during soundcheck.

Curt ripped the guitar over his head and shoved it at Holden. "Get your shit together."

It took a lot to get Curt angry, but Jack understood. Curt's guitars were being fucked with, but Jack was convinced it wasn't Holden. The kid was far too grateful to do it on purpose, but someone had it in for Holden or Curt.

Holden quickly tightened the strings and tuned the guitar. He was the best guitar tech they'd ever had, and Jack had no intention of losing him. "Hey, man, calm down." Jack gripped Curt's shoulder.

The audience chanted for them.

Curt shook his head. "What the fuck is going on? Guitars don't disappear on their own, and strings damn sure don't get loosened like that on their own." Nicki hugged him.

Something was going on, but now wasn't the time to figure it out. Jack was sure Em would've had something funny to say to defuse the situation. She had a great sense of humor. His blood pumped faster just thinking about her. Maybe the unease he'd felt earlier had nothing to do with her. Someone was definitely fucking with Curt, and it needed to stop.

"Curt, I really don't know how this could've happened,"

Holden said as he handed him the guitar. Poor kid looked scared.

Viv stood behind Holden with a worried look on her face. Jack suspected they were seeing each other. They were both sweet kids.

"Sorry I overreacted," Curt said, shoulder bumping Holden as he passed.

Elliot smirked. "Ladies, if you're done with your tea party, maybe we could get out there?"

Curt gave Elliot the finger, and the band took the stage.

The only other bump in the gig was when Holden gave Curt the wrong guitar. Since they were lined up in order of changes, that could only happen if Holden lined them up wrong, which Jack didn't believe for a second. Someone else had switched them.

Jack had a word with Jeff about it after the encore. Jeff would have his guys keep an eye on things, and they'd get to the bottom of this.

When he got to the dressing room, Jack took a quick shower. It was Saturday night, and they were going to grab dinner before going to see a local band, Invisible Pawn, at The Rock House. Jack had talked to the guys about it, and they all wanted in. He hadn't heard back from Kevin yet, but they all agreed something needed to be done. They couldn't let The Rock House close.

They were ready to leave when Jack's cell rang. "With You" was Emily's ring tone, and Jack's heart skipped a beat. Elliot and Curt made kissy faces at him, and Buzz just smiled.

"Hey, baby," Jack said as he connected the call. "How are you?"

"Hi."

Something in the tone of her voice set off alarm bells. It must've shown on his face because Elliot and Curt stopped. "You okay?" He swallowed hard. He knew she wasn't.

"No."

Shit, one-word answers were bad. He took a deep breath and tried not to panic. She'd been so upset this morning. "You want me to come over?"

Silence. She'd had too much time to think, but he needed to stop thinking of himself. Her pain was raw, and he should be trying to help her. He knew what she was going to say before the words left her mouth, so he braced himself.

"Jack, I'm confused and can't seem to make up my mind, so I think I need to stop trying to. I don't think we should see each other again. I'm not ready, even for slow."

Stay calm. It had taken all his willpower to leave this morning without begging her to be with him now. He needed to tap into that willpower to let her off the hook. "I understand." He sat on the couch because he didn't have the energy to stand.

"I'm sorry, I don't want to hurt you again." She choked on a sob.

Jack's heart cracked into pieces. "I know. Of course, you're not ready. It's too soon." The pieces of his heart crumbled as he said the words, but this was what she needed. He'd do it. Jack wouldn't ask her to keep in touch. He'd send her flowers before he left. She needed time. He'd give it to her.

"I—"

"Em, it's okay. Goodnight," he said and hung up. If he'd stayed on the line, he'd have begged her to not cut him out.

Nicki's mouth dropped open, and she gasped. "You called her Em." Her smile widened and she nodded. "Just give her some time."

"I've had enough of this shit. Where does that motherfucker live? He needs to be taught a lesson." Buzz stood in front of Jack, hands fisted and face covered in fury. Elliot and Curt stood behind him. They were all in.

Nicki giggled, so Jack looked at her. "I had to talk Vince

and Eddie out of beating the shit out of him. Vince knows a good place to bury a body and everything. Now I have to let the air out of your tires."

"Why is that funny?" Curt asked.

"That's not what's funny. Emi is always talking me off the ledge over one thing or another, I guess it's rubbed off on me. I'm not exactly known for being the voice of reason." She looked up at Curt. "Besides, if you really want to kill him, you'll have to wait three weeks. He left this morning for vacation with that slut he cheated with."

This just got worse and worse. "You mean he's taking his cheat on what should've been their honeymoon?" It hurt to say the words. How was Em even holding up?

Nicki nodded.

"Fucking piece of shit," Elliot growled. He walked over to the wall and punched it.

They'd all been through bad relationships, but what happened to Em was shocking. No wonder she was confused. His breakup with Christie was a long time coming. He'd known that if she couldn't clean up it would never work between them, and he'd seen it unfold. Emily had been totally blindsided. Even Nicki, who he'd judged to be savvy, hadn't seen signs anything was wrong. Em was being strong, so he had to be, too. "Let's get dinner." Jack smiled at their shocked expressions. "Nicki thinks Em will come around, and I'm going with that. We need to eat."

"What about Invisible Pawn?" Curt asked.

Jack shrugged. "The show must go on, right?"

After they finished dinner, Jack's positive attitude hit the skids when he saw a girl who looked like Em getting into a cab with a guy. He knew it wasn't her, but the thought of him losing her made his stomach turn. He begged off going to The Rock House, so Jeff drove him back to the hotel.

Jack couldn't sleep. He thought about going to her. Em

was miserable, he was miserable, why couldn't they be miserable together? Of course, if he did go to her, he'd be happy, and she'd be more miserable because he wouldn't back off like she needed him to. He turned over and tried to get more comfortable, but his hand kept feeling the bed for her. Maybe he should get another room. In another hotel. On another planet.

He closed his eyes, and her face appeared. He thought back to Thursday night, how aggressive she'd been in the limo once she'd made up her mind. He imagined her sitting across from him, sliding onto her knees and walking over to him. Her hands on his belt buckle. He turned onto his back and rested his hand on his abdomen. Her smiling up at him as she lowered the zipper on his way too tight jeans. Ahh.

His phone was on the pillow next to his head, so when it blared "With You" because he'd forgotten to turn the ringer down, he almost yanked his dick off. He grabbed the phone with his other hand and connected the call. "Hey."

"Did I wake you?" she asked in a weak voice.

"No, I wasn't asleep." He sat up and adjusted the pillows behind his head. "You okay?" She didn't sound okay.

"I don't know what I am anymore."

"Want me to come over?" Luckily, he'd just gotten started. He laughed. Talking to her was so much better than jerking off. "I can be there in—"

"That's not necessary," she whispered.

"Okay." He took it as a good sign that she called him. She was still fragile but wanted to talk to him. Maybe he'd send her flowers Monday, and he could include a copy of the picture that Ariana had taken of them in Casa Amici's. He'd checked his email when he'd gotten back to The Yorkshire, and Dex had sent it earlier in the day. Ariana's thank-you package was already on the way to her. He'd added their picture to Em's phone number. He'd already looked at it about a thousand times.

"Jack, I'm sorry about before, calling you like that. I was so sure it was the right thing to do for you."

"For me?"

"Yes, ending it before you get more—"

Jack sat up and said through his teeth, "Don't you think that should've been my decision?"

Emily sighed. "I don't want to hurt you."

"And yet you have, twice." Jack didn't know why he said it. It was true but mean to point it out.

"I know, and I'm sorry."

She didn't make excuses, just accepted what she'd done. His anger drained away because he wasn't mad at her. She'd called him because she had something to say, so he'd wait for her to say it.

"I'm sorry for calling so late," Emily whispered.

Jack pushed the phone closer to his ear. "Em, why are you whispering?"

"Because... I don't want to disturb your neighbors."

Jack bolted out of bed. "Where are you?"

"In the hallway."

EMILY HEARD HIS HURRIED STEPS, AND SHE TAPPED the keypad icon on her phone and pressed the one digit to get Jack's attention.

"What?"

"Pants."

"Thanks, baby."

Seconds later, the door to his room opened, and his head popped out. He smiled when he saw her. He used the security latch to keep the door from locking and stepped into the hallway.

Emily shifted. Her butt hurt and she was cold. She'd pulled on black yoga pants, a T-shirt, and a hoodie but had forgotten her jacket when the InstaRide arrived.

Jack sat opposite her. "Hey." His eyes sparkled, as his smile reached into her soul and warmed her through.

"Hi." She felt like a schoolgirl as a blush crept up her cheeks. He'd pulled on baggy sweatpants and a wrinkled red T-shirt, and his feet were bare. Smiling back at him, she probably looked like a psycho.

"You look beautiful," he said.

Emily looked down. She had something to say, and if she had the courage to say it, there'd be no turning back. She was scared, but she kept coming back to Jack over and over. She'd convinced herself that she was breaking it off to protect him, but as soon as he'd hung up earlier, Emily knew she'd made an epic mistake. She wasn't ready for a new relationship, but he was right—their chance was here and now.

"You okay?" His face shadowed with concern.

"Better now than before." This was stupid. *Say it already.*

"How long have you been here?"

Emily looked at the time on her phone. "Hour."

"Why didn't you knock? Afraid I wouldn't let you in?"

Emily gave him a half smile. "Well, since you almost ran out here without pants on, I never thought you wouldn't let me in."

Jack smiled. "Yeah, thanks again for that. Don't need my junk on the internet."

"How would your junk get on the internet?" She hadn't been able to sleep, but now she couldn't keep her eyes open.

"These hallways have cameras." Jack pointed to the one a few rooms down.

Emily sighed. *Great.* Of course, there were security cameras at a hotel like this, and security just watched her sitting in the hallway outside Jack McBride's room like a groupie.

"It's late, you want me to take you home?"

"No. But we shouldn't..."

"Agreed." Jack stood and extended his hand and helped her up. Her legs were numb, and she stumbled a little before Jack's arm snaked around her waist. She looked up at him and smiled.

With his cute, lopsided grin in place, he said, "Don't worry, baby, I've got you. I won't let you fall."

Jack pushed the door open, and she walked inside. This time when the door closed behind them, Jack locked it and walked past her to the bedroom. He returned a few moments later with a pillow and blanket. "I put a pair of sweatpants and sweatshirt on the bed for you to sleep in. They'll be too big, but it's better than nothing."

Emily went into the bedroom and quickly changed. When she walked into the living room to go to bed, Jack lay out on the couch, his knees bent so he'd fit. "What are you doing?"

"Going to sleep, it's late." Jack yawned. He'd turned the gas fireplace on, which did a good job of taking the chill out of the room.

"Jack, this is ridiculous, I'm not kicking you out of your bed."

He sat up and glared at her. Through gritted teeth he said, "There is no way in hell you're sleeping on the couch."

Emily grit her teeth. "You don't fit on the couch."

"I'll be fine," Jack said through tight lips. He lay back down. "I'm extremely comfortable. Go to bed, Emily."

"This is stupid." Emily fisted her hands on her hips.

"What's stupid is you thinking you're going to sleep on this couch. You're my guest, ergo, I'm sleeping on the couch. Go to bed."

He closed his eyes, so he couldn't see the glare she leveled at him. Fine, if he wanted to be stubborn, let him sleep on the couch. He'll wake up all cramped. Emily stomped off to the bedroom, moved the blankets aside, and crawled into bed. Damn him, the bed was comfortable. But he wasn't despite his assurances to the contrary. He was being a gentleman as usual.

She closed her eyes and expected to fall asleep but didn't. Not because Jack was on the couch, but she hadn't said what she'd come to say. Her nerves were frayed, and she didn't like this unsettled feeling at all. She was usually confident in her decisions. But she hadn't been earlier, and she wasn't now.

Jack didn't stir in the living room. She'd expected to hear him adjusting because there was no way a man his size would be comfortable on that decorative couch. Emily pulled the covers over her head. There was just no way to be sure if this was the right thing to do, and she wanted to be sure, for both their sakes. The sinking feeling in the pit of her stomach told her surety wasn't in her future.

She threw the covers off and sat up. She wouldn't be able to sleep until she had her say. *Fuck.* If he was asleep, she wouldn't wake him because that would be selfish. She'd wait until morning and probably not get any sleep, but that was what she'd get for coming here and chickening out.

Emily padded into the living room and over to the couch. Jack's breathing was even and steady. "Damn," she muttered. She turned and walked toward the bedroom.

"I'm not asleep."

Emily walked back and stood at the foot of the couch. Jack's eyes were open, and the flames from the fireplace danced in them. Her mouth went dry.

He sat up and swung his legs onto to the floor, patting the spot next to him. Emily sat, their thighs touching. Trying to ignore the warmth of him where they touched, she took a deep breath and exhaled. "I'm sorry about earlier—"

"You already apologized for that."

"Right. Well..." Emily swallowed hard. "The thing is—"

"Why did you sit in the hallway for so long before calling me?"

Emily cleared her throat. "Because I'm scared. I knew if I came here tonight there was no going back and—"

"You make it sound like you're going to the hangman's noose."

"Could you please stop interrupting me?"

"Sorry. I don't bite ya know."

Emily chuckled. "Actually, Jack, you do."

Jack gave a sly smile. "Well, that was in the heat of the moment."

"This moment feels pretty heated to me." Emily wished she could take off the sweatshirt, but she had nothing on underneath, and that wouldn't be playing fair.

Jack moved a few inches away. "I'm sorry, please continue."

"I don't want to hurt you again, and I'm afraid I will. And, I don't want to hurt more than I already do, which I didn't think was possible. I was so sure that breaking it off was the right thing to do, for both of us. But almost as soon as we hung up, I felt like I'd just made a terrible mistake. I'd expected to feel relieved, but instead, the thought of never seeing you again..."

Jack knelt before her, taking her face between his hands. "The thought of never seeing me again..." he prompted.

"Hurt. More."

Jack said nothing, just stared into her eyes, and she was lost in his, their blue depths burning with the intensity of his feelings for her. "I don't know who I am anymore."

Jack brushed his thumb over her cheek. "You're Emily Grace Prescott, whose world has been turned upside down twice."

Emily sighed, she wouldn't let him let her off the hook. "That's no excuse for what I've done to you."

Jack rubbed his thumb over her lips. "What do you think you've done?"

"Played with your emotions. This would be a lot easier if I didn't like you. You were supposed to be my first one-night stand. I couldn't even do that right."

Jack smiled at that. "You know I had no intention of this being only one night. Em, your head and your heart are at odds. Your head wants to protect you, your heart feels...being with me feels good?"

"It feels great, it's easy to forget. But it's not fair to you. You're ready for a new relationship. What if I'm just using you to feel good and can't move on?"

"I never felt like you were playing with my emotions. You've been hurt, and of course, you're scared. I'm a little scared." He kissed her gently on the lips. "I've never felt this much, this fast."

He wanted more, so she'd finish what she started. "That only leaves me one option." She swallowed the baseball in her throat.

Jack smiled. "Again, being with me has to be better than a one-way trip to the gallows."

"You know it's not just that it's too soon. It's what you are."

"I'm not the hangman."

"No, you're a rock star, Jack. You live in a spotlight."

Jack sat back on his heels. "I can't fix that."

"I know. The only way I'll know if I can deal with that is to be with you."

Jack lunged forward, somehow sitting on the couch and dragging her onto his lap. His kiss was warm and soft and hard at the same time. His hands slid under the hem of the sweatshirt and caressed her bare back.

326 JESSICA MARLOWE

When Emily pulled back for air, Jack's eyes were dazed. The light provided by the fire casting a warm, healing glow around them. Her chest heaved to draw in enough air, whether from their kiss or the look in his eyes, she didn't know.

Jack looked down, taking deep breaths of his own. When their eyes locked, his held tears. "Em"—he swallowed hard— "please don't leave me again. I couldn't take it."

Emily placed her hands on either side of his face. "Jack, I didn't come here to leave you again." She kissed his lips softly.

In a heartbeat, her sweatshirt was off, and Jack's hands cupped her aching breasts. He thumbed her nipples while he gently bit her lip. She found the hem of his T-shirt, and he sat forward so she could lift it up. His hands left her only long enough to remove the shirt and toss it away. Standing, Jack carried her into the bedroom, and within seconds, they were naked on the bed, touching, tasting, reacquainting themselves. It was heavenly.

They made love slowly. They both knew their one-night stand had turned into so much more.

Jack brought her to the verge twice with his mouth before letting her tumble over into ecstasy. He already knew how she liked to be touched, always finding the perfect rhythm and then changing the tempo at just the right moment. When her orgasm finally washed over her, pulling her under, Jack held her in his arms, whispering beautiful words that held the promise of a future together, allaying all her fears.

As Jack settled over her, claiming her, she wished she could make him the same promises. But she didn't know what tomorrow held, let alone the future.

And Jack being Jack, whispered to her, "Everything will work out."

Ever the optimist. Another pro.

Afterward, as she lay cradled in his arms, the fear returned.

But she wouldn't back out now. She'd made her choice, and she'd stick to it. She'd see this through, or she'd never be able to forgive herself.

"What's your plan for tomorrow?" Jack asked. "I mean today."

"More of this seems like a good plan to me." She stretched out next to him. She needed to move soon, but for now she'd just enjoy his body next to hers.

Jack laughed. "You are a very horny woman."

"Too much for you?"

"Nope." Jack took her hand that rested on his chest and moved it down to his hard cock.

"So it's a plan, sleep, then reconvene for more sex."

Jack groaned. "I can't. I'm having dinner with my family today. My mom is making all my favorites." Jack kissed the top of her head. "Come with me."

Emily froze. *Shit, he wasted no time.* She didn't want to. And she had stuff to do. Emily needed to figure out a new book idea before Meg had a stroke; laundry had piled up, and there wasn't any food in her fridge. Just say no, he'd understand. *No, he won't.* "What happened to all your patience?" Uncomfortable heat spread over her, so she turned onto her other side. She needed the distance.

Jack rolled behind her, pulling her to him. "I know it's soon to meet the family, but, baby, the reality of my life is we have to get things in when we're together. You'll have plenty of free time when I'm gone. I haven't seen my folks since Christmas. I'm flying in for Mother's Day, but then I won't be seeing them again until June over Father's Day weekend."

That was only two months away, which was too soon as well. She'd agreed to this relationship, but she was already overwhelmed. But, he had a point. He'd be away a lot, so she'd have to go with the flow, which wasn't her strong suit. "Shouldn't you call them first to ask?"

"Em, they're my folks, they'll be happy to meet anyone I'm dating."

"Still, maybe there won't be enough food." That was stupid; moms always made too much food. "They're expecting to have you all to themselves. It wouldn't be right to just show up with me." *Good one.*

Jack turned her on her back. "If you don't want to go, just say so." It was too dark to see his face, but he sounded hurt.

"It is too soon for me." Emily touched his face. "But you're right. I hadn't thought about anything past coming here, and I'm not great at going with the flow, but we'll go if it's okay with your parents." She felt him smile. Might as well get it all out now. "I think we need to talk about what it will be like going forward. I'll need your tour schedule so we can plan for the time we'll have together." His smile widened to a grin.

"You're the best, baby."

She wasn't, but she'd damn sure try to be.

Want more? Need more? Sign up to my VIP reader group, jessicamarloweauthor.com, and you'll receive access to exclusive cut and extended scenes only available to my subscribers.

Jack and Emily's epic story continues in book 2 of the *Rocked in Love* series. Keep reading for an excerpt from *No More Yesterdays*.

*****

Excerpt - No More Yesterdays

Months of planning the perfect meeting while the band was in New York for a week were not to be thwarted by some stupid groupie whore after all. Jack looked so sad last night when he left the Garden it nearly broke my heart, but now that she's gone, Jackie's vulnerable. This may have been fortuitous after all. He'll be happy to see a friendly face, and I'll comfort him. He's always the one to take care of everyone else, but finally, he'll be with someone who gives him exactly what he needs.

The Phoenix has risen from the ashes, and he'll see I'm not a weak, pathetic creature he needs to save.

No More Yesterdays - Chapter Two

Sunday morning, Jack was startled awake by his alarm, and he was alone. Terror gripped him, and he shot up. *Shit.* Em was still asleep but had moved to the far side of the bed. *Fuck.* He hated that; he wanted to wake up with her in his arms. Since he'd have plenty of lonely nights ahead of him, when they were together, he needed her next to him. The band would be leaving Thursday for Hartford, and he had no idea when he'd see her again.

Yesterday had been hard, but it all turned out in the end. Last night, Em had come to his room at The Yorkshire Hotel, and she'd agreed to give them a fair chance, and he had no doubt she would. He needed to remember she was afraid, and no matter how strong she was, she was fragile right now. She still had to work out what happened with the fucker, but Jack felt more secure in their future. Em was his. And today, she'd agreed to meet his family.

It was early, but his dad always got up at five, so Jack picked up his phone and dialed his dad's cell.

"Jack, you're still coming, aren't you?"

"Good morning to you, too." Jack glanced at his girl. "Absolutely."

His dad sighed in relief. "Great, what's up, son?"

What's that about? "I'm seeing someone, and I'd like to bring her today. Okay?"

Jack heard his father rub his hand over his face. He always did that when he was trying to break bad news.

"If we say no, are you still coming?"

What? Jack hadn't expected this. As far as he was concerned, asking had been a formality, but apparently, Em had been right. "Of course. I thought it'd be nice to have all the people I love in one place at the same time."

His dad sighed.

Jack's head dropped. "Look, it's okay—"

"Your mother's sleeping. Let me discuss it with her when she gets up, and I'll call you back."

"Okay." Jack paused. "Dad, everything okay?" Maybe there was a family crisis, and they didn't want any outsiders. Although, Em could probably help. She was great at that.

"No, we're all well. It's just this is last minute. We didn't know you were seeing anyone new. She is new, isn't she? You're not back with Christie, are you?"

Jack thought they'd loved Christie. "No. It's over with Christie. Her name's Emily, and she's a writer." *Shit.* He probably shouldn't have told him that. Em wanted to remain anonymous. He'd fix it later if it came up.

"Okay." Will sighed. "I'll call you back after I talk to Mom. Love you, son."

"Love you too, Dad." Jack turned up the ringer on his phone, placed it on the nightstand, and shifted closer to Em so he could spoon her. *Bliss.*

Jack woke at eight with Em in his arms. Much better. His hand cupped her breast, and his hard-on nestled between her cheeks. He rubbed his groin against her, and she moaned softly as her hips rocked into him. He kissed her shoulder, and she sighed.

"Mmm, that for me?" Her voice was still raspy with sleep.

"Sure is. Fuck me." Jack rolled onto his back, grabbed a rubber, and rolled it on.

"The only thing I like better than late-night dirty talk is early-morning dirty talk." Em settled herself over him and slid down.

Her warmth surrounded him. *Fuck, that feels good.* He wished he was bare. It drove him wild that she wanted sex as much as he did. He had a very healthy sex drive, but his past girlfriends hadn't always matched up to him in that area. Especially when they were passed out drunk or high as fuck on drugs. *Fuck.* Why was he thinking of Christie? Probably because his dad had brought her up.

He pushed all thoughts aside as Em leaned forward and kissed him while she continued riding his cock. He fondled her breasts and broke the kiss so he could take her nipple in his mouth. "Baby, your tits are fucking perfect." She smiled and contracted her inner muscles around him. Fuck, that did it. "Oh fuck, baby."

Her hands stroked his pecs as she rose and fucked him harder. God, she was perfect. He came hard and was so lost in his orgasm he hadn't realized until she collapsed on him that she'd come. If she hadn't, he'd have eaten her pussy until she did. He still might.

Emily nuzzled his neck and kissed his shoulder. He didn't want to move, but he needed to use the bathroom. "I gotta get up."

Em rolled off him and snuggled under the covers with a satisfied grin.

When he returned, she was on her back with her legs spread wide. Nothing turned him on more than a woman who wasn't shy about telling him what she wanted. He crawled up the bed and kissed his way up her inner thighs, careful not to linger near her scars. She was sensitive about it, but he hoped, in time, that she'd let him touch and kiss her freely. They were part of her, and he loved her completely. He dipped his tongue in. "Mmm." He was almost ready himself, but this was for Em, so he focused on her pussy, loving her sweet, musky taste.

Em groaned. "Oh, yes. I love that."

He knew she did.

Rush's "The Trees" sounded from the nightstand. "Shit. That's my dad." He'd hoped it wasn't bad news. Grabbing the phone, he connected the call. "Hey, Dad."

"Jack, we'd love to have your new girlfriend join us for dinner."

That sounded more like his dad. "Great. What time?" Em gestured to him. "Hold on."

"I have to go home first. I need clothes."

"Right. Dad, is one o'clock okay?"

"That's what I was going to say. See you then."

"Can't wait, bye."

She pulled the sheet up to cover her beautiful naked body, but he wanted to finish what he started, so he whipped them off her.

"Jack, we don't have time for this. We have to eat, shower, get to my place, change, and then get to your parents' house. I don't want to be late."

Damn. She was right. He licked his lips to get the last bit of her essence. "Okay, rain check. You'll need to pack clothes for here."

"Why?"

"Aren't you staying this week?"

Emily scooted off the bed. "I have to go to work." She walked into the bathroom and closed the door.

Jack stared at the paneled door. They needed to talk. He'd expected her to spend the next four days with him at the hotel.

Since Emily should've been on her honeymoon for the next three weeks, he'd assumed she was off. He wanted her to stay with him and not just time after she got off work. He needed more. They'd be apart enough because he was on tour. *Too much.* But most of all, Jack needed to stop pressuring her, like he had last night, to get her to agree to come to see his folks today. For the life of him, he just couldn't stop himself, and he didn't understand why.

After breakfast and an argument with Jeff over spending the day with Em without security, they left the hotel in the rental that Jack had ordered. Em's apartment in Oakdale, New Jersey, was thirty minutes west of Manhattan, and they arrived at eleven thirty. He parked in back and they walked hand in hand to her door.

Once inside, Em turned to him. "I'll only be a few minutes." She walked down the hallway and disappeared into the bedroom. He followed, waiting in the doorway, until she turned to see him.

"What?"

Jack walked in and sat on the bed. "I want you to spend the week with me."

Her brows drew together. "I thought that was the plan."

"I'd assumed that you were off all week."

Em sat next to him and took his hand. "You want me spend the week at your hotel?"

"Yeah."

She stood and paced, and he could see the wheels turning. "I canceled my vacation time."

"But you were off Thursday and Friday."

"Yeah, because my bosses told me not to come in until I got my shit together." Emily smiled. "They were nice about it, but I'd been screwing up everything. I'm usually reliable, but after I sent copy for approval to our client's competitor by mistake, who's also our client, which cost us both accounts, I really thought they'd fire me."

Jack stood and hugged her. "Hey, you went through something terrible. I'm sure they understand."

She rested her head on his shoulder. "They do. They've been good to me." Jack felt her smile. "I started as the receptionist, and they gave me the opportunity to move into copywriting."

"I'm sure you earned the opportunity."

"I didn't have a degree to back it up, but they didn't care about that. A lot of places would've."

"Can you take a few days off?"

Emily pulled out of his embrace. "That's what I'm trying to figure out. We have two new clients coming in this week, and I could probably miss those appointments, but the established client asked for me specifically, so there's no way I can miss that one."

He'd thought she was concocting an elaborate excuse to not be with him. His chest swelled with pride that one of their clients respected her work so much that he wanted Em on his next campaign.

"I have to call my bosses and see what works for them." She walked into the living room to make the call.

Her bedroom wasn't overly feminine, but there were touches here and there. The bedspread was purple with gold trim. *Oh fuck.* That fucker slept in this room with her, in that bed. Under that bedspread. Jack shook his head to dispel the images.

"You okay?" Emily asked.

Jack stared at the bed. "You need a new mattress." No way was he making love to her in that bed after—

"It's only three weeks old. I got rid of the sheets and bedspread too. They made me sick."

He was such a prick. He should be worried about her not himself.

Emily smiled. "I had a hard time hauling the mattress out, but the box spring was easier."

"Why didn't you ask for help?"

Emily looked down. "I was humiliated, Jack. I didn't even tell Nicki until Monday. Besides, Vince lives in California, and I couldn't wait for Eddie to drive up. It exited the apartment shortly after they did."

Vince and Eddie were Emily's friends who helped her survive the aftermath of the accident, and Jack remembered what Nicki had told him about how Em had thrown he fucker out. He was proud of her, and he couldn't help but grin.

"Nicki told you, didn't she?"

"Yeah. Naked, huh?"

"They were lucky they got out in one piece." Emily took out an overnight bag and packed. "I have to be in the office Thursday by one and Friday. Damn."

"What's wrong?"

"I never called Vince."

"Call him now. I'll call my dad and tell him we're running a little late."

"I hope Vince isn't at the airport." At Jack's puzzled expression, she added, "He threatened to get on a plane if I didn't call him this weekend."

Jack liked Vince already and couldn't wait to meet him. "Take your time." Jack went to the living room to give her privacy. He was on the phone with Buzz when Em walked in. Unfortunately, Buzz had a bad night but had just left a NA meeting. Since Buzz was going to visit his family later, they might see him because their families were neighbors.

"Ready?" she asked.

That bag didn't look full, but he was used to traveling with Christie. "Uh, one more thing."

Emily raised her brows.

"I'd like to read your books, but I don't know your pen name." Emily's shocked expression surprised him until he remembered that the fucker hadn't been interested in her writing career. *Asshole.*

"Paperback or e-book?"

"Paperback."

Smiling, Emily turned and went into her office. She returned with a canvas bag. "Here."

Jack opened the bag and pulled out the first book. *In A Heartbeat* by Emma Ryan. The cover featured a bare-chested man and a woman in a skimpy bikini. They were kissing, and his hand rested close to her breast. Her arms were around him, her hands disappearing below his waist. Jack swallowed hard and looked up at her. "I meant so I could buy them."

"The four on the bottom are the most recent ones, the others are all out of print, so don't lose them, okay? They're my only copies." Em smirked at him. He knew she understood his reaction and was enjoying his discomfiture. He'd like nothing more than to bend her over the kitchen table and fuck —shit, they had to leave. "Nice cover."

"People do judge a book by its cover." Emily headed down the stairs.

Jack adjusted himself and followed.

Get your copy of *No More Yesterdays*.

*****

Exclusive Offer

Building relationships with readers is the best part of sharing my writing. I send a newsletter about twice a month with details on new releases, special offers, and other fun bits.

I love my subscribers, and to thank you for joining my reader group, you'll have access to exclusive bonus content: epilogues, cut or extended scenes, cover reveals, and insider updates.

Sign up: jessicamarloweauthor.com

Enjoyed this book?

YOU CAN MAKE A BIG DIFFERENCE.

Reviews are one of the most important things readers can do to help authors. Especially indie authors. It's a tough business, and getting readers to take a chance isn't easy.

If you enjoyed this book, please consider leaving an honest review—no spoilers, please. Reviews on Goodreads and BookBub are also helpful. I would be grateful if you could spare five minutes to do that. Long or short, it would really help me out.

Thank you very much.

Jessica

About the Author

Jessica Marlowe has always loved reading. Inspired by a story that wouldn't let her go, she has written her first three books. She loves music (especially hard rock), animals (all kinds), autumn trees and jacket-weather walks, naps (after all that walking), and wine (certainly unrelated to napping).

As a side hustle, Jessica writes instruction manuals for glamping equipment. Just kidding.

Jessica is the author of the wildly popular Rocked in Love rock star romance series. (What? It could happen 😊)

You can connect with Jessica at jessicamarloweauthor.com or by email at jessica@jessicamarloweauthor.com.

Novels By Jessica Marlowe

Rocked in Love **– Rock Star Romance Series – Must be read in order**

With You (Jack and Emily - Book 1)

Rock star and all-around nice guy Jack McBride is single but not for long. Emily Prescott is newly single and not interested in a relationship, especially with a rock star. But the attraction demands satisfaction, so she offers him one night. Jack agrees but has no intention of letting Emily get away.

No More Yesterdays (Jack and Emily - Book 2)

Emily has agreed to this relationship, but she has no idea how hard it will be. Jack drops in whenever he has a two-day break from touring, but things never seem to go as planned. Emily's nightmares are getting worse as the truth pushes its way to the surface. Jack has never struggled so much with being apart from a girl. His stalker is still out there, and Jack's not taking any chances. He'll do anything to protect Emily even if that means going behind her back to keep her safe.

All Your Tomorrows (Jack and Emily - Book 3)

Jack can't imagine his life without Emily by his side every day and in his bed every night. And with the six-week European leg of their tour looming, Jack has a hard choice to make. Emily makes a decision about her future, but will it be the biggest mistake she's ever made, or will it allow her to fulfill all her dreams?

Found Family Series
Night and Day (Eddie and Sheryl - Book 1)

Sometimes, the perfect life isn't as good as it seems. Seventeen-year-old Sheryl Thompson has every advantage, and her parents have her life planned out to the nth degree. But Sheryl has other plans. Looks can be deceiving... At nineteen, Eddie Burris's life sucks. Growing up with an abusive father, he believes all the lies that were beaten into him. Until one night, on a dark highway, he pulls over to help a stranded motorist...When Eddie and Sheryl meet, the chemistry is electrifying, but the odds, and Sheryl's family, are against them. Will they fight for their future or be torn apart by their differences?

Night and Day: Ever After (Eddie and Sheryl – Book 2)

Eddie and Sheryl have endured everything life has thrown at them. With the help of their found family, they've not only survived but thrived. They're living their happily ever after, and for Sheryl, the next step is obvious. But how will Eddie feel? Two new patients in one day will test Eddie's recovery to the limit. He's going to have to revisit his painful past to best serve them. And with Sheryl's help, he'll do everything in his power to see his patients through. But they have to want it.

Lavender Roses Series
The One (Axl and Mara)

Mara dumped him two years ago, and Axl had moved on. Or so he thought. Seeing her again, has old feelings bursting back to life, but she's married now. Now that her divorce is final, Mara's greatest mistake is behind her. But when she sees Axl again at her great-grandparents vow renewal, the chemistry is as hot as ever. But Mara believes in moving forward, and Axl is in her past. But Gigi knows better, and she's not above using her party to give them the opportunity to see it.

Printed in Great Britain
by Amazon